Young Writers

Creative Writing Competition for Secondary Schools

From The Eastern Counties
Edited by Lynsey Hawkins

Disclaimer

Young Writers has maintained every effort
to publish stories that will not cause offence.

Any stories, events or activities relating to individuals
should be read as fictional pieces and not construed
as real-life character portrayal.

First published in Great Britain in 2005 by:
Young Writers
Remus House
Coltsfoot Drive
Peterborough
PE2 9JX
Telephone: 01733 890066
Website: www.youngwriters.co.uk

All Rights Reserved

© Copyright Contributors 2005

SB ISBN 1 84602 238 X

Foreword

Young Writers was established in 1991 and has been passionately devoted to the promotion of reading and writing in children and young adults ever since. The quest continues today. *Young Writers* remains as committed to engendering the fostering of burgeoning poetic and literary talent as ever.

This year, *Young Writers* are happy to present a dynamic and entertaining new selection of the best creative writing from a talented and diverse cross section of some of the most accomplished secondary school writers around. Entrants were presented with four inspirational and challenging themes.

'Myths And Legends' gave pupils the opportunity to adapt long-established tales from mythology (whether Greek, Roman, Arthurian or more conventional eg The Loch Ness Monster) to their own style.

'A Day In The Life Of ...' offered pupils the chance to depict twenty-four hours in the lives of literally anyone they could imagine. A hugely imaginative wealth of entries were received encompassing days in the lives of everyone from the top media celebrities to historical figures like Henry VIII or a typical soldier from the First World War.

Finally 'Short Stories', in contrast, offered no limit other than the author's own imagination while 'Hold The Front Page' provided the ideal opportunity to challenge the entrants' journalistic skills, asking them

T.A.L.E.S. From The Eastern Counties is ultimately a collection we feel sure you will love, featuring as it does the work of the best young authors writing today.

Contents

Amberfield School, Ipswich
Eleanor Faulkner (13) — 1
Olivia Wilkerson (13) — 2
Sophie Kennelly (13) — 3
Charlotte Jones (13) — 4
Jenny Blay (13) — 5
Rebecca Hasler (12) — 6
Josie Hughes (13) — 7
Sophie Maitland (13) — 8

Beaconsfield High School, Beaconsfield
Maria Mahmood (14) — 9
Hannah Felt (14) — 10
Sita Karia (14) — 12

Hadleigh High School, Ipswich
Ben Hart (12) — 14
Zoe Griffiths (12) — 15
Ryan Talbot (13) — 16
Lisa Guest (14) — 17
Zac Clark (13) — 18
Django Robinson (14) — 19
Alana Durrant (13) — 20
Alex Gosling (14) — 21
Jessica Oliver (14) — 22
Rebecca Butler (14) — 23
Rob Marsland (14) — 24
Sam Churchyard (14) — 25
Luke Bunce (12) — 26
Jessica Evans (11) — 27
Christopher Neill (12) — 28
Zoe Jeeves (12) — 29
Jack Butler (12) — 30
Chloe Gregory (12) — 31
Claude Claireaux (12) — 32
Shân Bendall (12) — 33
Ryan Ellis (13) — 34
Sarah Spice (13) — 35

Rachel Louden (12)	36
Connor Bentley (12)	37
Hannah Main (12)	38
Gena French (12)	39
Matthew Powell (12)	40
Bryony Clarke (12)	41
Jasmine Carter (11)	42
Chantelle Ward (12)	43
Lucy Lester (12)	44
Lauren Gant (14)	45
Oliver Benton (14)	46
Victoria Gray (14)	47
Peter Bridge	48
Daniel Page	49
Kyle Collins (14)	50
Jaki Freeth (14)	51
Flora McLennan (14)	52
Grace Kebby (14)	53
Peter Bartram (13)	54
Kirsty Farthing (14)	55
Lauren Bridges (14)	56
Hadley French Gerrard (14)	57
Ami Simpkin (14)	58
Mica Finch (14)	59
Charlotte Gregory (14)	60
Leon Slater (14)	61
Sam Cook (14)	62
Naomi Webb (14)	63
Susannah Barraclough (14)	64
Zachary Kerr (13)	65
Leanne Riches (14)	66
Natalie Rosemary Snowling (14)	67
Mark Littlewood (13)	68
Katie MacLeod (14)	69
Stefan Vincent (14)	70
Ashleigh Moore (13)	71
Alisha Keveren (14)	72
Natalie Bell (13)	73
Stacy Herbert (13)	74
Emma Jeeves (13)	75
Kirsty Benee (14)	76
Alice Farrall (14)	77

Rebecca Lewis (14)	78
Luke Green (14)	79
Luke Chesworth (13)	80
Kayleigh Gleed (13)	81
Hannah Petts (13)	82
Isabelle Lewis (14)	83
Claire Wright (14)	84
Natasha Ludbrook (14)	85
Gemma Squirrell (13)	86
Rachel Fraser (14)	87
Leigh Thornton (13)	88
Afsana Miah (12)	89
Jessica Shrimpton (12)	90
Aidan Bignell (12)	91
Josh Broadbent (12)	92
Yolanda Rankin (12)	93
Zoe Alleyne (12)	94
Matthew Snowling (12)	95
Ross Bray (11)	96
Melissa Parker (12)	97
Rebecca Le Grice (12)	98
Andrew Stuart (12)	99
Ella Rodwell (11)	100
Georgia Kerr (12)	101

Hardwick Middle School, Bury St Edmunds

Rachel Seymour (12)	102
Katie Riches (11)	103
Paige Mitson (12)	104

Kings Langley School, Kings Langley

Jake Adams (11)	105
Bryony Saletes (12)	106
Amelia Parkins (11)	107
Alexandra Oakley-Smith (12)	108
Jemma Green (12)	109
Jodie Doyle (12)	110
Ryan Thrussell (12)	111
Lucy Dillingham (12)	112
Kirsty Owen (12)	113
Luke Higham (11)	114

Sohail Sadiq (12)	115
Katie Walsh (11)	116
Nikki Carlisle (11)	117
Lauren Joyce (12)	118
Nick Couzens (12)	119
Rosie Dyte (12)	120
Jordan Pope (12)	121
Joe Hughes (12)	122
Joe Oldham (12)	123
Josh Ellison (12)	124
Joanna Butterfield (12)	125
Thomas Parsonage (11)	126
Ross Hudson (12)	127
Amy George (12)	128
Ryan Pamment (12)	129
Frida Becker (12)	130
Blondell Franklin-Beck (12)	132

Lea Manor High School, Luton
Daniel Harris (13)	133
Salema Khatun (15)	134
Simon Hayden (13)	135

Lincroft Middle School, Oakley
Ailene Gray (12)	136
Katherine Sykes (12)	137
Marta Lewicka (12)	138
Conor Craig (12)	139
Jennifer Buchanan (13)	140
Ashleigh Balodis (13)	141
Melissa Morgan (12)	142
Jenny Janes (13)	143
Charlotte Warren (13)	144
Richard Warren (13)	145
Sarah Hale (12)	146
Gabrielle Harding (12)	147
Harrison Barnes (11)	148
Alex Brown (11)	149
Alice Eaton (12)	150
Thomas Kiddy (11)	151
Christopher Paterson (11)	152

Tom Anderson (12)	153
James Rodger (12)	154
Rachael Southam (12)	155
Ahsan Bokhari (12)	156
Joyce Kwok (12)	158
Josh Walker (12)	159

Mayflower High School, Billericay

Sarah Maunder (14)	160
Melissa Newnham (13)	161

Netherhall School, Cambridge

Geraldine Morrisroe (12)	162
Jonathan Jongkind (13)	163
Raphae Memon (12)	164
Reuven Jongkind (12)	165

Newnham Middle School, Bedford

Mathea Armsden (13)	166
Jessica Smith (13)	167
Abby Alexander (13)	168
Cameron MacAskill (12)	169
Joshua Smith (12)	170
Tara Wheeler (13)	171
Josh Groom (13)	172
Abby Blake (13)	173
Tom Funge (13)	174
Isaac Fargher (13)	175
Daniella Caruso (13)	176
Iona Swannell (13)	177
Lily Waugh (13)	178
Patrick Meniru (13)	179
Benjamin Fearon (13)	180
Owen Cowley (13)	181
Holly Monk (13)	182
Tom Faden (13)	183
Ayesha Holden (13)	184
Keira Cruickshank (12)	185
Madison Fisk (13)	186
Raman Bhangle (13)	187

Ruby Baker (13)	188
Laura Mclean (13)	189
Joshua Boland (12)	190

Norwich High School for Girls, Norwich

Alice van Hattem (12)	191
Francesca Hodac-Nichols	192
Lara Cator (12)	193
Sarah Cochius (12)	194
Gabriella Ghigi (12)	195
Mollie Hyde (11)	196
Rebecca Morris (12)	197
Kate Robinson (11)	198
Hannah Barber (12)	199
Helen Falkner (12)	200

Park School for Girls, Ilford

Elizabeth Rose Cowell (13)	201

Quarrendon Upper School, Aylesbury

Benjamin Pearson (14)	202

St Bede's Inter-Church School, Cambridge

Christina Pettit (15)	203
David Kaye (15)	205

St Francis' College, Letchworth Garden City

Lucy Rahim (11)	207
Emily McGhee (11)	208
Nazlee Sabahipour (12)	209
Gemma Turner (12)	210
Katie Ritchie (12)	211
Rachael Barker (12)	212
Sarah Atalla (11)	213
Gemma Hall (12)	214
Claire Chapman (12)	215
Marie Davis (12)	216
Lauren Davies (12)	217
Susannah Cichy (11)	218
Charlotte Graham (12)	219

Courtenay Forbes (12)	220
Dreene Jamil (12)	221
Kanmein Kaur (11)	222
Rhiannon Griffiths (12)	223
Sophie Coleman (12)	224
Sophie Batchelor (11)	225
Rosie Kirbyshire (12)	226

Shenfield High School, Brentwood

Sarah Wright (14)	227
Harriet Austin (14)	228
Connor Coxall (13)	229
Stephen Clews (14)	230
Jayden Bowling (13)	232
Conor Robinson (14)	233
Alex Dean (14)	234
Jonathan Burns (13)	235
Kaz Melvin (14)	236
Oliver Hazell (14)	238
Charlie Joseph (14)	239
Kirsty Hough (14)	240
Christina Smith (14)	241
Sophie Mihailovic (14)	242
Stephen Cozens (13)	243
Billy Bolton (14)	244
David Mais (14)	245
Ryan Spurge (14)	246
Ryan Gunning (14)	247
Tommy McGroder (14)	248
Alistair Bygrave (13)	249
Liam Colverd (13)	250
Jeremy Williams (13)	251
Edward Starr (13)	252
Joshua Ashton (13)	253
Billy Bone (13)	254
Frank Austin (12)	255
Rebecca Morement (13)	256
Chloe Isbell (13)	257
Sophie Harding (13)	258
Lydia Reeves (13)	259
Natasha Warren (12)	260

Laura Mackenzie (12)	261
Hayley Macfarlane (13)	262
Anna Howard (12)	263
Emily Hall (13)	264
Elise Norton (13)	265
Hannah Page (13)	266
James Loveard (14)	267
Vincent Morris (14)	268
Francis Lind (14)	269
Joe Abbitt (13)	270
Anand Pandya (13)	271
Scott Fenn (14)	272
William Church (14)	273
Matthew McNaughton (13)	274
James Lind (14)	276
Dominic Clark (13)	277
Mitchell Clarke (13)	278
Oliver Field (13)	279
Jack McCarthy (12)	280
Steve Payne (13)	282
Daniel Gunning (13)	283
Rebecca Young (12)	284
Emma Conlon (13)	285

Sir Christopher Hatton School, Wellingborough

Amy Luke (15)	286
Aisha Opoku (17)	287

Smithdon High School, Hunstanton

Marvin Nicholl (13)	288
Ashleigh German (15)	289
Sophie Cribb (13)	290
Christina Sanderson (13)	291
Zoe Coton (13)	292
Amrith Malhi (13)	293
Helen Parkinson (13)	294
Dan Robinson (14)	295
Anna Goodchild (13)	296
Lauren Thrower (14)	297
Lewis Kimber	298
Oscar Allington (14)	299

Rachel Kennady (14)	300
Emily Mann (14)	301
Kelsey Rushton-Large (14)	302
Ellen Witley (13)	303
Kelly Mellor (13)	304
Faye Coles (14)	305
Samantha Bromfield (14)	306
Maria Woods (13)	307
Catherine Drewery (14)	308
Charlotte Ford (13)	309
Annaleigh Foreman (13)	310
Callum Lawrence (14)	311
Fred Marsh-Allen (14)	312
Jenna Hussey (13)	313
Matthew Kemp (13)	314

Thomas Mills High School, Woodbridge

Alex Hayes (14)	315
Rebecca Walker (14)	316
Hannah Gillott (16)	317

Walton Community School, Peterborough

Aimee Plumridge (14)	318
Thomas Seager (12)	319
Bryan Hoadley (12)	320
Heather Garton (12)	322
Ashley Mulbregt (12)	323
Hannah Lewis (13)	324
Callum Westbrook (13)	325
Saskia Bailey (12)	326
Victoria Morland (13)	327
Alfie Bell (13)	328
Jade Wheeler (12)	329
Matthew Andrews (13)	330
Chyna Bonham (12)	331
Georgia Cavender (12)	332
Chris Ogden (12)	333
Sonia Ferdous (12)	334
Hayley Clark (12)	335
Laura Cliffe (14)	336

West Hatch High School, Chigwell
Jessica Scully (12)	337
Safoora Safaei-Keshtgar (12)	338
Charlie McCann (12)	339
Abigail Lennard (12)	340
Jack Farley (12)	341
Hannah Sibley (12)	342
Peri Ozkeskin (12)	343
Danielle Woodcock (12)	344
Vriddhi Chopra (11)	345
Emily Green (12)	346
Amy Cross (12)	347
Michael Beswick (12)	348
Oliver Lumb (12)	349
Haniyyah Anwar (11)	350
Georgia Harris-Burdis (12)	351
Ambika Chopra (12)	352
Shannon Maris (12)	353
Joanna Harris (12)	354
Rebecca Dymond (11)	355
Julius Drake (12)	356

Woodbridge High School, Woodford Green
Lucy Smith (12)	357
Aidan Scott (12)	358
Ballal Chaudery (12)	359
Jane Holder (12)	360
Marianne Mahendra (11)	361
Elizabeth Sode (12)	362
Rebbecca Neofitou (12)	363
Ben Marks (12)	364

The Creative Writing

Creature

The carriage rolled along the uneven ground as it made its way up to the big old house. Beth, who was 14, was staring out the window into the darkness. All she could see was the light from the lamps on the side of the carriage. Apart from the faint sound of the horse's hooves, it was silent. All of a sudden, a silvery colour could be seen, reflected off the light. Beth couldn't see what it was, but it moved, sending a slight shiver down her spine.

It rustled around in the bushes. The carriage slowly overtook it, but Beth twisted round in her seat to catch a better glimpse of the object. It slowly pulled its head up from grazing and gave Beth a shock. 'Stop the carriage!' Beth cried, almost startling the creature. The drivers pulled up the horses in amazement and the fat, jolly groom came to see if she was alright.

After telling the groom what had happened, they both crept out of the carriage. There, straight ahead of them, was a wonderful creature, shaped like a horse but with a small, dark, golden horn on its forehead. Beth had read about unicorns in books but never thought they were real. The creature let out a quiet whicker that sounded grand in the night sky. It was similar to a horse's but this one sounded as if the creature was very proud but had a secret to tell.

Eleanor Faulkner (13)
Amberfield School, Ipswich

Nothing

I looked up. He was standing right there, ready to kill. I woke up, sweating. I turned to my side to look at my pink fluffy clock that was beeping and flashing the time, 7am, at me. I had been dreaming. It was just a dream. Wasn't it?

I climbed out of bed, bleary-eyed, and stumbled to the mirror. I saw the mess that greeted me. I heard Mum calling my name and chanting to hurry up. *'Roxanne, your breakfast will be ready in ten minutes, if you're not ...'* Her voice drowned as I turned up my CD player, which was blaring out 'Usher' at full volume. I quickly got washed and dressed and ran downstairs. I gobbled my breakfast up and ran out the door, shouting a 'thank you' as I left.

I had thought about telling Mum about the strange dreams I'd been having but she'd only try and make me see a psychologist. I didn't want to tell my personal problems to a stranger.

I ran all the way to school and as I sat through maths and all the other lessons, I still couldn't stop thinking about the man who was in my room that night. He seemed so real and I swear I had seen him before. I didn't want those dreams to keep haunting me but I knew that the man would be there again tonight. Why won't these dreams stop? What have I done to deserve this? The answer is *nothing!*

Olivia Wilkerson (13)
Amberfield School, Ipswich

A Day In The Death Of A Fly

I had no recollection of what had happened to me, but felt exceedingly weak and vulnerable, a tiny insignificant creature, drowning in blackness. I tentatively twitched a leg and suffered excruciating pain, a thousand burning metal pins searing my feeble body. Blinded by the overwhelming darkness, I scrambled to my feet, incapable of taking more than a few steps before I collapsed once more. I attempted to fly, but to no avail.

I came across an obstacle in my path. A dim light seeping through the hard transparency that blocked my escape enabled me to make out the shape of another fly that had evidently not been as fortunate as I when the 'monster' struck. At the sight of the square marks in the mangled body, it seemed incredible that I had survived the onslaught that had killed it. For now I remembered the monstrous thing that had knocked me out of the air and flattened me against the wall.

Suddenly, I saw the monster lying asleep nearby, pieces of wing and skinny legs clinging to its jaws. I recoiled to see chunks of the fly's body stuck in the square holes when I realised that the same chunks of flesh were missing from my own body, the same piece of wing was torn from me. Then I realised! The body before me was my own, and as I looked down at my ghostly legs, and found I could no longer feel the pain, I knew I was dead.

Sophie Kennelly (13)
Amberfield School, Ipswich

Sliders

Sliders are a great and complicated mystery.

You see, since the dawn of time millions of universes have co-existed without interference. The doors between worlds are inside other worlds and only chosen individuals can unlock these passageways - Sliders. Sliders have to keep people out of each other's worlds. Some Sliders don't know of their power and sometimes they unlock doors without realising and stumble into unknown universes. Sliders are not immortal but can only die at the hands of another Slider.

Unfortunately, humans cannot fully see them. If you see a slight shadow in the corner of your eye, it means a Slider is jumping betwixt universes.

As hard as it is to believe, there is only one evil universe, Sliprot - and this is the one that Sliders pay most attention to. Sliders that have turned to the bad side enter this universe and open doors to other worlds so the inhabitants of Sliprot can move between worlds and create havoc.

All good Sliders must band together to try and close all doors to Sliprot and kill all bad Sliders. But their most important task is to find the door to the universe that contains Kilpar. She is the one who can destroy Sliprot and allow all Sliders to find their power.

Sliders must try to find the magical tools that can help find Kilpar. These are hidden in different worlds.

I hope you now understand Sliders.

As I have said ... they are a great mystery.

Charlotte Jones (13)
Amberfield School, Ipswich

It's A Bug's Life

I awoke then to only one sensation, hunger. I was excruciatingly, ravenously hungry! The eggshell which had been my imprisonment for no more than a few weeks, was already down in the depths of my ever-requiring stomach. I then, naturally, turned my attention to food; the enormous leaf which had been my birthplace seemed to fit the bill rather nicely, but as I began my meal, I realised I had chosen the wrong time for my birth for it had taken place right in the middle of the bug rush hour. Bugs of all kinds made their way purposefully through the blades of grass that soared like skyscrapers up into the big blue sky.

But it became clear to me that this was no safe world as I peered down fearfully from my leaf. For behind nearly every corner lurked a shadow, which would creep silently to and fro until it found its prey …

I was brought abruptly out of my reverie as I realised to my horror that I was almost being thrown off my leaf, due to the fact that the wind was getting alarmingly strong, and as I made my way hurriedly towards shelter, I realised yet another misfortune. Raindrops, the size of meteoroids were making their way steadily down, transforming a busy, bustling bug world into one of desolation. I then looked out from beneath a rock and it became clear to me that this was a bug's life!

Jenny Blay (13)
Amberfield School, Ipswich

The Last Breath

Slowly, she opened her eyes, yet all she could see was darkness. Maisy didn't know where she was. She sniffed the air - but all there was was this thick smell, a bit like the garden when her father had just finished digging over the flower beds. The texture of the dark smelly cell in which she was trapped was clammy and dank. There was a humid feel in the air that she was breathing, like there wasn't much of it. In fact, Maisy knew in the deepest depths of her heart that the air would soon run out, and that before then, nobody would come to rescue her. Maisy Griffiths realised that she only had a few minutes left on Earth.

The air around her grew thinner and thinner, and Maisy knew that she had little time to remember what she was doing in this dark prison. Maisy struggled to think of what had happened the previous evening. Maisy remembered the distant screams and pleas of her parents and the thud of something hard against her head.

Maisy wasn't a great believer in God, and felt that she hadn't had a chance to do the good deeds that she would need to do to go to Heaven. After all, Maisy was only 13. Much too young to die!

Maisy tried to save herself - she screamed and screamed, but it was too late, with every breath she took, the air grew thinner until Maisy's final breath ended ...

Rebecca Hasler (12)
Amberfield School, Ipswich

Acting Life

It was about six o'clock and I had been working for eight hours. I went into my house and into the living room to put my feet up. As I went in there was a eerie sensation, my instinct told me there was something wrong. As I looked around the room I saw my dad tied to the chair! I screamed, he was trying to tell me something but I could not hear because there was something tied round his mouth. I ran forward and started to untie him, I was trying to think straight. Suddenly out jumped a man dressed in black, I screamed again, a hand was clamped over my mouth!

'Cut,' cried the film director.

I breathed a sigh of relief; today had been a hard day and just thinking about my tea made me feel hungry. I walked home after refusing the offer of a lift.

After walking for five minutes I began to wish I hadn't turned down the offer. Oh well, that's hindsight for you. My feet ached, I had been on them all day and had only had a snack lunch, *but only three days to go,* I thought.

I put my key in the caravan's lock and turned it, there was an eerie sensation, my instinct told me again that something was not right. I looked round and saw my mother and father tied down, my pulse rate went up, I screamed. This time it was for real!

Josie Hughes (13)
Amberfield School, Ipswich

A Day In The Life Of Maria Sharapova

'Wake up, wake up!' is the first thing that I hear in the morning of another long, stressful and hardworking day. It is the voice of my coach trying to wake me up, which isn't always successful. As I get up, I hear my coach telling me tactics about my match, and weak points about my opponent.

So anyway, we set off on another dull journey to another tiresome tournament. We are followed by the news vans virtually the whole way there and when I get out of the car there are microphones and cameras pointing directly at me asking me about my personal life!

After being escorted away by my coach, I meet with my opponent and I get on court. To my dismay there are many British supporters coming to watch my match and cheer me on. They all look so excited with smiles on their faces but when I start losing, everything changes. They get unreasonable with me and start getting angry. The thing is I'm the player, so it is not their duty to make me feel bad, as if they could do any better!

After being booed off court, which I really didn't appreciate, the cameras are there again. This is getting *tedious.* Now all I want to do is go home and relax. The only problems now are the headlines in tomorrow's papers like, 'Sharapova: Sexy but Stroppy' and 'Will She Ever Win Again?'

Sophie Maitland (13)
Amberfield School, Ipswich

A Day In The Life Of 'Morality'

A human is the material counterpart of the soul. One's soul lies near the heart and controls how the individual reacts in situations. Within the depths of thought processes, it lurks and tests the strength of one's moral principles. In life, many of us sit on a fence of decision; the soul trying to sway our mind to the correct path.

Paul sits on this fence today. He is lonely and has not eaten for many days. Orphaned not long ago, a constant memory resounds through his mind: the flames and his loved ones' screams. Life has become so barren that tears are the only thing that remain fruitful.

Entering the marketplace, the multitude of colours surrounds and suffocates him in a rainbow. His stomach gurgles as a sign of malnutrition and gazing down at his frail body, he notices the defined contours of his ribs. Breathing is heavy and all faith is diminishing. The victuals around taunt and tease Paul, *'You are a hunter. Look around and select your prey, when the conspicuous merchants become occupied ... pounce!'*

He snatches the plump mango from the stall and walks away. Sitting in a corner, Paul surreptitiously devours the juicy yellow fruit; the body's thirst for food has been quenched. But a once pure soul has been tainted with the label of 'thief' though material being is fulfilled for the moment.

Full-bellied, Paul laments his actions as the world continues to revolve. Guilt and emptiness immerses his body as his hands begin to shiver. 'Morality' was summoned and defeated by its enemy ...

Human nature.

Maria Mahmood (14)
Beaconsfield High School, Beaconsfield

Matrus And The Splenda Circa

Petra sat praying and asking the gods to protect her beloved Matrus. She prayed to Athena, goddess of wisdom to guide him well on the sea and use his knowledge to save him. She prayed to Aphrodite, goddess of love, asking her to keep their love alight and not make either stray while Matrus was away. She prayed to Apollo, god of healing and light, to brighten the dark days of his journey and keep him in good health. Lastly she went over to Matrus and warned him of the dangers of 'The Splenda Circa' and the Palace of Poseidon, god of the sea. But Matrus didn't take much notice. He was a cocky sailor and thought he was too good to crash. The cruel ocean was about to prove him wrong.

As Matrus set off he had an uneasy feeling inside him. From the moment he had awoken, he had felt it. It was there when he packed his things aboard the ship and when he kissed Petra goodbye. It was there as he brought in the anchor and set sail.

Matrus was thinking what it could be when he heard an almighty crunch. He saw the boat had hit a rock and was rapidly sinking into the dusky depths of the sea.

As Matrus plunged down with it he saw a woman, a beautiful mermaid. Her hair was deep chestnut-brown and flowed in the sea. Her mysterious green eyes entranced him and for a moment all thoughts of uneasiness and fear were gone. Her tail was a silvery colour and brought light to the cold sea. But Matrus couldn't breathe underwater and was soon struggling. She took his hand and pushed her lips against his. Into him she breathed a power and soon he found himself breathing by himself. Again she took his hand and led him through the water. Matrus wondered for a moment where she was taking him but again all thoughts were gone when he looked into her emerald eyes.

Finally they came to a huge circle of water that was different from the rest. As soon as Matrus entered the water he knew he had made a mistake. The silent sea around the circle stirred, and started twisting like an almighty undersea storm. Matrus turned round to ask the mermaid what was happening but she had gone. He was all alone and desperately wanted Petra but no one was there.

In the palace Poseidon was shaking with anger. The calm of the sea would soon be gone, and the raging waves would destroy anything in their path. The winds would howl louder than a wolf. The sunken ships would rise above their watery graves and smash against the rocks. Rain and hail would stream down from the skies. Thunder would roar and lightning would crash, for someone had entered his home, 'The Splenda Circa'.

Hannah Felt (14)
Beaconsfield High School, Beaconsfield

The Basking Beast
(An extract)

Long ago, deep inside the mystical and tropical Amazon rainforest, was a kingdom of animals. There, lived a powerful king. He was strong, confident and generous. He was the perfect king; everyone worshipped and praised him. All his subjects were very happy and content. The name of this magnificent ruler was King Aruna. He was a ferocious lion and he governed all of the animal kingdom. He had a fiery orange mane full of bright colours you thought didn't even exist. He was strong and muscular and had claws so sharp that when he cut a skull, it seemed like he was cutting a piece of cheese. When he opened his mouth and let out his almighty roar, it was so loud and so strong it was almost deafening.

He was a young king and, although confident and strong, he was easily led astray. As the years went by and he grew older, wiser and stronger, he also grew greedy, selfish, unkind and soon everyone started to fear him. Stories started circulating that the Haven gods came and stole his soul and gave him one of a ferocious monster. Anyone who approached the king and confronted him with his or her views on his ruling, would then be his dinner the next day. Anyone meant anyone, including his own children and parents. No one understood what had happened to the kind and loving king and how he had transformed into someone so evil and unkind. Something had to be done. Secretly the animals would go home and pray to the Haven gods to change their king or turn him back to his original self. The gods heard the animals' prayers and had a discussion.

There were five Haven gods and they consulted the ultimate god called Az. Az had been watching King Aruna for a long time and felt something had to be done. He knew that the king had been generous before and to test him he sent one of the gods down as a bright, beautiful and elegant peacock that was injured and needed some medicine. The goddess of beauty, disguised as a peacock, went down to Earth and asked the king for some medicine. The king ungraciously said that he did not have time for foreign strangers and that she should go elsewhere as he had a lot of work to do. She argued for a while until he screamed at her. She pretended to look frightened and limped away. She then transformed back to her original form and went back to the heavens and consulted Az.

They came up with a plan. This was the king's last chance. If he did not go along with the plan, he would be cursed forever and live a life so bad he would rather be dead. She went back again as a peacock and, yet again, she went up to the king. This time she offered him a potion. She said the potion contained the power to make him king of the world and have the power to command everyone and everything under the stars. Greedily, and without thinking, he took the potion from her claws and drank it until there wasn't even a drop left. Suddenly, he looked at the peacock that had revealed herself as Islina, the goddess of beauty. She told him that he had a cursed life now, and he had become a beast. If on the inside he was horrible and ugly, then he should be the same on the outside.

Suddenly a blinding, bright, bold flash of light struck the vast sky and down came the all-powerful, invincible god, Az. Az came down and exiled Aruna from his kingdom and appointed his younger brother as king instead.

Sita Karia (14)
Beaconsfield High School, Beaconsfield

Tales

Aragorn was in a war between two realms, one, Gondor and the other, Harad. He was angry with them for sending their army to destroy Minas Tirith and for killing King Theoden of Rohan, so Aragorn called for the Rohirrim, an army of horse riders with their leader, King Eomer of Rohan. Aragorn waited for Eomer. When they came, they rested for the next day.

In the morning they saddled up 50,000 men. As they rode out, a messenger came before them. He had at least six arrows in his back. Legolas looked at them, 'Definitely Haradrim arrows. They're marching with Orcs and goblins,' he said looking at two other arrows.

The messenger came to Aragorn looked in his eyes and said, 'They're coming!' and he fell to the ground, dead.

Aragorn sent rangers to find their numbers and where they were camping. When they reported back, they told him that there were at least 100,000, that they were camped at the crossroads; they also said that ten of their stealthiest men had stowed away on one of the Oliphaunts.

Aragorn sent riders to the misty mountains to find the dwarves. Aragorn was discussing with Eomer when an Orc horn sounded. Its noise shrieked throughout the entire camp.

Gimli woke up with a shout, *'Argh!* What's happening out there?'

'They're here,' said Legolas, with his bow at his shoulder.

Aragorn and Eomer roused their troops, who mounted up and they rode onto the plain.

Aragorn shouted, *'Chhhaaarrrgggeee!'*

Ben Hart (12)
Hadleigh High School, Ipswich

David's View

Even though David could see the sun shining through the dusty condensed windows, there was no light visible in his heart. Pain sat eagerly next to David prodding a large red-hot poker across his deep gashes that made him howl out in agony. Pity sat on the powder-coated window ledges, where he twiddled with his filthy string whilst trying to haul some sunshine into the abstemious bare room to fill David's heart.

David had fallen asleep towards dawn, cocooned in his sadness, but a faint tapping at the door, like a cat trying to get in for her saucer of milk, awoke him. A thin shaft of light started to appear around the door with a faint creaking noise, like the swelling and contracting of the beams and floorboards of the old house. The shaft of light around the door grew bigger, and suddenly an eye peeped around the door, seeking the occupant through the shimmering light filled with swirling dust particles, chasing each other, like little fairies playing a children's game.

The shadow entered the room. David let out a big sigh as he saw that the sly, scary shadow was actually his maid who was also his best friend. The maid's appearance was exciting for David to see as her teeth sparkled with glee and her smile seemed to light up the grey and pitiful room. It mended a little hole in David's heart.

Zoe Griffiths (12)
Hadleigh High School, Ipswich

Gone

There I was in the middle of the battlefield, shooting away at the enemy; a few of my fellow soldiers moved on to the front line … I was scared. The enemy was running towards us, shooting. I shot back, *'Argh!'* I'd been hit on my left leg. I felt all cold inside, I fell to the ground, an ambulance drove onto the battlefield, I was lifted into the ambulance.

The paramedics started to strap up my leg to stop the bleeding, I was screaming with pain, I was starting to feel dizzy. 'My eyes, my eyes!' I couldn't see anything! I went blank. I went into a fit, shaking about in the ambulance. I saw my life fly past me …

I was gone … !

Ryan Talbot (13)
Hadleigh High School, Ipswich

The Shadow On The Wall

I stop dead in my tracks. What is that? Slowly I turn around. Nothing. I try to forget about it but there it is again. Tentatively I walk on but an overwhelming feeling of being watched seeps through me. I quicken my pace, only to hear the sound of footsteps echoing my own. I stop. Silence. Nervously I carry on but the footsteps get louder and again I see it - clearer this time. Now I run. I fly through an open door just as the clock strikes midnight. The door slams behind me. Silence.

I look around, a china doll sits in the corner - eyes tightly shut. A jack-in-a-box lies a few feet away next to a miniature grandfather clock. The moon casts an eerie glow over the room making these children's toys seem somehow threatening! I try to convince myself nothing is there but menacing laughter breaks the stony silence. The temperature plunges. I run to the door and pull helplessly, desperate for escape.

All at once the room is filled with noise. The hands of the clock spin around madly; Jack repeatedly springs in and out of his box; the china doll sits silent, sinister, staring, but the worst is yet to come ...

I close my eyes in the hope I will wake up from this nightmare. It is all too real.

I come face to face with the shadow on the wall ... !

Lisa Guest (14)
Hadleigh High School, Ipswich

A Day In The Life Of ...

I woke abruptly; the soft pure white snow settling on my face. We were entrenched outside the small French town of Bastone. We had been there for three weeks with no relief. I put my head outside my foxhole. I saw some others doing the same or getting a brew on.

A few minutes later everyone was up and we were getting briefed for action, same as the last three weeks, 'Sit and wait for relief.' I settled into my foxhole and Matt gave me half a fag and some chocolate. It was all the battalion had, chocolate and fags.

I stripped and checked my Thompson and mags - three left, 60 shots. How long would they last? We knew a German attack was imminent as all we had seen for the last three days were more German troops arriving.

Thud! Crash! Two German 57mm anti-tank shells whizzed past my foxhole and into the trees behind. The small arms fire erupted all about. Sporadic MG42 fire came in from the farmhouse window then our 7.62mm Brownings returned the message.

The sound of half-tracks rumbling into life, carried troops into our position. The 7.62 Brownings did their best to pin them down but it was hopeless.

Before I knew it, a crack SS Storm Trooper was trying to bayonet me with his Mauser, but before he had a chance, I emptied my Thompson mag into him, all twenty rounds. It made a massive cavity in his chest. He slumped forward and fell straight on me, blood, guts and all!

Zac Clark (13)
Hadleigh High School, Ipswich

The Diggers

In 1649 to St George's Hill, a ragged band called 'The Diggers' came, mounted upon white horses and adorned with red cloaks. They came to fight for the common man. They defied the landlords and broke the laws, sharpened their sickles on the tithe stone and grew wheat and vegetables outside their caravans, like houses. They stayed for a year defying the laws.

'We're peaceful folk,' they said, 'trying only to live life serving ourselves, making the wasteland grow and serving no lord.' They didn't go to church, they refused to worship a god who let poor men starve while rich men gorged themselves on their corn.

Slowly people began to accept their ideas, 'After all, why should we be inferior to some lord?' they said. They convinced people to pull down their fences, open the land up for everyone and their 'dreams' worked.

The village changed, people helped each other, lent tools, people were happier and with more people working, food was plentiful. The lord's barn was declared property of the people and the land was declared a common treasury for all, all people in common, all people, one.

The summer passed fast under new rules and so did the next until, in December 1652. almost three years since 'The Diggers' arrived, a messenger clattered into the yard, abandoned his horse and announced to the gathering crowd that the crusades were over and Sir Henry, their lord, would return in the spring.

The diggers are gone now, long gone.

Django Robinson (14)
Hadleigh High School, Ipswich

Star-Struck

A lump of silver fell from the clouds followed by the wail of a newborn child. Tent flaps opened as a proud father unveiled his child. A tired mother emerged behind him and, seeing the lump of silver, she attached it to a woven cord and placed it around her son's neck.

Lena held her star. This piece of silver was guided down to every newborn by the gods, Firenze and Shadowenvy. The stars glistened in daylight and sparkled at night. Each person's star was their soul, each one unique. Lena hurried back to work.

It was later that day when disaster struck. A new tribe leader, Aldieb, had taken over. He was young and arrogant; he challenged the gods.

Firenze appeared before Aldieb roaring with anger, flames danced in his eyes, then transformed into a weak teenager wielding a sword too large for him. Flames ran up the blade of the sword. Shadowenvy materialised; darkness cloaked her, adding to her air of mystery.

The duel was over before it even began. Firenze jumped on Aldieb with unbelievable strength and with several quick stabs, Aldieb was dead.

Firenze morphed back to his original form, held out his hand and our stars were there. He gave the stars to Shadowenvy who threw them into the dark sky.

We have learnt. We are now meek. Never play God.

Alana Durrant (13)
Hadleigh High School, Ipswich

Necromunger Rescue!

The forest engulfed Jax. He rode on his horse towards the kingdom of Varira on a quest to free the army of Necromungers, captured by Ciarox. Jax continued on then he suddenly stopped, 'We'll have to set up camp here,' Jax said, after noticing a dark horizon. Jax got off his horse, pulled out his axe from his rucksack and made a fire on the side of the path.

In the morning Jax got onto his horse and with no haste, rode off along the path until he reached the Black Gate, the entrance to the Ciarox HQ. Jax hopped off the horse and slowly walked up to the gate, with bow in hand and arrows on his back; he continued to stride forwards.

'Hey!' shouted a guard as he ran away.

Jax pulled out two arrows and taking aim he unleashed them; the arrows hit the guard taking him down. Jax ran along the drawbridge and slinging his bow over his shoulder he struck out with his sword. Three guards charged at him, strike, slash, strike; all of the guards went down; he continued stealthily along the corridor until he reached the prison. Looking through the rails, he saw the Necromungers slaughtered. Anger raged through Jax; pulling out a bunch of ingredients he made an eternal spell in a jar, smashing it over the floor. The spell backfired and killed Jax instantly.

Alex Gosling (14)
Hadleigh High School, Ipswich

The (Last) Day Of A Desperate Man

I know he is here, I can feel his heartbeat thumping faster and faster. He won't be as easy as the others; I'll have to use brains, not brawn. I stroke the cool steel in my pocket (maybe I should have drunk a little more brandy before I came).

I try to concentrate on something else, to block out my emotions.

Closer, closer and I begin to think, *will decapitation be too messy? How about simply using poison?* Closer, closer, but how to do it? He obviously knows I'm coming, but how to make him swallow? Force? Threats? Bribery? No, a trick.

Closer, closer, I can hear only the silence of an evil deed beckoning nearby. Everything seems eerie as I glide towards the large door. I feel my blood run cold and my breathing become shallow. I grasp the brass doorknob and turn it slowly. As I step into the large mahogany room I see him: a fat, ugly, balding lump of a man just patiently waiting for his time.

I begin to have doubts.

His eyes are full of grief and remorse. I stumble towards him trying to look calm, although feelings like a thousand knives are ripping open my inside.

'So you're going to kill me?' he asks, blankly.

Without answering I give him the vial and within ten minutes, he lies there, dead.

I look at my father and weep!

Jessica Oliver (14)
Hadleigh High School, Ipswich

Where Was She?

Slam!

She was back right on cue. Although now the house was unusually silent, no hurried footsteps on the stairs or clatter of pans in the kitchen. Where was she? What was she doing?

Bang! I heard a gunshot. *Thud!* Now I knew where she was, now I knew what she'd done. But why? I couldn't move, I felt like I was shackled at the wrists and ankles. Paralysed with fear, I thought, although maybe I was just frozen in disbelief. There was nothing I could do, what would I find waiting for me if I went downstairs?

But a motive? There wasn't one that I knew of. Surely I would have noticed if she was unhappy. I was numb inside, like I was frozen in time. What was I doing? I could help her.

I fumbled for the door handle, it slipped through my grip where my hands were damp with cold sweat. I felt weak as I walked across the landing. Instead of jumping two steps at a time, like I usually did, I sneaked cautiously down the stairs. When I reached the bottom I swivelled to my right into the living room.

I was knocked back with shock; my mum was lying there on the floor, her eyes closed, a single tear running down her cheek, a gun clutched in her hand. But lying beside her was my dad, cold to the touch and blood pouring from his chest!

But why?

Rebecca Butler (14)
Hadleigh High School, Ipswich

Cat; Nips!

Agatha: 'I want a cat. I need a cat.'
Bill: 'No, they eat too much food; you can't afford to look after one.'
Agatha: 'I have money. Besides, it would protect the house at night.'
Bill: 'Yeah, I hear thieves are *really* scared of hairy sofas.'
Agatha: 'Please ... for me?'
Bill: 'Well, alright then, we'll go and see if the pet shop has any good deals in the morning. I haven't proved you wrong in a long time, got to start making up for it.'
Agatha: 'Not the pet shop; I want that cat! Isn't he most adora ... ?'
Bill: *'That* cat is *not* a pet! I've said you could have a cat, don't push it.'
Agatha: 'But he would make the most amazing dinner party subject and would be great with kids!'
Bill: 'He can't be left with kids! They'd be gone within seconds!'
Agatha: '... And I could teach him to do tricks and ...'
Bill: 'Eurgh! Did you just see that? He did his business right in front of everyone; he can't be kept in a house.'
Agatha: 'I could housetrain him.'
Bill: *'For the last time Grandma, you are not having the lion!'*
Agatha: '... Say that again and I'll set Kitty on you.'
Bill: 'Right, if you really want a pet, how about a bird? They don't take much looking after.'
Agatha: 'Would it have a fouler mouth than a Tourette's patient pumped up on caffeine?'
Bill: 'What? No!'
Agatha: 'Then leave me to die alone ... or if you don't want that maybe with some vampire bats.'
Bill: 'You just don't get this, do you?'

Rob Marsland (14)
Hadleigh High School, Ipswich

An Understanding

Another one. Another flash. Another scream as it hit them. It was too late. There were too many. They were strong, agile. Deadly. It was no use. More were coming. Guns were blazing. Another scream. They only needed a few more minutes. If only they could hold on. Another wave of them. How many were there? They must have killed at least a thousand. That's it, it's done. Another scream from behind. They were surrounded. The shooting stopped. No ammo.

It was quiet, whispering among the men. About dying. About your blood boiling as they hit you. At last they stayed back. Their long glowing limbs lashing at them. But they couldn't get past the barrier. At least for now. Only another minute until the shield gave out. 4 seconds, 3, 2, 1. This was it! There. The shields were down. Men started firing. 'Stop!' I yelled ...

The creatures are not advancing. They are just standing staring. Silently. They do not want war. They just want to understand us. My men are scared; for three days we have been battling and now they want peace. Why? They were winning. Why didn't they finish us off? They could have won. One walks forward, its long, flowing appendages behind it.

I walk forward. I touch it, feel its warmth. I close my eyes. I see a world. Their world. Destroyed by us. They are peaceful. They want a place to live, and we will let them.

Sam Churchyard (14)
Hadleigh High School, Ipswich

The Leaf Of Sackamia

The sky went dark as a ten-foot long creature swooped down and ripped an innocent, helpless man off the ground. The great golden chain that the man had been wearing crashed to the floor. The creature then dropped the man and fell on him gripping with its talons. The monster's beak ripped into the man's chest and proceeded to devour his heart.

This creature was called Viper, the sidekick of the twelve-foot-tall evil Killakanala. I saw it all happen and was horrified. People all around me were screaming. Then Viper left.

The hustle died down and council members announced the mayor had died. One of them said, 'We cannot keep letting Viper push us around. We have to stop it.'

Then another said, 'There is only one way to stop him. We need to get the Leaf of Sackamia and destroy Killakanala and Viper.'

Then the local tradesman replied, 'Impossible, no one could even reach the cave of Sackamia, they'd have to get over the mountains. Also that means getting past the goblins and Talons, Viper's black-hearted sister.'

Instantly I said, 'I will go. I know what could happen, I will do it for the town, but I don't want to go alone.'

The tradesman who had spoken earlier said, 'Do you know the town of Hillipania, because they are having the same trouble as us? There is a strong woman there who is travelling to get the Leaf of Sackamia. She is leaving at dawn tomorrow.'

'Yes, I know Hillipania. I will meet her tonight and leave with her tomorrow,' I replied.

The night dawned into a new day and the perilous quest continued.

Luke Bunce (12)
Hadleigh High School, Ipswich

The Missing Stone

Emerald and Jade travelled through the large, Elven town of Kingsly.

They were on their way to the mayor's village mansion. They had no idea why the mayor wanted to see them, although elves do normally have good ideas on why people want them, this one blocked out their minds like a migraine.

When they reached the mansion, Jade broke the silence. 'What do you think the mayor wants us for?' asked Jade.

'Don't ask me, you're the smart one!' replied Emerald, with a smile on her face.

The two young elves had not seen the mayor since their christening, although they were not sisters they were christened at the same time because their families had been friends, and not the richest of elves, so they decided it would be cheaper and easier to have it at the same time.

As the two elves were led through the hall of the mansion and to the office where the mayor was waiting, they grew more and more nervous. But when they saw the mayor himself, they just wanted to laugh! He was a short, stubby man. Although he was kind, he had a stern face, which always made him look angry, even when laughing.

'You wanted us, Sir?' asked Emerald, sounding more girlie and more stupid than ever.'

'Yes! I did!' shouted the mayor in very posh but rather loud manner. You see Steel Wizard who, as you know, is our worst enemy, has stolen the village's protective stone.'

With that Emerald's and Jade's eyes grew wide with horror.

'Without it, our village is in mortal danger, so I want you to go and retrieve it from Dark Country!' said the mayor.

Dark Country was where Steel Wizard's fortress was and the two girls knew that so they both shouted together, 'We accept!' sounding more excited than they ever had in their lives.

The major leaned forward to them both and shouted, 'The best of luck to both of you, you have three days to prepare!'

Jessica Evans (11)
Hadleigh High School, Ipswich

An Elven Adventure

There we were after strenuous training, standing by the fountain of Taverly. Four years ago, Barek, Niamh and I were sent to the seer, as is every other twelve-year-old. I can vividly remember the way Niamh flicked her fine, water-straight blonde hair, how calm her sapphire eyes were. And, as if in some comparison, there was Barek, my loyal, best friend who I have known for years and who was - in the nicest possible way, exceptionally clumsy. As the years have passed, I have not caught a glimpse of his face, as he went from helmet to helmet.

My given name is Omni. I am not extremely fast, not extremely strong and not extremely clever, but I am different. I have slightly strayed off topic a little and now I will return to the seer.

Dwelling in the temple of the sun, this geriatric woman has an extraordinary power. It could be said that she is clairvoyant. Others believe that she is a spirit herself. She can converse with spirits, bind them and control them. But she has a good heart and uses her powers with her better judgement.

We travelled furlongs, miles, kilometres. Whichever way you look at it, it was a protracted journey, becoming cumbersome with every step. It was worth it.

Archer. Warrior. Mage. These were the paths that she 'chose' for us. Our fate, our destiny. Our life. In this world you must use your talents just to survive. Archer. Warrior. Mage. I am one.

Christopher Neill (12)
Hadleigh High School, Ipswich

Niamh's Revenge

Niamh woke with a start, sweat trickling from her forehead and leaving fresh watermarks on her cheeks. Sinister dark was all around her, choking her as she sat up. Her pallid white eyes looked far into the distance as she remembered her grandfather's aroma - tobacco and peppermint - and his rosy cheeks that always looked like a bouquet of poppies, and how he permanently wore a cheeky grin.

She sat back but pain penetrated her body as a rocky surface lay smirking at her torture. Arduously she began to move forward on her hands and knees, crawling through the endless tunnel, not knowing which direction she was going.

The walls were biting her hands as she moved forward and the stones tripped her with every breath. Dimness swallowed her as she seemed to fall through time.

The lantern that she carried beside her smashed, as whispers washed around, words chanted in every breath, screams and warnings reverberated, 'Go back! Go back!' White spirits cascaded down the wall, their faces distraught and weeping.

The flutter of bat wings sounded off thick rock walls. A stone faltered her, screaming out in manic laughter. The rock floor growled at her as she crawled over its dusty surface. She was suffocating in its harsh climate. The air tasted sharp against her tongue like sour lemons.

As darkness began to descend upon her, she knew there was no escape from her destiny, or the danger ahead.

Zoe Jeeves (12)
Hadleigh High School, Ipswich

The Sacred Stone Of Tanjio

Bang! The thunder crashed against the cliffs. Sam was walking along the cliff tops by himself. The storm was worse than ever, the lightning lit up the sky like a light bulb and the rain looked like pins dropping from the sky. *Bang!* There was the thunder again. Sam started to jog so that he would get home quicker. *Crack!* Sam felt his legs fall from beneath him. On instinct he grabbed hold of the ledge of the cliff. The lightning had struck the cliff top and it had crumbled. Sam looked down and it made his stomach churn. If he was to fall he knew that he wasn't going to look pretty. With all of his strength he tried to pull himself back up to the top but he didn't have enough energy.

His hands were being sliced open by the rocks in the cliff top. He could see and feel his blood trickling down his arm. Sam knew that he wouldn't be able to hold out for much longer. He could feel his hands losing grip of the edge of the cliff. He tried pulling himself back up again but still he failed.

It made the situation that Sam was in twice as hard, due to the fact that it was raining. This was because the rain made Sam a lot heavier, plus his hands kept slipping and left him with only one hand to keep him up.

This was only the beginning …

Jack Butler (12)
Hadleigh High School, Ipswich

The Quest

One more step. I could see it glistening in the light that shed through the cracks in the rocky old cave. Reaching out I grasped the key. But why did I need it? All I had been told was to find the key that was in the old cave as it held a secret I needed to know. But what secret?

Suddenly the roof caved in before me. I turned round and fled for the entrance of the cave as the shelter crumbled behind me. I cried for help but the area around the cave was deserted. The sandy floor blinded me as I legged it for the opening.

I'd made it. I was out in the fresh mountain air. Just then, the cave collapsed!

I brushed the dirt off the key and saw the initials, 'LG'. The initials of my great grandmother. It was the key that opened that one door that no one had ventured into ... Until now ...

Chloe Gregory (12)
Hadleigh High School, Ipswich

Revenge

It was a stormy night when it happened, it was wet, miserable and gloomy. King Garak of the Elven realm had been in bed for just a couple of minutes when a clap of thunder made him jump. A strike of lightning made a dark figure clear. The dark figure looked like a gargoyle on the roof of the greenhouse-like palace.

The king was sitting up in bed when a pair of yellow glowing eyes peered through the balcony doors. King Garak thought he was seeing things so he closed his eyes. When he opened them the eyes had vanished, but the monster was still there. The rain had stopped even though there was thunder and lightning.

A flash of lightning struck the figure and he fell to the ground (or so the king thought). It had grabbed the base of the balcony.

The king grabbed an ancient dagger, that had been in his family for decades, from off the mantlepiece. He opened the doors that led to the balcony; he went to the edge where, on the ground, he saw blood in a puddle, then in the distance, with the help of his elven powers, he saw his children, Clarrise and Akrid, coming back with their mother, dead, in the cart.

With his dagger firmly in hand the king made his way back into his bedroom, the monster slid into the room, using the shadows as camouflage. The king heard the growl of the monster. He then came face to face with it. Then the king stabbed the monster in the arm. 'You must be Reptilimanog,' the king said.

The monster dived at him with his claws, then picked him up and threw him off the edge of the balcony.

Clarrise and Akrid had only just reached the gate when they saw the monster climbing onto the roof and then jump into the distance towards the rising sun.

The city smelt of death and torture. The prince and princess ran towards the dying king, but by the time they reached him, he was already dead, along with the guards.

Claude Claireaux (12)
Hadleigh High School, Ipswich

The Quest

'I hate you! I hate you! I hate you! Why did you have to give birth to me? I hate you!' Tom slammed the door, ran down the stairs of the flats, sprinted round the corner and into his hideout. He was safe there. Only Will and he knew about it. It was a small, abandoned sweet shop that shut years ago. When they'd found the shop it was layered with dust and it smelt, but now it was clean with a sofa and a chair. Tom and Will often spent time in there talking about things and doing their homework.

Tom texted Will and told him to come to the hideout immediately. Will arrived on his BMX bike.

'What's wrong?' Will asked.

'I hate my mum, she such a little ...' Tom paused and then sighed. 'It's my dad.'

'What about him? He's dead ...' Will asked curiously.

'He's alive, perfectly safe. He's alive.'

Will gasped with shock but stayed silent.

'I came home early from school and Mum was on the phone. She was saying things like, 'Just stay out of our lives, you were the one who left us,' and 'No, you're not coming to see Tom, leave us alone Paul.'

'I crept closer to the phone and she asked him what his new address was. I wrote it down as she repeated it aloud. Look it's here in my pocket.' Tom reached into his pocket and took out a scrap of paper. He gave it to Will.

Shân Bendall (12)
Hadleigh High School, Ipswich

The Fire Boy

The headlines read 'Fire In Barn Affects Baby'. I did that, all of that was me, that huge fire that was in the barn was all my fault but I must tell you how I began liking to start fires.

It was a cold, wintry night and I had only just moved into my new house in the countryside. It was about five o'clock in the evening when my mother said she was going to light the coal fire. I had never seen a coal fire before or seen anybody light one so I wanted to watch Mum light it; that is when it all started.

First of all I started with small fires like grass in the back garden and then went on to light bigger and bigger fires. It was a TV programme that gave me the idea of starting a fire in the big barn at the end of the road. It was my biggest job and it gave me such a thrill watching it burn, every colour of the rainbow could be seen in those flames. It was really cool and good to watch.

How was I to know that the house next door would also catch alight and that a newborn baby was in that house and that it would be affected by the smoke? I did not want that to happen nor any harm come to anybody ...

Ryan Ellis (13)
Hadleigh High School, Ipswich

Incendiary

I did it. That was me. The massive orange, leaping mountain firing away in front of me was my entire fault! One match was all it took to create a ball of destruction. The smoke was covering the night sky, smothering everything higher than five metres.

Hundreds of people were surrounding me and the fire. Some were standing in shock, others were shouting at me. I tried to turn and look at who was shouting but my eyes were stuck on the blazing fire which I had caused. When I struck the match, a bullet of power went through my body; I had complete control of what was going to happen, I felt confident that I knew the consequences and how to handle them. Now I realise I was wrong. I am glad I did it, just to see the look on their faces.

Two years ago was when it all started. At home my dad had left my mother with five children. My mother couldn't cope and she sent me and my sister away to different foster homes. She promised us she would come and see us a lot but she never did.

My foster home didn't want me but still kept me; they did it for the money. They got the money which they were meant to spend on keeping me but instead they kept it for themselves.

Revenge, was my object. Some might say stupid, spiteful or even attention-seeking, but all it was, was sweet revenge!

Sarah Spice (13)
Hadleigh High School, Ipswich

The Life Of A Tiger

I wish I was at home with my dear family, instead I gazed as they took me away from my homeland. Voices shouted and eyes glared as I curled in the corner of my steel cage.

It was like a frozen lake, the van I mean, the crisp wind from the miniature square wood window shot through my ruffled, stiff fur. Those terrible monsters with bone earrings and hanging cork hats were always observing me with every bit of their minds. I heard whistles, crying animals and I wondered what they would do to me.

Then I saw my sister, hurt, in her little tin cage. I turned very slowly and saw those shattered animals, their hearts broken. Then this tall man with gleaming boots which reflected in my tired eyes, stood on my weak tin cage, squashed it and his flared trousers flapped in the fresh wind.

I heard a click, then a rattle, they took me!

Rachel Louden (12)
Hadleigh High School, Ipswich

Deadly Dreams!

I tossed and turned trying to get some sleep in the old wooden bunk bed. When I moved, it creaked. Trying everything to get to sleep, I even tried staying still with my eyes shut and counting sheep, but nothing worked.

Suddenly I heard a car pull up, well at least I thought I did. Moving silently down the bed, I did not hear my bed creak that time, that was strange.

I flew out of the window and landed by the front garden. A black car pulled up; at first glance it looked like a limo but further inspection revealed a hearse. Meanwhile, I stood there motionless staring at the two people inside the vehicle. Two very large men stood there, both of them were dressed in black suits. At first I only saw the shoes, black, polished to perfection. As I moved up to the rear of the hearse they were unaware of my presence. *Weird,* I thought, because I was standing next to one of the men. He was either blind or just plain stupid.

The men opened the boot and pulled out a *coffin!* Fear struck me like a lightning bolt, my legs turned to jelly. The men carried the coffin on their shoulders over to my front door, they laid it down carefully and drove off.

Then I heard my front door open. I turned to see myself standing at the door. As I watched myself, the image of me opened the coffin and examined the body for a while ...

Engraved on the coffin lid in bold letters was 'Chris Newman, loved by all, RIP'.

That is my name, Chris Newman!

Connor Bentley (12)
Hadleigh High School, Ipswich

A Day In The Life Of A Salamander

I heard a strange noise. Not the usual tropical rainforest sounds like the dripping of the leaves or the constant twittering of exotic birds; it was a different sound. The sound of men shouting and the thud of footsteps behind me. They were getting closer. I tried to hide, darting behind a leaf and curling my tail around my scaly body but it didn't work. Before I knew what was happening, I was snatched up, grabbed by my tail and flung into a small, dark crate.

I'm not sure what happened next as I fell asleep, but when I awoke I had no idea where I was. I was petrified; all I wanted to do was run home. I darted across the strange wood chippings, I could see the outdoors, I was going to make it! *Smack!* I hit some sort of transparent force field, standing between me and my freedom.

My vision was blurred; the whole world was spinning before my eyes. I heard voices; I looked up to see three human faces pressed up against the glass.

'What is it?' said one of the faces.

'I dunno … some sort of lizard thing,' replied another. 'It's boring, make it move!'

Suddenly the walls around me began to shake and the ground shuddered beneath my feet. I hid under a leaf, shivering with fear.

'Come on, let's go,' I heard one of them say, as they disappeared to torment some other poor creature.

Hannah Main (12)
Hadleigh High School, Ipswich

The Frail Old Woman

My parents have recently bought a nice house. The house itself is not that old. It sits on top of a large hill surrounded by trees. Recently, for no apparent reason, we've had many strange things happening.

While practising on her piano, my sister, Monica, heard a voice behind her say, 'Come on Monica, you can do it. Keep trying.' She turned around to see this frail old woman dressed in black sitting in the lounge. Monica screamed and went to get Mum and Dad but the woman had gone.

A week later, Monica was taking a shower when she happened to take a glance in the mirror only to see this large face of the same woman. She ran out screaming and crying.

During Christmas Day, we thought it would be funny to hypnotise Monica just by playing. She started counting, she started to skip numbers. 30 seconds later she started screaming at the top of her lungs, 'She's going to kill me, she's got a knife!'

'Oh my God! She has gone mad!'

When Dad finally woke her up, she could only remember a lady with red hair chasing her with a knife.

Gena French (12)
Hadleigh High School, Ipswich

The Ruins

The gloom hanging over them, a curtain of silk brushed across their delicate faces, watching their every move cautiously, watching their every move. Mysterious groaning, coming from the desolate darkness. Moving closer, the moaning getting louder. They came to the clearing, a deep, eerie groaning starting from behind the clasped rotten door. Daring not to move, daring not to breathe.

A distant howl shattered the silence; the door exposed innards. The smoke ascended and evaporated leaving a tense atmosphere behind. It was deserted. A shadow proceeded over them like a shooting star flying across a midnight sky; they backed into a corner, it picked them off one by one, showing no mercy!

It took them to a prison cell. The smell of rotting flesh was overwhelming; the oxygen was thinning, leaving a dank, disgusting smell. There was a tiny crevice in the wall. A weed was sprouting. They brought the wall down with the cracked, dusty bones from the aged yet solid floor, revealing a desolate forest leaving a trail of destruction behind. They came to a lake filled to the brim with precious metals; they urged to touch them, their hands had minds of their own. They reached out slowly.

The shadow hid behind an immense leaf, watching, waiting, but this time it wasn't sparing them!

Matthew Powell (12)
Hadleigh High School, Ipswich

The Tiger That Tried To Defy Nature

As I lie in the mud surrounded by tall bright grass, I think to myself, *do I have a purpose in life?* For everything around me seems to have one. Why did God make me? What does He want me to do? I guess I haven't found out yet. Everything seems so pointless. I feel desolate, because my mum and dad have gone. Abandoned me in the big world.

I spot another tiger lurking nearby. Then it stops, slowly raises its head and, as quick as a flash, leaps over to the antelope and lands directly on its head, making it scream. By now the tiger has clawed the antelope's throat and the antelope is struggling to survive. It painfully utters its last squeals of help and then it finally passes away as the tiger eats it. It's mean. Sadness comes rushing to me. I feel as if it's evil to kill like that. There must be something else I can survive on.

I attempt to look for different foods. I've spent three hours looking now. There's nothing, nothing at all. Then luckily I spot a dead animal lying on the ground. I think, *at least I don't have to kill this one.* I stride closer to the animal. It's a warthog. I'm just about to have my dinner when I'm attacked by a tiger. I fun in fear for I don't understand how to fight. There's only one thing I can do …

I have to kill tonight!

Bryony Clarke (12)
Hadleigh High School, Ipswich

A Day In The Life Of A Working Child

My name is Zac, I'm thirteen and I live in Ethiopia. Work plays the most important part in my life. My job is to stitch footballs. I work twelve hours a day, from seven in the morning to seven at night, except on a Sunday when I play football with my mates. I live with my two-year-old sister, Lara. My mother and father both died two months ago with a serious illness. I take Lara to work with me and when I go out with my mates, my cousin Anya looks after her.

My dream would be to have been a professional footballer and be able to go to school but at my age it's a bit late now. I can't afford to go to school because I only get fifty pence for each football I stitch and I stitch one a day. When my mother and father were here, I didn't have to work because they had earned enough for clothes and food. Having to go to work is like being in prison. You can't leave until you've finished.

As I walk back home from work I see young kids on the streets alone with blankets covering their heads. Lara and I are very lucky to have a home even if it is just a hut. At least we're safe.

When Lara is older I don't want her to have to go to work. I want her to have the life I never had a chance to live.

Jasmine Carter (11)
Hadleigh High School, Ipswich

A Day In The Life Of An Elephant ... In The Circus

The blinding stage lights burned into my eyes, my leg was encased in a thick, rusty padlock. I was hauled into the spotlight and forced to rear up towards the congregation of spectators. Their contented, smug faces cheered, they loved seeing me unhappy, alone and having to perform night after night, with several humans at a time mounting my exhausted back and prancing about with sticks of burning devastation. They destroyed my home.

Every night to save myself from starvation, I had to indulge on a thick, slimy, gritty paste which tasted foul. They also occasionally gave me fruit, but not anything like the fresh, moist fruit I used to select in India, my homeland, where I long to be at this very moment.

At dawn, it was like a motorway rush hour. Trapeze artists, hot-footedly darting around in their second-skin leotards, glinting joyfully in the morning sun, the dew sparkling like 15-carat diamonds. Clowns slapping on eccentric make-up and oversized shoes. Fire-eaters fuelling themselves with highly protective liquid, the ringmaster practising his sonorous tone. His elegant velvet coat shimmered, the rich plum tint of his glossy boots reflected his fastidious nature.

Chantelle Ward (12)
Hadleigh High School, Ipswich

The Worst Day Of My Life!

On the 14th April, 1912, my mum and I boarded the Titanic. It was a lovely sunny afternoon when I first set foot on that death trap, I was excited. It was my first journey over the ocean.

A girl, Polly, her mum, my mum and I shared a room; we had to share because we were second class. But I didn't really mind. I never thought I would like Polly, but after a few hours it seemed as if we had been friends for years. We went searching the ship for a den; we found a lifeboat covered with a purple rain cover. It was brilliant. We stayed there for ages.

Suddenly the boat shook, it felt like we had hit something. We got out of our den; it was dark, people were screaming. I didn't understand what was happening.

We went to find our mums, they were running up the stairs, they told us the Titanic had hit an iceberg, the ship was sinking. As we were second class we had to wait until all the first class people had gone. It took three hours and the water was up to my chest. I didn't know whether I would survive.

Then when we got out, everyone was pushing and shoving, I was nudged to the back with Polly. After half an hour, there were no more lifeboats left.

The ship broke in two, everyone slid into the icy waters.

Who would live? Who would die?

Lucy Lester (12)
Hadleigh High School, Ipswich

Silver Unicorn

A waterfall of beauty flowed from her long mane as she galloped into the darkness. The moon shone down on her silver back, reflecting moonbeams into the night sky. A cold wisp of wind swept the nearby leaves into the air; they danced together across the derelict plains. Her horn was as sharp as a dagger piercing through the sharp air as she continued into the vast emptiness.

I gasped as the creature reared up with an almighty noise. She rose up in all her glory. She stood alone; the spotlight was on her as she lifted her silver body up to the moon. Just the one thing, shining with radiance, standing alone in a world of darkness. She was like a beacon, a ray of light to the blanket of black fog.

She would often come out at the dead of night and gallop alone. Her streamlined body would run until the break of day. She was never seen by any other creature and when the sun started to creep out, something so mysterious and magical would happen ...

A gush of wind would envelop her body as she slowly transformed. The whirlwind slowly decreased unveiling a hideous creature. It scurried into a dark shadow, lurking under the cover of safety. The small grotesque body slowly slunk out of sight. Daylight could never catch this hideous creature.

When the sun finally started to set, the magic of the transformation would start again. Stones were plucked from the ground and spun around the 'thing' and through the mist of dirt, out stepped the magnificent creature. The silver unicorn!

Lauren Gant (14)
Hadleigh High School, Ipswich

Infinite

It steamed, the light grey wisps expanding and contracting in the warm, humid air. The soft wisps lengthened, stretching towards the dark, rolling thunderclouds that were about to emit their tremendous boom over the comparatively silent screeches of small animals being eaten, the loud, deafening roars that accompanied them - those which told the listener what, or who, was about to eat the small, terrified creature.

The boom cracked out, the superheated air radiating from the bolt of light that was hurtling down towards the green waving treetops and the muddy river. It undulated over the shaking canopy, sinking into the wide river basin, but enveloping everything. Nothing could withstand its terrible wrath, the now black skies agreeing, harmonising with the thunder and adding another flare to illuminate the windswept, rain-torn hillside, to superheat more air, create another sonic boom.

The new lighting was the type of flare that left its imprint upon your eyes, your brain, your conscience, blinding you and remaining with you forever. An ethereal howl filled the interminable space between the shockwaves of thunder, filling the hole that the thunder had created, and expanding it further, again ripping down, through the ears, through the brain, to the now ravaged soul. The perpetual scream shredded what resolve any man would have had left, if any man had been there.

But there was. Her resolve was ripped into little tiny pieces and she would flee, if she had any idea where to flee to, or where she was, or if she was conscious.

Oliver Benton (14)
Hadleigh High School, Ipswich

Rise Of The Phoenix

Centuries ago, after the reign of dragons and dinosaurs, lived great creatures that ruled the skies. A phoenix is a beautiful bird of fire, but has long since died out. Rising from the ashes, a phoenix can reincarnate itself. Thought to be long extinct, the phoenix has become a myth, but now it's back! Back for revenge against the thing that wiped out the last phoenix.

A phoenix cannot be destroyed by anything, but one force can destroy a phoenix. A phoenix is a bird of fire; water can obliterate fire so a phoenix cannot swim. The force that destroyed the last phoenix was the sea. Once a phoenix drowns, it sinks and reincarnates, but drowns again immediately. Stuck in a vicious circle.

Scientists have recently discovered a phoenix egg at the bottom of the sea, this egg has been incubated, has recently hatched and has broken out of the laboratory in which it was held.

Flying across the sky with swoops of its colossal wings, scorching the clouds and burning the very air itself, the phoenix hurls fireballs the size of buses at the sea, who bubbles and steams whenever the beast is near.

For years the battle goes on, humans scared to go near the furious creature until one ... 'I must do this,' the phoenix explains. 'I will carry on until my fire dies, only then can I find peace.'

For a phoenix, revenge is sweet; so the sea boils and the fury of revenge burns inside the heart of the great creature, until it finds peace and lies down to rest.

Victoria Gray (14)
Hadleigh High School, Ipswich

The Old Mill

The white van pulled up. It was three o'clock, yet it was already dark. Rain smashed onto the roof. I was led out into death. My chains rattled as I waddled closer and closer to the end of my life. I stopped, looked how my life would end before being knocked out and carried inside.

I awoke to a blank, dull room with four blank, dull walls and a beast hanging over me.

'You're back.'

I could barely see him through the thick blood dropping over my eyes and face. I spat my blood over him, only to receive a punch in return. Then he left, leaving me alone. I lay there for a moment wondering why? Why would Danny do this? Why would he betray me? Why would he betray the force? All I knew was I had to get out. I was tied to a bench.

Two men came back in looking around frantically, only to find I was no longer there. Then in a hurry they both left again. I jumped down. There was nowhere to hide, so I made a mad dash for the door like a cheetah after its prey.

I ventured into a new room, a much more interesting room, filled with huge, loud machines. More men rushed back to the room I used to occupy. I shut the door of my trap, locking ten men inside, but I knew more would come. I wandered carefully around this room, looking at the product of these machines.

I saw it. Now I knew I had to get out …

Peter Bridge
Hadleigh High School, Ipswich

The Mansion

The full moon was the only source of light illuminating the creepy, rundown old mansion. The thick mist was a carpet laid over the front lawn of the house which was practically screaming, 'Stay away.'

'Still don't think it is haunted,' whispered David. 'There's no such thing as ghosts, I'm not scared and to show you, I'm going in there, if you're too much of a wimp, then you can stay out here in this creepy garden, all on your own then, alright?'

'But you're welcome to come with me,' Seth confidently muttered.

David just followed Seth without saying a thing. Seth turned on his flashlight. It seemed the closer they got to the house, the colder it got. Finally they got to the massive oak door, holding two steel gargoyle knockers, which were staring at the young boys with their evil eyes. Seth tried the handle. It didn't move an inch. But he didn't give in there, they tiptoed around the perimeter of the large mansion seeking a way in. Then, in the corner of his eye, David saw a window ajar. Both the boys stopped and pushed together. The window flew open much easier than they expected, mostly because the pine frame was extremely rotten. They made up their minds. David grabbed Seth's foot and gave him a boost up. Then Seth pulled David up. They fell on top of each other with a loud *crash!*

Daniel Page
Hadleigh High School, Ipswich

The Redcoats Are Coming

'The Redcoats are coming,' were to be the last words my lord would hear before he died facing them. He had prepared a great army of Scotsmen armed to the teeth with weapons. However the sword and shields were no match for the English weapons.

But here I am five years later, armed the same as my lord. Day after day I wait to hear the voice of the guards shouting, 'The Re ... the Redcoats are coming.'

The women and children rushed inside to hide from the inevitable.

'Ready the archers! Close the gates!'

The gate slammed shut as men rushed to the wall to take position.

'Light arrows! Fire!' A hail of arrows lit up the night sky to reveal five thousand Redcoats and ten English cannons all aiming and ready to fire on us. The Redcoats had walked straight into our trap, a freshly soaked field in oil. When the field lit up, it revealed an extra fifteen thousand Redcoats and thirty cannons.

The cannons started to open fire.

'Take cover!' Some men started running down the wall, some just ducked. It didn't matter. The ones on the wall got crushed under it when it collapsed. The men that managed to get off the wall were ripped to shreds by the splinters from the gate as cannons smashed against it. The only men left were the guards in my keep and there were only ten of them armed with pikes ...

Kyle Collins (14)
Hadleigh High School, Ipswich

A Day In The Life Of Migration

The sun was beckoned into the earth by the pleasing and welcoming horizon, there to hide for the hours of slumber. Thick, doggish clouds formed over the moonlit sky and thunder hurled across the land. My future stalking each step, guiding me to the path I'm about to take ...

At last I've finally got my chance to shine. Great monsters that spend their whole lives preparing me, until the five minutes of falling through a heavy hypnotic atmosphere of enticement have vanished. My neighbours are all migrating with me. All objects appear distorted. I can't picture anything that surrounds my feeble self. Nothing but an obscurity.

A tree, I think, *or a forest, fields maybe?* Now the adrenaline is pumping through my weak, negligible body, faster and faster. But now it feels so much different. An overpowering ball moulded around my slender shape. So what if my life is short? Every moment is beautiful, every second is a memory that I will treasure forever.

The ground is becoming clear now, the whole landscape is like a detailed painting of a painting. And yet, at this point in my life I feel anxious. All I do is fall aimlessly, to die would be my adventure killed at its grandest. The wet ground looked hard and evil, his eyes melting into me, blistering my flesh. Tales were all that I dreamt of about the earth and to see all these dreams fold into oblivion, the lies on which I forced myself to believe.

My stony grave lay before me. Splashes and pounds, thuds, trickles. None of them welcoming, none of them friendly. All my thoughts, every happy, sad, fearful, elated, curious, angry and betrayed thought. All of them stop.

Jaki Freeth (14)
Hadleigh High School, Ipswich

Reflection Of A Raindrop

The raindrops slapped the window aimlessly, then ran away just to leave the only lonely one to drip and fall haphazardly off the edge of the window to the longing pavement below after colliding twenty times or more with other raindrops.

This pretty normal rainy day scene was the very painting of my life.

Yesterday she fulfilled her daily threats and hunted me down, armed with an army of twenty plus: all stalking and following my panic-stricken tracks exactly, as if she could smell my fear in the humidity of the air, lingering in the pavement and whispering in the wind. If only I hadn't accidentally tripped up her best friend on sports day two weeks ago, disqualifying her automatically. What part of 'accident' doesn't she understand, the 'acci' or the 'dent'?

Dart. Dodge. Dip. Dive. Will I ever get away from her ever-growing gang? Or, as she likes to call them, 'My group o' homies!' Her fake accident echoed through the shopping centre with such a high-pitched squeal, it was as if I were escaping from fifty of her. If cloning ever caught on she would have to be the most unlikely guinea pig.

Gone. Disappeared. Where had she gone? Relief. I had escaped ... *bang!* Her foot thundered to the ground, 'And where d'ya fink you're goin'?' Where had she come from? I was so absorbed and cocooned in my own thoughts of wonder and dismay I didn't realise that I had become that raindrop ...

Flora McLennan (14)
Hadleigh High School, Ipswich

A Lost Soul

'What's your name?' asked a middle-aged woman; she then sighed and tried again to get the man to talk. 'Where have you come from?' Still there was no reply from the young, afraid man who sat before her.

The man was shrivelled up, clutching onto his arms, he had a single tear running down his face; however he did not sob loudly, he simply rocked back and forth on the chair. He had long, mysterious hair which draped across his shoulders; he had dark, bold eyes which were full of fear and dread. Only he knew who he was, he had not yet shared his secret with anyone.

Professor Harding was holding a clipboard in his right hand and in the other, he held his pen; he was unaware that he was tapping the board; he was tapping a familiar tune, a very famous one by Mozart.

'Professor, look,' Nurse Adler whispered. She gently pointed to the man sitting at the desk. He was lightly tapping his fingers on the table, imitating someone playing the piano.

The lost man was taken to the cathedral where there was a grand piano; the moment he sat down, it was like he remembered everything he had ever known, he was back in his life. Tears were streaming down his face as he began to play. He played: Mozart, Bach, Beethoven. He played so softly but with immense power. He cared for the piano, it was his passion and maybe the one thing that kept him sane at Hardingway Hospital.

This great man was a scared, whimpering child away from the piano, away from his life but once he sat in the piano chair, he was whole, normal, confident, happy.

Grace Kebby (14)
Hadleigh High School, Ipswich

Hercules With A Modern Day Twist

The sun shone through the window as the first ray of light was absorbed into his bed. Hercules sprung out of his bed and swept his curtains shut. Disliking the sun first thing in the morning was not a good thing for Hercules.

Hercules was a tall man; ginger hair with a red cotton band holding long wavy locks back; so it didn't sway in his face. Baby-blue eyes and rosy-red cheeks were the main features of his triangular-shaped face.

When ready, Hercules stepped out of the newly built building onto the dusty concrete floor. As soon as he took his first step outside, a blue racing Subaru car came zooming past with one white man, Stephen, driving the car and a black man, Will, with an old western gun in his oily hand, pointing it at the police car chasing them.

Hercules started running as fast as he could, full speed the other way. The Subaru took a sharp spin around the corner of the building, taking half the other car coming the other way, with it. Jumping out of his seat, Stephen ran up to the road near the Tower Bridge and jumped into the water. He swam as fast as he could away from the bridge.

While Stephen was running away, Hercules ran up to the Subaru and put some handcuffs on Will's wrist. He rang up the police station for some back-up …

Peter Bartram (13)
Hadleigh High School, Ipswich

Merry

'Alex. I need you with me. It's Janet. She's ...'
'She's what?' I shouted. I expected a reply. But, of course nothing came - an answerphone cannot reply.
I grabbed a bunch of keys from my pocket, shoved them into the ignition and forced my numb foot onto the accelerator. Meredith; I'd never heard her voice like that - so soft and so fraught.

'Merry, it's good to be afraid. You shouldn't hide it from me - I'm scared too.'
'Don't' she replied bitterly. She spat the word at him and her voice was cold and stony. It startled her husband.
'Don't do what?'
'Call me Merry. My name is Meredith.'
'Who were you calling, Meredith?'
'Alex.'
Tom sighed profoundly and almost whispered when he said, 'Oh Merry why?'
Meredith leapt to her feet, launched herself at Tom and forced him to the floor. She put her mouth against his ear and screamed. It pierced Tom's head and he began to moan. She drew her head back sharply but then lowered it again to his ear. She shouted, 'He's my husband! And he's Janet's father!'
Now it was Tom who screamed out his anger. 'Ex-husband! He's your ex-husband! I'm your husband. You ungrateful bitch!' Tom struggled, and ran from the house - just as Alex pulled into the driveway.

'Merry, what's happened?'
She ran over to me and flung her arms around my neck.
'Merry, Merry, what's happened to Janet?'
Her voice suddenly fell to a hoarse whisper, 'She's dead.'

Kirsty Farthing (14)
Hadleigh High School, Ipswich

Keep Your Enemies Close To You

As I watch this woman, I take pleasure in her not knowing ... that I am her stalker. She thinks that I'm her best friend. That's wrong, in fact it's totally the opposite. I'm her enemy. And as I watch her now, all I feel is hatred and jealousy. Then, as these feelings boil over I have the sudden urge to kill her right now. But then I relax again, when I reassure myself that it will soon become a reality. You see, she always takes what I want, and this time, she has something that is far too precious for me to lose. Her husband. Although he doesn't know it yet, I love him. Except there's one big problem - her. She can't love him as much as I ever will. She doesn't deserve him. She can't see the pain I am going through. So the only way I can have him, is for her to be ... *dead!* I know how I'm going to kill her; I'm going to pierce her heart repeatedly, just like she does to me every time I see them together. You know you always keep your enemies close to you.

Two hours, sixteen minutes and nineteen seconds until he's in my arms forever. Very soon, we will live without her presence looming over us.

Sitting on her foul fern-coloured couch, her front living room was a complete replica of mine. I was her stalker. I stared across the room until I met her pale face. I asked myself, *how could he love her, not me?* Hatred and jealousy came flooding back to me, but I could not relax myself this time. I had to finish this.

She was finished.

Lauren Bridges (14)
Hadleigh High School, Ipswich

Love

Love can turn the most noble men into brutish monsters and can make poor men feel like kings. Women who have been gentle and kind become fierce and unruly. Women who are cynics find the world full of romance. Love changes everything. Grey skies turn blue. From despair comes hope, and trust can turn into monstrous jealousy. Love is kind but cruel, miracle or madness.

The most transforming and loyal love is that for your child. The love you brought into the world. So when a police officer comes to your door to tell you that your daughter has had a car accident and is dead, no woman acts the way she should. They don't embrace sympathy and tenderness or let a friend hold out a comforting hand. They don't care for others, yet they don't care for themselves ...

Her small hands clasped my swollen breasts. Her tiny feet kicked and wriggled. Her soft eyes closed in contentment and she sighed softly.

What does a policeman think of you when you fly at him with flailing arms and vicious screams?

Her plump golden curls bounced as she ran. Her cheeks turned rosy with cold. She fell; but jumped right back up.

What will your neighbours think of you when you refuse to cry?

Her eyes glowed with happiness. Her wedding dress flowed behind her, her laugh echoed through the church; and everyone was silent.

Hadley French Gerrard (14)
Hadleigh High School, Ipswich

Theseus And The Minotaur

The story began thousands of years ago when Athens was at war with Crete. Even though the war was over between the two, Minos who was still King of Crete and King of Athens, made Athens pay an awful tribute as a sign of peace.

Half bull, half man, the Minotaur was the most fearsome monster of ancient times. Its horns were sharp as knives, its great hooves could kick the life out of the strongest of heroes, and its food was human flesh. The Minotaur lived in the labyrinth, a great maze of winding passages on the island of Crete.

Each year seven men and seven women were sent from Greece as food for the beast to contribute their peace on a ship which set sail with the deadly, black sail hoisted.

But one year, Theseus, the greatest of Greek heroes said that he would go to Crete and fight the monster. 'Let me go as one of the victims,' he said to his father. 'I'll kill the Minotaur and free Greece from this peril.'

Aegeus was unsure. He remembered how others had promised to kill the beast and had ended up dead, but Theseus insisted.

Soon his ship was rigged with black sails, which was the custom when Greeks were sailing to meet their doom. 'Watch out for when I return,' said Theseus. 'I will hoist white sails to show that I've succeeded.'

Theseus' ship arrived at the harbour of Knossos, near the palace of King Minos of Crete ...

Ami Simpkin (14)
Hadleigh High School, Ipswich

Why Were You ... ?

'Why were you walking down the seafront?' Mr Smith shouted.

I was thinking to myself, *I am not going to say anything to anyone.*

'I am going to ask you one more time, what where you doing down the seafront?' He kept on asking these questions.

I'm not going to answer. They just don't get it!

Nurses kept on giving me paper, should I write something or not?

I just drew a piano, if they didn't understand they must be ...

'Come on Sir, we have something to show you,' said one of the nurses.

I didn't know what to expect. Was it good? Was it bad?

They took me into a church, yes, in the hospital. They sat me on the piano bench. How did they know that I liked playing the piano?

'Do you like the piano?' said one of the kind nurses.

Why are they talking like I am a little child? *Hey, sweetie, you must think of something better than that because I'm not talking!* I looked around, they were all glaring at me like I was some sort of animal, a rare species that no one had ever seen. In my eyes, everyone else was gone, it was just the piano and me.

'Wow, he can play!' said one of the nurses.

'He should be famous, seriously he is really, really good,' Mr Smith sighed.

No one knows how much I love to play this instrument. Playing the piano means everything to me.

'We should really contact his family,' Mr Smith said nicely.

'Yeah, that would be great, if he would or could talk to us,' the kind nurse answered.

Mica Finch (14)
Hadleigh High School, Ipswich

A Day In The Life Of An Explorer

The Beginning

Mosquitoes buzzed above and below me whilst exotic birds chattered in the distance. The electrical roar of chainsaws echoed around the valley as bark underneath was noisily squashed down as creatures trampled over it.

I opened my eyes and gradually turned my head to see a mass of green and brown growth. Trees. Peering down the reddish-brown coloured hairy trunk, the bugs disappeared and all that could be seen were dead leaves, soil and bark. In-between the overhanging branches were a few wisps of slightly silvery smoke, weaving in and out of the atmosphere.

Cautiously, I stretched out each cramped foot and started descending downwards. Each branch took a turn of holding my weight by two feet and, over time, I reached land. Once there I stood still and tilted my head upwards. Amazing. Extraordinary! I had never known the rainforests to be so indescribable. Trees and bushes of all shapes, sizes and heights, were towering above me. Lianas climbed up and down the sides of mossy tree trunks. Some blossomed at the top, showing off magnificent flowers, with diameters of twelve centimetres. I felt like a mouse in a giant's land. Each and every plant had its own way of reaching and stretching limbs, strangling them around each tree. I had never known rainforests to be so exquisite.

Gradually I brought my head back down and started to advance forward. Sensing, after a while, that someone or something was nearby, I sped up. Excitement was now bubbling up inside, about to burst. What was it?

Charlotte Gregory (14)
Hadleigh High School, Ipswich

Frozen Speech

The night was frozen; the swift wind felt like ice as it touched warm flesh. There was no movement within the grounds of the mansion, all you could feel was the chill of the wind and the sinister sensation of an invisible eye scanning its prey and awaiting the perfect moment to strike.

The mansion stood tall above the courtyard, its silhouette loomed threateningly over the horizon. Heavy drops of blood began to fall from the bleeding clouds; bones of streamed light thumped at the floor and illuminated the grounds beneath the silhouetted manor.

The ground soon became a reeking bog, the mud sucked up the small plants slowly feasting on them, its appetite was endless, it swallowed up anything it could into its endless gut.

A shadowed figure gradually revealed itself from the mansion. It was the figure of a small person. It seemed to be lugging something across the floor. As the huge beams of light streaked up from the floor, its figure became more visible. It was wearing a hooded black cloak. The only visible feature of its face was its pale lips and a few scars were also visible.

As it moved closer to the recently created swamp in the grounds, the item it was lugging across the floor became more visible. It was a man!

The thing dragging him along the floor spoke in its frozen speech, 'Mealtime!'

Leon Slater (14)
Hadleigh High School, Ipswich

The Emperor And Horus

Even through the shields the impact makes the Imperial Palace shake. With a screech of tortured stone an angel topples from its alcove high on the throne room wall and crashes to the marble floor a kilometre below. It shatters into a million pieces. Splinters of stone flash across the hall like shrapnel.

From his throne the Emperor watches his warriors mill around in confusion. This hall holds ten thousand men, seasoned veterans, and all are now panicking. He knows they are more frightened by his silence than by the enemy. They look to him for leadership and he can give them none.

For the first time in his millennia-long life, the Emperor knows despair. The magnitude of his defeat stuns him. The lunar bases have fallen. Most of the Earth is under the war master's heel. Rebel Titans surround the palace and are held at bay only by the desperate efforts of a few loyalists. It is only a matter of time before the palace's defences fail and the last bastions of resistance fall.

'Sire, what are you orders?' asks Rogal Dorn, massive dark-haired Primarch of the Imperial Fists. His golden armour has lost its lustre, it is dented in a dozen places by bolter shells. The Emperor doesn't answer. He is lost within himself seeking answers to his own questions.

He has come at last to the dark place, the time of testing, the era hidden from his precognitive vision and beyond which he cannot see.

Sam Cook (14)
Hadleigh High School, Ipswich

4C Child

There they are, laughing again, looking straight at me with their small piggy eyes, glaring guardedly.

I walk on, with my head cowed, shivering against the vicious sparks flying at me. Tittering, garish laughter squawks from them in a hysterical tirade but I manage to block them out. Pretend I am not there. Not being me.

I blink, glazed watering eyes, tears that threaten to over-breach their boundaries and roll unkempt down my whey cheeks, falling on my broken cuffs and ripped skin. Pulling myself back up to my ungainly feet, I stumble back from them as they jeer excitedly, expecting another round.

I whisper to myself, 'I am not here. I am not here,' blinded by the lack of colour in my life, blinded by harsh reality.

Lessons jar on, filling my day with a ribald amount of shouting, screaming, leaving me shuddering for peace and quiet as I sit at my desk, lost in this week's assignment. Stuttering wrong answers, mesmerised by the shades of grey that swim before me, I tire of the noise.

I trip over words, rewriting my first sentence over and over again, frustrated by the images that won't be unlocked, shut behind barred doors in my head.

Naomi Webb (14)
Hadleigh High School, Ipswich

Incendiary

The yellow flames roared in front of me. The orange glow of the fire burned my dull eyes and fragile skin. The clatter of the fire engines was enough to deafen any passers-by.

I remember striking the match, spreading the petrol, I had a thousand feelings rushing through my shaking body: joy, anger, revenge. Revenge was the strongest feeling of all; I can't remember what they did but it was a deep feeling, as deep as the ocean itself.

The fuss made by the owners of the barn made it all worthwhile. As I saw them in the distance, running, screaming around, 'Help!' a smug smile spread across my face, I think they knew who it was, but were afraid to press charges, now nobody will know.

There's always the little baby who's probably grown up now, if he survived the fire, but I don't think he'll remember who it was, I hope he won't …

They never did catch me, they thought they did but it was someone else. I have full faith in myself not to be found out, and I won't be. Ever!

Susannah Barraclough (14)
Hadleigh High School, Ipswich

A Day In The Life Of Private Smith

Fzzp! The bullets flashed past the squirming bodies, which writhed helplessly in the bloody water. A mine exploded a hundred yards to my right; a carcass was flung sky-high. In front of me the water ran red and slowly ebbed back and forth. I swam frantically towards the skeleton of a once proud landing craft. I stayed low in the water and clung to the hull like a twig stuck on a fast-flowing river, not daring to poke my head above the surface for fear of a bullet between my eyes.

I floated there for what felt like a year, trying to muster the courage that would force me to swim towards the mines and bullets that were peppering our position. *'Jesus Christ!'* I yelled. I splashed towards the beach and my feet crunched on the millions of tiny pebbles. I surged towards a hole in the ground. Around me I could hear the screams of hundreds of men lying helplessly whilst the Nazis with their smoking barrels zoomed in on the survivors. I snatched a look, I could see the barrels out of the crumbling battlements on the hills above. A radio lay some way in the distance by a mutilated body. I eased myself over to it, inch by inch, trying my hardest not to draw attention to myself, till my fingers grasped the cold metal; I dragged it back.

For the dead, the hardship was over, for me it had just begun.

Zachary Kerr (13)
Hadleigh High School, Ipswich

Myths And Legends - Description

The dazzling sunlight is glistening down upon the mystical creature. The diminutive object, delicately placed, her cheeks a dusty pink, she sits upon the radiant red toadstool. Her soft wavy hair that sways from her head is like the hazy cornfield. Her velvety heather eyes gaze right through me. Her pale skin reminds me of a bleak winter's day.

The elephant trees look over her as if they are the kings of this spectacular woodland, where the fairies dance and sing. The lustrous cucumber-green leaves are swinging in the subtle winds that fly through the treetops. The birds are happily chirping their favourite song, in the fresh sunlight beaming through the trees. Not a single cloud will dare to roll in on the turquoise sky.

The bottle-green grass is spread over the forest floor; the blossoming flowers are creeping through the lime grass, searching for sunlight. The deep purple plants are stunningly beautiful; the blossom has elegantly fallen from the trees way up high. The graceful toadstools are placed in a perfect circle, filled with dancing fairies, their fragile petal skirts moving softly.

Leanne Riches (14)
Hadleigh High School, Ipswich

Fear

I stepped up to the brown-painted chipped door. It was covered with a thick blanket of cobwebs, so shiny, so delicate yet so sticky. I pulled away a small area of this that was twisted around the brass door handle. I reached out and turned it fearfully, my heart beating faster and faster and faster as though it was trapped in a tightly-packed cage like a lion trying to break free. I opened the old door slowly and fearfully. I imagined something behind the door, waiting to jump out and knock me flat on the floor.

I looked down the hallway and saw a small grey mouse scurry across the floor. I jumped backwards, with fear tangoing round me. I stepped carefully down the hallway, dodging the dead rats until I came to a large room. I walked cautiously into the room that seemed as though it was a romantic room, where a couple once sat and dreamt of their future together. On one side of the room was a grand piano with a small spider perched on one of the keys, and there was an old piece of music standing upright on the stand, coated in dust.

I decided to go upstairs to adventure but suddenly, as I stepped up to the first step, I heard a chopping noise, I started to worry and I went to where the noise was coming from - the kitchen and there it was, to my amazement ... a ghost of an old lady standing by the dusty worktops chopping her vegetables.

Natalie Rosemary Snowling (14)
Hadleigh High School, Ipswich

Nightmare In The Undergrowth

My heart was having palpitations as I sprinted clumsily through the knee-high undergrowth that suffocated the glistening blue lake; my short, gangly legs were like spiders' legs cutting through the soft undergrowth but my legs were cut. I felt the blood oozing from the small incision. I had not expected to get into any danger.

I didn't know what was behind me but at a guess I would say the legendary Nightcrawler. It was a strange delinquent of an animal, with its bloodshot eyes and its shaggy mane and its plaque-filled mouth. The only thing I knew was that whatever attacked me had an aura of violence and aggression.

Suddenly, I hit a dead end, a cliff. Embedded in the rock face was the face of Fear leering at me, begging me to come and join him! I turned around and my worst fears were realised as a huge werewolf came out from the bushes, I was facing almost certain death!

As the monster pounced, I rolled away and kicked hard with both feet and I felt my hard trainer collide with soft, meaty flesh. The werewolf was uninjured as I got up and was running again. My muscles were aching painfully. I was put out of my misery when something big and powerful swiped at my legs; my calf muscles were now covered in congealed blood. That was when something grabbed hold of me and threw me into the dew-covered bushes …

Mark Littlewood (13)
Hadleigh High School, Ipswich

Fear, Fury And fortune

He glared at me scornfully. His ponderous breath caused me to oscillate repetitively. I stood, scared, deserted. Companions having previously abandoned me caused a cramped, constricted blanket of fear to form, fixed around me.

Rays of radiant light reflected from his golden defensive scales, and as my eyes wandered towards them helplessly, I squinted cowardly in pain.

Cautiously I attempted a steady sideward step, maintaining eye contact in case of an abrupt reaction. He made not a solitary move, however, his blood-curdling eyes remained fixed upon my own.

As I inquisitively drifted to face the floor upon which I so nervously stood, to again steadily step sidewards, I gazed eternally at what I had so unexpectedly found glistening beneath my bloody, filthy feet.

Crystals; gold, fortune!

My grated, penurious, arid hands reached for it uncontrollably. As I clutched it cautiously, a sudden stream of control swayed swiftly down my spine. However, my lake of control rapidly came to an end, like a leaf at the edge of a towering waterfall, as I realised, once my eyes had returned to once more search for fury in his villainous eyes … I had found it!

Katie MacLeod (14)
Hadleigh High School, Ipswich

Troubled

His harassed mind had driven him to extravagant consequences. The final straw had been drawn and his once jubilant state had sunk to a heartless case.

His ghost-white face and beady eyes revealed how exposed and vulnerable he had become, all due to a heartless upbringing. He walked with loathsome intentions, almost as if his desperate situation had to conclude, and in his case, with desperate measures.

He began his heartless mission by striking a match with great aggression. He grinned with a sinful look. Then softly pronounced, 'This is what it has come to.'

He then released the lit match with devastating effect. Waves of ash and deep black smoke revolved into the cold, howling wind. His cowardly actions caused a school full of young, jovial students to retreat from the source of their learning to the safest area in sight. A blazing ball of light struck fear into everyone around it. A debris of rocks engulfed helpless students and, with this, he departed to his residence to resume his unfortunate routine to carry on his loveless life.

Even as he returned home, not a 'Hello, how are you?' or 'How was your day?' to greet his troubled feelings, whereas all that would be needed to improve his heartless caring, would have been a loving kiss.

He will strike again!

Stefan Vincent (14)
Hadleigh High School, Ipswich

Can Your Foundation Cover This Up?

In recent foundation ingredient experiments there is some cause for concern that the effects of some could cause cancer. Experts have said, although they are still in the early stages of their tests, there is a definite need for concern.

Only three types of foundation are being tested at the moment; each type contains at least four of the worrying ingredients, but there are several more ingredients needing to be experimented with, but not all of those are present in the popular foundations.

In a recent conference one scientist said, 'So far with the evidence we have found, I cannot believe people wear the stuff'. Which shows only one week into the testing, bad results.

The make-up brands' foundations that are being tested have not been named for legal reasons; but it can be said the current three suspect foundations are from major worldwide companies.

Even before the cancer-causing claims, foundation was not looked upon lightly by skin experts. Most foundations contain alcohol and perfumes which irritate the skin. Other ingredients can be impossible to wash off without the use of alcohol - these block pores and lead to spots and sometimes infections.

So although we are told by companies they have created products which are oil-free and completely safe and good for your skin - this is not true. In most cases harmful ingredients have been found but at the moment we are not sure just how harmful they are.

Ashleigh Moore (13)
Hadleigh High School, Ipswich

My Heaven

Smack!

'It's your fault.' My father's hand sent me backwards. 'It's your fault she's dead.' He crashed drunkenly through the house throwing random rubbish from the darkness that littered the house with saddened memories that echoed 'Mum'. My father raised his hand sending me to the ground, knocking my head on a cabinet on the way down. I was left in darkness, imprisoned in a cage of thoughts which taunted me, repeating my father's words, 'It's your fault she's dead!' Inside I was screaming, but like bells ringing in an empty city, my words, without anyone to hear them, seemed pointless.

Light! Light shone so brightly into the darkness that was my life that I brought my arm up to my face. A soft hand gently returned it to my side and whispered, 'It's OK, there's no need to be afraid.' I paused, who was this woman's voice who warmed me inside? And then it hit me.

'Mum!' It was her face, her smile, it was her. I opened my arms throwing them around her, hugging her so tight as if I was never going to let go. I could feel a lump forming in my throat as she kissed me on the head and held me tight, pulling back my hair.

'It wasn't your fault,' she whispered gently into my ear sending goosebumps all over my body. My eyes filled with water; I held her tighter. I was so happy, I was with my mum, it was my heaven.

Alisha Keveren (14)
Hadleigh High School, Ipswich

Forever A Gypsy

Fresh dew glistened in the morning sun. Crisp air crept through my half open window shutters followed by dawn's sunbeams.

Misleading thoughts sneaked into my mind from years ago, being huddled up in my warm, snuggly bed, not having to worry about what will happen that day. As I get up and stretch, I'm bounced back to reality, stumbling outside in my thin nightgown, sitting down on the bottom step of my trailer and soaking my feet in the cool dew. Everything doesn't seem so bad.

As I scan the horizon, there is no civilisation to be seen except for a small prairie house, though more of a small dot in the distance, looking up into the clear blue sky, only seeing thin wisps of candyfloss cloud. I drift into a silent daydream. I've never had my place in society, all my life being bullied for who I am, all I am, forever a gypsy.

Scrawny young girl, the outcast from the others. Never neat and tidy, never with the right equipment or uniform. Never cared for as a real living being. Never treated normally.

For me to forgive is a simple task of realising they did not understand. But to forget, to forget is an impossible task. I will always be a gypsy.

Natalie Bell (13)
Hadleigh High School, Ipswich

Seeking Nessie

Click! I shut the lid of my packed case. I'm preparing for my new life. I just know what my heart desires - money. To achieve my aim I need to find the most mysterious 'being' known to man. The Loch Ness Monster. I load my belongings into my car. It sat with its eyes in a kind of trance. Do I want to leave my home? It could just be a dream.

Speeding along a motorway is surprisingly tiring. All I see is cars tearing past me like children running to an ice cream van. Is a middle-aged, money-crazed businessman supposed to chase after a childhood dream, or in some cases, nightmare? It would be as real as the ... as the ... oh I don't know, the point is it probably isn't real.

After eight hours travelling I arrive. I'm at the loch. The cold creeps in, lashing me with a cruel wind, soaking mist drenches me through and through. Freezing and soaked my fingers fumble as I try and put up my tent. The ground is like bog. The loch is silver steel. It glares at me watching my every move.

Morning

Cold and shivery. I get my equipment. I walk around watching and waiting for my catch. Black shapes slip around me like snakes. I'm caught in the beauty around. I forget ...

Stacy Herbert (13)
Hadleigh High School, Ipswich

The Truth About Hercules

Oh for goodness sake! Here he comes again in his armour, ready to become some kind of hero; it never happens. Head held high, practically dragging the saddle across the floor towards me. His old leather sandals catching on the cobble floors, his too-big armour swamping his small, nimble body. He's such a disappointment to his father, always messing up. You begin to feel sorry for him, Hercules - pathetic.

I spat my haylage out as the girth is wrenched up about my chest, thrusting her air out of my lungs. You would think he would give me a chance to wake up. I turned my head to glare at him as he jumped onto my back and spurred me into a magnificent gallop, if I do say so myself.

'The killer goat of Birgh!' Herc exclaimed. 'That's where we're going, to become a true hero.' *Sigh!* another plan. 'The murderous goat killed two chickens, just over this hill in the mighty cave; ravenous for more blood and grass - a true killer.'

I galloped past Woodthorpe Woods to this 'mighty' cave - which turned out to be an old railway bridge. The goat stood looking at me, munching grass. Hercules leapt off my back and drew his sword. The goat kept munching.

'Be afraid, I'm the mighty Hercules.' He thrusted his sword to the goat, who just walked away back to the nearby farm.

The wrong goat.

Emma Jeeves (13)
Hadleigh High School, Ipswich

A Day In The Life Of Shirley Cortez

Why me? Every night when the stars are glistening and the moon is shining brightly, I will be found on a rough wooden floor, with a filthy blanket which will lay upon me. I have my younger brother's warm sweat, when I cuddle up to him, which keeps me company; plus the sound of snoring coming from my mother who appears to me as a drunk, an embarrassment and an abhorrent woman.

My bedroom is my home - four walls shared between the only family I have, which is situated in the back of a stranger's garden, it's not a home, it's a shed. There is no money, or if there is I have never seen it. I've certainly not been to school, so in my life there is no way forward, just backwards. My mother prefers to scrounge money off the last friends she has to buy alcohol, while the only job she has involves her selling her body.

I dream most nights about why I couldn't be the Queen's daughter, with money and elegant clothes. Instead I am the opposite, the bottom of the lower class. I have tried suicide, however I failed at this, and ended up in hospital. In fact it was more of a holiday for me; there was healthy food, which hadn't been chewed around the edges. I'm lucky enough to even receive any food these days.

Why should anyone live like this? Why should my younger brother live like this? Why should I live like this?

Kirsty Benee (14)
Hadleigh High School, Ipswich

A Day In The Life Of Astrid Achim
(A Jewish Prisoner Of War)

Screech! Screech! The cattle train ground to a halt, we all knew our fare; we all knew we had reached Auschwitz. The stench coming through the bars was like burnt meat. The air was ice-cold. We had indeed reached Auschwitz. The huge wooden doors were opened. Suddenly light poured into the carriage, and I could now finally see everyone standing together clutching onto one another.

We all got off the train too hurried to even look at each other. They made us line up, women on one side, men on the other. Children had to stand with their mothers; if they didn't have a mother they had to stand next to a woman able to look after them.

From the sky something was falling. At first I thought it was snow, but I soon realised it was ash coming from gargantuan chimneys.

My friend Sandra had told me that the officers at Auschwitz made you strip down, gave you soap; then took you to a shower room, locked you in and released poison gas into the room. They'd take your body to a huge furnace and turn you into ash.

I looked up and in front of me I saw a man in Nazi uniform looking along the line, preying on the innocent with judging eyes; it was as if he had already sentenced us to death. From that point on I knew that I had arrived at death, I had arrived at Auschwitz.

Alice Farrall (14)
Hadleigh High School, Ipswich

The Boat

It was sinking fast and the sharks had me surrounded, their mouths were foamed and their teeth were enormous. You could see what they had previously eaten. I was scared that I would be dessert.

The deep, dark sea was pulling me down into the mouth of the ocean and the sides of the boat were collapsing. I was going to drown. He was scared as well, he stared at me as if had seen a ghost, his eyes were large and beady, he was only three, he didn't even know what was going on.

Suddenly the boat was shaking, I didn't know what to think, my head was spinning and Josh started to scream. The sharks obviously were getting hungry; the ocean had already eaten half the boat and the half left was going down too! I held Josh high for his own sake as the large fish had their white teeth above the water, they were going to bite and it was going to be nasty.

Over the horizon I could see the odd bird, never a plane or a boat. At this point I knew we didn't have very long to live.

The boat was filling up with water as the sharks were going mental. Water was splashing everywhere. The boat was rocking again; I was holding Josh tightly. I wasn't going to let him go.

For a second I was wondering just how we had ended up in such an awful situation, if we were to live I would never forget this moment!

Rebecca Lewis (14)
Hadleigh High School, Ipswich

Train Incident

I was waiting at Market Street Station waiting for a train to go to work and a man with glasses was standing on the edge of the platform, too close to the edge. The man was crying and then the distant sound of a train came closer and closer. I wasn't really paying attention when the train finally came but I heard a kind of squelch, I looked back again and the man had gone! There was a bloody patch on the platform and in the middle of this bloody patch, were his glasses.

I hadn't been on a train since that little incident until two years later. I waited at the same station, except this time, everything seemed normal. The train slowed down this time and gradually stopped as it got to the station. The doors hissed open and I stepped on. The doors then hissed shut again and it gradually got faster and faster until everything started to go blurry.

The train zoomed through the mountainous countryside and it was coming up to a massive opening with a mile-long bridge going across it. There was no sign that the train was stopping. However, I looked around and there was a sign saying, *Bridge Out.*

Luke Green (14)
Hadleigh High School, Ipswich

My Nightmare

I looked out the window and what I saw will stay with me for the rest of my life, haunting me whenever I close my eyes. We were 15,000ft in the air. I was halfway through my journey to my destination and what I saw from my window was the enormous jet engine burst into flames. I saw it, saw it slowly fall to the water below.

My eyes darted around looking for a way to escape this horror. I had no time for that because all of a sudden the plane took a nose-dive. Down, down we went, falling through the air, gaining speed every second, hurtling towards the water below with burning speed. I looked down the cabin to see my fellow passengers gripping their armrests with intense anxiousness. Waiting, waiting for the scariest moment of their lives to grab and take them and escalate into the nightmare of their future.

Thud! We were submerged in the desert of water and flaming pieces of plane surrounding us. I could hear the screams of distressed people crying for the help of the captain and hostesses, who were trying their best to remain calm and retrieve the rafts and flares from the flaming plane.

Though some were struggling quietly, wondering what would happen to them, thinking of families and friends, wondering whether anyone would see them or would we not be given our chance to say goodbye …?

Luke Chesworth (13)
Hadleigh High School, Ipswich

Cable Car Chaos

I don't like these cable cars. I want to get off! I knew I shouldn't have agreed to meet Danny at the other end. I should have just walked. Everything was going fine until the cable car juddered and ground to a halt, I could see the gnarled cables. This couldn't be safe! I sat there thinking to myself, *what happens if I die? I might never see my family again or what happens if I don't get to the other end? I won't be able to meet Danny and he will think I have stood him up.* All these thoughts were going through my head when all of a sudden I heard some unusual noises; these were completely ominous as I could see nothing but hear everything. My eyes started wandering when they froze on a sign *25 People Maximum.*

At this point my heart was coming into my throat, were there more than 25 people using these cars? It certainly didn't seem like it; well I couldn't see anyone else. I mean how could there be? There were only a certain amount of cars, surely there must be someone at each end checking to see who gets on and off? More thoughts started to rush through my head again; what happened if the man who is in charge got beaten up and then a massive gang thought it would be funny to put more people in a car than you're meant too? What's going on …?

Kayleigh Gleed (13)
Hadleigh High School, Ipswich

Chaos In The Sky

Slowly, slowly, slowly; then suddenly as if it appeared out of nowhere the cable car started juddering and clattering on the cable. Immediately after the clattering my attention was drawn to the cables at the top of the cable car, they were worn and tatty and gnarled in places, it was so awful, my life was in the hands of a cable car. I thought to myself, *this can't be safe, why did I agree to this? What's going to happen to me?*

As these thoughts were rushing round and round in my mind I was having visions of my life, I mean you know what people say about your life flashing before your eyes when you are at death's door, then I started to hear unusual noises, they were completely ominous, no sign of anything making them just some high-pitched groaning noises; they sounded as though a bear was stuck in a cave or had been shot out in the wild by a passer-by. My eyes were glaring round trying so hard to find a simple explanation to where the strange noises were coming from.

But, it was as though I had forgotten about the noises when I noticed an attention sign at the back of the cart, it read, *Maximum 25 People*. At this point my heart was knocking at my ribs, had the maximum number of people been exceeded? What was going to happen to me, but not just me, everyone on the cable cars?

Hannah Petts (13)
Hadleigh High School, Ipswich

A Day Of Panic

A small shudder disturbed me. I opened my eyes from what had been a deep sleep; looked around; everybody was silent. Everybody was still. It was probably nothing but I had a tingling feeling on my neck: an inkling was telling me that danger was near. Once again I looked around. Everybody asleep peacefully, the faint sound of an action film being played in the economy class and the quiet talking of the air stewards and hostesses which distracted my rest.

An hour passed, my mind was at rest and no more worries. The journey was running smoothly. *Ding-dong!* An announcement from the captain, probably declaring the final destination was approaching.

'We ask you not to panic, but we have just received signals from the radar suggesting strong storms ahead. We ask you just to enjoy the ride, the storm may slow us down by an hour or so, but given that everything goes well, we will be arriving at Sydney airport, Australia at 0700 hours, thank you.'

Very comforting news to someone who is already paranoid about flying! A sudden bang startled me; the plane swerved violently; that soon woke up many passengers. The pilot was losing control, I closed my eyes tightly trying to forget what was happening and pretend it was simply a simulator at a fairground. Screaming children from behind me soon increased my concern and loud bangs, clashes and flashes from the thunderstorm totally overwhelmed me. What seemed like a rock hit my window. It suddenly occurred to me, the plane was falling apart ...

Isabelle Lewis (14)
Hadleigh High School, Ipswich

That Day

As she started to cry the rain started to pour, sweeping across the rooftops, down the gutter onto the cold, hard concrete. Then as she wailed in pain lightning struck and the thunder growled. As dark clouds formed she screamed, 'How long will this go on for?' The lightning struck and the thunder growled again.

I could not stand to see her like this. I could not let her be in so much pain. But there was nothing I could do, there was no way that I could change what had already been done. As what has been done is done. And it's surprising that in hours, minutes or even seconds your life can change; for the good or even in our case the bad. Very bad.

How could I have been so stupid! In my eyes I made it worse not better. However to her I presumed that it was a whole lot worse than mine! And after all this, all I wanted to do was make things better, not worse. Of all the things that I could have done. Of all the things I had to do that.

After she'd found out it was worse. Even though you're only supposed to take two a day; I took 2 weeks' worth. My head was like a twister spinning round and round, the sofas with their wide mouths ready to grab me and eat me. It was as if everything was alive in my head. What would happen to me?

Claire Wright (14)
Hadleigh High School, Ipswich

The Woods

'No! Don't go that way!'

Emma stood and stared at her friends as they ran off into the woods. Emma knew that part of the woods was dangerous.

It was beginning to get dark and Emma knew that she had to get back home before it was pitch-black. However she didn't know whether to go find her friends or go home. She decided that she couldn't leave her friends in the woods. She started to walk further into the woods to find her friends, her heart was beating fast but she knew she had to find her friends. As she walked she started to hear sound coming from around her. She just ignored them and looked straight ahead and carried on walking.

She started to shout their names out. 'Sarah! Katie!' There was no answer so she continued to shout their names. She carried on walking, she wanted to turn back but she knew that she couldn't. She turned round and didn't know what direction to do next. She was lost. She started to panic. She started to shout for her friends again, but still no answer. She got out her phone and tried to ring her friends but she had no signal, so she ran in any direction. It was getting darker and darker and she couldn't see where she was going. She didn't know what to do so she stopped. She sat on the ground and started to cry …

Natasha Ludbrook (14)
Hadleigh High School, Ipswich

Story, Guess Who?

She quickly walked into the dark room wondering what to expect. Yes, the note says, 'Meet me on the twenty-first floor'.

Yes, this was the twenty-first floor. My eyes darted around the dark room that I thought was empty. I listened carefully; I suspected there was someone in the room though. I looked, trying to focus but it wasn't working.

I knew who the note was from. It was from the man across the road; he was going to give me a job even though I didn't think he liked me since I'd moved in opposite a few weeks ago.

All of a sudden I heard the door slam behind me, it was even darker than before, I didn't know what to do. I looked around frantically. I didn't know who was standing behind me but I didn't have any choice when she turned the light on. It made me jump, she moved in front of me. It was ... my sister. It turned out that she hadn't forgiven me for stealing her husband. I didn't mean to, he had been cheating on her for a long time.

Over three long years of fighting over him she married him but things didn't work out; they always argued over silly things that were not important ... like me.

Gemma Squirrell (13)
Hadleigh High School, Ipswich

Maui-Of-A-Thousand-Tricks - A Polynesian Myth

In Polynesian myths there are many stories of Maui the sun god or Maui-of-a-Thousand-Tricks and how he helped mankind. Maui is the god who fished up the islands in the South Seas from the bottom of the ocean. Maui also went down to the Underworld and brought back the secret of fire for mankind, but this story is how Maui lassoed the sun and gave humans more hours of daylight.

One day Maui said, 'The days are too short there's no time to get anything done!' Maui set to thinking how the sun could be made to move more slowly across the sky. From coconut shell fibres, Maui had made a great noose with which to catch the sun, but the sun burnt it up. Then Maui cut off the sacred tresses of his wife, Hina, and wove them into a rope, fashioning the end into a noose. He travelled to the eastern edge of the sea and waited for the sun to rise.

At dawn, Maui flung his rope and caught the sun by the throat! The sun struggled and pleaded, but Maui refused to let go. Eventually the sun grew so weak it could no longer run across the sky but only creep.

In his way Maui brought mankind more hours of sunlight.

Rachel Fraser (14)
Hadleigh High School, Ipswich

Red River Reveals Secret

A terrible incident has occurred off the south coast of Cornwall on Monday 5th of May. Passers-by were rooted to the spot when the waters turned blood-red Special Forces were called in to discover why such an unnatural occurrence has taken place.

It was originally thought that the sudden colour change was due to competition within the sea, however, it is now clear that it would have taken more than a few fish to die to turn the water that putrid colour.

After forensic testing it is clear that the substance dyeing the water red is human blood. More tests are being carried out now to discover the source of the blood.

Scientists are trying to find a link between the red waters of Cornwall and the disappearance of nine families that have gone missing within the past week. It is possible that under the murky depths of the water a cave or hollow would have stored the bodies until such a force made the blood rise to the surface by changing the water pressure? However, even if this is what happened, the subject of why and how the bodies were placed there still remains.

The water has not yet been classified 'safe', so no divers have been able to explore what lies beneath.

This has been one of the most horrific sights in England for 70 years and it is not recommended that you take a family trip to the seaside until this case has been cracked!

Leigh Thornton (13)
Hadleigh High School, Ipswich

Beth's Diary

Dear Diary,

It's great here. It puts my mind to rest after all that has happened. I know it will never be gone but it's a start and I have to get on with my life. I did try fixing things, before it got out of hand. I have never told anyone about this. I needed something to stop my mind from completely shutting down, so that's why I wrote this diary.

We're on our way to Ludington, that's where Grace lives. I feel sorry for Grace in a way. I know we both went through the same thing but she couldn't move away from the problem like I could. I mean my mum sensed I wasn't happy in Ludington so I simply moved away. On the other hand Grace had to stay back in Ludington. But that wasn't it; she lives near the places where it all happened.

It was about a year ago now; Grace and I were walking along the beach eating ice cream; like usual. But this wasn't a normal day; we saw something we shouldn't have. There was a lady holding Ludington's biggest tourist attraction. Although this island was small it had one of the most famous and valuable paintings ever. We turned back but it was too late. This mysterious lady was chasing us up the rocks until we got to the edge of the cliff. My life flashed before me.

She, she ...

Anyway we're into Grace's drive now ...

Unfortunately the girls' secret drove them insane and therefore this diary was never finished.

Afsana Miah (12)
Hadleigh High School, Ipswich

A Day In The Life Of A Barn Owl

I was patiently perching on my musty wooden beam drowsing fitfully, until a considerably immense explosion erupted. Petrified and stricken I swiftly flew away. Whilst soaring the dusky wood I overheard a perplexing babble, was it humans? Nevertheless it took me no time to take a look at them. I was right, it was humans except one thing. It was a distinctive shape, almost shaped like a mini hut but what was it? I swooped through the dotage trees.

I placidly lurked around observing this astonishing being. It was beautiful; red, yellow and also green. It felt silky against my feathers. All of a sudden a rustle came from the distant bushes, struck by fear I briskly flew away and retreated back to my musty wooden beam, drowsing fitfully until a considerably immense explosion erupted. Petrified and stricken I swiftly flew away ...

Jessica Shrimpton (12)
Hadleigh High School, Ipswich

Football Article

Jose Mourinho's complaint was with the ref taking drugs. Jose Mourinho asked the FA to back up his complaint on the referee taking drugs in the Chelsea Vs Liverpool match, because of his dodgy refereeing, him falling over and scoring for each team! The FA agreed with Mourinho's argument and decided that they would do something because of the referee's actions.

In the referee's locker room after the game, the ref was getting changed; the FA and their bodyguards came in with Mourinho by their side. The referee was shocked to see them. He asked why they were there. The FA spokesman spoke to the ref and mentioned to him about his performance on the pitch. They said that they had received a complaint from Chelsea and Liverpool managers about the bad decisions and errors made by him. He was swaying and his eyes got wider. The FA spokesman noticed this and questioned him as to whether he had taken anything illegal. He said, 'No', but they said that he had to take a drugs test and have his bag searched. He disagreed but was told he would never referee again.

The search revealed a plastic bag containing drugs. The police were called out, the referee was arrested and taken away from the ground. The football match was declared a draw and was set to be replayed.

The referee appeared in court, was fined and never allowed to referee a game again.

Aidan Bignell (12)
Hadleigh High School, Ipswich

The Champion's Shield

'Come on Chelsea,' bellow the away fans at the corner of Old Trafford.

'Come on lads, kick 'em in!' screams a true *Red* as the teams run out for the first half. The whistle blows and Man U are trying to get forward early now. Here's Gary Neville, he hits it hard right up to Scholes who lays it off for Rooney. He decides to be clever and take it round Carvalho. He belts it low and hard … What a fantastic start from Manchester United, that well-worked move from Rooney made it just too easy for the Dutchman van Nistelrooy. The score is now Manchester United 1, Chelsea 0, with only four minutes gone.

This game has been pretty average since that early van Nistelrooy goal. Chelsea have tried their very best to try and break down the rock solid Manchester defence. They've tried: through balls, long shots, crosses and even attempts to win penalties but it just hasn't worked. Oh, but here's Lampard; he chips it over the top to Drogba. He turns one man and another, but …

It's 1-1 here at Old Trafford as we kick-off after Lampard's beautiful penalty. Drogba was brought down in the box after a dazzling run which left Lampard to smash it past the keeper. Not long left in this game now and the score is deadlocked between these top two teams. But we could be wrong because it comes to Tiago who shoots!

Yessss! He's won it for Chelsea!

Josh Broadbent (12)
Hadleigh High School, Ipswich

Tense

Jo always knew it could happen, but she didn't want to see it, not in her lifetime. Teardrops stained her face as she stood gloomily in the cold weather of November. She couldn't think of who the person was but she felt as if she had something to do with them; well she was there when it happened. Police were approaching now, gathering around the body. The atmosphere was tense as the whispers continued throughout the village square. A couple of people crept out of the village post office to join the growing crowd including police, detectives, villagers and Mrs Pip walking her dog.

Soon enough the village hall was opened ready for them all to be questioned; but as soon as Jo thought that it was her turn to go through a detective interrupted, requesting that it was time to examine the body. This was the part that Jo was dreading the most.

It was time to see who the victim of this murder was. The detectives checked the victim's shoes to compare the shoe prints with the footprints they had found nearby.

That's strange, thought Jo daydreaming, *I'm wearing those shoes and I haven't seen anybody else wear them before.*

Next the detectives studied the victim for a deep injury in the chest. Jo once again noticed the similarity, her clothes and the victim's ... were the same! *This is very extraordinary,* thought Jo, bending over to see the victim's face when the recognition dawned ...

Yolanda Rankin (12)
Hadleigh High School, Ipswich

Forest Attack

'Chloe, Zahra's mother is on the phone for you,' my mum calls from the bottom of the stairs.

Zahra's mum? Why would Zahra's mum want to speak to me? Still I turn off my TV and shuffle down the stairs. I grasp the phone from my mum's warm, gentle hands and press it to my ear.

'Erm, hello?' I murmur into the phone.

'Zahra's gone missing! I've phoned everyone, even the police, do you know where she is? Oh please tell me you know,' splutters the voice from the phone.

'Zahra's gone missing?' I stammer. Then I suddenly realise! 'Oh, erm, I'll tell you if I find anything out.' In a daze I put the phone down; I grab my rain mac and slip on my shoes.

'Where are you going?' exclaims my mum.

'Out,' I murmur, and I stomp out the front door and make my way up to Ghostly Woods. They must be there, I'd overheard people saying that they were going to meet there, and they were taking a knife! I couldn't warn her because she wasn't at school.

I am now standing in front of the old rickety gates with an old rusty padlock. But there is a dip under the gates, which perhaps a fox has dug. I can just about squeeze underneath. I can hear sniggering; I creep towards the noise. Then I hear a scream …

Zoe Alleyne (12)
Hadleigh High School, Ipswich

Play-Offs

Ipswich are hoping to get promoted through the long, nail-biting times of the play-offs. They have to play West Ham at Upton Park. Then Ipswich host West Ham at Portman Road on Wednesday 18th May. It is supposed to be a sell out already. Ipswich hopes to win the all-important second leg at home. If they win they get to go to the Millennium Stadium in Cardiff.

Ipswich were unlucky not to get promoted automatically when they drew 1-1 with Brighton away, when Wigan won 3-1 against Reading.

Sunderland won the Championship by far when they were crowned champions on their last league game of the season. Sunderland won against West Ham at the Stadium of Light. Jim Magilton told the press conference that he was looking forward to the first leg at Upton Park and the return leg at Portman Road on the 18th May.

Last year Ipswich won 1-0 at home and lost away. But in the final West Ham lost to Crystal Palace at the Millennium Stadium Cardiff. He also said that Ipswich were unlucky not to get promoted automatically, and they also hope to go up through the play-offs against West Ham next week. He said, 'I hope to sign the new contract. We are getting new talent coming through the academy'.

Matthew Snowling (12)
Hadleigh High School, Ipswich

FA Cup Final

On the 21st May the FA Cup Final will be against second and third places in the Premiership, Arsenal versus Man United. Man United players are all in shape like Cristiano Ronaldo who is playing better than ever. Van Nistelrooy is back from injury. The only disadvantage Man United have is their keeper, Tim Howard has been a bit dodgy this season so Arsenal will have a lot of long shots. Arsenal's one problem is Cristiano Ronaldo's step overs. He's so quick on his feet. Paul Scholes' shots are going to be a problem for Arsenal's keeper, Lehmann.

Arsenal's players are all top notch except for one big problem, the French star striker, Thierry Henry, might not be able to play because of an injury.

This will be Arsenal's squad ...

		Lehmann		
Lauren	Campbell		Toure	Cole
Pires	Veira		Edu	Ljungberg
	Reyes		Van Persie	

Man United squad ...

		Howard		
Neville	Ferdinand		Brown	Silvestre
Ronaldo	Scholes		Keane	Giggs
	Rooney		Nistelrooy	

Arsenal's captain, Patrick Veira will be leading out Arsenal. This is Arsenal's only chance to win a trophy this season. Man United captain, Roy Keane will be leading out Man United and this is their only chance to win any trophy as well. It will be an afternoon match at the Millennium Stadium in Cardiff. Who will win, Man United or Arsenal?

Ross Bray (11)
Hadleigh High School, Ipswich

Diary

Wednesday 5th June 1901

Dear Diary,

    I thoroughly despise my mother! Just because she's ill I have to go and work at the big Oakmore House. I won't be able to see baby Millie for months. If they like me, Mother says they may want me to stay for longer, and for what, a few shillings that won't even be spent on me. It will go on food and clothes for the family. I doubt the food will be half as good as mother's home-made cakes. I'll be a nursery maid looking after the children; they'll probably be stuck-up brats I really hate my mother for making me go.

Thursday 6th June

Dear Diary,

    Today I arrived at Oakmore House. I met Mrs Oakmore, James, Charlotte and baby Theodore. Mr Oakmore was away on important business. There are lots of other maids and cooks working here. There's one maid in particular that I made friends with, she was so helpful showing me around. I started off by dressing and organising the children for breakfast. (What fancy clothes they have!)

Friday 7th June

Dear Diary,

    I'm beginning to feel homesick and I pine for the days when me and baby Millie went on walks. It's just not the same with Theodore. At least I know they're well, Emma sends me letters each week, her handwriting's getting quite legible.

Saturday 8th June

Dear Diary,

    The absolute worst has happened! Baby Theodore's been kidnapped ...

Melissa Parker (12)
Hadleigh High School, Ipswich

The Escape

I watched the clock, tick, tick, ticking, counting its every second, waiting for 3 o'clock to arrive. No one knew Marnock Manor better than Scarlet Drowans and Scarlet was up for a big escape. The clock struck three just as the bell rang. Various members of the class jumped up and cheered, though silence was followed by the announcing of homework for the half-term.

'Scarlet, Scarlet,' I said, tugging at her long tartan pinafore. With a quick swish, her long chestnut-brown hair swung round and she emerged from a comic saying, 'Pop Talk' on the front.

'What? Where?' she murmured sounding drowsy, yet surprised.

'I'm down here,' I called tugging at her skirt again. 'I just wondered when the escape was?'

'Shut it!' she growled, dragging me out of the classroom by the scruff of my neck.

Perhaps Scarlet was not as brilliant as I thought she was.

'Who told you about the escape?'

'Oh everyone - everyone knows.'

'Right! Tell me who you actually are.'

I held my chin up high and announced, 'Jasmine Jones, but my friends call me JJ. I'm in my first year here. So when is the big escape?'

'What a first year wantin' to come on my escape. I don't think so.'

I had been pestering Scarlet to let me come for hours on end, though she was obviously not convinced about how much I wanted to escape form school.

Eventually Scarlet gave in though she warned me that I was my own responsibility.

Rebecca Le Grice (12)
Hadleigh High School, Ipswich

Area 51

15 years ago in 3019, my troops and I, armed with plasma cannons and mini machine guns, went into the most top secret military base, Area 51. We were searching for a scientist that worked there. As we went in we heard a noise, a sort of groaning. We walked slowly into the darkness.

We were walking towards the elevator. Suddenly the elevator started to come up by itself. Two of my men stepped lightly forward to search the elevator as it opened. But there was nothing there. Soon after a clink came from the ceiling, we all looked up. In half a minute we carried on and walked into the deep, dingy darkness.

Later a mangled creature burst out of a vent in the ceiling. My men and I started to fire but it was too late for some of them. As it was killing my men, my friend and I ran to the elevator. Later I found out that my men weren't killed, just infected. One by one they mutated into foul beasts. They had yellow eyes, crooked bones and scaly skin.

On the way down my friend got killed and I got infected, but for some reason I mutated slower. I managed to get to a safe place, but day by day I'm mutating more so I need to get out and find a cure.

Andrew Stuart (12)
Hadleigh High School, Ipswich

Diary Of Joan Smith

9th January 1920

I hate my life! It's so unfair, I have been sent away to work as a maid at this stuck-up posh lady's house. I used to be so happy, I would run around in the street with Henry and Jane having fun and enjoying life. Today is the first day of a new era in my life. I now have to work long hours cleaning this huge mansion. I have no friends, I have to obey orders and I am just fourteen! I have to do this whilst I could be at home taking advantage of my childhood and I have now lost all dignity - I have been reduced to obeying Ma'am - 'Yes Ma'am - no Ma'am'.

9th January 1920 (later on)

It's now midnight, I have just made my way down into the servants' quarters - because that's what I am now - a *servant!* It's dark, dingy and most of all it's freezing cold! There has been one good thing about today, I've managed to make a friend, Mary, she is just like me but she has been suffering here for the past year.

It's been such hard work today, how am I going to cope with tomorrow or the next day or the next even? Well if I am going to cope tomorrow I need to get some sleep because I am going to be woken at 5am

I don't think I'm going to get much sleep though, this bed is as hard as rock but I'm going to have to learn to live with it.

Ella Rodwell (11)
Hadleigh High School, Ipswich

The Quest

'Pay attention Samantha!'

'How many times have I told you to call me Sam? Samantha sounds so posh.' I was sitting in a chair overlooking the river; teacher's chair was facing mine. She was reading to me, but I was not listening. I was thinking. Not about my schoolwork, about her. She had only left a few months ago, leaving me and my father broken-hearted. We had no idea whether she was dead or alive. She just upped and left; 'Gone without a trace', my father always used to say.

Soon the already distant words coming out of my teacher's mouth were a blur. The ripples of the river slowed down, and gradually stopped. I closed my eyes. They must have been closed for a while, because when I opened them teacher was gone. As I looked round, I could see her pacing up the hill towards my house. I turned, a few yards down the river, I saw something. It was a bridge, but I could have sworn it was not there before; I was very intrigued by this sudden landmark. It was a rusty old bridge; nothing special to look at, just a rusty old bridge. As I walked nearer to it, I had no idea that as soon as I stepped onto it that it was the start of the biggest adventure I was ever going to endure.

I let my feet carry me to the bridge, I was so excited, like a kid in a candy store. I could taste the excitement. When I stepped onto the floor of the bridge; it was soft to touch. From looking at it, you wouldn't be able to tell. As I followed my feet onward; the bridge started to move, I jumped on it and we were off!

Georgia Kerr (12)
Hadleigh High School, Ipswich

Black Cats

I don't think I will ever forget what happened that night, Friday 13th - the worst day of my life! It all started when I decided to go out for a walk in the woods, 'It won't hurt,' I told myself, as I walked into eternal doom.

Before I entered the mass of dark green leaves, it was bright, the sun was shining and the sky was blue. I stepped into the woods. Then it went dark and deadly quiet. A whispering in the trees made my heart pound. Then it happened! A gunshot rang out; it whizzed past my ear and made me scream!

'Where are you little girl?' A voice came from nowhere. It sounded husky, and it was definitely a man's. I jumped - what else could I do? I started to run but tripped and fell. I started crying; I didn't want to die! The man caught up with me and picked me up as if I were a feather. His unshaven face reminded me of my dad, a thought that made my shoulders shake with grief. *I'll never see him again,* I thought. I took a closer look at my captor's face; his nose was hooked like Snape's from 'Harry Potter'. This made me think of my brother, Harry, whose glasses were black-rimmed and always broken.

Then the man took a gun out of his pocket - probably the same one he had used before. He aimed it at my head ... *bang!*

No more.

Rachel Seymour (12)
Hardwick Middle School, Bury St Edmunds

Never Again

Looking back on what I did, I knew I never should have done it; why did I? It didn't help me at all, in fact it made things worse. I never meant to harm anyone, I mean how was I to know that madmen lurked in the woods at night? I bet you're wondering what the terrible thing was, well let me tell you.

I needed to prove to my mates I wasn't a wimp so I told them to meet me in Blackgardens Woods at midnight. Except my plan didn't run smoothly. You see I was late arriving and others got there early - except they weren't my mates.

I was listening to my radio before I went and heard that a prisoner had escaped and was on the run and it just so happened he was in the woods my mates were in. I sprinted to the dark woods and heard a scream in the distance and stepped back in horror. Thoughts started drifting through my head, *had I put my friends in danger* or *is this just a dream?* I pinched myself, like they do in cartoons - it hurt, like a needle poking through my skin.

I scuffled into the woods, not knowing what to expect. There I saw my friend lying on the ground. *Dead* on the ground ... !

I ran back in astonishment, what should I do? What would happen to me? I mean the police would investigate, wouldn't they ... ?

Katie Riches (11)
Hardwick Middle School, Bury St Edmunds

Darkness

Tanya was walking home when suddenly everything went dark, like a jet-black veil had covered the sky. She felt two cold hands on her shoulders; she tried to scream but a third hand clasped her face. They pushed her and she edged forwards.

They walked for some time before stopping. Tanya could hear something talking in a rasping voice. A door creaked open revealing a dimly lit room coated in dust and cobwebs. It was a relief for Tanya to be in the light but it only provided her with a little comfort. She plucked up the courage to turn around to see what it was that had grabbed her on the shoulder - a big mistake! She looked round at them and let out a high-pitched scream!

Their faces were red as blood; they had no noses, instead there were two gaping holes running down their faces. Then she stared into their beady black eyes; she saw a fire appear in each of their pupils and soon after she felt her eyes burning; it was the worst pain she had ever felt, worse than breaking any bones. She yelped in pain; Tanya heard a loud crunch as the wall crash down beside her. She sprinted away as fast as she could. When she turned and looked back, she saw one of the creatures limping away.

She never told anyone about that day, so you may be wondering how I know about this - well, that's because I was there, I am one of the only two who survived!

Paige Mitson (12)
Hardwick Middle School, Bury St Edmunds

Space News Report

This morning news has come through that the six astronauts who went up into space ten days ago are now camping and living on the moon. The space agency NASA have developed a new super thin, light spacesuit, also breathing equipment which is much lighter in weight.

The astronauts are now living in an oxygenated dome similar to the Millennium Dome, made and designed by the British.

When the astronauts come back, in six months' time they will be awarded a medal by the Queen. We will keep you fully updated on all the news and developments from the moon.

Six months later ... Breaking news, we have an exclusive report and live filming from the landing bay of the six 'Moon Inhabitants" return to Earth!

Jake Adams (11)
Kings Langley School, Kings Langley

Mysterious Mystery

He stepped into the bitter cold, not knowing what he was looking for, only that they were after him.

Mikey was in a small alley, at the end was a rusty dustbin. Around it stood a group of tramps warming their cold and blistered hands on the blaring fire that came from within. He felt a pang of sympathy for them and himself, for a minute ago he was sitting cosily in front of the TV with a cup of cocoa when the next, he was in a deserted factory alone, except for those men watching him from every corner. Anyway he'd have to figure it out and soon, before Mum got back from her trip as stress on her heart could be fatal for her. From behind him stepped one of those haunting men with his haunting, deathly smile. Mikey crashed to the floor as the giant's hand fell on his head; a ton of bricks.

Again he woke up, but this time things seemed to be different. His body ached and people were starting to crowd the sudden misfit, him. They spoke with an accent, they wore weird clothes, as if in a play but no, they weren't. His hand, which had been throbbing for some time kicked in at full thrust. 'Argh!' He fainted from the unbearable pain. The coldness taking over his body, whipping him, tearing at him. He tried not to black out as his life flashed by his unconscious, closed eyes.

Bryony Saletes (12)
Kings Langley School, Kings Langley

A Day In The Life Of Me!

Diary - Saturday 23rd July 2005

Today I'm going off to Wales with my dance school (Life and Soul Theatre Academy). Holly and Rachel are going, I can't wait until we get there. It will be so fun.

Sunday 24th July 2005

Yesterday we unpacked our stuff and settled in. Today we went to have a look around and that, then we had something to eat and bed. I think tomorrow that we will be having a water fight, that will be fun!

Monday 25th July 2005

Today is the water fight, we are just getting up and some people are already outside waiting for us. Miss Sally, my dance teacher, always says that she always wins, but I don't think she will this time.

We have just finished the water fight. Miss Sally didn't win, we did. Everybody got so wet, it was so much fun. Having dinner now, then going to bed.

We stayed there for a week and we came back on the Saturday. Tomorrow is my birthday. I am going to be 12, I can't wait!

Amelia Parkins (11)
Kings Langley School, Kings Langley

A Day In The Life Of Beyoncé

Friday 7th June 2005

Dear Diary,
 I went shopping today with my girls. I bought loads of clothes and shoes because I'm going out with friends tonight.
 When we were leaving a group of people were following us, we turned round, made a pose and they took a picture. Some girls were waving our new album at us, so we signed a few then left.
 I went to my mum's afterwards, she's making me, Kelly and Michelle some outfits for tomorrow's video shoot. Well, after that I just chilled in my crib watching TV.
 Later I got dressed into my new black dress from Bay Trading and shoes from New Look. After I was ready my chauffeur came to pick me up. Once he'd collected the others we went to the best restaurant in town.

We got in really late, so I chilled while watching 'What Lies Beneath', it's very scary at the end!
 At about half twelve I went to bed, because I've got a busy day tomorrow.
 Love you loadz - Beyoncé xxx

Alexandra Oakley-Smith (12)
Kings Langley School, Kings Langley

A Day In The Life Of Jennifer Lopez!

Dear Diary,

I woke up at 6am to be at a video shoot for my new song. I got there at 7.30am, and got ready. After 11 hours of hard work at the shoot, I went home and had a shower, then went shopping.

I bought two designer outfits with matching shoes, 3 bikinis and two sarongs.

I went home, had a long bubble bath, had a cup of tea and watched a film on TV.

I ended up going to bed at 11pm. I was so tired the next morning!

Jemma Green (12)
Kings Langley School, Kings Langley

The Life Of Usher!

21st July 1.04pm

It's so hot! I'm loving it. Well I'm gonna make the most of it, I'm going in the pool and I'm gonna sunbathe for a while.

1.25pm

Right time to get out! Oh no time to sunbathe. I'm going out for dinner at 7, to celebrate the new single coming out! Did you know it's sold about 100,000 copies and it's only been out for 2 days?

4.30pm

I'm out the shower now and I need to decide what to wear. Ben Sherman? Nike? Adidas? Smart? Casual? Erm I know, I suppose it's casual so I'll wear my Nike Air (limited edition, not in shops yet!), FCUK jeans, Schott Jacket and Schott T-shirt.

5pm

I'm dressed now. Well I need to get Jodie, she's my erm ... the person that makes sure I look right and she also does my hair. 'Jodes can you sort me out please?'
    'Yeah, coming!'
    'Cheers!'

5.30pm

Well Jodie has sorted me out now, I need to get a Coke, hang on let me just get one out of the fridge ... Back now, well let me just see if Jodie wants any food.
    'Oh yes please, spaghetti Bolognese will do thanks!'

6.07pm

Well we have to leave now, I'll see if my chauffeur is ready ... Yeah he is, I've got to go. Bye!

Jodie Doyle (12)
Kings Langley School, Kings Langley

A Day In The Life Of A Cat

6.35 Tuesday
I'm sitting in a hedge, there's a badger sitting next to me, for some reason it's dribbling and growling at me. I miaowed at him. He pounced! I ran all the way up the hill and rolled back down. Wheeee!

6.40
I went through the cat flap, it's fun going through the cat flap, *clickety-clank!* I go through the cat flap like money going into the bank.

6.45
I'm bored. No one is out. I know, I'll climb the stairs. It'll be an early wake up call.

6.50
Sitting on the landing I'm hungry now, I'll go back downstairs.

6.52
There's no food in my bowl. I think I will go and have a nap.

6.55
This looks like a good spot. I will nap here.

7.30
I'm dreaming. I'm dreaming of a cow eating a dog, good cow.

7.55
Someone's refilled my bowl.

8.31
Back to napping.

3.59
String, I like string. I love a bit of string.

4.05
Go through the cat flap, hey look a bird, I get it and then go back to sleep.

4.35
'EastEnders' is on. I'll go back to bed I think.

8.30
I'm dreaming of a cow, a cow eating a dog!

Ryan Thrussell (12)
Kings Langley School, Kings Langley

A Day In The Life Of Ashanti

I woke up at 5am to be at a video shoot for 6.15am. I got dressed and put my hair up, and got there at 6.05am.

The producers gave me an outfit to put on, and the make-up artists did my make-up for me. The hairdressers curled my hair for me so I was ready to go!

I got set up and did my first scene of my video. Eventually I got most of it done. I haven't finished it yet though.

I got home for about 9.45pm. I got in the shower when I heard a huge bang on the door. I quickly got out with a towel round me and looked through the spyhole.

I saw about 25 people outside my door screaming my name and waving paper at me for autographs.

I put my music on full blast, so I couldn't hear the banging and I got back into the shower. By the time I got out, they were gone. It's 10.40pm and I'm going to bed to do it all again tomorrow.

Love you guys - Ashanti xxx

Lucy Dillingham (12)
Kings Langley School, Kings Langley

A Day In The Life Of Mariah Carey

Dear Diary,

It's about 6.45 in the morning, it's really early and I'm tired. The reason I have to get up so early is because I have to go and shoot the first part of my new video. I'm really excited but then again really tired. I wish we didn't have to get up so early. Anyway, I'd better go and get dressed or I'll be late. Write in you later!

Dear Diary,

It's 3.24 and I've just got home! I finished the first part of my shoot. It looked great. There were big bright lights, great outfits, I loved it. I've got to do it again tomorrow but I don't have to get up so early, thank God!

I'm going to buy a new car later. I wonder which one I'm going to buy. After that I might go clothes shopping 'cause I've got a party to go to tonight. Everyone is going to be there so I have to look my best. I'll probably get surrounded by lots of people. I hate it when they do that. Sometimes I wish I wasn't famous because I could do without the aggro, LOL! Anyway, I'll write in you later and tell you what I bought from shopping, bye!

Kirsty Owen (12)
Kings Langley School, Kings Langley

Dragon Wars

The red dragon tribe fell out with the yellow dragon tribe. The young and strong yellow leader was in charge of the yellow dragons. The old and wise red leader was in charge of the red dragons. He set traps around the village and river to stop the yellow tribe getting water. The yellow leader sent spies to the village but were killed by the trolls. The few that did return gave the yellow leader information about the village. There was battle after battle.

The red dragon leader was inventing machines for the war and wishing for peace between the tribes. It was wrong to control them. The yellow leader sent dragons to attack the village. The dragons did terrible damage to the village.

The red leader's wife was killed. He was heartbroken. He remembered the story of the Trojan horse, he made a Trojan dragon. He sent his entire army inside the Trojan dragon. He employed actors to act as guards, they took the Trojan dragon right past the city and in a loud voice said, 'This weapon of mass destruction should not fall into the enemy's hands.'

The yellow leader heard this and charged to steal the Trojan dragon. The actors had fled back to the village, screaming. The yellow leader did not pursue them, he was more interested in the Trojan dragon.

At night they came out, killed the guards, captured the yellow leader and the dragons could be free and happy.

Luke Higham (11)
Kings Langley School, Kings Langley

A Day In The Life Of Tony Blair

It is really cool being Tony Blair because I'm Prime Minister. I can do whatever I want. It has been hard work for me in the past couple of weeks because the General Election is taking place. I have to make up long speeches for a couple of weeks.

General Election Day

It is the day of the General Election. I have woken up early to give more speeches and make more people vote for me.

It is now the end of the day, thank God, but I am not going to go to sleep due to the results of the General Election. I am really scared that I will not win, but I have been told by my wife the more positive you are, the more chance there is of winning.

It is now nearly 3 o'clock in the morning and they are just about to say who has won the General Election …

'The winner of the 2005 General Election is … the Labour Party.'

Sohail Sadiq (12)
Kings Langley School, Kings Langley

A Day In The Life Of A Rabbit

Bang! I was woken up this morning at 8am, feeding time. I had my plan all laid out in front of me, literally. Well I did until *someone* moved my run and I got up late.

I'm checking my plan again, 7am get up, 8.30am she leaves, 9am *action!* It's now 8.31am I can hear the door closing as she's going out. I've been waiting nearly half an hour, time to do my plan!

I've started to dig under my run, soon I'll have a big enough hole to get through. I squash under my run and through the gap in the fence. I come to a wood, I hop over the winding roots and over the dry leaves. As I stand still I hear raspy breathing and a paralysing chill goes down my spine. When I turn round I see a dark red coat and a sly grin. I run and run, over the dry, curling leaves, over the winding roots, through the gap in the fence and under the run. At last I'm safe. Now, what shall I do tomorrow?

Katie Walsh (11)
Kings Langley School, Kings Langley

A Day In The Life Of A Fish Called Lou-Lou

It's 6.30, little Lou-Lou is asleep, she is laying still, she is not making any noise.

It's 7.00, little Lou-Lou has woken up as Mum has fed her. Now she is swimming around.

It's 7.30, little Lou-Lou is swimming around. I'm getting ready for school but I can't hear her because the music is on and it is very loud.

It's 8.00, I go to brush my hair. Little Lou-Lou is swimming and is making a lot of noise. Then I go downstairs to go to school. She's asleep ... *silence.*

4.00, I get home from school. I go upstairs and get changed. Little Lou-Lou is swimming but it's silent ... *she stops.*

4.30, I go to do my homework. Little Lou-Lou's not swimming, she's *not* asleep ...

5.00, I go to check on her, she's not there. Then I notice that Lenny the cat has been upstairs ... 'Lenny's got blood dripping from his mouth ... *argh!'* I scream, 'Lenny's eaten little Lou-Lou!'

Nikki Carlisle (11)
Kings Langley School, Kings Langley

Life As A Great White Shark

I don't like being a great white; people try to kill me for fun and for my fins.

This morning, my friend Bob, who is a hammerhead shark and me, went to the coast to get some breakfast which was a tall man for me and a small child for Bob. Afterwards I swam away but when I looked back I saw Bob with blood around him.

Bob didn't see the nets and got caught. I did try and help but someone saw me so I swam away. When I looked out of the water I saw him hanging, having his picture taken with the person who caught him. After that they took his jaws out and chopped his fins off. There was blood everywhere.

The next day I decided to kill the person who'd killed him. It was stormy with waves crashing about. The man was at sea fishing so I grabbed the bait and pulled the line and when he pulled it up he saw nothing. I was on the other side of the boat. I swam back as far as I could and crashed straight into the boat and as the boat capsized the man fell out. I grabbed the man and there was blood all over the place.

When the people came out they wanted to know what had happened …

Lauren Joyce (12)
Kings Langley School, Kings Langley

A Day In The Life Of My Fish

I'm a goldfish, I think anyway. I wake up and blow some bubbles and look out of the window.

It's dark so I go to sleep (6.30am). I wake up again, swim around again, blow some bubbles again, look out my window and ... guess what? It' still dark.

I wake up at 7am again, swim round again and blow some bubbles. While doing so I realise it is light and that's my day. Oh wait it's breakfast time. I've just had a lovely breakfast.

What did I just say?

Nick Couzens (12)
Kings Langley School, Kings Langley

A Day In The Life Of A Dog

I wake up, look at the time, it is 6.30am, too early for me so I'm going back to sleep, *yawn!* Ah! just the right time, 9am, yes breakfast's already there. Hopefully I'll get my treat now and my belly rub.

The door's opening it's my owner and my brother, he's already up, he gets up at about 7am because my owner's up already.

'Angel!' My owner's calling me. 'Shadow!' He's calling my brother. 'Time for walkies.' We both jump up and wait by the front door. He takes us for a play in the field where we chase each other or race to the ball.

We get home, it is about 9.30am. At 10am we get in the bath, then have our teeth brushed, then we'll go out for the day to Whippendale Woods, we love it there, we get so much attention it's really fun.

11.15am we go home to watch a bit of television. We love the cartoons, our favourite one is *'Tom & Jerry'*. We like *'Roadrunner'* as well.

After watching TV it is 12.30, yes, lunchtime! I run through to the kitchen, lots of food is in my bowl, mmm! I eat it all up and a little bit of my brother's.

It's 2pm I am getting tired so I go to sleep. 9pm I'm still tired, I'm going to bed. Night!

Rosie Dyte (12)
Kings Langley School, Kings Langley

Paul The Goldfish

My name's Paul, I'm a goldfish. I will tell you my normal life.

10.34. The family have gone out with Mum. Quite quickly in fact. Mum looked to be in pain. After they had gone I swam round the tank. I followed some bubbles. It was boring so I went to sleep.

11.18. I woke up. Still the family were not here. I went to the top of the tank and I ate some food that the family had put there.

12.01. I heard a bang outside. I thought the family were home. They weren't, it was some boys out the front playing football against the fence. I started blowing bubbles.

1.09. I woke up and came out of my house and looked at the TV and it was blank. Then I saw the cat, it is called Smudge. I'm always scared when Smudge is around. It tried to eat me once. I went and hid in my little house.

1.59. I didn't go to sleep. I was too scared of the cat. finally I saw the reflection on the door, he was gone. I came out of my house. I went to sleep.

3.49. I woke up and hoped the TV would be on. I swam to the edge of the tank and looked. It was, they were home. Then mum came in, she was holding something in her hands. Then I saw a face, it was a baby. Mum had a baby. It was called Alex.

Jordan Pope (12)
Kings Langley School, Kings Langley

A Day In The Life Of A Monkey

When I woke up one Sunday morning I found that I had been sleep-swinging again. By the way my name is Duncan for anyone who was wondering. Anyway, I found myself in wildebeest territory which is not a good thing because they wave their legs around like mad if they feel like you are invading their property and if one hits you that's the end of your adventure. So I got myself out of there before it was too late. Then I thought, *let me go and get some food, some of the Amazon's finest bananas I think.*

I had some bananas. When I had eaten I felt very full and satisfied with my morning. At about 2pm, 3 hours after I'd eaten, I felt a bit hungry again but I could not find anything so I went to torment the alligators. Just as I was passing over the lake, I slipped on a branch and fell in. An alligator bit my tail but I escaped. I then ran right into a tribe's spearing session and I got speared in the chest. I then plodded a short way and then passed away.

This story was written in monkey Heaven.

Joe Hughes (12)
Kings Langley School, Kings Langley

A Day In The Life Of My Lizard

07.00:
I woke up, saw some broccoli and cauliflower, went down to take nips at the broccoli and cauliflower. I had some. I was thirsty after, I saw some water so I drank some but I was still hungry.

09.30:
Live locusts entered my vivarium so I ate them because they were teasing me, saying, 'Yummy, I'm all nice and fresh aren't I?'

About 5 minutes later I needed the toilet. I had a poo under the sand. Afterwards I was really dirty so I had a bath.

14.38:
After my bath I was really cold so I ate some more broccoli and cauliflower to warm up my blood! After, I started basking.

16.61:
My vivarium was cleaned out by my owner (slave). When it was clean I buried myself in the sand, then ran about for some fun.

20.16:
Time to shed my skin. I went to my bed and I shed my skin. I shed my whole head skin.

22.23:
I went to bed. Suddenly it was dark.

23.59:
I knew why it was dark! It was time for bed!

Joe Oldham (12)
Kings Langley School, Kings Langley

Life On The Moon

It is my first day working on the moon. It is fun, but hard. We are doing scientific tests to see whether humans can live here.

We have to sleep in tents, it is very cold. We've found some interesting things today. We've found samples of rocks and stuff. We have to wear special overalls to keep us warm. We're living off junk food. The drink is alright.

The aliens are alright. They have 3 eyes and ears like ogres. Their skin is green but they can talk like humans.

The job is quality. I am really enjoying it. I get lots of money for it. It is tough but worth it!

Josh Ellison (12)
Kings Langley School, Kings Langley

A Day In The Life Of A Snail

I woke up this morning and found myself in a pile of leaves as usual. Then I went for some breakfast. I had some leaves. After that I stood there for about an hour, then had a bit more to eat, then stood there, then I ate.

After that I went for a quick walk, well I say quick, when really it seemed like it took me forever. By the time I got back it was dark. It was time for me to look for somewhere to sleep. Before that I had a bit more to eat then some more and more and more until then I decided to find somewhere to sleep.

Last night I slept on the grass but tonight it was a bit cold so I decided to sleep inside. I didn't know if I should sleep in the house or which room to sleep in. In the end I decided to sleep in the bedroom in the plant!

Joanna Butterfield (12)
Kings Langley School, Kings Langley

The Golden Dragon

An age ago in a village in England, there was a knight named Eldor. He had won many wars, but he did not know something devastating was going to happen that very night.

The daughter of the king of the realm was visiting and coming down for the feast. It was the celebration of their victory in the last war, when the dragon was attacked. So everyone in the village was busy.

The knights and warriors of the village were no normal people: they had the greatest riders, the best knights and the best horses, but amongst great happiness.

Far away there was great evil awaiting the knights and the king. The dragons of Amohen were waiting for the night to come.

They lived in caves in Amor and were waiting for the Great Dragon's roar. The Great Dragon was also known as Gold Fang. He had a great soldier dragon named the Gold Dragon. He was covered in gold - that's how he got his name.

It was night; people were jolly and eating at their feast, when suddenly they heard a sound like a hurricane. All of Amohen was emptied and the dragons were coming for war. They looked up to the mountains, then it got brighter and brighter. The dragons were licking the side of the mountain in flames. They came swooping down in anger. People screamed - in seconds the village was gone.

Thomas Parsonage (11)
Kings Langley School, Kings Langley

A Day In The Life Of My Fish

6.30am
   Woke up, blew bubbles, looked a bit dark outside, went back to bed.

6.40am
   Woke up, blew bubbles, swam around a bit, looked a bit dark outside, went back to bed.

6.50am
   Woke up, blew bubbles, swam around a bit, saw bubbles come from a chest (I like bubbles), swam around the chest, looked a bit dark outside, went back to bed.

7am
   Woken up by a bright light, blew bubbles, swam around a bit, saw a big ugly cat's face, hid, went back to bed.

7.15am
   Woke up, blew bubbles, swam around a bit, ate some food, pooed, went back to bed.

7.30am
   Woke up, blew bubbles, swam round a bit, saw a finger in *my* tank, bit it, went back to bed.

7.45am
   Woke up, blew bubbles, swam around a bit, swam a bit more, got bored, went back to bed.

8am
   Woken up by a loud bang. Yes, peace at last. I swam around a lot, got really tired, went back to bed.

4pm
   Woken by another loud bang. *Great they're back,* I thought. I blew bubbles, swam around a bit, felt a bit lonely, went back to bed.

8pm
   Woke up, blew bubbles, swam around a bit, looked a bit dark outside, went back to bed.

8.10pm
   Woke up, blew bubbles, looked a bit dark outside, went back to bed.

Ross Hudson (12)
Kings Langley School, Kings Langley

The Dragon And The Treasure Cave

Up on a mountain was a dainty village. The birds sang in the tall trees, the children played happily with each other, everyone was happy.

One very hot day, everyone lay in the sun, tanning one side and then the other. Then, all of a sudden, the sky went dark. The villagers looked up and saw a fierce, fire-breathing dragon! They fled to their houses and locked the doors. Peering out the windows, they saw the dragon strolling into the treasure cave.

The next day, there were a lot of arguments about what to do with the dragon and how to get the treasure. Two brave knights came forward: 'We will kill the dragon and rescue the treasure!'

Everyone cheered.

The brave knights woke early. They crept into the cave and reeled back as they saw the giant sleeping dragon. One knight charged at the dragon with his sword, aiming for his neck and got burnt to ash.

The other knight hid and waited for the dragon to settle back down to sleep. Then, cautiously and carefully, he crept towards the dragon. He took a large gulp as he went to dig his sword into the dragon's neck, but the dragon was still awake and saw him creeping up. It took in a deep breath and gobbled him up.

The dragon is still sleeping on that massive pile of treasure. No one dares to enter because no one ever saw the knights again.

Amy George (12)
Kings Langley School, Kings Langley

The Face At The Window

It was a cold night. The trees rustled in the breeze, the wind howled, the houses creaked. Lucy was wide awake, she couldn't sleep, she kept seeing faces, faces at the window. The face was John Hamming, the gravedigger. The house is in a graveyard next to an old church that people say is haunted. The gravedigger used to live there a long time ago.

Bang! The bedroom door slammed shut with a mighty force and it nearly came off its hinges. Lucy jumped. She ran out of bed and tried to unlock the door but it was too hard.

Slowly the window started sliding …

Ryan Pamment (12)
Kings Langley School, Kings Langley

A Day In The Life Of A Cat

5.26:
> I woke up, opened my eyes, it was still dark so I went back to bed.

6.00:
> I woke up again, a bit lighter, looked around the corner. I went back to bed.

6.59:
> I woke up, looked around a bit, decided to get up.

7.05:
> Sneaked around a bit.

7.30:
> I heard a scratching noise in the kitchen. *A mouse!*

7.31:
> Caught it, mmm, nice one.

7.50:
> Bored, went back to bed.

7.55:
> Zzzzzzzzzzzzzzzzzzzzzzz

8.00:
> I was woken by a noise. One of my humans were getting up. I got up and went to see. The human had the bedroom door closed so I waited outside it.

8.15:
> I started scratching and miaowing at the door. It swung open and I jumped back. The human said something I didn't understand.

8.20:
> I went down to the kitchen for some food. I started scratching, miaowing and cuddling the human's feet because it's all I can reach! I hope to get some food.

8.21:
> Food, hurrah!

8.30:
> Finished my food.

8.35:
> Went back to bed.

9.00:
> Woken up by shouting and some strange words that sound like this: 'Oh it's Kitty!' and the little humans stroked me. Who is this Kitty? I am a cat not a kitty. Is there another cat in this house?

9.05:
   Started looking for this so-called 'Kitty'.
9.30:
   Was still looking, no sign of it!
11.00:
   Gave up looking for the strange, so-called 'Kitty'.
12.00:
   Most of the humans had gone.
12.30:
   All the humans had gone now.
1.00:
   Decided to go out.
2.00:
   Had a fight with another cat in my garden;
2.30:
   Went for a poo in the neighbour's front garden.
2.40:
   Got chased out of their garden.
3.00
   Went back to my garden and sat in the sun.
4.30:
   Tired, went to sleep in the sun.
6.00:
   Woken up by rain and thunder, ran inside.
6.01:
   Sat on the sofa to dry.
6.30
   Dry.
7.00:
   Had something to eat.
7.30:
   The human came home.
7.35:
   Got told off because the sofa was wet.
8.00:
   Had some food.
9.00:
   Went to bed.

Frida Becker (12)
Kings Langley School, Kings Langley

A Day In Space For Sam The Astronaut

Sam the astronaut went to space to visit a planet called Jupiter. He saw blue skies, he saw black skies, then lots of bits of a planet around him. Sam searched and searched for Jupiter! It was not there! It had gone! Sam got out of the rocket and went floating around, looking for Jupiter. He searched for ages, until he gave up and reported that he wanted to be pulled back in.

Suddenly a spaceship came! He glared and three knobbly hands came out. It was aliens. Sam screamed, 'Help!' many times but no one could hear him.

The aliens unclipped him from the rope. They took him to their spaceship where there were lots of gadgets. The aliens said, 'Don't be afraid, we need to return something.'

Sam saw the aliens holding a mini Jupiter and they took him to where Jupiter normally is and it grew bigger, bigger and bigger, then they said, 'We shall return you to your land, bye!'

Sam said, 'Wait!' but they were gone.

Blondell Franklin-Beck (12)
Kings Langley School, Kings Langley

Consoles

Yaki Yamamoto laughed to himself. He had invented the ultimate addiction virus for his new games console. Nobody would be able to resist it ...

Ben snatched the console from Joe and pushed the 'on' switch. A green light flashed on the screen. 'That's not right,' said Ben touching the screen. As his finger met the screen his scalp inflated like a balloon, his eyes bulged from their sockets and his clothes evaporated, showing pulsing red veins running throughout his body. Yamamoto's virus had mutated and infected Ben.

Joe screamed and ran. Ben followed, trying to infect him. Joe bumped into a man coming the other way. Fear drove Joe on without apology. Ben caught up with the man and touched him. He became infected.

Joe, out of breath, hid behind a wall. Meanwhile the thing continued to infect anyone in its path. It passed him without noticing him. Joe noticed a green trail. In a moment he decided to trace it back. He ended back at his house. He crept in and discovered it came from the games console. If he touched it, the console meant death. He had to destroy it. Joe reached for his large dictionary and hurled it at the machine. It smashed down and shattered it. The green light disappeared.

Joe left the house and was met by a trail of dead bodies. The last one he came across was Ben's.

Meanwhile, in Boston, Mike turned on his console. A strange green light appeared ...

Daniel Harris (13)
Lea Manor High School, Luton

I Dare You

My arm was beginning to sting now. I sat up on the bed glaring at the etchings I had just carved into my arm. God I hate them. The compass that was lying next to me still had bits of flesh on the metal. Blood was beginning to seep out. Events which happened earlier that day flashed through my mind. I was getting dizzy, or was that the pills I had swallowed taking effect?

I was giggling now, giggling hysterically. Soon my empty, hollow laughter became a soft sobbing sound. I began to cry, hot, salty tears were coursing down my face and droplets landed on my arm, where the stinging sensation occurred. I began to rock to and fro.

I could still feel the heavy blows that were reigned on me that day. Why do people have to be so cruel?

My parents were always too busy and teachers neglected the fact that I was being bullied, so why should I care anymore? It was a question I asked myself one too many times.

Clasping the compass firmly between my fingers, I began scraping on my skin again, daring myself to go deeper in. I switched the compass with the silver razor blade next to me. I dug the razor in deeper than any other time I had done it before. I let out a painful sigh. This was it. This time I had done it, I could feel the life within me seeping out ever so slowly. Blood was coming out at a tremendous rate. I could feel myself getting dizzy. I decided to write a note to my parents. Maybe they'd take a moment out of their hectic schedule to read it. Maybe not. I began scribbling down.

'Sticks and stones may break my bones, but words will never hurt me. God how they were wrong, they hurt just as much.

I love you, x x x'

And with that last word, I let go of the pen, leant back on the bed, closed my eyes and succumbed to the feeling that was overpowering me, making me cold, ever so cold …

Salema Khatun (15)
Lea Manor High School, Luton

St George And The Dragon (Rewritten)

Our story begins in a village that is home to a herd of dragons.

One day a farmer visited his farm animals, to find they had been killed by a blood-drenched sword being held by a platinum-clad figure called George.

Screaming, the farmer quickly ran to the village elder who formed a plan. However, no one was willing to carry out this plan so the name of each dragon was put into a hat, with one chosen daily, to kill George. This carried on for years until the herd faced extinction.

One day, as time was running out, the elder's name was pulled from the hat. Shaking with fear, he began to get ready but as night fell, George made an ambush on the village and killed the elder. The elder's heir was quickly crowned.

The new elder requested a champion to be called upon to stop George but the herd were too scared and no one came forward, so off the elder went to do his duty.

Battered, bruised and in need of rescue, the elder knew he was failing when a fierce warrior appeared and began to attack George with his blade.

An exhausting battle commenced, until a deadly cut was made on the warrior, turning him into a fire-raging dragon and using his long, sharp, dagger-like talons, he slew George.

The elder was saved. The herd cheered and the elder knighted the warrior, St Dragon.

Simon Hayden (13)
Lea Manor High School, Luton

The White Trout

Once, at a lakeside castle, there was a beautiful noble named Lady Evelyn. She was engaged to a royal prince and was to wed in a month. Yet, when the month was nearly up, on a gloomy, dark day, Lady Evelyn was killed by a band of thieves who, after she died, hid her body at the bottom of the lake.

Soon people from that part noticed a white trout in the water who seemed to swim back and forth looking for someone. Since this was a rare sight, the villagers promised not to catch or kill her.

One day, three booters along with some soldiers came to the town and flouted their rule about the trout. Yet one man, whose language was enough to make the Devil blush, said he would catch her and eat her for his tea and so he did!

He fried her in his home and after her screams slowed, he flipped her over to cook, yet that side was not brown! He tried a number of times to cook her but nothing worked! Losing his patience, the man got out a knife and fork and as his knife touched the scales, she screeched, jumped out of the pan and into the middle of the room. When the man looked at the trout, it was not there. Instead, a beautiful maiden stood before him, clothed in white, her right arm bleeding. 'Look what you've done! Why didn't you leave me in the lake to do my duty?' she asked. 'I shall turn you into a salmon and hunt you until I win! Return me to the lake so I may wait for my love!'

'Yes my lady! I shall give up my foul being to keep you happy!' replied the flustered man, 'But how may I return such a beautiful woman to such a cold dwelling?'

On the floor lay a white trout, its silver skin shining in the sun. The trout was returned and she waited for her love for a time, until one day she left. The villagers say she died but that is another myth …

Ailene Gray (12)
Lincroft Middle School, Oakley

The Soul Of Countess Kathleen

Once in the poorest part of Ireland, two strangers arrived. They stayed in an inn and many people tried to figure out who they were. All they knew was that every night they counted their money.

One day the innkeeper asked the strangers to use their money to help the poor, and they agreed, but the strangers were the servants of Satan and they sold the souls of the peasants to the Devil. When the ruler of those parts, Countess Kathleen heard of this she sold all she had and gave the money to the poor, so they wouldn't have to sell their souls to the Devil.

That night at midnight the strangers stole the rest of the countess' money. So she asked the king of the western country to send over some food for the peasants, but the fleet would take twelve days to arrive. So she went to the strangers and offered them her own soul for 150 ducets. When she got the money she gave it to her steward, Patrick, to give to the poor, so it would last until the ships came. Then she locked herself in her room.

Three days later they knocked down her door to find her lifeless body. She had died of grief.

Katherine Sykes (12)
Lincroft Middle School, Oakley

Where Thunder And Lightning Came From

Once there lived a princess. She strolled in the rainforests, hungry and homeless searching for her long-lost family. One night, she spotted a house and knocked on the wooden door. The door creaked open. A witch stood in the doorway. 'What do you want?' she snapped.

'Love,' the princess replied.

'Love? I'll give you love!' and with a wave of a wand and a whisper of words, the princess was a frog. 'Whoever kisses you will turn you back,' the witch sneered.

The princess wandered on the rainforest floor, searching for anyone to kiss her. Then one day she wandered into a clearing. A tribe stood still and stared. A frog with a crown? They gasped.

An evil curse! 'No!' the princess croaked. 'Kiss me, I am a princess.'

The tribe's people stared at each other. 'Bang our drums,' one tribesman said. The tribesmen banged so loud the whole world could hear. The Englishmen called it thunder.

The frog scampered away, scared of the drums. But soon, the frog leapt back and asked for a kiss. 'Fire!' a tribesman shouted. So the tribe piled up sticks and lit a fire. A fire so big it touched the skies, and spread into the whole world. Lightning, Englishmen called it. The frog ran away, but kept coming back.

So whenever you see thunder and lightning, spare a thought for that princess frog. And if lightning and thunder never come back, maybe, just maybe, a tribesman dared to kiss the frog.

Marta Lewicka (12)
Lincroft Middle School, Oakley

The Creation Of The Black Dragon

In a time before time there was a sorcerer doomed for eternity by God. He had done many deeds against God's will. He had been sent to the lonely mountain, not yet discovered by mankind. On this mountain there was only one thing to do. Suffer.

So far the sorcerer had been there for 8 days and already he was as thin as a stick. On the tenth day he woke up to see a black lizard sat in front of him, as still as a rock. The sorcerer lay there staring and staring. Suddenly a thought flickered across his mind. With lightning-quick hands, he grabbed the creature, caging it in his hands. He put it in the pocket of his crimson-red robes.

There was a log lying next to him and a razor-sharp stone on his other side. He picked up the stone and began chopping away at the log. Hours later he had made a dip in the log, like a bowl. He took it to the edge of the mountain where he had discovered a never-ending pool of water. He cupped his hands and scooped up the water and threw it in his makeshift bowl. Then he took out the lizard, which had fallen into a deep sleep and placed him in the water. The lizard did not move, it stayed in its slumber. Quickly before it woke up the sorcerer murmured a spell under his breath. Suddenly the log lit up like a bonfire, the flames blazing a golden-red. The sorcerer continued the ritual. The flames began to take the shape of a giant winged creature. The flames slowly extinguished revealing the jet-black beast. It had daggers for teeth, knives for claws and brilliant huge wings. This was the birth of the Black Dragon.

Some days later the sorcerer died, exhausted from the demands of his magic. His last deed was to seal the dragon away deep in the mountain. The seal would not open for three thousand years. When it did the human race would slowly diminish at the mercy of the Black Dragon.

Conor Craig (12)
Lincroft Middle School, Oakley

Why We Decorate For War

Do you know what I know? You don't! Do you want to? Alright then.

Years ago in this village there lived a boy Akecheta (Warrior). He was wild but he was also loyal to his people. His best friend was a horse called Amdahl (Forest Water). Her mane was as soft as water when it trickled through your fingers.

Akecheta was at the top of the mountain, when he heard cries from the village. Akecheta ran sliding down the paths, nests from the trees fell on his head as he ran past. As he was nearing the village he slipped in some clay that had become wet in the rain. His hands became plastered in the clay. He got up and raced over to the bushes and peered through. There were white men there, they were attacking the people of his village. They were dressed in blue with gold buttons. Some carried wooden objects that shot out deadly metal. Akecheta crept over to Amdahl and jumped on. He wiped his face and patted her face and neck. She raced through the undergrowth to the village. Akecheta was screaming. The men ran away shouting, *'Retreat!'*

Later Akecheta was walking by the river with Amdahl. He suddenly noticed his appearance. His hair was filled with feathers, his face was smeared with clay, and Amdahl was covered in hand prints. He realised how scary he must have looked. Through the centuries our people have honoured his bravery by *decorating for war*.

Jennifer Buchanan (13)
Lincroft Middle School, Oakley

Thunder And Lightning

Do you ever wonder who are Thunder and Lightning? How they got up to the sky? Well, listen carefully. Thunder is an old German shepherd, and her daughter Lightning is a German shepherd and Labrador cross. These animals were not liked in the village.

Other animals wouldn't speak to Thunder because of how bad Lightning was. Why you may ask, well, Lightning would burn down trees so they would fall onto people's cars, burn people's sheds down, so people's crops and gardens got damaged as well. You might say that it isn't that bad. Well, it is when people are killed for the fun of it.

Thunder would then tell Lightning off and make a terrible noise. So the neighbours got angry. They tried to send them away from the village, but it didn't work. So the king, sent them away from the village, and even off the Earth. He sent them into the sky. They were not happy. So, Lightning still loses her temper from time to time and sends her fury down to Earth. So, Lightning's mother Thunder will tell her off and you'll hear a rumble. But even Thunder gets tired of Lightning and will appear to be distant from her daughter.

So, next time you see Lightning you know that she is angry with someone. Let's hope it isn't you. Then know, that her mother will be close by.

Ashleigh Balodis (13)
Lincroft Middle School, Oakley

The Boy Who Created Weather

One day there was a boy called Tom. Tom was in the garden playing football with his dad, he was very happy. All of a sudden the sky opened up and out came the sun. No one knew what it was. No one had ever seen the weather before, the sky had only ever been blue. Tom went to get his mum to show her but he accidentally tripped over and cut his knee. Tom was now sad and it started to rain. Tom couldn't understand why it was sunny when he was happy, but it was raining when he was sad.

Tom thought he could be creating something, he called it 'weather', and that was his surname.

So the next day he made himself angry and he created thunder. People were amazed at what Tom could do, but they were also scared in case he created anything else. Tom was inventing more and more types of weather, he invented lightning by being horrible. He invented clouds by being tired. He invented wind when he was hot and he created a rainbow when he felt creative and artistic. Tom created even more different types of weather with his feelings and emotions. And since then we have always had weather.

Melissa Morgan (12)
Lincroft Middle School, Oakley

Why A Dog Is A Man's Best Friend!

Tom and Charlie were best friends. They did everything together. They had many things in common but the best thing was they both loved dogs.

In the middle of their village there was a huge green. Every weekend they played football on the green and had great fun.

The boys were on their way back from school. They had agreed that they would play football when they got to the green. As they turned the corner they spotted a well in the corner of the green.

They ran as fast as they could towards the well, to go and explore it. When they reached it, they had a look down. It was dark but they could see the reflection of themselves in the glistening water below.

Propped up against the wooden bucket was a white sign with black writing printed on it. It said, *Wishing Well! Do You Dare To Make A Wish?*

The boys looked shocked. Was it a prank by their school mates or was this real? Tom didn't believe it so he dared Charlie to have a go at wishing. Charlie couldn't back out, so he reached into his pocket and pulled out a 2p coin. As Charlie loved dogs he decided to wish that he was a dog. He had always wondered what life would be like for a dog, so he did!

Before anyone could say anything, Charlie began to grow a tail, ears, furry coat and big puppy-dog eyes. Charlie had turned into a dog, forever!

They were still best friends even though Charlie was a dog! This is why a dog is a man's best friend!

Jenny Janes (13)
Lincroft Middle School, Oakley

Pandora's Box Continued ...

But what happened after Pandora opened the box? Well, you can imagine. Everyone blamed Pandora for all the bad things that had entered the world. And Pandora was the most unhappy person I had ever met.

Epimetheus, who was furious, divorced Pandora and tried everything he could to catch all of the bad creatures but old age had caught up with him.

Pandora was teased by everyone she met, so she took to hiding in the Black Forest at the edge of the world.

Every now and then Pandora saw the little creatures that had flown out of the box, and no matter how hard she tried to kill them she couldn't because spite stopped her.

Though she couldn't stop thinking of the little winged creature she swore she had seen still in the box. And she was so angry with the people that had blamed her she thought she should steal into Epimetheus' house and let the last creature out of the box and let it out into the world.

So when she found the 'empty' box where she had left in Epimetheus' house she quietly lifted the lid. Out came the most beautiful creature she had ever seen, it landed lightly in her hand and smiled. Then it jumped out of the window and caught all of the horrible creatures and shut them up in the box. And everything was alright again for the world of men.

Charlotte Warren (13)
Lincroft Middle School, Oakley

The Creation Of The Earth

God had a walk through the solar system and He found a big gap. So He decided that He was going to create a new planet. It was to be the best planet ever created. So He got a huge piece of rock, picked up a shovel and began to dig and shape the countries and the sea. Then He filled up the sea with a huge watering can. Then He decided to have some plants and trees so He planted them and helped them along with Miracle Gro.

Then He decided to make the landscape more interesting by getting a chain with two hooks on each end of it. He attached one hook to the ground and one hook to the back of His flying car. As He drove away the hook pulled up hills and mountains, He repeated this over and over again.

Then He got a huge box of Lego and began to build towns and cities, but He had to build Big Ben twice because the first time He accidentally knocked it over.

To punish people when they did something wrong God filled some mountains with red-hot tomato ketchup. Then He put us on the planet and called the planet 'Earth'.

Richard Warren (13)
Lincroft Middle School, Oakley

How The Rainbow Came About

There were seven fairies that were good friends. However they always argued about one thing. When it rained and was sunny at the same time they wanted to change the colour in the sky.

Rachael wanted red, Amy wanted yellow, Isabel wanted pink, Nina wanted green, Beth wanted purple, Olivia wanted orange and Wilma wanted blue.

They all wanted different colours and they didn't know what to do.

Then one bright, sunny day with some rain as well, Wilma had an idea. They could all paint a strip of colour in the sky, so that's what they did.

> Rachael painted red
> Amy painted yellow
> Isabel painted pink
> Nina painted green
> Beth painted purple
> Olivia painted orange
> Wilma painted blue

And that is why there is a rainbow when it rains and it is sunny.

Sarah Hale (12)
Lincroft Middle School, Oakley

The Night The Angels Cried

A very long time ago all the angels were given a family to look after. In the summer everybody was happy and playing all day long, the weather was hot and everybody was kind to each other.

But winter was a completely different story, it was cold and dark. This made everybody sad because they couldn't play. People started arguing, shouting and yelling with each other. The angels tried everything they could think of, but the cold, dark days and long, dark nights didn't go away and the people didn't laugh or smile anymore.

One dark night they were so sad that all the angels started crying. They didn't like crying because their silver tears were so precious, but this time they couldn't help themselves. Their silver tears flew through the sky. The sky lit up with a flash of colour, the families looked up at them, amazed. Then the stars came up every night and lit up the dark winter sky.

Gabrielle Harding (12)
Lincroft Middle School, Oakley

How Lightning, Thunder And Rain Came About

There was once a god called Zepiria who controlled the weather. He controlled when the sun came out and when the clouds came over. One day he was deciding what weather the Earth should have, when Criticus the cloud god came to him.

'You can't make it sunny, I want clouds.'

Then a few minutes later over came Preistus the goddess of the sun.

'You can't make it cloudy, I want sun.'

For many long years they argued over which was better and why. Zepiria couldn't bear it. He tried to stop them fighting but it was no use. Eventually he went away and cried to himself. Drops of water hit the plants, rivers and oceans. This was called rain.

Finally Criticus and Preistus could wait no longer. They gathered their armies of gods and went to war. The fighting was vicious and went on and on. With every hit that Criticus and Preistus took, their power over the sun and clouds went. Slowly, Criticus turned into the thunder god and Preistus turned into the lightning goddess. Zepiria carried on crying from above.

From then on Criticus and Preistus came out and fought every so often, causing thunder and lightning, making Zepiria cry drops of rain.

Harrison Barnes (11)
Lincroft Middle School, Oakley

The Making Of The Rhino

God was sitting down when there was a knock on His door. It was His mum.

'I'm going out to do some shopping and I want you to clean your room and make a new animal for your Earth,' she said.

God heard His mum go out the door, tidied His room, picked up a pickled onion to carve an animal from and started to carve. He carved four legs with His pie slice, a head, a tail, a body, some ears, a nose, some eyes and put some cement on it. It was a perfect specimen, His best by far. But as He was picking it up His mum came in.

'Hi, my ickle shnooky wooky,' she said. As she said that He dropped the carving and the pie slice scraped a point into its nose. Because, as all the crazy people who carve pickled onions know, they're cut very easily. The cement-covered pickled onion fell into His duplicating machine.

'Uh-oh,' said God.

A clunk and a crash. The creature came out as ugly as all of the other things He'd made.

'Oh poo,' said God. But He still thought up a name for it. 'I'll call it a rhino,' said God.

But as He typed it His mum knocked on the door. God slipped and typed r-h-i-n-o instead and then pressed enter!

'Oh poopywoo,' he said and Tipp-exed out the 'Made In God's House' label. Then He shipped them all around the world. That's why the rhino's horn is white.

Alex Brown (11)
Lincroft Middle School, Oakley

The Four Seasons

Once upon a time there lived a couple. The man was called Ice and the woman was called Sun. They married and had four girls. The first they named Winter, she had long white hair and snowy skin, she always wore a white dress and a silver shawl.

The second daughter they named Spring, she had green hair, green eyes, she always wore a green dress and a daffodil hair grip.

The third girl they called Summer, she was extravagant. She had gold, glossy hair and her skin was kissed by the sun. She wore a gold dress and an orange shawl with a matching hat.

Their youngest child, Autumn, had long, red, feathered hair. Her lips were a dark, shocking crimson, she wore a red dress and a necklace made of orange leaves linked together.

One morning only Winter awoke and however hard she and her parents tried they could not wake the others. Winter pulled open the curtains to find a white blanket of snow lying on the ground. It was like this every morning for a few months and every morning Winter would run around the garden, as she did not feel the cold.

One morning in March only Spring woke, to find a warm, yet breezy morning and the garden filled with daffodils. Every day she ran through the fresh land and picked them.

The same sequence happened all year, every year, with Summer bringing sun and Autumn bringing wind. Some people believe that this is how the seasons come around and that these four sisters are still alive today.

Alice Eaton (12)
Lincroft Middle School, Oakley

How The Universe Was Created

Once upon a time there was nothing. Just blackness, not even a star. There wasn't anything just black, black, black. Then all of a sudden God decided to scratch His head and little bits of white fluff flew all over everywhere and stars were created. But even though it was very pretty, it was still boring so God decided to make things more interesting.

While He was thinking away His cat came up and sidled up beside Him. It started coughing and retching, 'Oh no, he's got a hairball!' shouted God.

The cat coughed up a hairball which fell into space and was stopped by an enormous star, held there by its gravity. It started to break up into nine pieces. It got so hot that these pieces grew a hard crust around them. God thought, *you don't get this sort of thing every day.* So He thought that He would name all the bits of hair. He named the star the *sun*, the closest piece to the sun, *Mercury* and as they got further away He called them, *Venus, Earth, Mars, Jupiter, Saturn, Neptune, Uranus,* then finally, the smallest bit *Pluto*.

Thomas Kiddy (11)
Lincroft Middle School, Oakley

The Loch Ness Monster

One day in the cold lands of Scotland a Scotsman called Bob decided to go fishing in the loch. His son wanted to go swimming in the loch at 5am because that was the only time it wasn't absolutely freezing.

Bob was fishing when his son ran out with shock and horror on his face. He said that he had seen a monster.

'You're saying there's a monster in Loch Ness? We could call it the Loch Ness monster, but there's no such thing as monsters.'

Bob returned the next day nice and early at 5am again and with shock saw the monster. It was green and had scaly skin that shone in the early sunlight of the morning. He ran into town shouting, 'There's a monster in the loch.'

Nobody listened, they were just complaining that he'd woken them up from their sleep.

He ran back to the loch and jumped into the water but the monster had gone. He went back every morning at 5am. The problem was that nobody would believe him. Eventually someone else came along with him one morning. They both jumped in the boat when they saw the monster but it had gone instantly.

The myth of the Loch Ness monster is still present. It only comes up at 5am every morning, but it can't be caught. It was only seen because a man and his son went fishing and swimming and today people are still looking for the Loch Ness monster.

Christopher Paterson (11)
Lincroft Middle School, Oakley

The Loch Ness Monster

Once upon a time, in the high old hills o' Scotland. Across the thistles and the heather and through the barren gorse was a loch. Loch Ness it was named and this loch was hidden by hills covered in brambles. After a long trek through mountain glens Barry and his wee bonny lass Jess had arrived. They pitched their tents in a wee cove just inshore, broke open the chocolate-flavoured Yazoo milkshake and sat among the heather by the lake sipping their icy milk and eating an old Scottish favourite ... Digestive biscuits. There the two sat for a few hours watching the pink sunset. Ultimately the day had been very boring ... but what would the night have in store?

The wind was howling and lightning fired through the fierce rain, the red sky at night had turned into shepherd's warning, or more appropriate, shepherd's shock. But through the night's darkness, the wind, the rain and the constant thunder, a shape was visible in the water, this shape at first looked like an old bit of hose piping. Up close the fangs and fins on its python-like body were distinct. Jess picked up a video camera and ran to the shore. The monster lunged at her, nearly taking her head off. Seeing Jess nearly killed Barry picked up a shotgun and shot the snake. The snake writhed and its fang snagged Jess. Suddenly the storm broke but with Jess and the monster lying in the water ... dead.

Tom Anderson (12)
Lincroft Middle School, Oakley

The Last Of The Dinosaurs

In the early days God made some very strange creatures. One day as He wondered what to make next, suddenly He thought of the dinosaur. It was perfection. He made thousands in all different shapes.

One day He came unstuck with one dinosaur, it wouldn't come out right and eventually He fell asleep. When He woke up, He found a furry creature in front of Him.

'I'm a bushbaby,' it said.

God was puzzled. Afterwards He started making bushbabies. But when it came to dropping them down to Earth, God couldn't because of all the monsters He'd created.

God killed the dinosaurs.

A demon heard what was happening. He went to God and asked Him if he could look for one of the dinosaurs and if he found one he could keep it. God agreed.

The demon found one - pterodactyl. He took it to a cave to look after its jewels. The demon fed it snakes. However, two humans came to take the jewels but they started fighting over them and the demon fled. Man complained there was so little gold it was making his wife ill. Suddenly a snake came out of nowhere and explained the situation to God. God laughed and snapped his fingers and all the jewels disappeared. The demon cried loud and the pterodactyl turned into nothing bigger than a goose. God called it 'heron'.

James Rodger (12)
Lincroft Middle School, Oakley

The Four Seasons

Once upon a time there were four little fairies that lived together on a sunny island. The fairies were called Summer, Autumn, Winter and Spring.

Summer was bright and colourful, Autumn was warm with brown hair. Winter was cold and pale and then Spring was gentle and fresh. The four fairies had been given the privilege to name the year and to say what it should be like. They always disagreed about what they should call it. Each fairy thought it should be named after themselves.

Spring wanted it to be called Spring. Summer wanted it to be Summer. Autumn wanted Autumn and Winter wanted Winter. They were fighting all day and night.

'I want it to be called Summer!' shouted Summer.

'Noooo, it will be called Spring!' protested Spring.

'I think it should be called Winter. It's definitely the best,' screamed Winter.

'It *will* be Autumn!' Autumn screamed as loud as possible.

God, who had granted this permission, was now starting to dread it.

'I know,' shouted God over all the racket, 'you can all choose part of the year to name.'

'Yeah!' shouted all the fairies at the same time.

So it was agreed. Each fairy chose part of the year, and named it after themselves. God called these 'seasons'.

Rachael Southam (12)
Lincroft Middle School, Oakley

The Blue Lion

In the sweltering wastes of Ethiopia was a village named Sypathy. It was known for its natural beauty and wildlife. Many elders from other tribes went there to relax and participate in their holy festivals. Sypathy was indeed a very popular village. What the people didn't know was the danger that lurked beneath the local river. The danger had always stayed in the shadows, isolated from the rest, just waiting to come back and wreak havoc upon the world.

The villagers were celebrating a festival in honour of the fire god, Aag. As the villagers circled around the statue of Aag, there was a sudden loud shriek which alarmed everyone. The sound was coming from the river. The villagers rushed to the river and saw the most ferocious creature imaginable. None of them had ever seen such a beast. It had razor-sharp teeth which were a foot long. Its navy blue fur was drenched and it had yellow glowing eyes which were similar to that of a demon. The beast's claws were suddenly visible as the villagers came towards it. It suddenly grabbed one of the children and dove back into the deep and murky water. The father of the child was a great chief warrior who was just devastated by the tragedy.

After that day the father of the child, Bahadoor which was Swahili for *brave* embarked on a quest to save his son and slay the evil beast. The goat named Manaqui was kind enough to give her magical horn for defence and as a good luck charm. His weapons consisted of a dagger forged in the fires of Metradon, which was said to possess magical powers. A goat horn and an oil torch to be able to see in water. Diving in the water with great speed he entered the unknown waters of the river.

As he got deeper and deeper there was the smell of rotting flesh and blood which alarmed Bahadoor greatly. In the distance he could see a figure that looked like a cage. As he got closer and closer he found that it was his son who was inside and beside him was the beast. Thinking that the cage wasn't very robust he tried to break the lock. It slowly broke off and he got out. Believing they were free, they swam up to the surface. Then suddenly there was a great roar that triggered an underwater avalanche and a tsunami effect. They tried to get out as fast as they could, but the beast stretched out his arm and grabbed Bahadoor by the foot. He struggled to break free but it was no use. Thinking quickly, he grabbed the dagger from his loin cloth and struck the beast in the hand. It suddenly let go and they finally got to the surface. Both of them were glad to be alive and that nobody was hurt. Due to all the splashing and kicking almost half the village had gathered.

They slowly came up to the coast, suddenly out of nowhere sprang the beast. Both father and son jumped out of the way. The circle of torches which were lit up the day before had fallen down and had created a whole ring of fire. As the beast jumped in the fire and burnt all his blue fur to a crisp and had somewhat shrunk.

Once the fire had been extinguished, out came another type of animal. It was similar to the evil beast, but instead his fur was bright orange and he seemed less ferocious. The animal never attacked humans as long as Bahadoor was around and was kept as the village pet. They called him Shair which was Swahili for *Big Cat*. As the years passed, the Shair had spread all across Africa and was now a new species and was given a new name, the lion.

Ahsan Bokhari (12)
Lincroft Middle School, Oakley

King Midas Of Phrygia

When King Midas returned Silenus back to the god he was offered the granting of one wish by Dionysus. Foolishly and without thought Midas asked for the ability to turn anything he touched into gold. His gift was granted and the consequences were laid out.

At first Midas was delighted with his gift. He went all around his palace turning everything to gold. It was later when he decided to eat that his joy turned into horror. His grapes turned into small golden balls the moment he picked them up. His meat turned into a solid block when he tried to eat.

In his fury, Midas pushed aside his servant. At once a golden statue replaced the warm, living body. Midas ran out of the room and tore away to the storage rooms. But nothing changed when he was down there. The sack of grain turned into gold, each storage jar turned to gold as they were touched, he would not be able to eat. Midas flung himself on the floor and wept and wept as the true meaning of the gift came true to him.

Wine god, Dionysus, returned a few days later and King Midas begged him to take the curse off him. However, Dionysus claimed that he could not take the gift off him. Instead he told him to bathe in the waters of the River Pactolus. Midas took his advice straight away and the power left him as he bathed. But later troubles were stirred …

Joyce Kwok (12)
Lincroft Middle School, Oakley

Thunder And Lightning

There were once two brothers called Thunder and Lightning who were gods. They had a dad called Zeus who was king of the gods and a mother called Aphrodite, goddess of love.

Life was fine until one day a war broke out between the mortals and the gods. It was a war that claimed many lives of both mortals and gods.

Just as the gods thought they had won, a terrible thing happened. A brave and talented human with the name of Zorlak (king of the mortals) came along. He had a huge army, billions of people, but he only needed three. He took them and crept into the god's palace where he murdered Zeus and his wife Aphrodite in their sleep.

When Thunder and Lightning woke up the next morning they were filled with anger to find their mum and dad had been killed. The two boys began at once to look for their parents' killer, Zorlak. They are still looking now. You know when they are near, by the rain which is their tears of sorrow, the thunder which is their mourning and the lightning which is their anger. They strike down humans as they go, hoping to find Zorlak. But as far as we know, they haven't found him yet and they probably never will.

Josh Walker (12)
Lincroft Middle School, Oakley

A Day In The Life Of Barney

I open my eyes as I hear the familiar noises of my family rising from bed. Their footsteps patter around upstairs as I lie in my basket, not wanting the warm, fuzzy sensation of sleep to leave.

Too soon, they're downstairs, making breakfast. The blanket of sleep has been lifted by the wonderful smells of bacon and I'm ravenously hungry. I plead with the humans, using my best puppy eyes, my desperation for my biscuits obvious to everyone. I sit transfixed at their feet, until one of them gives in and gives me my breakfast.

The event of my day is my walk. The children leave (where they go all day is a complete mystery to me) and Mum takes me out. As I've grown bigger, I have realised that my mum and I look very different, so she may not be my real mum, but I call her 'Mum' anyway.

Once I'm out walking, even restricted by the lead, I feel overwhelmingly happy. As the wind blows my ears back I feel I'm swelling to twice my size and I'm walking on air. The smells overpower everything and I can't sniff everything quick enough. It is over too quickly and the next thing I am focused on is my dinner and going to sleep.

I lie watchful in my basket until everything goes quiet and I drift off to sleep, exhausted by the day's adventure. One eye remains open though. My job is to look after my beloved family.

Sarah Maunder (14)
Mayflower High School, Billericay

I Decide Who Stops

Morning. The bitter wind nips at my bare feet as winter's chill seeps in. But Ravensbruck is always cold, no matter how hot it is in the open. The ice crunches beneath my raw toes, burning my skin as effectively as fire. The burning hatred within me makes the place I reside in more and more like Hell every day.

We stand in straight lines of twelve. No more, no less. There are hundreds of women here. My fear, my sadness grows in its suffocating splendour. And I hate it. Lord, forgive me ...

Work. We trudge in silence. The odd groan of pain here and there, yet we dare not stop. We fear what may become of us. A guard stands vigilant, whip cracking in the wind. A constant reminder of what we must never forget. Every day the prospect of escaping, breathing the crisp, free air grows distant.

The guard rushes towards us, her whip flying. I fear it is my error, but Betsie is the victim. Lash after lash is beaten upon my sister's back, a harsh tattoo, a 'souvenir' that will remain. Dear Betsie screams in pain and cries for God to save her. Why will God not save her?

The women restrain me. I fight, a futile battle to reach her, but my punishment for not protecting her is to watch now. Finally the terror ceases and the guard turns a greater chill upon me as I hold my tortured sister in my arms. 'I decide who stops ...'

Melissa Newnham (13)
Mayflower High School, Billericay

A Day In The Life Of My Granny

'Cissy, Cissy!' called Mum. I woke to find Mum asking me to go and collect turf from the shed. It was freezing outside and as I stepped out of the back door a shiver ran down my spine and I got goosebumps all over my arms. Ireland is always freezing!

As I walked back I spotted a sharp stone. I walked on it without care. Not wearing any shoes is very helpful, as the soles of my feet are as hard as donkeys' hooves.

In my family, there are lots of people to feed, so lots of jobs, but there's always someone there. Mostly my jobs are cleaning the house, collecting turf from the shed and feeding the chickens, donkey and sheep.

Today we are working our hardest to get all the turf home, as soon it will be winter and it will be too wet! Turf is bog, (muddy, wet soil) that has dried in the sun. It's back-breaking work on the bog, but riding there in the donkey and cart and being heated by its warmth when lit is something to be proud of. We cook everything on the turf fire.

Our few neighbours came round for a drink and supper of leek soup. We sat and talked for ages. Soon I felt tired and said goodnight to everyone before going to bed.

I love my life. Although it's hard work, I would not change it for the world.

Geraldine Morrisroe (12)
Netherhall School, Cambridge

A Day In The Life Of A Pearl Diver

I wake up at 6.30am to prepare my diving equipment. Most boys do without it but over ten pearl divers drown here every year. I like to be on the safe side.

After that I have a full protein meal for a healthy body and a cereal bar for energy. Then I exercise thoroughly using my arms and legs for the diving routine. It is important that you do this every day to make sure your body is warmed up and ready to dive.

I make my way to the beach. My boss gives me an exact spot where to dive. I look carefully when I dive as there could be dangerous animals nearby. When you first dive in the murky water, you can't see anything. An odd sensation tingles all over your body as you make your way to the bottom.

I skim my hand over the sand underwater to make sure I don't miss any shells that could contain possible pearls.

At dusk I finish diving as it is hard to spot the oysters. When I scramble out of the sea I find the boss and get my payment according to the number of pearls I find. On a good day I find about 200 oysters of which 30 have pearls in them.

It is rumoured that 'The Black Queen Pearl' is right here. I would give it to my mum if I found it. Who knows, maybe I'll find it tomorrow.

Jonathan Jongkind (13)
Netherhall School, Cambridge

The Escape From Island Doominy

Roger McKarton and Johnny Eldridge were best friends. They were next-door neighbours and they went to the same school.

'Roger, wake up!' shouted Mrs McKarton from downstairs. 'It's a big day for you junior!'

'Eh-uh, what's happening?' Roger said in a sleepy way.

'Haven't you remembered that you are going on a boat trip with Johnny? And Fluffy is going with you.'

'Fluffy! He-he-he's a dog!' Roger said getting out of bed.

'I know he is a dog, but I think it will be good for him,' Mum said.

'OK, I'm getting dressed!' replied Roger.

'Hi Roger, ready for the trip?' Johnny said.

'Yes, definitely,' Roger answered.

They went in the ship and off it sailed.

'What's that noise sailor?' Johnny questioned.

'I dunno, but it looks like there's a hole in the bottom of the ship,' the sailor replied.

'A hole?' Johnny said in shock.

Then the ship gradually began to sink.

'Everyone, get into the lifeboats,' the sailor shouted.

One of the boats was punctured and the two children with the dog were sitting in it.

'Oh look, an island,' Roger shouted.

The children got off and were happy to find an island, but they didn't know that the island was Doominy!

'This is the island of Doominy,' Roger said. 'Oh no!'

'But I know that there is a helicopter landing pad on the other side, let's go,' Johnny shouted.

Will they reach the landing safely?

Raphae Memon (12)
Netherhall School, Cambridge

An Astronaut's Day

2.19* Spacely hours

I'm very excited because this is the last day before I'll go back to Earth and complete my mission. I just have to get on Saturn's third moon and then my mission is complete. My one year investigation was worth it all right! For breakfast I'm having a piece of tinfoiled chicken and a bottle of lemonade to drink (well, what else could you do with it?).

2.58* Spacely hours

I got in my spacesuit and clambered in my pod. Then I landed on the third moon of Saturn (not that they have any order) and thought I'd discovered a new element.

4.17* Spacely hours

I have just come to base and teleported the element to Earth and am waiting for the results.

6.43* Spacely hours

I got good results, it is a new element! After a ceremonial upgrade and a red hand of shaking, I'm going back to Earth!

1am Earthly hours

As soon as I got to home, sweet (Earth), I jumped from my craft forgetting gravity and broke every bone.

7am Earthly hours

The doctors have made an estimate of how long until my bones grown back and it is 2 years! I take it very seriously because the estimate took six hours. Luckily this isn't Hell because there are plenty of pretty young nurses around.

Reuven Jongkind (12)
Netherhall School, Cambridge

A Day In The Life Of A German Soldier

After an early wake up call I went down to the station for our daily briefing. It was my turn to go on patrol. I gathered my equipment and headed for Germany's border. My job was to make sure that nobody left or entered Germany. I hated stopping Jews from escaping, but it was my job, if I disobeyed I was automatically sentenced to death.

Finally, after around four hours of boredom, people emerged. It was an army tank - the English. I didn't know what to do, but nevertheless, I had to do something.

'Sir, could you move from the area?' His strong English accent sounded as though it could shatter glass.

I refused to move, but looking back I wish I had.

Crash, bang, shatter. It was my bones. The noise was coming from my spine. As they bellowed insults at me I rolled up in a ball, I was too weak to defend myself, yet too conscious to blank it out of my mind.

'Good evening Bill. You're at Kiel Army Hospital, you've been in a serious attack. I'm afraid you're paralysed from the neck down.'

That was ten years ago; those words still haunt me. I'll never forgive my attackers for what they did to me, although my attack wasn't against British MOD's laws, I still can't help but feel that I've suffered a terrible injustice, the mental and physical effects will be with me forever.

Mathea Armsden (13)
Newnham Middle School, Bedford

Murder

Detective Inspector Samuel Smith is interviewing James Lovell on account of a serious assault and murder of Elizabeth (Lizzie) Lovell - James' wife.

DI Samuel: 'Why did you do it?' (Leans in)

James: 'I didn't do anything, I told you I was down the pub with a few mates.' (Holding his head, elbows on the table, looking down).

DI Samuel: 'We know you weren't down the pub with your 'mates'.' (Leaning right in). We have fingerprint evidence on her body and the knife.'

James: 'So you're telling me that I'm not allowed to touch my own wife, or use knives for cooking?'

DI Samuel: 'Well what about your fingerprints on Lizzie's blood and the footprints in the carpet … ?'

James: (Shaking) *'I didn't do it!'*

DI Samuel: 'Why do you keep denying it? Give yourself up James, you and Lizzie had an argument, you got angry, you hit her and hit her until she was unconscious, you couldn't help yourself, you reached for the nearest weapon which was a knife and stabbed her in the back *16 times.* She had made you really angry, you left her for dead. How could you kill your own wife?'

James: (Crying) *'I didn't do it, I didn't do it.'* (Covering his ears and mumbling).

DI Samuel: 'You did, You know you did! James, not only did you kill her but your baby as well … '

James: *'No!'* (Crying and thumping the table) *'No! No! No!'*

Jessica Smith (13)
Newnham Middle School, Bedford

A Day In The Life Of A Cat

'Morning ... already? Oh fish sticks. Hello there, my name is Tom cat. There are new people around me. Where am I? Oh my gosh, I've slept in my neighbour's garden ... they have a *dog! Argh!* Run, run as fast as I can, he can't catch me because I'm the um, um, oh, fish sticks, I can't think of a word.'

The dog continues to chase Tom cat and he speeds up. 'Simple, if I just pop through this here fence ...'

The fence doesn't open and the agitated dog is getting closer.

'Let me jump.'

He leaps over the broken fence and looks below onto the dog as he comes to a sharp halt.

'I'll get you next time if it's the last thing I do,' groaned the exhausted dog.

'Too bad I was too quick for you!'

'It's time for breakfast, now it's the task of getting my big body through the cat flap.'

He holds his breath and squeezes through the cat flap and hurries to his bowl for his value cat food, but anything will do for Tom cat because you can't stop him from eating!

'If you carry on eating you'll become Mr Podgy won't you my sweetie-kins,' says my owner, although I don't think she knows that I can hear her!

Cats aren't that clever are they ... ?

Abby Alexander (13)
Newnham Middle School, Bedford

Silent Killer

The assassin dropped from the sheer cliff face, his black cloak billowing out behind him. His entire body was covered in black clothing and there was only a strip across his face for his eyes. His skin was a light brown complexion and his eyes were a tranquil blue. A single red headband was the only part of his clothing that was not black. On his belt he carried two bombs, a pistol with a silencer and several knives.

He hit the ground at the base of the cliff and set off at a run. The building he was heading for was an old German castle, built in the Renaissance. Reaching the wall, the assassin began climbing, using the smallest crack in the stonework as a hand or foothold.

He managed to reach the battlements and climbed up onto them without a sound. The assassin leapt into the courtyard below. His pistol was suddenly out. Five of the guards were dead before they could fire their AK47s. The assassin ran to a door at the base of a tower, opened it and ran up the stairs. Reaching a room at the top, he found himself facing the back of the general he'd been hired to kill. The assassin quickly put one hand over his mouth and drove a knife into his back. Pulling it out of the corpse, the silent killer planted one of his bombs on the floor and leapt out of the window into the night.

Cameron MacAskill (12)
Newnham Middle School, Bedford

Large Eggs Found In South-East London

In south-east London, seven abnormally large eggs have been discovered.

156 centimetres tall, a metre wide. Found in a field, one mile from an archaeological dinosaur site, 3 metres underground by archaeologist Archie.

Scientists have no definite label for them yet, but hope it is a prehistoric dinosaur egg.

In 1955, one like this was found in Spain. One, with the most delicate care, has been opened. Unfortunately, grey matter is all that's left. However, one, presumably preserved by an Ice Age, has a faint pulse and will be X-rayed tonight. The dig has been closed off for searching. These shells seem to date to 100-140 million years ago. Just after the dinosaurs were said to have died out. Unfortunately, the nest itself is of no use to us, eaten away by underground vermin and mould.

We are relying on this one egg to help explain history. The last of the dinosaurs?

Joshua Smith (12)
Newnham Middle School, Bedford

The Journey Of A Dollar

Bank till in Los Angeles. Sold to a grubby businessman sent to San Francisco. Given away to a burger bar in San Francisco. Hands of a boy I am taken to Florida. Given to an ice cream man who takes me to California. Sold to the President's grandma who dropped me off in Washington. I was picked up by an Elvis impersonator and taken to Memphis. Given to a young man, taken to New York. Fell out of his pocket and dropped into a drain.

Now in the hands of a girl, wondering whether to use me to buy her school lunch. She thinks as she's in the queue, *where has this coin been? Has it belonged to a film star? A celebrity?* She let her mind wander as she was clever enough to know only the Dollar itself would know where it's been.

Tara Wheeler (13)
Newnham Middle School, Bedford

A Day In The Life Of A War Hero

Boom! I hear the sound of an exploding shell piercing the walls of the trench. We all stand waiting for someone to shout 'emergency'! But all my comrades are dead and all I can hear is the penetrating sound of bullets as they shatter the lives of my men.

I look out onto no-man's-land and I see debris of destroyed planes, mangled body parts and one man's whole body. Hang on, that man's alive and he's one of ours. I call out to the survivors in our trench to come quickly. I say to them, 'Cover me, I'm going to get him.'

I creep up the side of the trench making sure I am not seen. *Bang!* I put my hand on a mine and half of my arm has gone. I can't give up now, I have to save him. I quickly roll over to him and sharp piece of metal slashes my back, but I keep on going.

'Got ya,' I say and right at that moment I feel a faint relief of saving a life. I climb back into the trench and as I do so a bullet hits my leg. I scream out in pain, pull the soldier in and shout out for immediate help.

We all help him and check if he has any wounds, then move swiftly on to me. They cover my injuries and we start talking about the other soldier. They said to me, 'You were a hero out there …'

Josh Groom (13)
Newnham Middle School, Bedford

A Day In The Life Of 50 Cent

An average day of Cutis Jackson AKA 50 Cent is usually very busy, especially now as he has just released his new album 'The Massacre'. With interviews, photo shoots, performances and many other things, for 50 Cent this is just another thing on the list. He is known all over the world for his music. But how well do you really know him? In this short biography we tell you what a day in the life of 50 Cent is really like.

50 Cent starts his day at around 6.30. He gets ready and goes straight to the studio, where he has just finished recording his new single 'Just A Lil' Bit'. He is also recording another single due to be released soon called 'So Amazing' featuring Olivia, the newest member of G-Unit.

After finishing at the studio, 50 Cent takes his manager back to his house to start preparation for his party, which is going to be on MTV, he was very excited about this. Soon after starting he has to rush off to have an interview with TRL. After finishing the interview he goes back to his house to help prepare for his party.

When he returns there is a huge surprise in store for him, not only are all his fellow 'gorillas' there, his chief party planner has organised a huge art piece of all of them as a present for 50 Cent. After a few more hours the guests start to arrive and the party starts.

Abby Blake (13)
Newnham Middle School, Bedford

A Day In The Life Of A Lion

Waking earlier than the rest, I'm relied on to provide food for the family. Soon I need to teach my little boy how to capture and kill his prey. However, I will stick to doing the killing for now.

I lazily wander out, still being half asleep, to the hunting grounds. I leave the missus still sleeping happily in the cave with the little one tucked up in her arms.

Plodding through the fields I see my first target ... an antelope! Eyes sharpened, back hunched, teeth grinding, I pounce!

Damn it, what gave me away? The antelope escaped. Looks like I need to try harder. The missus won't be happy if I come home empty-handed. There it is ... another animal to feed upon.

Dragging the dead animal back, something doesn't seem right. There's a musty odour in the air, but what ... what is it? Hurrying to the door the smell gets stronger, my heart races, my ears steady. There he is. He has my missus, he's making a break for it. He's taking her!

Tom Funge (13)
Newnham Middle School, Bedford

The Exile Race Of The Humans

After dictator Rican was defeated and his followers/army, known as the Cetan, were exiled from Earth and the newly found planet Terra Minor. The Cetan managed to find a new planet that could only just let them sustain life, but at a price. Because of the atmosphere their skin mutated into a yellowish colour and many of the Cetan died when they first landed on their new planet, afterwards named as Cetanas.

Now, after many years, they have managed to create a grand army to attack Terra Minor with the help of a human traitor, who can shut down the planetary defences.

A month after the invasion the only man who can restart the defences has been abducted by the Cetan. Captain John Temples has been assigned to rescue the general. To John he is not just his general, he is his father. Special spy operatives have gathered Intel showing that after Terra Minor it is Earth that will be targeted …

Isaac Fargher (13)
Newnham Middle School, Bedford

A Day In The Life Of A Bird

Hello I'm Birdie; I don't have a real name because I don't have owners, which isn't a bad thing! I don't have to do what they say or be called a really stupid name like Chucky or Fluffy.

Anyway, you wanted to know about what I do in a day. Well I have six little chicks so I'm usually very busy looking after them!

I wake up at 7am and make sure that my chicks are safe and warm. I then leave them to have a lie-in and I go to fetch breakfast. I go to this big field which has lots of worms crawling around in it. I try not to go into people's gardens as most have cats and you know what cats are like when they see birds!

Anyway, once I have delivered my chicks' breakfast I try and give them lessons on flying, but only some days as this is a very tiring process! Especially for little things like them.

I then go and fly around looking for sticks that I can add to my nest as I always need spare sticks. You never know when the wind will come along and knock some sticks out!

By the time I get back, as it is usually a difficult job looking for sticks, it is time for me to go and catch some dinner for me and my chicks. That takes me an hour or two and that's the end of my day really, oh well. I'd better be off now. I have to go and start looking for dinner, bye-bye.

Daniella Caruso (13)
Newnham Middle School, Bedford

Fugitives - Chapter 3

Robert gasped and deeply inhaled a breath of fresh air. They were out of the danger zone, they were safe, for now. He slipped on the slimy moss that covered the interior of the cave as he tried to crouch on the hard, uneven, stony floor. He couldn't think, his thoughts were too muddled up; like someone had jumbled them all up. But one question wouldn't go away - *what about Jessie?*

Finally Simon spoke, 'You there Robert? Robert where are you?' He sounded worried.

Robert mustered all his energy and reply feebly, 'Yeah, I'm still here,' into the gloom.

Suddenly a faint noise came from above the pitch-black of the cave. 'Robert, Simon!' The familiar sound of Jessie's concerned voice resonated around the cave.

A feeling of relief rushed all the way through Robert, like a warm tingling sensation. He felt his way through the empty dampness of this rocky den and struggled to get up. He must get to Jessie - 'Jessie!' he cried.

'Robert is that you?' was the answer. Then he heard a tumble, grasping, a scream.

Jessie lay unconscious on the small grassy bank outside the enclosed cave. Robert picked himself up and blindly ran to the entrance of the cave, closely followed by Simon. There was Jessie, blood spattered on the grass around her. Robert knelt in shock.

They were fugitives from the police but they needed help. If they didn't get help soon ... well Jessie might die.

Iona Swannell (13)
Newnham Middle School, Bedford

A Day In The Life Of An Infant In World War II

20th October 1939 6.30pm

It was a bitter night. Mum was feeding me this new milk, I didn't like it but I was ravenous so I drank the powdery liquid greedily.

Recently a lot of things had been changing: much talk of air raids and shelters and my older brother and dad had left home. I don't know why or how long for.

20th October 1939 9pm

A loud continuous noise filled my head. It petrified me. Mother put me inside a plastic box and put a mask over her and my brother's face. She took me in her arms and held me close to her chest. She then ran out of the house with my brother's hand clasped in hers. The noise was pounding through my body; people were running everywhere. I closed my eyes, it was all too awful to take in.

20th October 1939 9.30pm

I opened my eyes, I found myself in a vast underground station. My mother was pumping air into the box I was in. It was cold and dim inside, all I wanted was my mother's warmth and her familiar smell to comfort me in this new place.

Suddenly a rumbling sound consumed the platform. The station fell silent. A louder bang rumbled across the walls. My head was saturated with these unfamiliar noises. What are they? I didn't know.

21st October 1939 8.30am

I awoke to the familiar scent of my mother. My mother held me close to her chest and she clasped my brother's hand; it was our turn to emerge into the real world.

I saw sights I was not ready to see or understand: houses reduced to rubble; grieving families and even injured or dead people.

Soon we came to our street. Our house was missing. The one with the shiny green door; the beautiful front garden full of flowers; the one with my bedroom; my family; our life - reduced to rubble.

Lily Waugh (13)
Newnham Middle School, Bedford

Martian Invaders Strike In Italy

Last night at approximately 11.15pm the deep space aliens struck again, this time in Italy. The little green men from the Andromeda galaxy are becoming increasingly aggressive. In the last four days there have been six aerial strikes at different locations around the globe.

The Martians attacked with Ion-cannons and high concentration lasers from their bastion that is in a deadly orbit around Earth.

The estimated damage is thought to be around $16,000,000,000. The European Union is currently discussing the best way to retaliate.

We suspect that they will launch a wave of Kamikaze pilots in space shuttles, equipped with atomic and plasma weaponry. These will fly up into the stratosphere and hopefully cripple the alien fleet. The air operation has already begun with millions of dollars worth of equipment and food being flown over from the USA and the United Kingdom.

An eyewitness account reveals the true horror of orbital bombardment: 'It was awful, the ground shook with every impact and everyone was panicking. I was lucky to find my way to a nuclear bunker before the main attack happened. Some of my family were not so fortunate. In the bunker you could hear the thud-thud-thud of the air defence guns, we all thought that we were going to die. After a while it stopped and I looked out of the hatch. All I could see was rubble with the odd half building jutting up out of the rubble like remnants of another time. Then I was forced by the local police officer to go back into the shelter'.

Patrick Meniru (13)
Newnham Middle School, Bedford

A Day In The Life Of Steven Gerrard (Liverpool FC Player)

We've flown over to Istanbul, the capital of Turkey. It's half-past five in the morning, my alarm has just gone off. We are playing in the Champions League final tomorrow; we're playing AC Milan.

It's really hard getting out of bed in the morning, as we are in a foreign country. I drag myself out of bed and into the fairly clean shower. Once I'm in the shower I'm awake. I lay out the best ever team's training kit on my bed - Liverpool's training kit.

It's like a furnace outside so we train for an hour and then have an hour to cool off. After our five hours on and off we have a coach to drive us back to the hotel. For the rest of the day the boss (Rafael Benitez) lets us have time to relax.

We are not allowed to have any food that takes too long to digest or any form of alcohol.

Me, John Arne Riisse and Djbril Cisse all like to play video games. I bought my Xbox, John bought his PS2 and Djbril forgot completely. We play on the games and relax by playing cards for the rest of the evening.

At ten the manager calls all of us to the meeting room. As I am captain he expects me to be there first. We are talking tactics for tomorrow's match. After talking tactics we go upstairs to rest for the next big day.

Benjamin Fearon (13)
Newnham Middle School, Bedford

A Day In The Life Of Tim Foster

10am	Wake up to the sound of my alarm clock.
10.03am	Get out of bed, clamber downstairs to have my breakfast.
10.15am	Eat my Coco Pops and check my timetable. Today I'm going to Newnham Middle School to give a speech! Have to arrive at 11.15am.
10.30am	Back upstairs to wash and get changed for my day ahead.
10.35am	Put on purple velvet trousers and pink lined T-shirt.
10.40am	Leave the house with my gold medal and speech.
10.56am	Arrive at Newnham Middle and I'm greeted by Mr Warmsley and the PE department.
11am	Wait for the children to file into the hall for assembly.
11.15am	Walk into the assembly hall where I'm greeted on stage by Mr Warmsley.
11.20am	After Mr Warmsley has his talk, it's my turn to do my speech! Very scary!
11.25am	Present the PE department with the sports award.
11.30am	Children leave the hall, I sign a few children's books and head to Mr Warmsley's office for a chat before leaving for lunch.
12.45am	Say goodbye to the teaching staff and Mr Warmsley and head home.
1pm	Jam sandwiches with crisps for lunch.
1.15pm	Watch some football - Man Utd v Aston Villa.
2.45pm	Go to parents to talk about tomorrow and have my dinner.
4pm	Realise I'm going to Bedford Modern School tomorrow to make yet another speech. Leave parents for home.
6pm	Have an early night ready for tomorrow.

Owen Cowley (13)
Newnham Middle School, Bedford

A Week In The Life Of Tim Foster

Monday:
Today we spent most of the day in the river therefore we were all worn out. I still managed to go out in the evening even though it had been a non-stop day.

Tuesday:
Today I got up at 6am It was an all work day today. It's an all work day most days. We had a team talk and a few races with others in the river.

Wednesday:
Today I got up at 10am We had a day off so we went down the river to watch some schools race. It was on for most of the day so we didn't get back until late as we had been to the pub afterwards.

Thursday:
Back to work today. Up early like most mornings. Today we were going to board our flight for Greece for the Olympics. I'm terrified as I hate flying. We board at 3.15pm. We said our goodbyes and then boarded. All the way there we were talking about Greece as Steve had been before.

Friday:
Today was a bit of a work and non work day. In the morning I was getting to terms with the flight and then had a tour around the rowing stadium. In the afternoon we had another tour, around the town that we were staying in so that we knew where everything was.

Saturday:
It was a late start today for the crew as we had all slept in. Can't write a lot for today as not much happened.

Holly Monk (13)
Newnham Middle School, Bedford

A Day In The Life Of A Soldier In World War II

I would normally wake up in the morning to the sound of gunfire, enemy shells exploding close to my friends and me. But not today. Today I will be having the job of a messenger. I will have to write letters to the parents and friends of the poor lads who have fallen in battle. I don't know how I am going to be able to write a letter to the parents like I actually knew the deceased man, like I actually liked him.

I am given a list of the names that have died in this battle: William Heratin; Josh Todle and Tim Minuter. I start with the fatal, scary words:

'Dear Mrs Todle,
I am sorry to inform you ...'

It is so hard to write these letters, as you are the carrier of this terrible news.

I finally finish the letter to Mrs Todle, the mother of Josh. I don't know how hard it will be for her to take this information, but Josh must have fought for his life in this war, all of us have. I send it off with another messenger and begin with another letter.

This job will never stop until the bodies stop falling, which I think will never happen.

Tom Faden (13)
Newnham Middle School, Bedford

A Day In The Life Of An Evacuee During World War II

I woke up suddenly to the sound of a bomb exploding. I looked around, frozen with fear. It was pitch-black - except for the burning house, just two roads away, that had been hit by an enemy bomber.

Today was the day that I was going to be sent away to live with another family. While I was huddled in the cupboard under the stairs with my family, I was thinking about this. Bombs were still being dropped by the planes above us. I dreaded what our street would look like in the morning. Eventually, the all clear siren went off and we all squeezed out of the cupboard.

Surprisingly, our house wasn't badly damaged. I looked out the front door and saw that immediately opposite was a huge crater. There was no sign of the house that used to be there.

I walked upstairs, trying not to think about leaving and started to pack. I was only allowed to take a small suitcase with me. I packed: a spare set of clothes, a photo of my family and some sandwiches that my mother made me pack for the journey.

At the train station, I started to realise that once I got on the train, I might not ever see my family again. I couldn't stop trembling and tears started to run down my face. Mother was hugging me so tightly, I didn't think that she would ever let go. I didn't want her to let me go. I wanted her to come with me - but she had to stay in London. She let me go and I stepped up onto the train. I was terrified. Would I ever see my family again?

Ayesha Holden (13)
Newnham Middle School, Bedford

Gunshots And Grenades - Chapter 3

I woke up to the sound of gunshots and shouting, 'Private 697369 has gone down - someone get first aid!'

Pete must have already woken up. I wondered where he was, he wasn't supposed to be on duty until lunchtime.

'Oi, Eddie, can you take over on lookout, we need a replacement!' called Connor's voice. 'I know you were on night guard but we really are desperate!'

'Yeah, I can't sleep anyway.'

'Thanks, I owe you one mate. How abouts when this damn war's over I buy a couple o' pints down the pub 'eh?'

'Great, well I'd better start looking out or ol' Mr Tash'll be causing 'avoc.'

Quickly I got to work, still wondering where Pete was. 'Grenade front left.' I called. 'They're retaliating, watch out they're firing grenades right left and centre. This is the worst possible job in the trenches - being on lookout. If a grenade or bullet is coming to the left then you've gotta tell everyone to watch out or there's gonna be loads of dead people that you're partly responsible for,' I told Connor.

'Well I 'ope you're looking out cos we already 'ad one dead un today.'

I was puzzled. 'You mean John died?'

'Nah, some other young lad woke up this morning and stuck his head up in the air. He got blown to bits!'

'What was his number?' *What if it was Pete?*

'Eh, 637571 I think,'

'Right, shape up. I don't want any more injuries today,' boomed the general …

Keira Cruickshank (12)
Newnham Middle School, Bedford

Asleep?

This is one of the ending chapters in a book. To summarise so far, a family has gone missing. When police were called and entered the house, everything was at a standstill. A clothes horse stood by the washing machine, half filled with clothes; an overturned chair ...

The following chapter takes place after the police have talked to the neighbours and figured out when the last sightings of the Gellar family were. Currently, police are searching the house and have found something suspicious on the door of the under stairs cupboard ...

A crack. A long slit slithered its way down the centre of the door. It looked like the door had been forcefully slammed shut. Cautiously, an officer opened it and gasped. Was it her? A small girl, aged about seven or eight, was on the floor. Curled up in the foetal position, with her thumb in her mouth and her long, vanilla-blonde hair falling gracefully over her shoulders, she lay there, undisturbed, with her eyes closed. She matched the description of the Gellars' youngest daughter, Erica: blonde hair; small build; blue eyes? Her eyes were closed; she looked so peaceful, as if she was sleeping. Both officers and the neighbour, Mr Rose, suddenly stopped. The officers removed their hats. They all wished that she was sleeping, but truthfully they all knew she was dead. Feeling somewhat emotional and with a tear in his eye, the male officer called for the undertaker ...

Madison Fisk (13)
Newnham Middle School, Bedford

A Day In The Life Of An Alien

I got out of my Brinthax chamber and stepped into the goo cleanser. I hate the sticky stuff, it's easy to wash off but it smells bad and slightly stains your skin. Mum insists that we use energy saving chambers even though they cost a fortune.

I went outside and saw it. War, death, destruction. A huge crater had been converted into a battlefield and a gang of terrorists were attacking the royal palace. Luckily the troopers arrived just in time and the terrorists were arrested.

I then went inside and put on the Cyberskool. A series of questions had appeared on the screen. Dad says that I must get my grades up or I will become a junkie. The questions were about the Salazar quadrant! In frustration I turned the screen off and watched TV for a while. 'The Lindin Show' was on. I watched that for a while.

It was feeding time already! I went into my Brinthax chamber and pressed feed. A small tube was pushed into my mouth and a pink gunk poured out into my mouth. It was fried Glorg. I went back downstairs and tried to watch my show again, but my dad saw me and said that it was my bedtime. Wearily I got up, trying to go as slowly as possible. I got upstairs and pressed the sleep button on my chamber and a blue goo started to fill the hollow tube I was in.

Raman Bhangle (13)
Newnham Middle School, Bedford

A day In The Life Of a Celebrity's Dog

I woke to the sound of my owner, cooing and clucking over me. Her strong peach perfume made my eyes water; her voice boomed like a broken drum throughout my miniature kingdom.

As soon as I poked my head out of my only refuge I was stuffed into a tight fitting Burberry coat and sprayed with a dog cologne that smelt of gone-off toothpaste. After having my nails clipped painfully short, I was carried into the sparkling kitchen. She pushed me to my bowl and wandered back to her bedroom, gazing at herself in every mirror.

I looked at the disgusting brown sludge in front of me. It was supposed to be the tastiest dog food: low in fat, vegetarian and full of vitamins. To me it was just like mud with rotting cabbage and a hint of newspaper. I ate it all! I was on the new 'Atkins' Diet' and was forced to eat this 24/7.

My day got even worse as I was stuffed into a stupid bag which smelt strongly of my owner's peach perfume. My owner visited a number of designer shops, dunking me down wherever she pleased.

I emerged from my bag prison to find myself in *my owner's* favourite dog parlour. More baths! How I longed for a walk in the countryside: jumping in puddles, rolling in mud. As a celebrity's dog it would never happen. My owner's pristine Gucci shoes in mud? No way would she even consider it!

Ruby Baker (13)
Newnham Middle School, Bedford

Together

Will he ever leave my mind? Beth thought to herself. Day after day she hoped that she would see him again. Although she knew she had no chance of ever being more than friends, her mind told her to keep waiting for him.

Driving in his car, James was contemplating his life. So many paths to choose from, which one would he take? Who would he take it with? Beth.

He loved her more than words could describe. Although she was younger, he wanted to spend the rest of his life with Beth, still knowing that their parents would disapprove.

Beth kept walking. Thinking of the one she adored, wondering where he was; what he was doing.

Both were drawing nearer and nearer to each other, without knowing James came to a junction and stopped. Beth came to the edge of the road and stopped. No traffic was coming so she crossed. No people were crossing so James started the engine. He turned the corner and hit something.

Beth was lying in the road unconscious. James was halfway through the windscreen. Both were rushed to hospital, together, without knowing.

Lying in a hospital bed, Beth came round. Her last words, 'Tell James I love him and will meet him in Heaven when the time is right.'

With his last breath James whispered, 'Tell Beth I have loved her since I first saw her.'

With that they both passed together.

Laura Mclean (13)
Newnham Middle School, Bedford

A Day In The Life Of A Hamster

8pm	I woke up and got out of my little house which I just about fit in.
8.30pm	I tried my wheel out but I stopped. When it stopped I was upside down.
9pm	My owner let me out of my cage to have a run around.
10pm	I sprung an idea. Despite my owners being quite kind to me, I decided I would do a runner.
11pm	I wrote my plan down on my hamster-sized notebook.
12pm	I had a quick drink.
12.10am	I started gnawing on the cage to make a hole.
2am	I finally found my way out of my cage.
2.05am	I started running for the door in my stage 1.
2.30am	In stage 2 I reached the door and jumped through the cat flap.
3.45pm	In stage 3 I needed to reach the dark alley, which I did.
4am	In stage 4 I needed to run along the path and go over the bridge.
4.15am	As I ran along the bridge, behind me was a drunk man. As he was walking his foot swung past and hit me.
4.16am	I was kicked in the deep river where I died.

Joshua Boland (12)
Newnham Middle School, Bedford

A Day In The Life Of Fred Flintstone

Monday, or is it Tuesday? Woke up about 3am because Dino needed the loo and Bubbles wanted her breakfast. Wilma (my really lovely wife) gave me my breakfast, cheese on toast with a steg egg on top, and I went and got dressed in a really nice pair of stegosaurus-skin shorts and a really nice and warm (though a bit tight) T-shirt with a long-sleeved sabre-toothed tiger skin with a blue tie and a green jacket, and went off to work.

The quarry is a nice place really. Mr Slate and I, well it was accidentally-on-purposely done, we have created some gooey mix and he named it after his daughter, Concreasure. The day went well, well, as good as a day usually did!

Later I came home to find Wilma and Betty hanging out the washing and Barney Rubble doing a barbecue. I mean, what was that all about? Oh well, I carried on like nothing was wrong, so I had my steak and went inside.

A few hours later Wilma came in. I got into my pyjamas and shoved our pet, the sabre-toothed tiger, Ade, out and then got into bed.

Alice van Hattem (12)
Norwich High School for Girls, Norwich

A Diary Entry From Ruth, 1942

Dear Emily,

From the day I was born, I have wanted to become a nurse to help people. And my mother has always supported me and has said it was a very sweet idea.

However, since the war started and Father was made to fight, my mother has tried to stop the idea of me becoming a nurse even passing through my head. I have heard recently on the radio that more nurses are needed as more soldiers are dying through being left untreated.

When I told Mother that I was going to work in the makeshift hospital set up near our village, she gave me a strong, hard slap around my face that burnt deep into my skin. I couldn't speak from the shock and my eyes filled up with scalding hot tears. I managed to make out her voice, 'Don't you dare talk about that ever again,' she said before turning on her heels and walking out of the room.

From then on I realised that I had to help immediately and do my bit to help win the war against Germany, and if my mother didn't understand that, then she was a total stranger to me.

I couldn't just sit here doing nothing, not when the next dying man in need could be my father! This is what I have been waiting all my life for, to save lives and show that I could be of use in this unbearable world of hate.

All my love
Ruth xxxx

Francesca Hodac-Nichols
Norwich High School for Girls, Norwich

Darling Susan

Darling Susan,

Dusk has fallen on this desolate land, my heart aches with the fear of the coming day. Hitler's forces are forever growing. I feel as though the British army is being crushed like an ant underfoot. I long to be out in the open and a family close at hand to love and care.

The glowing image of you shines repeatedly through my mind; of the day we walked hand in hand across the beach, skimming stones and paddling in the shallows. Tell Archie I love him and to look after the cattle as soon will be the time of calving. How's the winter been? Hope it was satisfactory because before I left I didn't stock up on fuel.

Many of my fellow friends suffered badly from frostbite, and in some cases they died. You're lucky to still have me fit and alive. Many were left behind as we couldn't spare time, having to trek through tough conditions, oblivious of any short-notice attack or planted landmines.

Some days are restless as fierce battles are sprung on us, with aircraft, tanks and guns of all sorts. But other days are calmer, maybe not even fighting on rare occasions.

My general says I could be home by autumn if all goes well so I have one hopeful aspect of the days to come.

I love you so very much and miss you a million times a million!
From your beloved,
Fredrick.

Lara Cator (12)
Norwich High School for Girls, Norwich

Dear Ging And Calli

Dear Ging and Calli,

Hope you're having fun, seeing that it is the summer holidays because I'm not! I'm at military camp here in Essex and getting tortured by the staff.

Every morning I have to get up at 3.45am just to do 50, maybe even 100, press-ups to get us going for the long day ahead.

At 4am we have to get our breakfast from the revolting smell of the kitchen. I hate the food, it's just watery vegetables.

At 4.15am we do an extremely hard exercise where you have to climb 30m ropes and put up with crawling through long, wet, muddy tunnels.

At 5.30am we have to put on different clothes and go swimming in the most freezing cold water you could ever go in. He says we should get used to it for war!

At 6.30am we finally get to wash in some warm water which I think is the best bit of camp life because it is the only part which isn't hard!

At 7am we have a race; not a race like the ones at school, I mean running the length of three football pitches and back, this kills me.

Anyway I won't say everything I do otherwise I shall be here for ages. Write back to me as soon as you can so we keep in touch. OK?

From your best friend,
Sarah xxx

Sarah Cochius (12)
Norwich High School for Girls, Norwich

A Day In The Life Of A Soldier At War

I was running, bangs were coming from everywhere and then I fell! There was a faint siren!

I awoke, I had just been dreaming, yet, this was no dream. Shouting, men running, bombs exploding. Germany had attacked! I grabbed my uniform and thrust it on. As I took my gun I thought of my family.

Out I ran into the darkness. The sight, chaos all around! I ran with my fellow men. Oh God, please help me get through this! I heard running, someone was shooting at me. I jumped and fell into a trench. I'd escaped that time but would luck strike again? I scrambled out!

Just before me lay my friend. My heart throbbed, he didn't deserve it! Yet I knew I couldn't stop, it was all too dangerous. Again I was running; high above was a bomber aeroplane. Narrowly I missed my fate!

All of a sudden there was a bang and I fell to the ground. Pain seeped through me. Oh how I longed for that feeling to disappear. My wife, my children, I would never get to see my beautiful family again. I felt the loss already. My breaths grew shorter and shorter. The world around me faded away. *Farewell,* I thought as my eyes slowly shut.

I was no more!

Gabriella Ghigi (12)
Norwich High School for Girls, Norwich

How The Worm Can Live Even When Cut In Half

It all started when Persephone was skipping happily through the wood picking flowers when she caught sight of a strange-looking flower; she picked it and took it to her mum, Demeter. It was a bright red colour with grey spots. When Demeter saw it she was astonished! Demeter had never seen anything like it before so she gave it to Persephone to look after . . .

It was getting late so Persephone fell asleep on Demeter's lap. When she awoke, she heard a little voice crying. Persephone looked around and on the ground on a leaf she saw two worms. One of them was leaking blood and the other was crying. When the worm that was crying saw Persephone, it said, 'Help, my mother has been trodden on and cut in two. Please help.'

'But how, Worm, how?'

'There is only one flower that will cure it, it has red petals and grey spots. You need to sprinkle the grey spots over my mother's body and she will be cured.'

Persephone suddenly remembered about her flower. She rushed to get it and when she got back, she did as the worm had said. The worm was cured and the other worm thanked Persephone.

'Persephone, now that you have helped my mother, because of your kindness, other worms won't die if cut in half.

Mollie Hyde (11)
Norwich High School for Girls, Norwich

The Government's Secret

After the recent election of a new Prime Minister, we asked him what he thought of the British public. He said, 'These people, they distrust those who they know nothing but the name of, yet gladly follow those whom they know nothing about. That's how I won the election. These people I'm ruling believed everything I told them, they're that stupid!' His promise to make the world a better place is the one thing he has failed to produce.

Anonymous

sources stated that the nameless one has been in power since 1976. Hiding in the background he has gradually been taking over. But who is this power-hungry being?

I have found that the only beings capable of producing this result in so little time are turkeys. Those delicious birds you eat for Christmas dinner have been in charge of the country for the past 29 years.

When I found this out I went back to the Prime Minister dressed as a giant turkey (I had to go in disguise or he wouldn't have told me anything) and he confided in me his plans.

'We first planned to get our own back on humans. It would only take a few years. Soon we had accomplished that. We then realised what we really wanted ... to destroy Christmas. Soon our 30-year plan will be complete and we will be eating them in celebration of this miraculous event'.

This is Rebecca Morris for the 'Daily Disaster'.

Rebecca Morris (12)
Norwich High School for Girls, Norwich

A Day In The Life Of A Beagle

10am - I have just woken up and I am wondering where my food is, it is normally here by now. I go looking for my owner and find her lying on her bedroom floor in a heap. I go up to her and lick her and when she doesn't respond, I know something is wrong so I run to the back door, which is usually open so I can get into the garden. I run up to the front gate and scramble over it. I rush to our next-door neighbour's front door and start barking.

After about five minutes the door opens and there, standing in the doorway, is our neighbour's daughter. I start tugging at the girl's skirt, indicating that I want her to follow me and she finally understands. I lead her to the back door of my owner's house. I then take her to the room that my owner is in and she rushes over to her. Next she goes over to the telephone and talks to someone.

About ten minutes later I hear sirens and two men come rushing in and go over to my owner. They say a few words and take her away.

Our neighbour's daughter congratulates me and then leaves the room. I follow her into the kitchen where she pours me some food. After I have eaten, a sudden wave of tiredness descends upon me so I go to sleep.

Not every day is quite so exciting!

Kate Robinson (11)
Norwich High School for Girls, Norwich

A Day In The Life Of Hermione Granger

I don't know why Malfoy wasn't expelled years ago! Levitating poor Professor Flitwick around the classroom! I have it seriously in mind to report him to Dumbledore right this minute. And Ron was being a complete ignoramus too! He actually believed Dean when he said the Forbidden Forest was built on an Indian burial site! I mean, honestly! Hasn't he ever read 'Hogwarts: A History'? The only sane person in this place is Harry and with him ogling Cho Chang all the time, I don't get much sense out of him either.

Breakfast today was awful. Fred Weasley managed to receive a Howler from his mum (I don't know what he has been up to this time!) and forgot to open it, so the whole of the Gryffindor table went up in flames. Professor Sprout was livid! The leaves of her Mandarin Mandeligols got singed by the fire so now Fred has to do detention collecting the pus from the Oober Tuber pods in greenhouse five!

The rest of the day was pretty bad too. Professor Trelawny discovered that Harry and Ron had made up their Divination homework and made them polish all the crystal balls in her cupboard. Ron got in even greater trouble when he smashed one trying to escape out of the window!

There are still a couple of armchairs left by the fire so I will go and do my Arithmancy homework. Better get it done before Fred and George get here. You know what they're like!

Hannah Barber (12)
Norwich High School for Girls, Norwich

Own Kind

Ching-ko Mung-li stared in frozen horror around him. It had begun to snow and an old instinct, a yearning to be in the wild, was calling him away, yet he dismounted and looked around him to confirm what he was seeing. Kalmanina had been burned, its people tortured. Ching-ko had been on the trail for two days now.

Chink-ko Mung-li, the samurai warrior, had always disagreed with the persecution and wars between tribes of Japanese. Unable to agree with his superiors, he had ridden into the wild to combat cruelty in any culture. A band of raiders from the west of Japan had been sweeping across the country killing civilians and burning villages. Ching-ko had been following them from Nunbar and, by the fires still burning, could tell he was close. He mounted his horse and set off to the east.

A scout hurried up and reined in his horse by the tent of Gan-yu, leader of the Re-vi raiders. 'The samurai has followed us and is coming this way, my lord,' he gabbled, 'he will kill us all.'

The raiders fled. By the time Ching-ko had arrived, the camp was deserted, but for one. Gan-yu stood, sword in hand, defiant. Ching-ko drew his katana blade. Gan-yu struck first, making a deep wound in Ching-ko's sword arm. Changing hands quickly, Ching-ko struck back, knocking Gan-yu off the cliff. Ching-ko doubted he was dead, he knew another combat would come soon. In fact it came sooner than Ching-ko expected . . .

Helen Falkner (12)
Norwich High School for Girls, Norwich

Agent Score Plus

Those agents not on a mission were meeting in St Bartholomew's. No agent was allowed to know the real name of any fellow agent. They would meet twice a week at a coded location. For security reasons each meeting would be chaired by a different agent. Agent Jar was holding tonight's meeting.

'So it is agreed. We meet at Rendezvous 6432! Agent Cheese will give you your assignments. God keep you safe!'

Smelly Cheese handed out bags of cakes, no one would think it odd if they were found carrying bags of cakes. Each bag had a different number on it, disguised as a price label, this told Cheese which bag went to which agent. Those with no mission would have fairy cakes, those with a mission, macaroons, their orders written on the rice paper; only the agents knew how to reveal the coded message on the rice paper.

The meeting ended just as the service in church did, the agents mingled with the small but regular congregation. This way no one would think it strange, a group of people leaving a church after a service.

The agents never opened the bags until they got home. Agent Foxglove let herself into her flat, shut the door and locked it. She entered her kitchen, and taking her coat off, opened her bag. Inside the macaroons sat waiting. She placed them on a plate, turning them over, read the coded message and, of course, ate them!

Elizabeth Rose Cowell (13)
Park School for Girls, Ilford

The Unlucky Boy

Dear Diary,

Today at the end of school, I got told that I had bad luck. I think I know what you are thinking, *why did they say that I had bad luck*? So I'd better tell you.

It was Monday, first day of my GCSE test, it was a very cold and wet day. I had the shivers but I still had to go to school because of my GCSEs.

When I was walking down the path I saw a gang of students and I knew, if they saw me, I would get bullied so I tried to hide myself somewhere, but it didn't work . . . they spotted me and put me into a garbage can which stank like dog poo, and they took my lunch money and my homework. I begged for Britain! But it didn't work, I tried not to cry ... too much ...

Anyway when I arrived at school, I was late for class and cold and wet and I stank of dog poo but I got an hour's detention for being late.

When I entered the GCSE room I was given my paper, but ten minutes before the end of the test, Troy threw something at me so I looked behind me and the teacher saw and I then had my paper torn apart and was disqualified from the tests. I tried to tell them but Troy's dad is the head teacher's son so they wouldn't have any of it!

So that is the reason why I got called 'Bad Luck Boy'!

Benjamin Pearson (14)
Quarrendon Upper School, Aylesbury

Death In The Docklands
(An extract)

Rain fell in sheets from the thick clouds that obscured the stars and moon. All that illuminated the winding streets of the docklands was the candlelight that spilled from the windows of the taverns, brothels and other houses of disrepute which occupied almost every corner of the infamous district. Nearer to the docks themselves, where thirsty sailors regularly disembarked from the incoming ships, there were few other establishments. Tonight they did a roaring business. Nobody wanted to be outside, where there seemed to be a small sea pouring from the heavens. The ships floated dark and empty, like dead shells, and the streets were nearly deserted.

Only the watch remained out in the hostile weather. They pressed along their patrol route, heads bowed against the rain and wind, hoping that the night would not be too eventful. Now and then one of them poked his head around the door of a tavern or inn, checking that the tenuous peace that existed in the docklands was being kept, and warming his waterlogged bones a little. The docklanders fell silent, and glaring stonily at the offending officer. Then the patrol moved on, blinded by the rain that stung their eyes maliciously, and deafened by the percussive din it made as it smacked the cobbles.

The docklanders mistrusted the watch. To them, it was another part of the hulking and oppressive creature that was the aristocracy, the part that was visible, creeping around with the intention of making the lives of the poor miserable. They saw it as another measure implemented by the rich to make sure that those at the bottom of society stayed there. The docklanders were by no means a tight-knit community, but as soon as the watch became involved, they were confronted by an icy wall of silence.

Rarely did a night go by in the docklands when somebody was not robbed, beaten up or killed; but by the time the watchmen arrived all the witnesses had conveniently forgotten what happened, become temporarily deaf or simply gone home. This often included the victim, where they were capable of doing so. However, the watch was still expected to pursue the case, despite the fact that, like a muddy puddle, the more you stirred it up, the murkier it became, as the docklanders came up with more and more elaborate lies in order to confuse them. The locals preferred to resolve their grievances in their own manner.

For this reason, the watchmen copiously avoided noticing anything awry, particularly when the weather was bad. And it was for this reason that a man named Sinus Ramstone had chosen the docklands as the grim setting for his activities that night ...

Christina Pettit (15)
St Bede's Inter-Church School, Cambridge

Darkness Is Victory

(An extract)

Imagine a dark, so black that it seems to suck in all light around it. A darkness that invades your head, clouds your senses, dulling your mind to the world as the thick black smog of it suffocates you. There is a point in darkness where neither shape nor movement can be seen, and it is here where darkness stops being just the absence of light and takes on its true nature. It becomes a force, an entity so powerful that no person could survive in it without the absoluteness of it overcoming them, driving them slowly mad.

The darkness around Pedro was the ordinary dark of night, but was complete enough that not even he, creeping amongst the gravestones, could see his way towards the tiny pinprick of orange light that was the master. The darkness swirled around him, closing in, throttling him to death. Tripping over a badly placed rock, Pedro nearly swore, remembering in time that the master got very unhappy when people made noise on his night-time visits. Picking himself up gingerly, Pedro continued his stealthy walk, barely emanating a breath for fear of what might happen if he did. Fear pumped through Pedro's heart, he knew he had failed, knew that the master could not forgive him this time, but was helpless to resist his call, as all dark things attract one another. You may as well have asked Pedro to defy gravity.

'I would stop there if I were you,' said the master's voice in his ear, 'there's some newly dug graves you'll be visiting if you walk much further.'

Though the light from the cigarette had been several hundred metres away when Pedro last looked, his master now stood behind him. Black as the night itself, he seemed to become one with the night, and only a deep hole in his robes where his face must be showed him to be at all human.

Pedro flung himself to the ground, grovelling in front of the tall robed figure. 'Father, sorry I have failed,' he whimpered.

Casually lighting another cigarette, the master pulled his trembling servant to his feet. 'You make more noise than an elephant, Pedro.'

Smoke curled around the master's hood as he moved the cigarette into the deep black recess of his hood. 'I told you failure would not be tolerated again.'

The master felt the familiar rush of excitement fill him, as the air of the graveyard seemed to breathe in, drinking the excitement up, and lavishing the experience. Pedro's neck found itself suddenly clasped in the freezing vice of the master's hand ...

David Kaye (15)
St Bede's Inter-Church School, Cambridge

Narcissus' Tale

I don't believe this, I really don't believe this. That goddess, Echo, or whatever her name is, keeps following me around everywhere! I just can't get rid of her!

'I will ask you again, what can I do for you?'

'... Do for you ... do for you ...'

She just keeps saying the same thing, whatever I have just said. She is *really* annoying me! What's this? Now she is putting flowers by my feet. I mean, come on. I know I am incredibly handsome and the delight of many shepherdesses' dreams and all that, but you would think that they would give me a bit of peace and quiet sometimes!

'What are you playing at? Why do you keep following me? Stop repeating what I am saying.'

'... Saying ... saying ...'

'You really are a stupid girl, did you know that? Well I suppose you are madly in love with me and have been struck dumb by my dazzling good looks. I've seen it before.'

' ... Before ... before ...'

'Oh yes, you know that goddess, Athena, I could see her eyeing me up too. I'm the most popular bachelor around Mount Olympus, so I see women desperate to have me as their own every day.'

' ... Every day ... every day ...'

'That's it. I am fed up, just look at yourself!'

' ... Look at yourself ... look at yourself ...'

'No problem!'

'... Problem ... problem ...'

There she goes, crying like a girl. I will do as she asks. I can never resist admiring my wonderful self. Wow, I really am amazingly gorgeous, amazingly ...

Lucy Rahim (11)
St Francis' College, Letchworth Garden City

Orpheus And Eurydice

This was found in a bottle thrown up onto the sand.

'I have been such a fool! Pluto, god of the Underworld, tricked me. He gave Eurydice back to me, but commanded that I could not turn back and look at her beautiful face until we reached the sunlight, or I would lose her. I was determined, for I wanted, I *needed* her!

So I started travelling back to the three-headed dog, Cerberus, all of the time playing my lyre and listening to my beloved's swishing dress behind me, not looking.

I reached Cerberus and played my tune until he was lolling around and had no thought of lashing at me with his enormous, bright white teeth. Still I had not, out of my love, turned back to look at her, although I was tempted many times.

I climbed aboard the ferry which had taken me to the underworld. The ferryman, cloaked in black with a battered staff and withering hands, stood there.

I shouted to my loved one, 'Not long now!' but she did not reply. I thought, *has Pluto tricked me? Has he sent someone else instead of Eurydice, or has she, from being in the Underworld, lost interest in me? Does she not love or care any more for me?* So I couldn't help it ... I glanced back ... and yes, it was Eurydice!

... I had just made the biggest mistake of my life.'

Emily McGhee (11)
St Francis' College, Letchworth Garden City

Persephone And The Pomegranate Seeds: Pluto's Story

Many years ago there lived a man called Pluto. Some said that Pluto was selfish and wicked, but really, Pluto was a very nice, but lonely god. For many years Pluto was blamed for devilry, bad luck and anything and everything bad. This was because he was ruler of the Underworld, the Kingdom of the Dead.

One day, when it wasn't as dark, gloomy and cold as it normally was (a miserable day for Pluto), he decided to go up to where Zeus ruled and everyone sang in happiness (ugh!). He decided that the weather might be better there, but as he arrived, he realised that he'd made a mistake as it was even worse! The grass was green and the flowers were in bloom and the trees were putting on their first blossom. Just as Pluto turned around to return to the Underworld, he heard a shriek come from behind the bushes. As Pluto was an extremely kind and caring god, he couldn't help but save this damsel in distress.

He ran up to the bushes, bravely jumped over them and grabbed the young lady, (who seemed to be very startled at her rescue). You see, poor Pluto did not know much about young girls and how they passed their days. He failed to notice that the girls were only playing and the screams were only screams of excitement.

'Don't worry, I'll save you!' Pluto said to her.

Nazlee Sabahipour (12)
St Francis' College, Letchworth Garden City

The Hydra's Heads

I'm Dory, one of the Hydra's heads. I've lived here for my entire life - since someone chopped off my father's head and I grew in his place - and life never seems to change.

The other day, the swamp was colder than usual, but that's about the most interesting thing that has happened in the past month. But hey! Life is life and I do not want to waste it ... Oh look! There is a frog!

It's so late at night now, and I can't go to sleep, I have this funny feeling inside me ... something is wrong. I just don't know what it is.

Did you hear that? The grass rustled even though there is no wind! Phew! It was only a frog. I must try to stay awake. Who knows what could be out here at night? Must stay awake ... must stay ...

Yawn! That really seemed like a long night. Well, the newspaper has just come. It says that a man called Heracles has been given twelve tasks to do by the king. I wonder what they are? What's that? I saw something ... it's Heracles, the man in the newspaper. He is charging at us! What a fool! He's chopping off our heads. Two more are growing each time he chops one off. Oh no! He is chopping off our heads and putting his hot club on them. However did he find out how to stop our heads from multiplying? He is heading for me! *Noooooo ...*

Gemma Turner (12)
St Francis' College, Letchworth Garden City

Orpheus And Eurydice

Long, long ago, Prethidic and his wife, Clerabothy, discovered they were having a baby. Prethidic went to a fortune teller to ask if his baby would have a good and prosperous life.

When he asked, the fortune teller replied, 'Your baby shall be a boy, name him Orpheus. He will grow up, become a wonderfully talented musician and will fall in love with a beautiful young girl named Eurydice. But beware, on the first day of the third month after they have been married, Eurydice shall go to her death in the deep Underworld, when the deadly adder bites her leg!'

At these words, Prethidic recoiled in horror, but the fortune teller carried on. 'Orpheus will be so heartbroken at this that he will go on a quest down into the deep Underworld and sail across the dark lake and find his way past Cerberus, Pluto's three-headed dog, and persuade Pluto himself to do something he has never done before and will never do again: release a dead soul up to the world of the living again. But, as Orpheus treks up to the sunlit lands, he must never look at Eurydice until they have reached their destination. As they draw near the finish, Orpheus will do a terrible thing. He will check that Eurydice is still there and by doing so, will look at her. Orpheus will lose her a second time and will be devastated.'

Prethidic hurried home and to this day, events occurred exactly like that.

Katie Ritchie (12)
St Francis' College, Letchworth Garden City

Why Does It Rain?

Zeus had a special water supply that only he could use. It was for his baths and for his drinking water.

One day, Zonacuse changed the route which the water took, to make it go into the forest so that all of the normal people could use nice clean water, just like Zeus' water. Of course, Zeus thought that this was ridiculous. He thought that he should have at least one thing better then everyone else.

He called for Zonacuse to come and see him right away, so Zonacuse came.

'Why did you steal my water?' he asked.

'I only wanted a clean and fresh water supply, I mean just some water to drink!' Zonacuse replied.

'You want water, I'll give you water!' Zeus said as he stormed away.

Zeus decided the worst punishment was to make it rain for a very long time, until Zonacuse apologised.

After a while, Zonacuse found some courage to apologise. Zeus agreed to stop the rain.

So why *does* it rain, you ask?

When Zeus gets angry or feels bad-tempered, he will make the rain fall out of the sky until he is in a good mood, but when he's in a really bad mood, he makes it rain so much that it may even cause floods.

So, that is why it rains.

Rachael Barker (12)
St Francis' College, Letchworth Garden City

Where Do We Get The Colour Of Our Eyes?

In the beginning, the gods ruled over the world from their home in Mount Olympus. The gods lived in clouds of sunlight and owned all they desired. Odyssey was the god of jewels and he had jewels of tigers' eyes, opals and emeralds to give all the other gods the gift of having colour in their eyes. Epimetheus stole the jewels to give to Man so they could have the wonderful gift, as he cared so much about them. The jewels were in a mahogany wooden chest with a golden lock, and inside the lock was a delicately made golden key. Once Man opened the chest, all of his kind would have randomly-selected, coloured eyes.

One day, Epimetheus gave the chest to Man and he took it to his home. Once it was opened, a fantastic swirl of wind trapped him and formed the colour in his eyes. Then all of Man was surrounded by the wind and they had the same gift, but each person had a different colour, and all of their young would have colour in their eyes. Once this miracle happened, the gods sensed that something was wrong. They looked down to Earth and saw everyone had coloured eyes.

Zeus knew exactly who would give this gift to Man. Epimetheus was punished for all eternity, so that he would never see the heavens again and would stay down on Earth.

Sarah Atalla (11)
St Francis' College, Letchworth Garden City

Why Humans Do Not Have Tails

Once, a long time ago, Epimetheus and Prometheus were told to create all the animals of the Earth. They gave all their creations tails for balance. The brothers decided to make three humans: Icarus, Spinner and Odysseus. They were told never to interfere with the other animals, by capturing them or killing them for food.

The humans obeyed this law for some time, living in the country, swinging from trees and sleeping under the stars, and the watchful eyes of the gods. But then a bear injured Spinner in the middle of the night. They decided to catch some wolves and use them to guard their home.

Zeus found out what they had been doing and decided to punish them by removing their tails, so they were unable to swing from trees anymore and were laughed at by everyone. This is why humans still do not have tails, to remind us never to interfere with the lives of other animals.

Gemma Hall (12)
St Francis' College, Letchworth Garden City

Why Animals Can't Talk

Long, long ago, after Prometheus created Man, there was one goddess who was not happy. Artemis couldn't think of one reason in the world why her beloved animals should be different from Man. Man could talk, yet animals could not and she didn't understand why Zeus didn't change all of the animals so that they could talk too. She was sure the animals didn't like not being able to talk, but she couldn't ask them because they couldn't talk.

So Artemis and Poseidon, the god of the sea, stole one tiny sliver of fire and gave it to the animals of Earth. Disaster soon struck. Because all of the animals could talk, it meant that they were also smarter than they were before. The predators were getting together and exterminating all the herbivores, and soon there were almost none left.

The small group that were remaining were those who had some defence, like the birds who could fly and the elephants with their size and strength.

It was a battleground; with almost all of the prey gone, the predators were fighting amongst themselves. When Artemis saw what she had done, she ran to Zeus and begged him to make things as they were before. Zeus agreed, although she had stolen the sacred fire. He forgave her because she had owned up to her sin.

Since then, no animal has spoken a word on this Earth, apart from the parrots. But that's another story.

Claire Chapman (12)
St Francis' College, Letchworth Garden City

Why Don't We Have Tails?

Captacous was like no other god. He was ill-behaved, mischievous and eight years old. He had the smuggest little grin and never did as he was told.

He was going out on his usual walk in the evening and suddenly had a great urge to do something really disobedient. Every day before Captacous' walk, Zeus would always tell him to never ever go down to the Underworld in fear for any evil that could escape.

Once he had got down into the Underworld, through nettles, brambles and poisonous bushes, Captacous' balloon had deflated a little.

He wandered round the dusty plains for a little while until he came to the most unusual thing in the world. It had a poisonous red skin and a tail that looked like a slithering snake. It looked like it had been trapped down there for way too long. It was whipping and thriving to kill. This thing was the Devil.

Captacous ran with all his might! He ran and ran, but it as no use, the Devil was gaining on him! Suddenly, Captacous realised what the Devil was after! He wasn't after him, he wanted the world! Suddenly, everything went black.

When Captacous regained consciousness, a deep, booming voice was shouting at him.

'How dare you! As punishment for going down to the Underworld after I commanded you not to, your tail has been removed!'

I hope that's answered your question.

Marie Davis (12)
St Francis' College, Letchworth Garden City

Why Does Gravity Pull Things Down Instead Of Up?

In the beginning, the ancient goddess Athena was the goddess of war. She was the most fierce, powerful, vicious and strong goddess in the land. There was not a day that other gods recall, that she was not in battle, or at least twenty other gods or humans were hurt or wounded in her presence.

When in 'The Battle of the Gods 3', where all the gods competed against each other with their own armies, she was struck down to the ground by a cloudball. Not very surprisingly, they thought they had defeated her ...

But she got up, and in anger she stormed off to Zeus on Fire Mountain and screeched, 'Make my spear deadly, as deadly as can be, to show them what it feels like to be defeated ... and for them to be wiped out. Make them see.'

So after calming down, Zeus finally granted her the wish of the deadly arrow ... then he said, 'You have had your wish. I will not let you go until you have thought of who and why you are killing.'

So when she finally flew down, she won the battle with no rage.

Lauren Davies (12)
St Francis' College, Letchworth Garden City

Why Rainbows Appear Only When It Rains

As long as the gods could remember, there had always been rainbows. At the end of every rainbow, there was a pot of gold, treasures and riches. Few people could see rainbows, and one vain emperor, Theseus the Almighty, had found many pots of gold before.

One day, Theseus decided to tell his people of the rainbows. This was not an act of kindness, he wanted them to think how clever he was. Soon after he had told them, hundreds of his people were taking the gold. The rainbows weren't a gift anymore.

News of this soon reached Zeus, king of the gods. He was furious. Immediately, Zeus sent Hermes, the messenger of the gods, down to Earth to find out who the culprit was. Hermes was soon back, and at once told Zeus that Theseus the Almighty was the one who had caused the trouble.

The next day, Theseus was down on Earth enjoying his new popularity. Suddenly, the doors of his great palace burst open, and in walked a creature more terrifying than anything seen before.

'I am Zeus,' roared the beast, with a powerful voice. 'You have sinned, and so you must be punished.'

His punishment was to find the pot of gold at the end of the rainbow once again, but this rainbow was a never-ending one. Sometimes, Theseus cries, and that is why rainbows appear when it rains, and a small glimpse of his fate is revealed.

Susannah Cichy (11)
St Francis' College, Letchworth Garden City

Why Don't Humans Have Tails?

Long ago, neither humans nor animals had tails.

Atlantis was working. Every day he was late home because he did not have enough hands to work fast and efficiently, so he asked Zeus to grant him a third hand. Instead, Zeus gave him a tail. But to keep the tail, Atlantis was only allowed to use it for difficult jobs.

Slowly, Atlantis began to forget his promise and used his tail for opening doors and picking fruit. Later he used it for stealing things from other people.

Zeus noticed this and asked Atlantis to come to his mountain for a talk.

'Atlantis, I gave you the blessing of a tail,' Zeus exclaimed. 'You have started to take the tail for granted, so the only thing I can do is take your tail away!'

So the tail disappeared and Atlantis scrambled solemnly home.

Zeus decided that as animals never take things for granted, they could be given tails. So he gave all animals a tail. Zeus told all the humans and gods that they could never have tails.

Atlantis then argued against Zeus' decision, complaining that creatures never use their tails, whereas humans could use them to work with. So Atlantis was punished. He was tied to the top of a tree for three weeks in rain and storms.

This is why animals have tails and humans never will. Humans would use the tail selfishly, whereas animals would only use them for necessary things.

Charlotte Graham (12)
St Francis' College, Letchworth Garden City

Zeus And The Dreamers

In ancient times, no one ever grew weary or needed to sleep. Ancient people were friends with the gods and helped them fight evil on Earth. But after the tragedy of Pandora's box, people grew tired and lost faith in life, thinking, *why should I keep on fighting, when I know the darkness will just win over me again?*

Zeus was very upset to see his people like this. Apart from the fact they were very useful to him, he had actually grown quite fond of them in a superior kind of way. It didn't take long for him to conjure up a plan; he would let the humans sleep when the sun stopped working at night.

But sometimes, the evil from the box would get inside people's heads and tell them in its sickly-sweet voice that there was no point in trying to fight the evil away. Zeus got Hope to help him solve this problem. She let the people wake up after these visions of the underworld, and never-ending pits of darkness, to reassure them that wherever evil was, hope would always be nearby.

In the end, this worked and people carried on fighting to please the gods, and many joyous defeats followed as a result.

That is why we dream, and we always wake up after a nightmare, and yet again, hope is restored.

Courtenay Forbes (12)
St Francis' College, Letchworth Garden City

Coloney And The Colourful Rainbow

In the beginning of the world, above Mount Olympus lived Zeus and his gods and goddesses. The most prettiest, happiest and kind goddess of them all was Coloney, the goddess of colour.

She lived on Earth to make it a better place and more colourful. Everyone loved Coloney and enjoyed her company.

Hades, god of the Underworld, was very jealous of Coloney and cooked up a plan to get his revenge. He asked for Coloney to come to the Underworld to make it a better place and more colourful. After a lot of persuading, Coloney finally agreed.

When she was in the Underworld, she realised this was all a horrible trap! She begged to be let out, but Hades didn't agree and kept Coloney as his slave from then on. This made Coloney unhappy and she lost her colour and became dull and miserable.

From then on, the world was a miserable place. But whenever it rained (which was dullness from the Underworld) and was sunny (brightness), this colourful stripe came up into the sky - now known as a rainbow!

This is the symbol of the goddess of colour, Coloney. It is said that when Coloney misses all the bright colours of the world, everyone in the world remembers her for this beautiful rainbow.

Dreene Jamil (12)
St Francis' College, Letchworth Garden City

Why Animals Can't Talk

Orisine knew it, the animals had attacked his house again, taken his dinner, and even knocked down his special vase. Orisine had sent complaint letters to Zeus, asking for help, but he never got a reply. So the only thing he could do now was go up to Mount Olympus himself.

Meanwhile, Zeus was watching the clouds move, and in his peace, he was disturbed by a knock on his door.

'Enter,' Zeus called out.

'Orisine, my Sir, I have come with complaint.'

'Well?' Zeus didn't want to answer questions, for the people from Earth came up with bizarre complaints.

'The animals, all the time they are attacking us, destroying our houses, all they do is make plans to make our life a misery.'

'Do they? Well I shall take this to court.' For this complaint was sensible to Zeus, so he decided to take it to court.

All the animals were called and the case began.

'Now, I believe that it is not fair for you animals to attack people, for all the work they do for your living.' Zeus was getting tired and made the punishment quickly. 'As your punishment, you shall have to speak sounds to communicate with each other.'

'But that isn't fair ... !' the animals shouted.

'Case closed,' Zeus called out.

The animals started to knock chairs and tables down.

'What are you doing? Your punishment starts now!'

That is why animals speak with sounds, and not words. Some have learnt their lesson, and some have not.

Kanmein Kaur (11)
St Francis' College, Letchworth Garden City

Why Do We Sleep?

In the early days, the sun always shone. It spread its wonderful golden light all over the world and there was never darkness, and no one ever slept.

But one day, the sun began to get tired and it just couldn't supply enough energy for the whole world. It could easily manage to light half of the world, so it had to give up and do that.

The people left in the dark half of the world were angry. Where had the sun gone? Had it deserted them? Yes, it had left them in the miserable darkness. They went to complain to Hermes, who delivered their complaint to Zeus. After a great deal of thought, Zeus ordered the sun to shine on alternate sides. Zeus ordered people to sleep when their side of the world was in darkness.

After that, everyone was happy.

Rhiannon Griffiths (12)
St Francis' College, Letchworth Garden City

Why Are The Grass, The Leaves And The Trees Green?

Once there was a Greek goddess called Persephone. Persephone's favourite colour was green. She had green silk slippers, emerald jewels and a green satin dress, which she wore all the time in the spring. Persephone's mother was called Demeter, and she was in charge of nature.

That spring was Persephone's 21st birthday, and Demeter wanted to do something that Persephone would never forget and that nobody else had done. So one afternoon she came up with the idea of making the leaves, the trees and the grass green. Demeter thought that she could mix the colour of the sand and the blue from the sky to make the colour green. Demeter asked Mardus, who was the god of the sky, if she could have a portion of it, then she walked down to the beach to find some sand. When she returned to her wooden hut she made a concoction of the substances which made a green dye. Demeter got all the village people to help her pour it on the grass and the trees.

The next day, Persephone was coming home but she didn't know that when she returned her favourite colour was going to be in the grass, the leaves and the trees. When Persephone arrived home she was flabbergasted, she could not believe her eyes and she wondered how her mother had done it.

So that is why we have green grass, green trees and green leaves today.

Sophie Coleman (12)
St Francis' College, Letchworth Garden City

Why There Are No Unicorns Today

Once there was a beautiful mythical creature. Its shining silver hooves pattered on the soft grass as it galloped through the forests on Earth. The gods in Heaven had made this creature to be king of the animals but the animal population was decreasing very fast, for the humans were killing them for their horns and tusks.

The unicorn wanted to be wild. The unicorn wanted freedom and peace between animals and mankind. He did many good deeds for his animal friends. The animals had to hide from the humans in the forests, so they were not captured.

Zeus, king of the gods, was worried about the unicorn because the humans had seen it and fallen in love with its horn. He knew that unless he did something, the unicorn would become extinct. So, Zeus held a meeting with all the other gods and arranged to transport the unicorn to live safely with them in Heaven.

The gods did this and the humans hunted other animals instead. That is why there are no unicorns left on Earth.

Sophie Batchelor (11)
St Francis' College, Letchworth Garden City

Why Do We Sleep?

One day, the mud people were working for Zeus and they were working very hard on a very hot day. After a while they were too hot, so they decided to sit under a tree. It was only for a couple of minutes but it helped and they began to work again. They did this every day and each time, the break got longer and longer and longer, until they were having a break for half an hour.

When the mud people were resting one day, Zeus saw them and he came thundering down and said to them, 'Why aren't you working? I will punish you for being so lazy. You might need only half an hour now, but I am going to make you need eight hours, so when you want to keep working through the night you won't be able to.'

The mud people stood there stunned not knowing what to do, so they waited until the next day.

Zeus came down and threw stormy clouds over all the mud people and when the night came they still had lots of work to do, but they couldn't and they had to rest. Before they knew it they were asleep.

The next morning they thought they were only to have half an hour of rest, not all night. So they had twice the work to do, but they couldn't do it all as they got tired and had to sleep through the night.

Rosie Kirbyshire (12)
St Francis' College, Letchworth Garden City

My War

I wake up every day to terrified, screaming people, the roaring of the over-flying planes and the sirens that echo through your brain, yet the house is silent and I am all alone.

As soon as I hear the threatening warning sirens, I just run, I don't have time to take anything with me. I run as fast as I can down to the cold, dark, lonely Andersen shelter. It is my only comfort, the only place that I feel I am protected.

You see I have no family, the war has taken them from me. My precious loved ones are now only distant fading memories. It all happened so suddenly. My mum, dad and brother all decided to venture out of our house and into the dark, distressing street to see the damage the bombs had done that gloomy night. Suddenly the sirens began to screech and as usual, I ran into the shelter. It was the first day raid we'd ever had. I cried and screamed for my family. They never returned.

As I awake in the muddy, sweaty shelter, I see the blinding sun peer through the door. I poke my weary, tired head out and I see emptiness. My house is still there, thank goodness. However, the trees, plants, wildlife and people have vanished.

I am only ten years old. I have no one; I have lost everything to the war.

Sarah Wright (14)
Shenfield High School, Brentwood

The Orange Witch

Mouldyfrocks is no ordinary witch. She lives up an orange tree, down my road, and likes to play snap with a monkey called Henry. The last time anyone saw here was when Grandmamma was a baby, and this is why.

Mouldyfrocks was a greedy child. If she saw someone with a lollipop, Mouldyfrocks needed three bigger lollipops. It was how she was brought up to be, by her three witch aunties.

After Mouldyfrocks had finished her third breakfast one day, an auntie stood up (after struggling to get the chair off her bum) and shrieked, 'I've had enough of slaving away to feed your gob. I'm twice as greedy as you, but can only afford four breakfasts! I'm going!'

In the same day, after Mouldyfrocks had finished her twelfth lunch, another auntie bellowed so loud at her that her chins wobbled, 'Why should I spend money on food for you? I'm seven times as greedy! I'm leaving!'

The third auntie was sneaky before leaving Mouldyfrocks. Whilst Mouldyfrocks was sleeping, the auntie put a curse on her so she turned the colour of anything she ate, and then she left.

When morning came, Mouldyfrocks didn't care where her aunties had gone. She was starving! She waddled around town looking for food, but everything cost money, and she had none.

After hours of waddling up a hill, Mouldyfrocks exclaimed, 'Blimey! There are the juiciest-looking oranges ever!' and she ate the oranges.

I think you know what happened next. You're not stupid, like her.

Harriet Austin (14)
Shenfield High School, Brentwood

The Secret Life Of A Cat

Mrs Robinson left a saucer of milk out for me and that will be my first meal of the day. I trotted over to my neighbour's garden to find my friend, Tweety. As usual he was singing and I had to slap him to stop his infernal racket. We then ran across the road, narrowly dodging the cars, and went straight to my friend Fluffem's house to get him to come out, as he is the strongest member of my gang (he is a bulldog). We went off to gather the other ten members of my gang.

After this, we set off to find one of our rival gangs, the South Side Budgies. We rolled up to their territory in my modified cat basket with built-in hydraulics.

'Get out of our territory, man,' said the leader of the budgies, BG Gard, as he and his clan pulled out their weapons (consisting of twigs and nuts) and their leader pulled out a sub-machine seed rifle. They were very surprised when they saw my gang armed to the brim with nut launchers!

The fight got underway when one of the budgies threw a stick at me and it narrowly missed my head. I was so enraged that I ordered my men to fire! The powerful array of bullets totally took the gang off guard and knocked them all out. 'Good work, guys,' I said, 'now let's go home.'

So we all went home and went to sleep, awaiting our next adventure.

Connor Coxall (13)
Shenfield High School, Brentwood

The Jungle

Sweat was trickling down my spine. The roof of my mouth was dry, my tongue hanging out in the humidity of the furnace jungle surrounding me. I gripped my Lee Enfield rifle tightly, as though my life depended on it. My life did depend on it. This small clip of bullets was my barrier between life and death, seeing my loved ones again and surviving this pathetic war.

My platoon leader ushered our unit to get down on the ground and take cover quietly. Our unit spread out into the jungle, disappearing into the many shades of green, blanketing ourselves from the hidden enemy. I knelt down and hid behind a large tree. I glanced around. I couldn't see the rest of my unit. I didn't know if that was a good thing or not. I squinted through the slits of my eyes and searched for the 'bad guys'. All I could see around me was large trees and rope-like plants winding their way up to the canopy of the jungle. On the ground, I could see large bush-like shrubs of many different shades, through the darkness that surrounded me.

It felt strangely quiet. All the creatures of the jungle had suddenly stopped. Like turning off music. 'Use nature to spot your enemies', is what Colour Sergeant Watts used to say. The quieter the nature was, the more likely there were enemy around.

Time to move on. I arranged my helmet on my head properly, and lifted myself up and followed the squad through the darkest parts of the jungle. My platoon leader gestured to us to stop and listen. All was quiet. Unusually quiet. I could hear a bell-like ringing in my ear, when there was no sound to listen to. My stomach tightened. Something wasn't right.

Bang!

Out of nowhere was a gunshot and a bullet ripped into Ryan's flesh in front of me, spraying blood all over my face.

'Get down!' I could hear my platoon leader cry as he turned fire.

All hell broke loose as bullets poured through the jungle like water from a tap, hitting trees and whizzing past my ears. I dived down and noticed the platoon leader go down, his helmet being shot off and his skull cracked in two, pouring scarlet blood from his now brainless head, again spraying me with blood. I couldn't escape.

A bullet punched into my knee, splitting the kneecap right off. A searing pain swept through my leg; unbearable pain, like lightning. I couldn't feel my leg. I tried to get up but I couldn't. I tried to run, but I couldn't feel my leg. I tried to escape, but I couldn't. This was the jungle.

Stephen Clews (14)
Shenfield High School, Brentwood

D-Day

The water splashed up high against the boat, cold and brisk on the side of my face, reminding me I'm still here.

As the U-boat approaches the bullet-riddled shore, all of my surroundings become blurry and undefined. Mortar. The last word travelled through my rusty metal helmet and into my ears. Suddenly, the boat is violently flipped and I'm cast beneath the icy water. As I stare up at the surface, time stands still. All quiet, bar the silent bullets streaming past me, like miniature torpedoes with jet trails behind them. Then I lift my head from the abyss.

I scramble out of the shallow water and onto the crimson, blood-soaked beach. I take cover behind a stone pillar that has fallen from its sandy foundations. I peer my head round the pillar; it takes some time for my brain to process what my eyes are seeing. Total destruction, carnage. Men being killed, not three feet in front of me. I am convinced that I am witnessing mankind at its lowest form. Men acting with basic instinct, no rank or order. I step out from beneath my bunker, searching for the enemy. I'm overwhelmed by the fact they're not fighting on the beach; they are in watch towers, pillboxes, nests. They have huge, unbreakable fortresses, with automatics and rockets. I have only my rifle to protect me.

This is not a battle, it's an ambush, a slaughter just waiting for us. It's so hard to believe that this is what we must endure for peace and prosperity.

I load my rifle, look ahead, and charge. I keep running. I almost reach the gate, but I stumble. I pick myself up. Aim, aim, *fire!*

Jayden Bowling (13)
Shenfield High School, Brentwood

Battle Of Oak Pass

This war had been inevitable, the omens had told of it. The seer had spoken of his own demise within this war, and yet his voice held no fear. He gave hope to his armies, giving speeches that made the earth itself shake.

The seer wore armour of enchanted gold and rode a great white steed. His sword had condemned thousands of beasts and men to death. He had carved his own legend, using his blood as writing. His light had consumed many shadows; he had fought mighty vampires and fiery demons, and could still walk the Earth.

Yet this immortal being now spoke of death, the very thing he had fought and won against so many times before. It had even been told that the seer had once been part of the Gold Templars, a guild that held the secrets of the gold dragons. The Templars were finally crushed after fighting an army of ogres for six years. Yet it was said that some were saved by a dragon that matched the emblem of the Templars.

The seer acted as a guiding light to his people and army, protecting and commanding them.

After every battle, the seer would walk among the dead and say a prayer for every one of his dead men. This could take weeks, but it was only done during the night. After the ritual was done, he would command his men to feast and he would join them. To his men, he was a legend.

Conor Robinson (14)
Shenfield High School, Brentwood

We Are Soldiers

I am Jimmy Patterson. I am sixteen years of age, and already I feel my life is over. It is the 6th of June, 1944. we are on our way to Normandy - Omaha Beach on the French coastline. Already I can hear the explosions, see the pain, feel the anguish, smell the fear. We are armed and ready for combat, but none of us actually have time to realise what is going on around us.

The boat sways from side to side in the rough current as the beach head draws closer. We are all nervous, seasick and afraid of what lies ahead of us. Some are praying for help and hope on the battlefield, others are crying, and some are concentrated on the front of the boat, waiting for the gate to drop, leading us all into Hell.

Explosions send water and fish flying into the air, showering us, distressing us even more. A boat to the east of our craft explodes, flinging men into the air. The stench of death grows stronger, the need to survive the attack becomes urgent. Bullets hit the front of the boat as we approach the beach. Adrenaline sets in, my heart beats faster and faster, as it slowly rises in my throat.

The signal is shouted ... '30 seconds!'

We prepare ourselves hastily for what we had waited for. The door shudders. As it opens, a hail of bullets kills the first men in line.

We are soldiers on the frontline. This is D-Day.

Alex Dean (14)
Shenfield High School, Brentwood

The Legend Of Stelios

In the great metropolis of Athens there once lived a smart young boy called Stelios. He worked for his father, who sold everything from abacuses to zodiac charts. Stelios delivered heavy goods all around the city.

One day, whilst on an errand, Stelios caught sight of a burning building in the distance. He ran towards the smoke that was filling the sky, and as he got closer he heard the screams of a woman. When he arrived, he saw that everything was ablaze, but the woman was still screaming. He grabbed a blanket from the nearby market stall and jumped into the house.

Smoke filled around him everywhere and he couldn't see. He heard the woman's screech again. He forced his way upstairs as that was the direction the scream was coming from. He got to the door that the woman was behind and violently kicked it open. He saw the distraught woman was tied up by a rope, but there was also a hunched figure in the corner.

'Help me, help me!' shrieked the woman.

The dark thing in the corner drew a sword and thrust it at Stelios, who jumped out of the way. Then again it jabbed, aiming for his torso and above, but this time Stelios was ready and grabbed the sword away from the hooded thing, and in one swing chopped the creature's head off. Stelios then rushed the choking woman out of the burning building and everybody cheered.

Jonathan Burns (13)
Shenfield High School, Brentwood

Beneath Skin Deep

Monday, 27th September 2004
    Dear Diary,
    Someone told me that I should start a diary because you'd become a friend to me. I don't have any friends, so it's worth a shot. I don't trust you, so I'm thinking why should I write the truth to someone or something that I don't even trust?

    I have secret places. I find comfort in the dark. It used to be, I loved to lay in the grass in the middle of the yard on a hot summer's day and watch the clouds float past. But not now, everything is different now.

    I cut my wrists last night. It was my first try, so next time I'll do a better job. Mr Demon visited last night. He sits on my chest and torments me in the middle of the night. I can't breathe when he comes. I wake up in a sweat and I'm terrified. I wish he'd leave me alone - like everyone else. He comes while I'm asleep and I never know when to expect him. All of a sudden, I wake up in terror. I guess if he would warn me that he's coming, it wouldn't be a fun game for him, would it? You don't help me either. You're not the friend they said you would be. You're a brick wall just like all the rest.

Thursday, 30th September 2004
    Dear Diary,
    I'm on the lookout for tools. Everything I see becomes a potential tool. A piece of broken glass, a safety pin, a match. What I do to my body seems surreal. I watch my own hand take a weapon and carve my flesh out. The sharp point digs into my skin and makes its way past the nerves and into a vein. I feel pain. It becomes a challenge to me - I can withstand physical pain equal to the emotional pain that I live with. Tomorrow I will increase that pain. It's a secret I have from the rest of the world. I thought it would bring attention, but I was wrong, and now it's an obsession. I hate myself. I'm living a lie. This whole messed-up life is a lie. Sometimes I would just love to die. Why do I do this to myself? I can't even do a good enough job to kill myself. Maybe part of me wants to preserve my own life. I'm in control of myself. *No* one else cares.

    Today I took a can lid to my hand. I did it slowly and watched my flesh part. Then the blood oozed out. I came home and showed it off. I still got no sympathy. This life sucks. I talked back to my mum once and she threatened to cut out my tongue with a can lid. I imagine the bloody violence of that scene. She would have to use all her strength to keep me down on the floor as she cut out my tongue. Blood would be everywhere. She doesn't want to hear me talk.

Friday, 1st October 2004

Dear Diary,

Mr Demon doesn't stalk me as much anymore. Sleeping with a light on helps too. He's an evil, ugly man who perches right on my chest. What does he want from me anyway? You never answer me. I have plenty of 'friends' just like you, so why do I need one more? Answer me!

Silence and darkness, that's the world I live in. I can't be a friend because I don't know how to be one. I live in loneliness and pain. Why won't this end? How can I make it end? Day after day, I go to school and I work - I even do some social stuff. But nothing ever changes. I'm still desperate. I'm still hated by the people who are supposed to love me.

Tuesday, 5th October 2004

Dear Diary,

I'm tired of you. I'll cast you out of my life. Like I said; I'm in control. I will cast you out before you cast me out. It's better that way. I have the choice and I'll choose first before you have the chance to. I've built a wall around myself, I'm encased in my own shell; I have no one to turn to. It's just me and Mr Demon.

Today

Dear Diary,

I don't even know why I said 'dear'. You didn't help me. I put my trust in you, and you failed me just like so many others. I found out that I can't trust you or anyone else ... just one person. I became so desperate and you let me come to the end of myself. Only then, when I reached the complete end, is when He could reach down, scoop me up and rescue me. I found out that Jesus is a real friend. He was there all along ... just waiting for me to notice Him. All the time I was living in such darkness and desperation, I was crying out for help. I cried out and it seemed that no one heard me. So, I would abuse myself in frustration. Hatred and bitterness haunted me.

Humans fail me. I fail others, it's an imperfection we all have. I found out that God never leaves me or fails me. Even in darkness.

Scars on my body bear witness to my past. But no one bears witness for my future; that is something only I am responsible for.

Kaz Melvin (14)
Shenfield High School, Brentwood

The Spider

It was there, he could feel it, sense it. He couldn't get to sleep, he didn't close his eyes for fear of the spider engulfing him in a mass of web, or eating him without him knowing it. *Scuttle, scuttle, scuttle.* It was coming to hunt its prey, coming in for the kill. Harry suddenly had images in his mind of a mass of jet-black, rough hair and thousands of eyes watching his every move. The pincers clicking away like typewriter keys. It was coming nearer and nearer, he couldn't bear it, he had to close his eyes. This was it, the monster was going to kill him. He pulled the covers over his head and waited. This was it, this was it.

Everything went suddenly quiet, not a sound. *It must be coming,* Harry thought. He carefully, cautiously, nervously peeped out, expecting the horrible mass of hair. He groped for the lamp and hesitantly turned it on. The bright light pierced the darkness like a knife. There was no escape now, he would see his fear and face it head on. Harry's legs turned to jelly and he started to shiver all over his body, even though it wasn't cold. There it was, his fear - just a little money spider. Harry breathed a sigh of relief. It was nowhere as big as he thought it would be, but he daren't go near it!

Oliver Hazell (14)
Shenfield High School, Brentwood

A Day In The Life Of A Squirrel

I woke up early in the morning. The sun was bright and it hurt my eyes, but I was very hungry. I went searching around my tree for where I had buried my nuts. After a long, long time of searching, I found my nuts. I ate nuts till I was full.

After I was full, I went out for a walk in my forest. It was a nice day and there were many humans about. A small human started throwing sticks at me, so I ran up a tree and hid. A large human grabbed the small one's arm and pulled it away.

I stayed up in the tree for a while eating acorns; they were delicious.

I left the tree and began walking around again. Suddenly, a fox jumped out of a bush at me. I ran and ran as fast as I could. When I looked back after a while, the fox was gone. I was safe.

I returned to my hollow tree. It was getting dark, the owls would come out soon. I went into my tree and slept.

Charlie Joseph (14)
Shenfield High School, Brentwood

Cruelty Or Conservation?

When the anti-fox hunting ban was passed in 2002, everyone thought that this was the end of the chase. But two years on, our countryside is still being used as a war zone; huntsmen and dogs versus foxes.

What was once used to protect livestock is now being classed as a 'sport' and 'good fun'. But what about the fox? He is chased for miles, then torn to pieces by his cousins.

Huntsmen claim that this is the 'only way to keep fox numbers down', but is there a more humane way than this?

The law has done nothing to protect the foxes from their deadly end. Foxes can still be hunted on foot or by car, and hunts still continue despite the law.

People have begun questioning whether passing this rule was intended to keep the peace without keeping the foxes' best interests at heart. Susan White, an animal activist, says, 'When was the last time a hunt was stopped? Never! Action needs to be taken immediately to prevent the fox from becoming extinct'.

Claire George, 18, a student, asks, 'Who gave us the right to decided on the foxes' future?'

No one knows how this fight is going to end, but we can only hope that a solution will be found before it's too late. But for now, two separate battles will continue, one for survival, one for rights, until something is done.

Kirsty Hough (14)
Shenfield High School, Brentwood

A Day In The Life Of A Footballer's Wife

So, here you are reading part of my life, being a footballer's wife. It's not really that interesting; most of the time I go shopping. I bet you're thinking, well, doesn't she have someone to do that for her? I do, but I like going myself. When I go myself, I can get the things I actually need, instead of the idiot that buys something the wrong colour, or the wrong sized shoes. I don't go shopping all the time on my own. I might meet up with some of the girls, like Colleen or Victoria, it depends really because sometimes they're busy getting their hair cut, or having their nails done. I get mine done every other week on a Friday.

On a Thursday, I might meet up with some other mates and go out for a coffee, and then go shopping. I like shopping for designer clothes and new shoes, and maybe the odd bottle of Burberry perfume, depends what sort of mood I'm in.

On a Wednesday, I have a spa day: massages, facials ...

On a Tuesday, well it's a stay-in day really, you see me and my husband (the footballer!), we might stay in together and watch a film, or he might have a meeting with the manager, so I go along too.

Monday is a training day, so I drop him off at the stadium and go and visit my mum, if I'm not too busy shopping or buying a new ring or necklace, which takes me all day to choose the colour I want!

My life is quite hectic. I'm on my feet all the time, so on a Sunday I might go and watch him play football. Well I'd better take part somewhere, he does earn all the money to pay for my very expensive shopping bill!

Saturday, well I don't really know what I do on a Saturday. Once I did go and do a photo shoot and was on one of those children's TV shows.

Well really, the mansion needs a clean, so I call the cleaner in while I take a dip in either the hot tub or the indoor pool. The reason we have an indoor pool is because there is always paparazzi outside, probably trying to take a photo of my good looks!

Well that's my life. I told you It might not be worth reading, as it's quite boring. After a while, you get bored of the money, so what I do to help is buy a brand spanking new convertible, or Range Rover. I've got three cars to myself now, and he's got five. It's not fair really, but that's life I suppose!

Christina Smith (14)
Shenfield High School, Brentwood

Chapter 9

What has happened so far ...

Molly Winslow is 17. She is popular and clever, but very unhappy. When she was six years old her mother abandoned her and her father, and hasn't been in contact since. All her life Molly has wondered why her mother left and what she did wrong. One night, Molly and her dad had a terrible row and he blurted out that Molly was a mistake and her mum had never wanted her. Molly was devastated and had to know for herself if this were true. So she set out on a long journey to find her mum and discover the truth. On the way, she got 'lumbered' with Jake, the class nerd. However, they discovered an unlikely friendship ...

Chapter 9

'This is it,' breathed Jake as they pulled up outside the house.

Molly sat in her seat staring ahead.

Jake looked at her. He'd never seen her like this - at school she was loud, chatty. He felt protective of her, and wondered if they should just go home. 'Look Molly, maybe this isn't a ...'

'No! I've got to Jake, I need to know.' Molly looked at him pleadingly, tears in her eyes.

Jake hesitated, then shrugged helplessly. 'OK,' he sighed.

'Thanks Jake, you've been amazing.' She kissed him softly on the cheek and got shakily out of the car.

Jake still lingered, but as Molly turned towards the house, he slowly drove away.

Molly stood shivering in the November wind and looked around. It was a nice area; detached houses along the private road, with neat hedges and lawns. 'No wonder she left us,' Molly whispered. It had gone over and over in her head - why her mum had left her and what she'd done wrong. Now she understood. She didn't belong here.

A middle-aged woman with neat blonde hair got out of her car and started walking up the next drive. She frowned when she saw Molly, obviously wondering what she was doing there, with her tatty jeans and messy hair. Molly scowled back. 'Who does she think she is? I'll show that smug-faced witch,' and before she could change her mind, she strode up to the front door and rang the doorbell ...

Sophie Mihailovic (14)
Shenfield High School, Brentwood

Troy And The Wooden Horse

The golden beaches shine in the distance. The sun beams down on the white city. The King of Troy stares at the army of Persians, the ships slowly rowing forward, and the army of thousands ready to fight. 'They will not breach the gates of Troy.'

'Fire!'

The arrows of the Persians slide through the air, a fire burning into flesh and bones. Swords clash, boats moor and men shout, but the dead are soundless, their souls already drifting to Heaven. Alexander the Great, a leader of men, orders the Persians to attack.

Odysseus charges forward, ready to kill all men in his way.

The Trojans fight bravely, and are talented, with many men. Paris is a coward and he caused this war, for he stole the beautiful wife of a Greek king, Helen of Persia, but he will not fight.

The fourth day of fighting continues. The Trojans have forced the Persians back to the beach, having seen them off at the gate of Troy. A sigh of relief flows through the crowds, but they shouldn't think it is over; the battle is still unpredictable.

Night falls; the Persians have a plan. A wooden horse, a gift to the Trojans, left on the beach, with no boats to be seen. The king unwisely lets the horse in, for he doesn't think it is a trick. As the Persians hide in the horse and attack at night, Troy is overcome and the dead curse Paris.

Stephen Cozens (13)
Shenfield High School, Brentwood

Untitled

Long, twisted veins creeping up past your thighs, winding around your waist; pulling, dragging, suffocating. Down; your toes being nibbled, damp moss rubbing on your scratched mortal skin as you are pulled ever deeper towards the jaws of death. Your fingers are raw to the bone as they scrape along the floor, trying to delay your slow and painful demise.

Slowly you inch towards the edge, weeds pulling so stubbornly on your legs, infesting themselves in your knees and ankles. You are unable to scream, your breath has long gone.

Upon hearing the slashing jaws, you feel nauseous, vomit relieves itself on the wrecked turf in front of you. The plants all around you leer, they wobble in an unearthly manner, as if working in unison. Once innocent flowers now become snarling hyenas, bobbing with laughter in the chilled wind; the wind that pulls at the roots of your hair and penetrates your clothes, as if they were not there, leaving you feeling naked.

Your life flashes in front of you on an invisible screen, showing and replaying your experiences. But now you see them differently. possibly more vivid? Or just now you see the underlying sinisterness.

The tingled glint in your clown's eye, and the gleaming braces on your friends' pale faces. Now you feel the scraping on your bare soles, your senses hit you at full steam, knocking you backwards.

The coldness of the water you are in nibbles through your trousers, rips through your shirt, tickling your neck. Pointlessly you tip your head back, gasping petrified breaths that never reach your lungs. The water level reaches your lips, you can taste the sour, bitter taste in the water. Then your mouth is covered, and your nose is your sole breathing apparatus.

Insects wallow and slime through mud, creeping into your ears, making a beeline for your brain.

Now you can't breathe, the carbon dioxide builds in your lungs, you feel it burn, scorching your frozen body, limp, in the off-colour sludge.

Your vision spirals, you can't see, you can't hear, you can't think. This is it, you cannot live.

Billy Bolton (14)
Shenfield High School, Brentwood

Writing In The Style Of Susan Hill

This is the opening to a story written in the style of Susan Hill, author of 'I'm the King of the Castle'. It's about a fear of a walkway and what lies beside it:

I walk along the eerie walkway, submerged in darkness. The darkness hangs over me like a dark black shadow following me. I see the tall, dark shadow of a tree and its branches. The branches hang over me menacingly, like a claw waiting to reach down and grab me. A terrorising hoot of a nearby owl sends a shiver up my spine, attacking me like daggers.

The path winds to the left now, along a riverbank. I can just about see the river but I can clearly hear the water as it roars ferociously along the riverbank, eroding away the sandy rock. A large bat swoops down silently, yet unexpectedly, startling me as it seems to skim along the top of the water as it flies off into the dark night's sky and away into the distance. I hear the terrifying shriek of a nearby train, making me jump with fright.

I come to an opening to a wood which would lead me to my house. A small sign is dimly lit by the fading glow of a nearby lamp post. The sign reads: *'Danger, Avoid Use Of This Pathway At Night'*. I grew even more afraid now, but I told myself that I must continue, as I was so close to home. I knew this opening to the wood was like a gateway to Hell, as this wood brings terror to me. I stepped into the wood. There were trees crookedly stooping menacingly over me, bushes along the walkway and sounds from the creatures which inhabited the dark depths of the wood.

David Mais (14)
Shenfield High School, Brentwood

The Incident Of The Innocent Man

I wake, my head hurts. I look around me, but I have to strain my eyes as the place I am in is filled with darkness as there are no windows. I see not a pretty sight; bare, dense, damp walls with marked carvings. The foul suffocating stench of decaying corpses fills my nostrils. I try to release my arms from the tight rope that restricts them to very little movement, but the struggling only seems to tighten the ropes. I try to remember how I got here, but my memory is blank. I listen out for any sounds and hear footsteps coming closer, and closer, and closer.

Suddenly my heart races and a bead of sweat from my forehead drips onto my lap as I tensely watch the door handle slowly turn. Who could it be? My heart jumps as the door swings open and a masked person advances towards me, carrying a crowbar. I struggle as hard as I can, but I still remain trapped in the wooden chair.

'You feel like talking now, Malakian?' the masked thug spoke.

'I don't know what you want with me. I don't know why I am here,' I stutter as I feel the fear shoot straight up my spine.

'Liar!' he spat.

I fell the sudden blow to my head and I feel the blood rush to my head as I stumble to the floor and my eyelids solemnly shut as I lie on the floor …

Ryan Spurge (14)
Shenfield High School, Brentwood

Good Or Bad Glazer?

Yesterday, the American billionaire bought 75% shares in Old Trafford. A total cost of £650 million. As soon as the fans found out about this, there were demonstrations around the ground. The American billionaire has borrowed all of this money and used none of his own.

So what do the fans think of this? I have spoken to two Manchester United fans and they are disgusted. 50-year-old Joanne Moore and 51-year-iold Eddie Moore have packaged all of their Manchester United possessions and have sent them back to Old Trafford.

Glazer borrowed the money to buy Manchester United and now they have been bought with borrowed money, whereas before, Manchester United were debt-free.

Alex Ferguson's job was in the balance, but he has now been assured that his job as a manager is safe. But what if Glazer cannot pay the £650 million back?

If Glazer cannot pay this money back, Manchester United will end up like Leeds United and West Ham United, who are now in the Coca-Cola Championships.

Yes, Sir Alex Ferguson has been assured of his position as manager, but will Malcolm Glazer be forced to sell Manchester United's big names such as Wayne Rooney and the world-class striker, Ruud Van Nistelrooy, or the young Cristiano Ronaldo?

All will be revealed as time goes on and on.

Ryan Gunning (14)
Shenfield High School, Brentwood

Pitiless Stones

Drake stood, trembling. Blood trickled out from a gash above his left hear, leaving the whole side of his face caped with the thick scarlet liquid. Before him lay a limp figure. The figure made no movement or sound; all that could be heard was the trickling water and the vicious beat of Drake's heart pounding in his throat. Drake glanced about suddenly at the darkness consuming his surroundings, as vivid black clouds began to smother the sky above. He began to edge towards the body, stepping carefully around the sharp, slippery, moss-infected stones, which he had fallen victim to earlier that evening. Oh those stones, so cold and pitiless, deliberately sticking out or smoothed to trip the unwary.

Now a tall, desolate plain of them surrounded him on either side, a bombarding army lying in wait from the other side of the window. It was them that had made Drake remember that dreadful day. The day on which he witnessed his best, and only, friend die in front of him. He shivered as he remembered the slow moving stream of congealing blood running steadily across the stones from Buckeson's skull. He had not wanted to go on this trip up through the mountains, but it was impossible to change her mind. He tried to close his eyes. That just seemed to deem the situation worse, as ever more clear came the picture of his friend's neck awkwardly twisted to reveal the stone-grey eyes staring straight through him, without expression.

Tommy McGroder (14)
Shenfield High School, Brentwood

A Day In The Life Of A D-Day Soldier

15th May 1945.

'We are about to embark on a great fight. Anyone turning back will be shot.'

The sound of craft splashed through the waves, as everyone thought about their loved ones.

'Take cover.'

As we were all silent, the loud roar of an aircraft swooped down and let out gunshots. It hit the metal of the craft next to us. It struck the fuel tank and sent the craft into flames as it leapt into the air. Shrapnel splashed into the water and some struck our craft.

'Go, go, go,' commanded the generals.

We flooded out of our craft into the shallows of the Normandy beaches. Gunshots rang around the air. The sense of danger ran up my spine. The troops splashed over the water to take cover. Already soldiers had been left to die in the shallows.

I found cover behind a ruined wall. I could see behind another wall on the top of the hill, a German with a machine gun, shooting. I leapt out and fired a few shots. They struck him in the chest and he fell to the ground. A bullet flew past my face. I ran back to the wall and collapsed. Fear took over me.

'What do you think you're doing, soldier?' my colleague said. 'Pull yourself together. On three we'll go. One, two, three ...'

We made a dash for the next wall. That's when ... it felt cold. There was pain as I fell to my knees. I lay, dreaming of my loved ones. I could hear shots still, but they faded out. I lay there, lifeless.

Alistair Bygrave (13)
Shenfield High School, Brentwood

A Day In The Life Of A World War II Fighter Pilot - Liam Colverd - ID 3457

I woke very early and went down to North Weald. I usually sat with Bill, Bob and Rob, smoking and playing cards. I always felt nervous waiting for the 'scramble' signal.

I was just about to win a pound from Bob when the siren blared. We ran to our Spitfires. I thought about Linda, my fiancée, who worked in an ammunition factory. We hoped to get married after the war. My inspiration was always my dad, Danny, who was killed in World War I.

As I took off, I heard the Messerschmitts were not far away. Suddenly, we were having a dog-fight. I had shot down two enemy aircraft when a Messerschmitt attacked me, peppering my Spitfire's tail with bullets. We were just about over France by then. I tried not to panic and to remember my training, but my brain seemed to have frozen. Rob was screaming through the radio, telling me to jump. I hurled myself from the cockpit and thankfully, my parachute opened. A German aeroplane came swooping towards me and I thought I was done for, but luckily he didn't shoot.

I landed safely and made my way to a French bar. Recognising me as English, the owners quickly hid me. Terrified, I heard some German voices. They were searching for me! I was certain I would be discovered, but they left after ten minutes. A man looked through the hay where I was hidden. Fortunately, he was a member of the French Resistance. He told me he would take me back to England. *Thank God for my lucky escape!*

Pilot Officer Liam Colverd ID - 3457
Honours: DFC (Distinguished Flying Cross)
Birth location: London
Age when joined: 18
Survived: Yes

Thousands of men died fighting for their country in World War II.

Liam Colverd (13)
Shenfield High School, Brentwood

A Day In The Life Of A Famous Football Player

The big game was at 3 o'clock everybody was saying. It was the final of the FA Cup. 'I can't wait for it,' I kept saying. It was Southend versus Manchester United.

I went training in the morning and the whole squad was nervous, even the team manager! I just kept thinking about playing in the Southend team that won the FA Cup for the first time, that famous Southend team.

I played in goal, so it was all down to me to save all of Manchester United's shots. We were the underdogs, so I had to put in a good performance, or otherwise we could get thrashed! I kept repeating that in my head.

At 2 o'clock all of our team were in the changing rooms and the manager was going through our tactics and strengths. The manager was always saying that we could win the game, but would have to get stuck in from the kick-off.

At 3 o'clock the atmosphere was insane. All the fans were cheering and screaming. As the two teams and I ran out onto the pitch, my heart stopped. *It was magnificent!* Wembley looked terrific. As the game started it was fairly even. As it got to half-time, disaster struck as Wayne Rooney had a great shot and it hit the back of the net, and Southend were 1-0 down. At half-time we were very disappointed because they didn't deserve their lead.

The second half was the same, but in the 90th minute, Floyd Smarten scored our goal and the score was 1-1. The game went into extra time and nobody scored. It was *penalties!*

It was 5-5 in the penalty shoot out when I saved Wayne Rooney's penalty. Then Bob Thomas put in our penalty to make us win!

We'd won! It was the best moment in my life, I won us the game!

Jeremy Williams (13)
Shenfield High School, Brentwood

A Soldier's Thoughts, D-Day

This is it, all the battles, all the deaths leading up to this. We cannot afford to lose. If we lose, the war is lost. If we win, the war is won. We've heard the Germans don't even know we're coming, let's hope that's true, else there will be trouble ahead.

We are only an hour away from the Normandy coast. There are thousands of us, but I'm still not sure. We don't know how well-defended the Germans are. We have tanks, but they will be difficult to land.

We have very little armour; if they've got machine-gun posts, we'll be slaughtered. I've got my gun, it's a good one, but if the Germans have tanks, it'll be useless.

I'm not much of a religious man, but I'm praying, it's the only comfort I can get on this ship. We're all nervous, I can hear thousands of teeth chattering; the cold makes it even worse.

I'm part of the fourth wave. Our objective is to help keep the beaches secure, if we can even take the beaches in the first place. If we can't, it's all over. Let's hope our bombers can take out their coastal defences, else we'll all be dead in the water, literally.

I remember what my mum said. She told me to be brave. I don't know if I can be brave, I don't know if I'll even survive.

Edward Starr (13)
Shenfield High School, Brentwood

A Day In The Life Of A Soldier In World War II

It was a was a warm and clear night on the 3rd January 1942. Everything was calm, until a loud, roaring bellow that rumbled the floor, shattered the silence. There must have been twenty, no thirty bombers, and at least 60 fighter planes. Then I saw black; chaos was all around, I couldn't see anything! Then I couldn't feel the floor. What was happening? I smashed into a brick wall of some sort, I couldn't quite see. It took me five or so minutes to come to my senses, and then I realised what had happened. I must have been swept off my feet by an explosion. Everything was clearer, apart from all the soot and debris.

All I could hear were screaming men crying, and the air raid alarm. I was so scared. It had all happened in half an hour or so, but the most frightening thing of all was if they would come back again, and if they did, when? I couldn't move my back and I could not feel my left leg. I did not do anything. I could not do anything but scream, and that's what I did. I could hear people saying, 'Where are you?' but I did not know where I was either. I just screamed, hoping they could follow my voice. *'Help! Please help me!'* I kept screaming.

Dawn started to rise, but no one could tell because of all the debris.

Joshua Ashton (13)
Shenfield High School, Brentwood

Bobsil And Jimmel
(Inspired by 'Hansel and Gretel' by the Brothers Grimm)

Once upon a time there were two little children, a boy named Bobsil and a girl called Jimmel. They had parents, but they were very poor and couldn't afford to keep their children.

One day, Bobsil and Jimmel were taken to the city by their parents. Their parents gave them a brain licker sweet each and they scampered off down an alley next to McDonald's, not to be seen. Bobsil and Jimmel didn't know what to do, so they walked around the city of Dover in search of their parents. As the children were walking, they decided it would be a good idea to make a trail with their brain lickers along the pavement. This was a brilliant suggestion by Jimmel, because then the children could find their way back.

Jimmel and Bobsil walked for about half an hour, when they saw a Mercedes-Benz made of edible gold and silver. Bobsil ran straight over to the car and started eating one of the wing mirrors. Jimmel was weary at first, but when she saw Bobsil tucking in, she didn't hesitate to join him.

Suddenly from around the corner, came a vicious burger creature. The creature came straight at them with brute force and unknowingly, knocked Bobsil and Jimmel into a rubbish heap. Jimmel and Bobsil hid in the heap silently. They had to get away. Bobsil said quietly, '1, 2, 3, *go!*' and sprinted as fast as he could out of the heap, closely followed by Jimmel. Bobsil and Jimmel didn't stop running until they were back at the alley next to McDonald's. Their parents were sitting in a Lamborghini Merchiolago. Bobsil and Jimmel were amazed, their parents had won the lottery. So their parents took them back to their brand new mansion.

Billy Bone (13)
Shenfield High School, Brentwood

A Day In The Life Of A Gangster

My name is John, John McCall. Today our major bank robbery is taking place. Our months of preparations have all come down to this day, but I have a gut feeling that something bad is going to occur.

My crew are James he's our new recruit. He is inexperienced and anxious, but is the sneakiest man to my knowledge. Then there is Brains. His name is the giveaway. Every move which will be performed today, was chosen by him, he's even made three back-up plans in case things go wrong. Finally the twins, Sharp Eyes and Dr Drive, they're impossible to separate. Sharp Eyes sees everything and is a great sniper, and Dr Drive can turn U-turns at high speeds.

We met at Starbucks. We checked the plan, then set off. The bank's delivery was coming in a truck and guess who were in the truck? Sharp Eyes and Dr Drive! We then departed down the road that led to riches.

Our plan was perfect. We were all in position and everything was running as smoothly as a sanded piece of wood. The delivery truck pulled in. The text came through to go. I checked that all systems said go; they did and we were about to leave when ... *nee-nor, nee-nor!* Police sirens. We were surrounded, devastated, but worst of all, stitched up.

'Put 'em in the cars, boys,' I heard a familiar voice say.

It was James, our new recruit; James the copper and James the grass. I'll get him. Just watch this space ...

Frank Austin (12)
Shenfield High School, Brentwood

A Day In The Life Of It

She looked at the ground as she moved. She wouldn't dare look up. Her long black hair covered her pale, blank face. Her hungry eyes starving for attention, stayed on the floor. Her slow, awkward steps made her seem almost invisible. She didn't want to be seen, hidden was best. She didn't deserve to be seen. She didn't deserve anything.

That's what they'd told her. Over and over again. Their words killing her, until her memory of life had gone and all that was left was a blank canvas for them to mould into a weak nothing. As she moved, they watched her. Their unblinking eyes forever watching. Then it came. The lashing snake tongues, that whipped her fiercely and constantly. She just stood there looking into a vast open space. And she dreamed of a life that was not of her own. Of a life where she was something more than an 'it'. But that was a dream and she was in reality, and in reality there were no other chances. This was it.

Her wounded soul flew when she entered the room. She was safe, but did not feel tranquil. Instead, she felt alone. She knew what she had to do. She entered the kitchen with the same slow steps as before and she found the thing that she had been searching for in her heart for eternity, but had been too afraid to find. Now she was not afraid, now she was determined.

As she drew the blade into her soul, she felt the ending pain. And as she fell and the light faded from her eyes, she dreamed of the life she never had, felt the peace she had been longing for. She wasn't an 'it' anymore. She was something real.

Rebecca Morement (13)
Shenfield High School, Brentwood

Untitled

I woke to the sound of crashing.

'Please don't hurt me! Please!'

'Tell us where she is!'

'She's in the room next door! Please let go!'

I closed my eyes trying to get back to sleep, telling myself it was only another dream. I heard footsteps coming closer and closer.

'Kate, or should I say Jennifer? I've got some friends I'd like you to meet!'

'You killed my daughter, you filthy piece of s***.'

I couldn't realise what was going on, until I remembered my past. The past I was trying to forget. 'I'm not Jennifer Jones! I'm not! I'm Kate!' I pulled back the covers from my bed and stood up. I could have made a run for it. I tried, but my legs wouldn't move. They had found me. Me, Jennifer Jones, a killer.

'You're gonna pay for what you did b****!'

'I didn't do anything, I didn't, I ...' I fainted to the ground

My head was killing me. Where am I? What am I doing here? Too many thoughts were running through my head.

'Jennifer, Jennifer ...'

I hadn't heard that name for ages.

'Jennifer, it's OK now. Jennifer, we're going to move you again. I'll just find the details.'

Oh dear Lord, please help me, this is not worth it. No more identities, I can't take it anymore.

I reached out for the nearest sharp object. I dug it into my thick skin. Blood seeped out, it felt nice, so warm and ...

'Oh God! She's dead!'

'Jennifer Jones, time of death, 13.07pm.'

Chloe Isbell (13)
Shenfield High School, Brentwood

A Day In The Life Of A Piece Of Bread

Well today started off like any other day, stuck in the bread bin in a bag with all my family.

It was incredibly cramped lying here in this bag, I mean I had to lie on my side and you know what that did to my back. I really needed to go to Dr Pitta for that.

But then something happened that would change my life forever. I was taken away, kidnapped. My mother tried to grab me but she just fell over. (Do you notice when you take a piece out of the bag, the next one falls over?) I tried to get away, but it as no use, I was trapped!

As I hung there on the white table I noticed I was in the outside world. It was, it was ... disgusting! It was clean, white, and smelt of disinfectant; it made me sick.

I realised I was about to die. I lay there paralysed like a frightened deer struck in the middle of the road. I was to die. I had so much longer to live; my use-by date wasn't till the 31st.

As I began to move, I was put into a blazing machine. It burned! I became hotter, it burnt my beautiful white coat and I became yellow and crisp. I burned for a whole two minutes. So this was what Hell was like, burning for eternity.

But then my hope was restored, I was lifted, lifted to Heaven. I had a warm yellow blanket placed on top of me, it smelt of cheese?

But then my hope vanished; I was eaten by the burning jaws of Hell!

Sophie Harding (13)
Shenfield High School, Brentwood

Time Of Your Life

I always get so depressed around Christmas, any holiday for that matter - where you have to be merry and full of joy. I hate it when people get so excited about irrelevant illusions.

Every year I'm forced to look like I enjoy receiving childish, over-sized, itchy jumpers from great auntie someone, whom I've never met before (and will hopefully never have the 'pleasure' of meeting).

I could vomit every time people put on phoney, cheery voices to avoid arguments, just because it's meant to be a 'special' day. What's so 'special' about eating so much that it takes you another fifty-two weeks of hard labour to work off all the mince pies, or spending the night before all the relations (that you never knew about until Christmas) come round, searching for the one faulty light bulb that annoyingly turned off the whole set on your over-sized, smothered in tinsel, non-drop (which seem to drop more pine needles than the ordinary, cheaper version) Christmas tree? All that palaver just to find that it was the wrong bulb! Thus the panic search starts all over again; until, another five minutes later - once you thought that the fairy lights could not be beaten, that yet another bulb has blown.

Poor old Santa can't think it's a bundle of laughs either; getting stuck down the chimney. On the other hand, he does get Dad's secret stash of brandy in return (sometimes I wonder how nobody's ever picked him up for drink-driving.

Lydia Reeves (13)
Shenfield High School, Brentwood

A Day In The Life Of A Spider

The drip, the drops of the leaking tap. Silence is golden, but it won't be for long. The sun is rising and a new day is dawning on the massive house of four children in the suburbs of London. I scuttle onto the ceiling over bumps. I can hear the children waking up from their sleep in a warm, soft bed, and I have got the hard, damp bathtub. Another day with the fear of being killed. It's a hard life, everybody screaming at you, stuffed in a tissue and then flung out the window at the top of the mansion in the middle of a deserted field with overgrown grass and plenty of weeds. I don't know why everybody hates me, all I want to do is find a corner where I can spin a web.

Every day is a new adventure. Today, I want to go somewhere, I want to be somebody. As usual there will be an obstacle in the way. I've made my plan; I will get flushed down the sink and end up in Australia. The further away from here, the better!

If I were a human it would be a lot easier. Walking down the street without a care in the world, not the constant reminder that you could be dead any second. However, I know that will never be the case, there is no point dreaming. I must make the most of what I am; a small stick insect, with an ambition to catch a bee. There is no point wallowing in self-pity!

Natasha Warren (12)
Shenfield High School, Brentwood

A Day In The Life Of A Baby

Why are they ignoring me? Can't they hear me crying? I've been sitting in this dirty nappy for over an hour now! I hate being a baby; nobody understands how I feel. They just thrust toys and food in front of me and expect me to shut up! Plus, you know when relatives and family friends come over? They always make a massive fuss of me. It's as if I'm a baby! I am a baby.

I can't wait to start walking, talking and making friends. I'm fed up of seeing the exact same faces craning over my cot to wake me and give me my morning bottle. What's wrong with these people? All the coochi-coochi-coos! I thought *they* couldn't understand *me!*

Each night, when I'm snuggled down in my cot, I hear my mummy and nanny talking about me. Complaining, Mummy said, 'It's too much work, I can't do it anymore.'

Then the night came when I heard the words, 'Should we put her up for adoption?'

That's what Mummy said to my nanny. She wants to send me away to an unknown place.

My nanny has been looking after me quite a lot recently. Mummy hasn't been around. There's a frosty atmosphere about the place. Something's not right. I don't have a daddy. At least I don't think I have. I try to picture what my daddy would look like. It's hard though, because of not seeing him, having no memories, as if he doesn't exist.

Laura Mackenzie (12)
Shenfield High School, Brentwood

A Day In The Life Of A Baby

I look ridiculous! It's so unfair! They dress me up like a little doll, making me look as pathetic as possible. I'm helpless, all I can do is scream and cry, and that gives me a headache after a while. They treat me as if I'm not human. They talk about me and think I can't hear them, and when they *do* talk to me, they don't talk properly - they speak in a stupid voice and embarrass themselves. They always bore me with the same stories that are not interesting, and throw me around when I want to sleep. Also, they invite visitors over, who won't leave me alone. These strangers are obsessed with me and keep passing me around like a toy, and then moan when I'm sick on them - they had it coming! They're all over me like a rash and then suddenly, as soon as I need to be changed, they all disappear for some peculiar reason.

On the other hand, when I want to play, they're not in the mood. They put me upstairs out of the way in my bed, which is basically a cage, turn the monitor off and shut the door.

The worst thing is when it's meal times and I can't breathe with the ten thousand bibs and aprons she wraps me in. Also, the lame clothes she dresses me in are all colour-coordinated and accessorised. When we go out, I have to sit in this pram and she doesn't even go fast! People always peer into the pram and say, 'Isn't *he* cute!' *He!* How can people think I'm a boy?

I can't wait to grow up and go to school! Then I can do things *my* way.

Hayley Macfarlane (13)
Shenfield High School, Brentwood

Rapunzel Rewritten

'Giddy up, boy.'

Cor, this Rapunzel bird had better be worth this journey. Is that ... it can't be ... it is! It's the tower. Finally! Whoa, I don't remember it being this high in the description.

'Er, hello? Is anybody there?'

'Oh finally! Do you know how long I've been waiting for you?'

'No, and to be honest, I'm not that bothered.' Oh now I've gone and done it. 'Look, I'm sorry. Can you just throw down your soft golden locks please?'

'Well, you'll have to wait a while, I need to brush my hair.

Half an hour later ...

'OK, I'm ready now. My hair seems a bit greasy, as I've been locked up in this tower for heaven knows how long.'

Urgh! Her hair is worse than an ogre's hair. I'm surprised I didn't fall. Oh well, just as long as I get my beautiful girl. OK, not that beautiful. Fine, ugly!

'So, what do you think of me? And please be honest!'

She's expecting me to stay positive. She has that sort of smirk.

'Well honestly; you need to wash, you need a haircut, dresses are so first century and overall, you really need to change your style.'

Well, after all that, she went off crying. Then, her witch came up to see what all of the kerfuffle was about. She was very nice, so I asked her out to dinner, and here I am, sitting at home with my lovely wife and our three young wizards.

So fairy tales do happen!

Anna Howard (12)
Shenfield High School, Brentwood

Blondilocks And The Three Bears Incident

You probably know Goldilocks. You know, the sweet and innocent little girl who goes to the three bears' house. Well, this story isn't about her. It's about her cousin, Blondilocks, who you probably haven't heard of.

Blondilocks is the complete opposite of Goldilocks. She goes around burgling people's houses. She is the most common criminal in Bearville. She wears a leather jacket and leather gloves. She has a sky-high, blonde Mohican, a nose ring of a bull and earrings, so many you couldn't count them! Even the police are too scared to go near her!

Anyway, it was a normal day for Blondilocks, searching the town for a new spot to burgle. Then she came across it; the most secure building, the highest building, the most challenging building. Blondilocks was determined; she would make it.

As she mounted the 555th flight of stairs, she started to panic. She could hear a noise, a churning noise. And then all of a sudden, d*ing!* Argh! Panic. Someone was trying to kill her! She had blisters on her feet, but she ran up to the next level, into the nearest flat. At last, she was safe. She took her first look around. *Hang on a minute - this looks familiar,* Blondilocks thought. Then the penny dropped. Three bowls of porridge, three chairs, three beds. Oh no, she was in the three bears' flat! Now everyone would think she was a goody-two-shoes, the bee's knees, the teacher's pet. It would ruin her reputation! Suddenly the door opened and Blondilocks did what she had to do!

Emily Hall (13)
Shenfield High School, Brentwood

A Day In The Life Of A Captured Gorilla

Bang! The last time I saw my mum. *Bang!* The last time I saw the jungle.

Tap, tap! I awoke to hundreds of unfamiliar eyes. *Tap, tap!* I looked around and saw ... nothing.

That day, I remember. This was how it continued; my life, every day, eyes watching me, things flashing at me, no one caring for me.

Watching me. Flashes at me. No one caring for me.
Watching me. Flashes at me. No one caring for me.

Will every day be the same?

I have no purpose, no one to give me a purpose. Every now and then I catch a glimpse of an elephant or a tiger, and remember home. The sounds, smells and my mum.

I hate the food here, it's not like home. I can feel myself getting weaker and weaker. I can't be bothered to play, I can't be bothered to eat, I can't even be bothered to stay awake. What do I have to live for?

No! No! I must stay strong; not for me, but for my mum. She's out there somewhere, she needs me, I need her. I must stay strong!

As I am looking up, I can see a small being, like the ones I see every day watching me, but smaller. As I am looking at it, it's looking at me, into my eyes, as if it's feeling my pain. As I'm sitting mesmerised, I feel something pulling me. Where am I going now?

What is this? Other gorillas, just like me, more eyes around me now as I'm sitting here trying to find my bearings. I wonder, is this my life? Will it ever change?

Elise Norton (13)
Shenfield High School, Brentwood

A Day In The Life Of A Teenager

OK, so I know what you are thinking, 'It's another teenager complaining about her sad little life and her sad little friends!'

Well maybe if I was an average, boring, normal teenage girl. But I'm not. I am special. I am a superhero. OK, so now I suppose you are a little shocked, and maybe you don't believe me. Maybe you are in denial. It doesn't surprise me that you don't believe me, but it's true, and I will prove it to you.

Right, so first thing, I wake up at 6.30 (well we superheroes have to get an early start!) and I brush my teeth, get dressed, eat breakfast, you know, all the normal teenage things. Then I rush into school, get to form with minutes to spare (I use my superhero speed). And then it's off to my first lesson.

Second lesson comes and I have to use my superhero negotiating skills to explain to my history teacher how I lost my homework on Mars when I was saving alien creatures from a missile! However, she doesn't believe me and I spend my break time in detention. But they will not crush my happy spirit!

Come bedtime, I have helped my friend hook up with a boy she fancied, with my superhero charm, done all of my household chores and written about a hundred essays on 'Napoleon' and 'My Day Trip To France' (in French, obviously!) and all in time to watch 'EastEnders'.

So next time you hear a teenager complaining about how hard and unfair their life is, don't immediately think that they are just very dramatic and that they are exaggerating an awful lot, just remember, *not all teenagers are superheroes like me!*

Hannah Page (13)
Shenfield High School, Brentwood

A Maelstrom Descends
(An extract)

A sea of darkness engulfed the forest, the inky blackness drowning the final sparks of light, descending into a void of utter silence. The tension was almost tangible, shackling the atmosphere, making the air still, hot and unmoving. Waiting, pressure increasing, captured rainwater sliding tantalisingly slowly from the leaves above, falling, impacting soundlessly on the ground.

The menacing shape of trees rose from the dark, forming rows of jagged teeth that snarled at the sky. Their branches a complex lattice of emerald-green needles and thin-veined leaves linking and intertwining to create a massive canopy that moved like a mighty ocean spurred by a tempest. Towering over the landscape were think spikes of stone, piercing the seething mass of black, grey and dark indigo as a storm embraced the grief-stricken sky. It was a window to a void of tortured souls, screaming in defiance at the lightning that streaked across the heavens. A harsh wind shipped the clouds creating immense structures of unparalleled intricacy, formed from a fluid opalescent marble that flickered with a blue luminescence. The maelstrom swelled as its pulsating heart swept across the valley accompanied by a sharp crack of thunder that sent intense ripples of sound punching through the air.

From the depths of the aerosphere came a dark torrent of rain plummeting to the ground with an inexorable force, exploding as it collided with the ground. The steady dripping of water became a roar of unbridled fury, constant and resolute.

James Loveard (14)
Shenfield High School, Brentwood

The Flames Of A Dying City

Chaos. Total anarchy swept across the city, the now dilapidated houses rising up in flames. The fire spread with considerable speed, devouring anything in its path into a well of raging inferno. Shrill screams echoed in the distance as shadowed figures ran helplessly in a hope to escape. Smelling the heavy fumes, the black smoke, the burning remains, I knew death was inevitable. Stormed by an enemy onslaught, armour-clad knights raided the city, mercilessly slashing at any living thing that was in striking distance of their blades. The city was engulfed in a sea of flames, submerged in burning destruction and suffocating clouds of black smoke.

I reached the courtyard, panting, looking for a way out of the enflamed labyrinth of streets. Searching frantically for a way to escape, but with every second that passed, my demise drew closer. Suddenly, I heard yelling, ringing above the crackling flames, and within moments, two knights came into vision directly ahead, approaching with unnatural speed. They charged fearlessly, raising their weapons. Instinctively, I turned, running immediately, knowing that I could not match the skill of those knights. But to my dismay, my path was obstructed when three other knights appeared, in which all hope deteriorated. I swerved out of the swing of one of their swords, and avoided death by a fraction, which was all too close. Then darting through an alley, stumbling through the debris, I came to another street. There was no way out. I was surrounded …

Vincent Morris (14)
Shenfield High School, Brentwood

Dead Memories
(In the style of Susan Hill)

The moon hung, lifeless in the sky. A vast field covered the land, its grass torn, and burnt. A tree, leafless, black, stood in this field. The tree was engulfed in many birds, worming their way in-between each other, until, stillness. The crows stared blankly out of their cold, red eyes, waiting.

A house was the only other feature of this landscape, white in colour, and each window was shattered and sharp.

A man was trudging up to the house. He knocked softly on the door. It opened, slowly, deliberately. No one. The hall was empty. He stepped in.

Inside the house, the walls were charred, but the actual place itself was in pretty good shape. Photographs lined the hallway, photographs in black and white, and of a family that perished long ago.

The man walked nervously into the first room. The light was on. A ruffling could be heard, directly from an old, ragged chair that faced away from view. There was something there. Holding his breath, he walked to it, his head pounding.

On the seat sat a little girl, wearing a white dress. Her head was buried in her hands. The man walked up to her, relieved that it was a harmless child, but curious as to why she was in this place. His hand went out to touch her. She turned. Facing him. Her eyes were missing. Deep scratches tore her face. Blood slithered down her wide, gaping mouth. She vanished.

He was alone, once more.

Francis Lind (14)
Shenfield High School, Brentwood

The Assassin
(In the style of Susan Hill)

The assassin crept slowly towards his target; the only sign of life was the vapour of breath protruding from his mouth, lingering momentarily in the overhanging mist, before being consumed into the night. He didn't want to kill the target; the man seemed to be happy, with children and a loving wife, but he was a professional and he was being paid; he must do it. *Why do I agree to these things? Why do I get myself involved with all this dirty work? Money, that's why,* he answered himself, and he remembered the cheque that would be cashed into his account when his work was completed.

The assassin moved forward into the darkness, cautiously, every inch of the night swallowing him up. He carried on along the road, the headlights of passing cars revealing the lines on his face, so intricate it looked as though they had been carefully engraved. He turned back as a row of vehicles followed the street, each ensuing the other's path. It was then that he saw the car of his target, moving placidly towards the driveway of his home.

The assassin increased his pace and skipped behind the trees in front of the home, only the slight orange glow of his cigarette giving any indication of a figure standing there. The car had been caught in a row of traffic at the lights, and so the assassin had more time to contemplate his plan. He would do it as he stepped form his car, it had to be done before he got inside his house, but not before he had shut the car door. As the vehicle escaped from the traffic, the assassin twisted his silencer onto the end of the pistol, stamped out his cigarette on the pavement and loaded just two bullets into the barrel. His shadow appeared almost sinisterly onto the floor, created by the lamp overhead as he moved from behind the trees, still engulfed in darkness.

The car pulled into the driveway. *This is it,* thought the assassin, the pressure increasing as the seconds passed like hours, *now it's time.* But as the man stepped from his car, the front door opened and his family ran to greet him. He couldn't do it now, maybe tomorrow, and he smiled gently to himself.

Joe Abbitt (13)
Shenfield High School, Brentwood

The Painted Dog

The dog howled as the masked men dragged a sack out of the building. It stood, perfectly still, anger in its eyes, muscles tensing, veins throbbing.

Bang!

Like a flaming lead from a gun, the dog darted across the road towards the men. The black-clothed figures glanced to the left to be horrified by the sight of a ferocious dog.

The rain thumped the dull grey concrete. The dog lay on the ground, motionless, silent, dead, scarlet drifting from beneath its cold, lifeless body.

'Mummy! Mummy! Look, there's a dog, someone tried to paint it red!'

Mrs Smith turned her head around the rusty doorframe of the newsagent's, as her eyes processed what she was seeing, her neck became tight, she gasped for air. She reached into her purse and took out her inhaler. 'Come here, Joe, come here!' said Mrs Smith, wheezing, forcing each word after every breath.

Joe got up from beside the dog and ran to Mrs Smith. 'Mummy, why is the dog not moving?' asked Joe intently.

'Well,' said Mrs Smith, clawing the oxygen from the air, 'it's sleeping Joe, sleeping.' Mrs Smith clambered to obtain Joe's hand, she held it firmly.

'Shouldn't we clean it, Mummy?' suggested Joe.

'It's better we don't, dear, let's go home,' replied Mrs Smith.

Holding his mother's hand, Joe walked down the damp street in the direction of his home, every few metres, turning his head to look at the 'sleeping' dog, wondering when it would wake.

Anand Pandya (13)
Shenfield High School, Brentwood

A Day In The Life Of U-Boat Commander Eric Topp

Topp woke with a start. The overwhelming fumes of diesel and the nauseating concoction of sweat and waste filled his nostrils. Next to him sat the lifeless body of a torpedo, above him slept pipes and valves. Occasionally everything would shake and rumble as the ballast was adjusted, it was this that jarred him from his troubled sleep.

He jumped down; he landed in a sticky pool of diesel and seawater. Beginning to walk the length of the U-boat was not an easy task; the floor was wet, and littered with boots, gloves and other debris.

Moving to the control bulkhead, he adjusted his hat and now shabby uniform. 'Reporting for duty, Herr boot-Fuhrer.'

Boot-Fuhrer removed his cap, he looked half dead, the extra long Atlantic patrol had taken its toll. 'You have the boat,' he said behind a sigh.

Checking the depth-meter was the first task to be performed, then stirring the ballast tanks and testing the dive planes.

The sonar operator sat quietly in his cupboard-like station, twisting the rotation wheel, listening. It was hard to detect an enemy ship, especially their arch adversary, the destroyer. Their narrow hulls cut through the water like a knife through butter. Occasionally the operator would sit bolt upright, an intense look on his face, each time Topp would nervously reach for and finger his Iron Cross, holding it close to his chest.

Now he was squeezing the life from it. The operator had been bolt upright for a good ten minutes now, then, 'Merchant with escort, Herr boot-Fuhrer, 10,000 tonnes plus, bearing three-zero-nine.'

Instantly he rang the alarm. 'All forward, switch to battery, full ahead. Load tubes three and four, crash dive ...'

Scott Fenn (14)
Shenfield High School, Brentwood

In The Lair Of The Gremlins

His brown coat dragged along behind him on the sodden earth. It was getting almost as saturated as the muddy ground itself. The man, however, showed no signs of caring. He continued his march through the dense and ancient terrain that was Samelkiar Forest. His rough, bland clothing was retrieving all sorts of decoration from the forest: interesting green smudges of moss from the strong, slender, tall trees and dew from the waxy, sticky leaves of the bushes. They were reaching out, wanting to make their mark on the man. This possessive, desperate landscape seemed to prey on idle beings trudging through its roots, sucking life out of all who walked on its precious feet.

Wisps of activity flew past him. The man, breathless, continued on what he intended to be a stress-relieving country walk. Spirits innocently watched him through invisible eyes and clasped their invisible hands innocently around his neck, trying to suffocate him.

Predators were not welcomed.

Inaudible chattering brought this dreary place to life, animating the very souls of the trees. Evil, high-pitched laughter would have been heard by the man if he had been sufficiently conscious. The noxious toxins that leaked into the air took hold of the man's concentration, losing him his recognition of grave danger.

Hours later he was still stumbling on through the same hypnotising forest. Little did he know that he had fallen prey to the invisible gremlins of Samelkiar.

William Church (14)
Shenfield High School, Brentwood

A Day In The Life Of A New York Gangster

I have only one clean outfit that belongs to me. I walk the streets with all black clothing. My delicate Chicago Bulls jersey covered my highly valuable bullet-proof vest. I positioned my hat sideways, with loose fitting trousers that had a very compact but detailed logo on them. My enormous gold chain dangled from my neck and put quite a lot of pressure on it.

It was night, the all so crucial time where many thugs and sometimes innocent people were murdered for foolish reasons.

As I made my way to find my colleagues, I passed many tramps trying desperately to sleep on such a chilly night. I spotted my friends in the distance all sitting in a large vehicle with huge amounts of smoke escaping the inside of the car and drifting through the air.

I remained staring at the fogged-up car and I was about to approach it. When suddenly, I was grappled by one of my most angered enemies.

He explained how he was going to take my life, while he put a sharp and terribly dangerous knife to my throat. He then said he'd rather me suffer and just as he finished that sentence, *smack!* I was hit with a remarkably solid baseball bat. I fell to the floor and was assaulted one by one by the members of my enemy's highly villainous crew.

As they deserted the area, I still recognised my companions in the dark vehicle. I struggled to crawl to the car. I rapidly thumped the window. The door flew open. My crew members demanded to know why I was bruised and bleeding. I explained to them how I was brutally attacked.

I was dragged into the vehicle and my gang and I went desperately searching for the culprits. As we drove, three of my ruthless friends loaded our remarkably loud firearms. We discovered the gang standing outside the liquor store, blasting sinful hip hop from a stolen boom box.

The car pulled to a halt, four of us leapt out of the car with our loaded guns. Everybody at the crime scene was shouting and screaming. I fired exactly eight shots, they mainly struck my enemies in their backs, heads and legs. Many of the deranged enemies crashed to the ground in an attempt to race to safety.

I heard sirens and my comrades and I dived into the vehicle and rushed to a quiet and safe location.

This is just another day in the life of a New York gangster!

Matthew McNaughton (13)
Shenfield High School, Brentwood

Fear Before Death
(In the style of Susan Hill)

The train pulls into the station, it slows down to a careful stop. The sound of the track underneath the metal beast gets slower, before twisting into a deep growl.

Silence.

I clamber out of the train, carefully, amid the resounding echo of an empty, artificial voice. The flat puddles lay isolated, their surfaces glistening with the calm glow of the street lamps above.

I pull the zip of my coat up higher, my hair blowing violently in the wind. My woollen hat, loosely knitted, barely stretches over my head, before the wind claims it, and it becomes lost.

The crusty grass, damp with dew, shimmers like a distant star with a weak glow. The twisted trees block my journey home. They are protecting their territory, and yet they fail. Sick with defeat, their thin branches are bare, black and still.

It begins to rain.

A torrent floods from the skies as I traverse deeper into another world. Overgrown weeds and insects; limp with death, dominate the pathways. The silence claws at my sanity, until a few minutes later, I hear rushed footsteps approaching.

I quicken my pace. I can't look back; I don't want to see them. I pull my hood quickly over my head. The rain beats heavily down like bombs, in a ceaseless attack on the Earth. My quick and heavy breaths drown the sound of my obscure pursuers, and, as my black, shiny shoes enter a puddle - the ripples expand, and then finally diminish - I see them.

James Lind (14)
Shenfield High School, Brentwood

Achilles

His breath stale, cold; enraged. He had nothing. Since the conflict of the day before, when he had received news of his cousin's death, he had wanted revenge. Achilles was the greatest Greek warrior, he knew that, but Hector, he also was the greatest warrior from his country; Troy.

'I will kill him!' the warrior's promise sharp, piercing.

He flicked the soft leather reins. This was to be the most strenuous challenge he would ever face. Corealus, his steed, led Achilles through the Greek post, a complex assemblage of shacks and boats. The chariot was Achilles' throne. decorated with the merits of his successes, it boasted the threat Achilles oppressed.

Over Troy, an orb of immense light rose from the ashes of the night. Its radiant light bathed the city in a pool of glory and triumph. The clouds which framed the sun focused the light onto the Trojan chapel which sat on the peak of the city, reflecting the intensity of the heavens onto the world it towered above.

As Achilles moved ever closer to his prey, a mist of tension moistened the walls of the mighty city. Horns of warning announced his arrival and arrows of lead were poised, ready to impale Achilles' dominating figure.

'Hector!' his voice, punishing his victim. 'I am ready.'

Dominic Clark (13)
Shenfield High School, Brentwood

Shadows Of The Night

A day in the dark is all they know; a day in the light is all they want.

The streets are filled with children. Playing, laughing. Women hanging out their washing, men walking to work, salesmen going from door to door selling things for their existence. But what they don't know is what lies down below, feeding off wandering life-forms, yearning the light, but all they know is darkness. Coldness, grimness.

Night comes again to the streets of the world. A black cape thrown across the sun, a black cape is swept across the pathways; a black cape, as black as their hearts. Colourless, lifeless. The shadows of the night once again retain their true forms. The souls that were lost to this dark force wandered the Earth. Homeless became lifeless, non-existent to this world. Their mangled bodies stiff still on the ground. Bloodless, soulless. Shadows stolen from good-hearted beings, seeping through the cracks in the ground. Dawn is near, now the shadows live in fear. Screams and tears as the dead are now found. Murder, murder.

The humans are now second in the food chain. Shadows outnumber humans two to one. The shadows are waiting. For night will come soon, and they will strike again. Resting, sleeping.

The clock strikes twelve, the bells in the church chime. The creatures come out of their dark graves, ready to devour more flesh, more blood, more souls. Crawling, creeping. Stalking the unwary prey like an eagle, flying high in the sky, casting a shadow over the victims below.

No one can hear your scream!

Mitchell Clarke (13)
Shenfield High School, Brentwood

A Day In The Life Of A World War II Soldier

Today we broke through the Normandy landing and are heading into France. We expect heavy resistance, but after surviving that beach I know we can survive anything.

We're expecting reinforcements, but with the lack of supplies, we're not holding our breath.

We just had a heavy fire fight but like I said, we survived, but we lost two good soldiers. From the look of the enemy I'd say we're near an enemy camp, so we're not letting our guard down in case we come across some more scouts.

We can just perceive the enemy encampment through the dense vegetation; we are going to mobilise and take up positions and fire while they're at the dinner table.

Bang! As a heavy flurry of pervasive bullets flew into the camp, cutting, ripping and rending the enemy, all there was, was red mist flying everywhere and blood-curdling screams; screams that would haunt me for the rest of my life.

We endeavoured cautiously into the camp. *Bang!* I leapt with horror as a German soldier fell to his knees.

We split up and searched the camp, but found no enemy soldiers. We found a radio transmitter and this was the first good luck that we had had since we were put on this suicide mission, since our radio was broken.

We called HQ and not to our surprise, no reinforcements were coming. So we gathered all the supplies we could and camped for the night.

Oliver Field (13)
Shenfield High School, Brentwood

The Magical Planet

A long time ago there lived a small race on the planet of Gongan. The Gongans were little elf-like creatures that lived off plants that grew on the planet.

One day, a little Gongan named Tonton, was walking through the wood that were nearby. Tonton had green wrinkly skin like crumpled-up paper, and a short green hat. He was enjoying a walk through the woods when he slipped and fell into a dark tunnel. As he slid down the slimy sides he saw a light at the bottom and fell out onto the ground with a thud. He looked around and found himself staring into one of the busiest places he had ever seen. He stood up and found himself standing on a concrete floor. There were people of all shapes and sizes passing by from every direction.

He got up and walked ahead, being knocked into by lots of busy people. He was heading for the only building he could see amongst the crowds of bustling people As he walked on, a big red transport ship came hurtling towards him carrying lots of people. Tonton dived out of the way quickly. 'Wow!' he exclaimed. 'You don't get those where I come from,' he said, open-mouthed.

He continued along to the building ahead and walked inside.

'Now, you're an odd lookin' little fella, ain't ya,' said a man behind a counter. ''Ow can I 'elp ya?'

'I am looking for a way to get back to my planet, Gongan,' said Tonton, a little scared of this man.

'Well, I've neva 'eard of it, but you could always try the local airstrip. The man there can be very 'elpful.'

'Thank you,' said Tonton, and off he went.

After asking around a lot, at last he came to the airfield. 'Excuse me. Could you help me get back to my planet, Gongan?' asked Tonton of the owner.

'Er, yeah. I got a rocket leaving in a minute. It's going right your way. Hop on and I'll take you to your planet.'

'Thank you so much,' replied Tonton.

As Tonton climbed onto the ship, he felt slightly nervous. He sat down shaking all over. He had never travelled on a ship before. He sank into the cushioned seat and relaxed for the journey. It took ten hours before the ship landed and Tonton got shaken out of a deep sleep. When he walked out, he took a whiff of the fresh air, happy that he was home again. He thanked the driver and walked home to his village.

His father was so pleased to see him and asked him where he had been. Tonton pulled out his map and remembered seeing a picture of where he had been on the wall of the building he had entered. He pointed to it and his dad said, 'Ah, I know. That's Earth that is. Strange folk are the Earthlings.'

Tonton look surprised and asked, 'Dad, when I was on Earth, I saw a red transport ship. What was it?'

'I remember the first time I saw one of those. That is what Earthlings call a 'bus'. Now enough about that and off to bed. You look exhausted.'

Jack McCarthy (12)
Shenfield High School, Brentwood

Local Students Held Hostage During A Bank Robbery

Yesterday, some Year 10 students were held hostage by some armed bank robbers. 'I was terrified when the robbers ordered me to open the money vault. Then they took two Year 10 students and pointed their guns at them', said the manager of the bank.

The students told us that there were four men. All were quite tall. They were all masked and wearing hoodies. They also had gloves.

They had a driver waiting outside, who was also wearing a mask and a hoodie. The car was a silver Audi and the number plate was half broken.

A female student told us, 'They held me in the car and said if I tried to move I would die. They then stopped and told me to get out. They quickly drove off'.

The descriptions were given to the police and it is said that over £5 million was stolen. There have been some sightings of the car not far from the bank, but not many. 'We still have no idea who the men are', reported the police sergeant.

This gang of robbers may be linked with seven smaller robberies around the country. So if you have any information, please go to the police immediately.

The students are suffering from shock, so have been given the rest of the week off school.

Steve Payne (13)
Shenfield High School, Brentwood

Cup Final Horror

Man U favourites as Henry is crocked!

Yesterday, more bad injury news was announced for Arsenal. Arsenal may now be without five influential first team players for their showdown with massive rivals - Manchester United. Thierry Henry, José Antonio Reys, Fredrick Ljungberg, Robert Pires and Lauren all look set to miss the cup final.

There may be some hope though, as Paul Scholes also looks set to miss the cup final, and nerves may be setting in as Malcolm Glazer looks likely to axe Alex Ferguson, Cristiano Ronaldo and Ryan Giggs. We spoke to Arsene Wenger earlier to see how he feels about the cup final, this is what he said: 'We have a lot of top class players out injured, but we have a lot of talent throughout the squad, so I have no worries. We can still win'.

We also spoke to Thierry Henry about his tragic injury, we quote: 'I can't believe I can't play, I had just got back from injury, and then I played 45 minutes and suffered a reaction to my injury. I still believe we can win, although we have five big players out. We are strong and will continue to be strong. If we are not playing to our best, we may not win, but I believe we can win'.

Although Arsenal has a lot of big players out, they still believe they can win. Manchester United are the favourites at 3/1 and Arsenal are the underdogs at 8/2. We can only wait and see what the outcome is on Saturday.

Daniel Gunning (13)
Shenfield High School, Brentwood

A Day In The Life Of A Prisoner

I awoke. The bright sunlight shone through the tiny barred window into the dark, bleak cell.

How I wish I could be out there right now. Playing in the sun, socialising. I sighed and threw the filthy blanket off me.

It was three weeks since I'd started my ten-year sentence. I didn't do it. I just call it being in the wrong place at the wrong time. I must admit, my life wasn't at its best when it happened. I just got fired, my husband died and I got evicted from my house. I'd gone for a walk in the park to clear my head. There was only one other person. Well, so I thought. There was a gunshot. The man in front of me collapsed. I looked around startled. I heard a rustle in the bushes. I ran to see what it was. Then I saw it. Something black in a pile of grass. I brushed away the grass and stumbled back, stunned. I stood there staring at it, then at the man, lying there still as a log.

The police sirens surrounded me and they took me away. From that moment on, I knew my life was over.

The court case went by quickly. All the evidence pointed to me. What could I do? My fingerprints were on the gun, I was the only other person there and the man who was shot was my old boss. So they thought I wanted to get revenge.

So now I'm here ...

Rebecca Young (12)
Shenfield High School, Brentwood

A Day In The Life Of A Murderer

He lay on the ground, he did, on that bitter morning of November. I don't normally stand waiting, but he was always a strange one, we had a connection. So why did I do it? I walked away.

'Cowards walk away.'

I listened to the wind taunting me. The garage was now a distant memory. I mean that's what you have to do in this business ... forget, or you will be overcome with guilt.

The dingy pier and its ghost-like town awakened me. Paul was here, in the shadows. He is like the air, always there watching ... waiting, like an eagle interrogating its prey.

Before I reached him, I stared at those bottomless eyes, all of the warmth drained out. His black hair ruffled by the wind showed the only sign of movement. I looked at the solemnly shut, cracked lips and thought of him ... *daddy,* and the lips that had once spoken, ''Ello Princess.'

'How di' go?' he said in a gasp-like whisper.

'All right,' I replied.

'What di' ya get?'

'His wallet.'

No reply.

'And of course, his memory, we are safe now. The cops won't find him till five-ish, and by then Abs will have buried him.'

I went away. My black hair, once blonde, waved about. The only question rattling around in m y brain was, *why did we kill him?* I mean, Lewis was a friend.

Anger filled up inside me. Paul had made me kill him because ... Was it hatred or guilt that made me stay awake that night? Well, whatever it was, he was going to pay ...

Emma Conlon (13)
Shenfield High School, Brentwood

Kimi Raikkonen - Ready For The Off

The sweat from my colleagues could be tasted at the back of the queue. The fumes from the engines salted the air that blew towards me. I felt ill and nauseous. I felt so ill that I didn't think that I would be driving in today's race.

As my fingers went to their accustomed places, I knew I was to follow my dream to the end, whenever that may be. With a pulsating engine behind my back, I knew where my rightful place in the world was. The engine appeared to keep time with my heart, although I did wonder whether I had a health problem, because my heart was beating normally under stressful circumstances.

The roar of the stands did its best to drown out what appeared to be a feeble attempt at making some noise. The engines revved, impatient to be off and whizzing round the track.

The fumes from the engines tickled my nose and made me feel more ill than I had ever felt before. The food mixed with the drinks smelt wonderful, but I knew that I could not eat or drink until after the big event because of the rules of this 'game'.

The other cars were all ready while my team were performing last minute checks on the car. All were waiting for the lights to be lit and the horn to sound.

The grid no longer bustled with activity.

The lights lit up and the horn sounded to signal the beginning of the first race of a new Formula 1 Grand Prix season.

Amy Luke (15)
Sir Christopher Hatton School, Wellingborough

Diagnosis

All day I could feel *its* solid presence enveloping my thoughts. *I've got cancer* - crazy I know. I have not got it. Probably. Maybe. What did Sir say again? My concentration's wandering, looking at the clock constantly. I've got to meet Mum at the doctor's in a minute. Each moment stretches to ripping point when the bell rings. I jump and clutch my chest. I can feel *it* there, as noise reverberates round my skull.

Left. Right. Left. One foot at a time. Mum waves and smiles, like we're on some pleasure jaunt. Doesn't she care? Isn't she worried? I get a grip on myself and smile. It's strange how the mind distorts a simple visit to the doctor. Entering the waiting room, as one entity, everyone waiting looks at me warily, unblinking, examining. Mum and I sit together - me holding our number plaque tightly, and looking up at the nameplate: Dr P.

Tick-tock, tick. Bing! We're next. The pit of my stomach tightens.

Dr P is really nice. She reminds me of those jolly, round people-toys that go round and round on the spot.

'What's the problem?' she asks.

OK, deep breath. So I explain about *the lump*, keeping my fear beating against my ribs. The next stage is the examination. Funnily, I wasn't embarrassed, I just wanted to know. Is it the big 'C'? Will I die? Shh ...

Ten minutes later ... I'm fine. Relief is a cold wind in the face as I walk out the door.

Aisha Opoku (17)
Sir Christopher Hatton School, Wellingborough

A Strange End

As the lift door opened 7 agents lay waiting behind boxes and crates. A volley of fire came pouring out of the lift killing all of them, whilst clearing a path through the barricade of crates.

A solemn character walked through the onslaught, dropping his empty guns he reached out and ripped the safety deposit box off the wall. A single agent started to get up when the box was wrapped around his head.

As the lift reached the lobby, a rocket hit the doors as they opened. A blast flew back burning the reception. No one was there.

A shaded figure leapt off the bank, diving straight off the ground, halfway down the figure opened its coat, allowing them to glide into the next street. As he landed storm clouds drew near, as he ran lightning struck buildings on either side.

Shock took the crowd when a police officer launched a rocket. The mass of explosives hit the shaded figure causing him to launch into the nearby window.

Injured, he was arrested for theft, treason and murder, identified as Laurence Lefercent. A most wanted, he was put on trial and killed in the electric chair.

Crime stopped for weeks as an impact struck the villainy world as one of the best or worst villains, depending on which way you flip the pancake, had died.

After a while crime regained its speed and people went about their business forgetting the whole ordeal.

Marvin Nicholl (13)
Smithdon High School, Hunstanton

Second-Hand Dreams

I must explain; the events I'm to describe happened a long time ago ...

His eyes locked on mine as I slowly paced towards him with the blindfold in my hand. Thoughts crossed my mind of this being wrong. *Am I the right person to give the command for his killing? Am I the right person to judge whether what he did was unforgivable?* My hands trembled and his head shook from the tightness of the knot. 'May God forgive you,' he pleaded.

I calmly marched across the wide-open muddy field to my position. I could hear the echo of firing guns, however I blocked out the death-drenched sounds and prepared to give the order.

Is shell shock such a crime? Does he really deserve to die? There it was again - my conscience.

I did it. I steeled myself and gave the order, 'Take aim, fire!'

Unwillingly I drew my revolver from its holster and stumbled over to the limp body to administer the coup de grâce.

I killed him. Not the soldier who fired, it was me that demanded it happen. I killed my mate. We had enlisted together, fought together and when we went over the top to attack he just lay at the bottom of the trench, crying. Cowardice they called it. He didn't deserve it. My mate ... I killed my mate.

The psychoanalyst said to me, 'So that's it, you were a World War I officer in a former life.'

I replied, 'Now the dreams make sense.'

Ashleigh German (15)
Smithdon High School, Hunstanton

A Day In The Life Of Anne Frank

Monday: we have been found, we had to be taken away in an old, dark, horrible train. I felt so scared, frightened and confused. It felt as if we were on our way to Hell, but we were actually on our way to a concentration camp.

Children around with pale faces as if they had seen a ghost, they were screaming for their parents but they were not there, they were confused and had no idea where they were going. I knew where we were really going, we were going to a monstrous place, where people were murdered because of their religion.

Tuesday: the Germans were shouting at everybody, they were holding long pointing guns. I knew that they were not afraid to use them on us. When we departed the train I was petrified, confused and I didn't know what was going to happen next. Then suddenly a large soldier ripped me away from my family, I felt as if I had been stabbed in the heart repeatedly. My throat went all dry as if I had just swallowed a huge pill, and I went dizzy and felt so sick.

I have been split up from my family. I'm on my own to try and be safe and stay alive. All I can think about is if I'll ever see my family again.

Sophie Cribb (13)
Smithdon High School, Hunstanton

No Escape

That's when the engine went dead. Great. I should've known this would happen.

Howling wind and rain battered the car violently. A brief flash of fluorescent lightning illuminated the towering ruins before me. Stumbling up the rough stone path, I huddled deeper inside my coat. The torrential rain whipped my back. Grasping out for the door, I felt just twisted, gnarled, rotten wood beneath my fingers, before it swung ominously inwards, creaking.

Rubble littered the floor. An oil lamp flickered in the gloom, its flame writhing like a snake's tongue, spluttering dully. It cast long shadows over the high stone walls, filling the cavernous chamber with a surreal, eerie glow.

My dishevelled hair fell roughly at my shoulders, echoing the sorrowful aura enveloping me.

A glittering orb quivered in a corner. It danced playfully in the shadows, like a carefree fairy, teasing me to come closer, intriguing me. In a wisp of curling black smoke it was gone.

'Be my friend.'

I spun around, breathless with shock.

Hovering before me, suspended, feather-like, in mid-air, was a child. Her pale, papery skin omitted a shimmering light. Clear, glassy saucers blinked at me, bewildered.

I glanced hastily at the door. A thick, rusty bolt was drawn across it.

Suddenly, the girl morphed into a haunched, wrinkled hag. A wizened nose protruded from an engulfing robe, the rest of her features hollowed and shrivelled.

My feet turned to lead weights.

Hobbling towards me, wheezing, she snarled, 'There's no escape …'

Christina Sanderson (13)
Smithdon High School, Hunstanton

Keats

When I arrived home from school at 3.45pm my dad had a phone call. It was Julie, one of my parents' friends. She said she had seen a ginger tomcat, being hit by a car!

We had a ginger tomcat, so my dad went to the main road, and there he laid. It was our cat.

Julie said that the driver just drove off, probably didn't even realise that he had hit anything at the speed he was going. Keats was quite old, my cat, he was 17, and going to be 18 on the 17th of May.

I knew from that moment that everything would be different. It was like losing a member of the family, a human.

I was always quite close to Keats, as he was 5 when I was born, it was even like losing a brother.

My dog, Bobby, was really close to Keats too. They even used to share the same dog bed at night. They used to fight as well. Keats would hit Bobby round the face with his claws, but they never got hurt, just play fighting, like brothers.

It has now been 5 months since the death, but Bobby still looks for him, behind the sofas, in the garage, in the dog bed. He's probably thinking, *where could he be?*

Zoe Coton (13)
Smithdon High School, Hunstanton

The Closed Door

I went back today, to the day when my life fell apart and my childhood ended. The day I realised adults weren't perfect and that I had to stand on my own two feet.

It was a boiling day and I had spent it with Mum. We were playing on the carpet. Barbie was getting married. I could feel the itchy, synthetic material rub against my smooth skin.

The door slammed open and in walked Dad. He towered over me, red eyes unfocused and he smelt funny. Sometimes when he was like this, he would be happy, smiley and fun. Other times he turned into a monster, shouting and swearing.

It was a monster day. Mum scooped me up in her arms, carried me upstairs, put me in my bed and whispered, 'I'll be up in a bit.'

It was too hot to sleep. I tossed and turned, trying to relax. Then I decided to go down and find Mum. I sat at the top of the stairs, looking down at my parents. Suddenly Dad shouted, the words slurred. He raised a fist and rammed it hard into Mum's jaw.

I screamed. They looked up. Dad snarled, turned round and slammed the door. He'd closed more than one door though. He'd closed the one on my childhood too.

Amrith Malhi (13)
Smithdon High School, Hunstanton

Disappointment

She woke up with a shock, it was just a dream. Although her mum had precisely told her not to get up before eight o'clock, she couldn't wait any longer.

Creeping slowly along the creaking floorboards she tiptoed around the hallway towards the living room.

What happened next was something she would never forget. She had imagined huge mountains of presents perfectly wrapped in shiny paper and the walls decorated with balloons ready for the party. There was nothing. She didn't want to believe it but it was clear her mum had forgotten again.

Storming down towards her mum's room, she didn't know whether to feel disappointed or angry.

Jenny knew deep down that this was always going to happen. She slammed open the door only to find her mum giggling along to an early morning TV programme, totally oblivious to what day it was. She had done it again.

Jenny didn't care about the last five birthdays. Her mum had always got the wrong day. It wasn't her fault. Jenny had always wanted her birthday to be special. In another couple of hours her friends would be knocking at the door expecting a spectacular party. Weeks of planning wasted as it was clear she would have to cancel the party, her mum hadn't even bought a card. This had to be the worst birthday she had ever had.

After feeling sorry for herself, her mum came to ask what the matter was. After Jenny had explained, her mum couldn't help but laugh. Jenny's birthday wasn't until tomorrow!

Helen Parkinson (13)
Smithdon High School, Hunstanton

School Vote Decides Election

Schools across the country have voted in mock elections this week to decide who they thought would make a good party to run the parliament for the next four years. Students had to register to vote, select candidates to represent each party and then follow the normal voting procedures.

It was shown afterwards that schools often reflected constituency types, for example one fee paying school in Essex returned the Conservative candidate almost unanimously, they could not get anyone to stand for either the Labour party or the Lib Dems.

However, across the country the overall results were as follows, 42% of the seats went to the Liberal Democrats, 24% to the Tories whilst Labour were beaten into third place with only 17% of the seats, the same total number of seats as won by all the smaller parties combined. One seat went to a candidate for the Monster Raving Loony Party and one candidate standing for Veritas forgot to register, so couldn't vote for himself.

When interviewed many students stated that they voted Lib Dem for their policy on scrapping university tuition fees because students did not want to start a career many thousands of pounds in debt or be a tremendous financial burden to their parents. Others gave the proposed removal of the AS tier of examinations as a reason for giving the Lib Dems their vote.

Perhaps all party leaders should take note of these results as in four years time as many as two thirds of these students will have the vote themselves.

Dan Robinson (14)
Smithdon High School, Hunstanton

A Day In The Life Of Queen Elizabeth I

I was woken up at 10 minutes past seven on a cold February morning by a loud knock on my chamber door. My chambermaid hurried over at my command and opened the door to reveal Lord Langfre. He marched up to my bed accompanied by two guards, and bowed deeply.

He boomed, 'Your Majesty, the Spaniards have sent word that their ships have already set sail for England. They should arrive in a few days with the intention of war.'

I arose from my bed at once and commanded Lord Langfre to inform the head of the guards to ready his troops for war, to get them to board the ships as soon as possible. We would meet the Spaniards at sea.

I called my maids at once to get me ready. I hardly even winced as they put my corset on as I was so deep in thought.

I hurried down to court where all the courtiers were already assembled. I sat upon my throne as the room was called to order. I addressed the court. 'The Spaniards are to invade.'

There was a noise of shock amongst the court. It was called to order, my ministers took over. As I listened it was unbelievable, it was like the stories I'd been told when I was a little child, not a situation I had to rectify.

I was to go and bid our soldiers farewell. It was a tradition for the monarchies to wish them luck. As I went down and looked at the army, I knew it was hopeless, these men could never win this war, but I gave a speech about honour and watched the men board the ships and sail away into the distance. My only thought was … *it has begun.* What, I did not know.

Anna Goodchild (13)
Smithdon High School, Hunstanton

The Selchanté

The wind curved through the bay and ruffled the hair on Connla's head. His deep, blue-green eyes were focused on the waves. The waves that brought a myth back and forth every day.

A live Selchanté had not been sighted for almost one hundred and fifty years and because of the stories, more and more people were eager to see one.

Although today only Connla watched the sea, hoping to glimpse the glimmering tail of a Selchanté. A glorious creature with a human's upper body, the tail of a fish, the wings of a butterfly and the voice of an angel. Pale in complexion, long wavy hair, mesmerising violet eyes and a pearly-scaled tail. This creature was a beauty to hold in one's memory forever.

Many times had reflections from birds, ship sails and young maidens been mistaken as a Selchanté. Connla had already been deceived countless times, but there was something different about that shimmer that caught his eye, just by the Okuri caves.

Cautiously climbing down the rocky slope, Connla edged toward the cave and sidled inside.

Perched on a throne of coral was something so beautiful even the sun looked dim. The melody that trickled from her lips was so harmonious that the cave seemed more like a wondrous paradise.

Ending her song, the Selchanté gracefully dived into the depths of another heaven, only deeper blue, with secrets that must remain silent for eternity.

Lauren Thrower (14)
Smithdon High School, Hunstanton

The Sport Express

Adidas Release Top Of The Range Football Boots!

Yesterday, Adidas confirmed reports that they are releasing their new 'super boot'!

The first glances of the boot were revealed last night after their emergency press conference. The boot was set to be released in November but due to rivals 'Nike' releasing their new range of boots, Adidas boot sales have decreased. Nike's new boots feature top quality leather, a new safe stud and a fantastic design.

The Adidas boot aka 'Super Boot', has a super lightweight structure which only weighs 100 grams, but even though it is lightweight, it still has the same top quality protection as the previous Adidas Predator. Adidas have been concentrating hard on making their blades on the boot safe as there has been uproar on safety of the old blades. Cases were taken to the English FA but nothing occurred from it.

The boot also has special soles for different needs as the F50+ boot. But the best part of the boot has to be the microchip! Yes, this is the first ever boot to have a microchip.

It gives you the option of telling you the distance you've run and how fast you've run. You read the data by connecting the boot to your computer.

Lewis Kimber
Smithdon High School, Hunstanton

Road Rage?

A car can't possibly start on its own can it?

The Rogers were on holiday, so it couldn't have been them. But then how and why was smoke scraping itself from the sides of the garage doors as though it were possessed, or was it just my imagination, a statement of the mind?

A menacingly green glow slowly clawed against the doors as it seeped out into the driveway as if daring me to step any closer.

Suddenly what sounded like an engine bellowed, hidden behind the garage doors. It seemed to be trying to escape. From what, I did not know. Were my eyes deceiving me or was the door beginning to bulge slowly outwards?

Quickly as I could, I took a step back, yet it still crept forward demonically. Suddenly there was a loud bang, crack and then a long creaking noise. Everything had stopped; the lights and the engine had gone, slurred to a stop. Whatever it was had suddenly retreated back into the darkness from whence it came. Never to be seen again. That was what I had thought, this was how it had seemed.

Why is nothing ever as simple as it seems?

Oscar Allington (14)
Smithdon High School, Hunstanton

Back To My Past
(An extract)

The room shook. The furniture jerked violently.

After what seemed like an age, the old lady fell back to her seat and regained colour.

'I said I would see her again, didn't I?' the old lady said sarcastically.

'I apologise ... what was said?'

Rhiannon had been visiting Mrs Turner to research one of her ancestors, Miranda Goldman. Rhiannon met Mrs Turner every Wednesday to listen to her stories.

'She said to tell you why she died. She was a medicine woman, she helped people with ailments and would grow plants for medicines. Everyone liked her until a year when rain refused to come. Famine struck the village. When villagers saw her plants still growing they accused her of being a witch and sent for Matthew Hopkins: witch-finder general. In 1646 she was burned alive. An innocent woman.'

Rhiannon mulled it over. 'She was a medicine woman and then she was killed,' Rhiannon muttered.

'Yes,' Mrs Turner replied.

That's when the room began to shake again. It shook much worse, the furniture was vibrating terribly. The old lady began to rise out of her seat ... she was floating! Just as quickly as it began, it stopped. Rhiannon turned to the old woman who slumped back into her chair.

Mrs Turner looked up but her eyes were different; glowing green.

'Mrs Turner ... you alright?' Rhiannon mumbled over her throbbing heart.

'Hello Rhiannon.' The old lady's voice wasn't normal.

'Who are you?' Rhiannon stammered.

'Miranda Goldman!' came a reply ...

Rachel Kennady (14)
Smithdon High School, Hunstanton

A Day In The Life Of …

As I walked down the high street I felt at unease, I felt as though I was being watched, but not by the odd couple of people but the whole street had stopped and stared.

I dived into the nearest shop to escape from those burning eyes. After a few minutes of looking around, I soon left. I made my way down to the latest fashion shop round the corner. On the way I passed weird kids taking pictures of me and asking for my autograph. I waltzed into the shop and grabbed a basket, which was soon whisked away by one of the store's staff. I thought I had done something wrong until he explained he would carry my basket for me. Must have been to promote the new shop, but funnily enough no one else had anyone carrying their baskets for them. Strange.

I went on further through the shop picking up every other item. I heard someone shout.

'Kate.'

I looked up and as I did a gigantic flash zoomed across the room like a camera flash. I kept hearing my name so I turned around but there was no one there except a poster, a poster of me.

Was I famous? Am I famous? I couldn't be. Was it all just a dream, a fabulous dream? Was I really Kate Moss?

Emily Mann (14)
Smithdon High School, Hunstanton

Pies Are In!

A recent study in the modern-day world of celebs has shown that the most craved-after dish is none other than the good old traditional English pie!

A survey was carried out throughout the globe on the most famous and well-known celebrities and it was concluded that 7 out of 10 preferred pie to Thai, Indian or Italian foods.

Stars such as Kylie Minogue and Orlando Bloom confessed that when they are on the road, taking part in tours or promotions, one of the main dishes they crave is pie and chips or apple pie. The legend, Elvis Presley, also had a fetish for pies in the late stages of his life and found it hard to go a couple of days without consuming one.

'My favourite type of pie has got to be chicken pie topped with gravy and with vegetables and chips on the side', said EastEnders' bad boy Nigel Harman, (Dennis Rickman).

This is what the manager of one of London's busiest supermarkets has to say about the recent pie obsession: 'During the last two or three weeks, the pie demand has been so high that we have, on more than one occasion, had to refill the shelf with new stock twice in one day!'

Hotels have had to send employees out on errands to the local food store because guests have been following in the steps of their favourite stars and ordering a vast quantity of pie at mealtimes!

So, to all readers - happy pie eating!

Kelsey Rushton-Large (14)
Smithdon High School, Hunstanton

A Day In The Life Of A Field Vole

'Argh!' squeaked a terrified rodent, running for its life.

The little field vole was frantically running from his archenemy. He narrowly escaped a life or death situation, literally by a whisker, as he managed to scuttle down into his nest. Heart beating, panting, nose twitching, adrenaline pumping through his veins, he shouted, 'Yes, 0.58 seconds past my record!'

This is not a 'usual' vole, as you might have realised. Whilst a 'usual' vole would have probably died of shock from the event that happened at breakfast, Splinter simply nipped down to the stream to meet his friend, Tiger, who was indeed a cat. This to you must sound strange and to other animals this was also a phenomenon. But Splinter was strange and fearless!

'Eeeek,' screamed a screech!

Splinter and Tiger jumped out of their skins and swiftly span around.

'Sounds like a barn owl,' miaowed Tiger.

Curious, they ran over to the direction of the noise. There on the field floor lay the barn owl that had recently hunted Splinter.

'What's happened?' Splinter asked.

'A cat ... my wing,' replied the owl in shock.

Splinter ran off to get a splint.

Tiger secured the splint on to the owl's wing. The owl thanked Splinter and Tiger, and promised to not eat any field voles in the future and managed to fly back to its barn.

Splinter squeaked goodbye to Tiger and ran (eating tea on the way) home to his nest to dream of the records to break tomorrow.

Ellen Witley (13)
Smithdon High School, Hunstanton

A Day In The Life Of Lindsay Lohan

I woke up at 6.30am with the sound of the alarm clock. I had to leave at 7am to go to the shoot of a Coca-Cola advert. My hair and face were a mess, as I got into the car.

Once I'd arrived at the set at 8am, I went to the trailer to have my hair and make-up done. That's one of the best things about being a movie star, you get pampered.

After about an hour I was ready. I looked amazing! The make-up and hair artist were brilliant! Then I had to choose my outfit. There was a whole rail of beautiful clothes and shoes. There were leather, fur and denim items. How could I decide? At 9am my mum and sister turned up. I don't get to see them much because I'm always on the road. They helped me choose an outfit; black leather trousers and a lovely red top.

By 10am I was ready and looked absolutely brilliant! I headed for the photo shoot. I was told what to do, sing, walk, etc. The usual advert. By about 1pm, the shoot was finished.

Mum, my sister and I all went for lunch at McDonald's. It's hard to go out because everyone asks for autographs.

After lunch, I went back to my hotel to relax. I don't get to do that often. At about 7pm I had my tea, then had an early night. The next day was an early one also!

Kelly Mellor (13)
Smithdon High School, Hunstanton

Road Rage

A car doesn't start by itself. Or that's what I thought anyway.

I was standing outside the garage when I heard an engine splutter into life. I then saw ribbons of pitch-black fumes slither out of the cracks around the door. I gagged as the bitter stench reached my nose. Fear started to trickle through me as I saw the gleam of headlights seep towards me like blood. The rusty red garage door pulsated in time with the engine.

I jumped backwards in terror. As the tires screeched, a small dent appeared. As I turned to run, I noticed my brother standing a few feet away.

'What were you looking at?'

I spun round and looked back at the door. I smelt nothing, heard nothing and saw nothing unusual. 'Nothing,' I said without much thought.

I didn't know why I was keeping it to myself, all I knew was that the whole thing had finished as quickly as it had started.

As I stared at the car, something extraordinary happened. The car moved away from the wall and straightened out its bodywork. The remaining blood-red paint spread itself evenly over the surface of the car. The windows webbed themselves back together. The car looked as good as new. On the windscreen appeared another message.

'Honey, I'm home!'

As I turned to leave, I saw out of the corner of my eye the livid headlights turn my way.

Faye Coles (14)
Smithdon High School, Hunstanton

Sunny Express

Ghost Robbery

Ghostly happenings occurred late on Thursday night as £7,000 was stolen from the LDS Bank in Thetford Road ...

On the 15th May, £7,000 was taken from the LDS Bank with no witnesses or suspects.

But the most unusual happening was that when the security cameras were checked, there was no one on them at the time of the robbery!

Bank owner, James Lloyd, was mystified how this could have happened. 'The cameras were, and still are, working perfectly well. I check them every night before I leave. It is impossible how this could have happened'.

James told the police that no doors had been damaged when breaking in, so they are now holding interviews with employees to find out if any of the staff knew the security code to get in.

Everyone is shocked by it all and are now calling it the work of ghostly spirits.

What else could it have been? The doors were opened and the money was stolen, yet there's no trace of any person stepping foot into the building.

We spoke to the head police officer at Linden Station.

'We are taking this matter very seriously and urge anyone who knows anything about this to come forward'.

The bank are now running a further test with their cameras to make sure nothing like this happens again.

Samantha Bromfield (14)
Smithdon High School, Hunstanton

A Day In The Life Of Toby

'Toby! If you don't stop barking now you're going to the pound and I mean it!'

That's what I hear every morning, my mum shouting at our new puppy. However, one thing I never expected was to hear my mum shouting that at me.

It was around 6 o'clock in the morning. That's when (for some strange reason that I cannot explain) I transformed into my dog. I am not going mad, honestly, it really happened. I now know for myself how annoying it is to eat on the kitchen floor.

'Mum, what time is it?' my sister cried, jumping up and down. It was her sixth birthday.

Mum sighed, 'Lucy, you have two hours before your party.'

I jumped on a chair, hoping I wouldn't be noticed.

'Toby, down, you naughty dog.'

Mum pushed me off the chair and threw down a green bowl which contained what looked like brown sludge with bits in it. There was no way I was eating that. I laid on the floor staring at my new breakfast while Mum, Dad and Lucy enjoyed their mouth-watering pancakes.

That's not the only experience I had to live through. Have you ever tried walking? Yes, most of us have, but I bet you weren't tied to a lead. It nearly strangled me and worst of all, Lucy was tugging at it. I pulled at the lead, trying to escape her evil grasp, but it was impossible. I was small; she was big. I knew I couldn't win, so in the end I settled for being led by my sister (how embarrassing).

Anyway, even though I have just been through the worst experience of my life, I am happy because I don't have to live with it, (poor Toby).

Maria Woods (13)
Smithdon High School, Hunstanton

The Sunny Times

120mph Winds End The Perfect Flight

Yesterday afternoon at 4.16pm, 120mph winds caused a horrific accident for a plane heading to Malaysia as the strong winds caused the plane to lose engine power and plummet towards the field below causing a major tragedy.

It was a warm day when the plane, heading to Malaysia, lifted off. Only an hour into the flight the plane ran into 120mph winds. The winds were so horrifically strong that they caused the plane's engines to fail and the plane to plummet towards a sheep field. Three people died in this disaster including the pilot, Alfie Madison, also many people were injured.

The plane was very badly damaged in the crash and the trauma will stay in people's minds for a while. The company which made the plane will be under investigation about why the winds caused the engines to fail and we will find out what happened soon. It appears the winds were just too strong for the plane but if the plane wasn't made to the highest standard there is a chance that the manufacturers will have a fine to pay.

Jennifer Layton was a passenger on the plane when it crashed. This is what she had to say about it. 'The plane plummeting was the scariest thing I have ever witnessed. I felt like the world had ended for me, I am very glad that this situation is over even though the nightmare will stick with me forever'.

Another passenger, Kevin Mort, said, 'Flying to Malaysia was my first ever flight and even though I know it's not very likely to happen again, I don't think I will be going on another plane in the foreseeable future'.

Co-pilot, John Madison, declined to comment about this disaster, as he was upset about losing his brother, the pilot.

Catherine Drewery (14)
Smithdon High School, Hunstanton

No One But You - A Day In The Life Of A Freddie Mercury Fan - 24th November 1991

'Only the good die young' they say.

Oh, how they laughed at us when we queued up for hours to get tickets to Queen's latest gig but nobody was laughing now. Only yesterday, Freddie had announced he was HIV positive; it was almost like he knew he was going to die the next day.

I sat with my brothers and sisters for what seemed like ages before I realised how late it was. None of us were dressed; we'd been sitting in our night clothes all morning, sobbing into each other's comforting embraces.

'The show must go on', as Freddie once famously sang. our lives had to go on; although they were shattered by the death of the most fabulously over-the-top showman we had ever known. His music had touched all of our lives, the touching emotional lyrics of 'Friends Will Be Friends' to the uplifting 'Crazy Little Thing Called Love'; there was something for everybody in the Queen collection.

But now there will be no more new music. As we walked to the house where he lived and died, The Lodge, to pay our respects and lay flowers, we could hear strains of 'A Kind Of Magic'. Some people might think playing music after the death of somebody is disrespectful but with Freddie the song was so fitting, and music was his life, why shouldn't that carry on after his death? We'll move on, find another band to listen to, go to other gigs, but the musical genius of Freddie will live on, I'm sure of it.

Charlotte Ford (13)
Smithdon High School, Hunstanton

A Day In The Life Of Ellen MacArthur

3 o'clock, time to have a snack. I set myself times in the day to keep my energy level high and to keep me awake through the long, exhausting night. I grabbed a high-energy bar from the box and a litre bottle of water to drink. I knew I had to eat it, but I didn't want to force myself for the third time that day.

I strapped the bottle to my belt that Mum gave me, as it was extremely windy and very rough at sea. I couldn't risk losing my precious drinking water overboard. The wind was cold and gave me chills down my back. I could feel the joints in my hands aching and freezing up.

Later I lay down in my bed to keep warm. I eventually fell asleep. I could hear the wind bellowing, beckoning me to wake up. I pulled myself out of bed, food and supplies were on the floor, that's when I heard a massive bang, something huge was hitting the side of the boat. I trailed up onto deck to discover the sail down and the mast broken in half. I went into panic mode, I didn't know what to do, I just stood there. After half a minute I remembered the drills.

It was difficult without anyone else to help me haul the mast upright, but I realised it was going to be like that as I had come on a long journey on my own.

Annaleigh Foreman (13)
Smithdon High School, Hunstanton

Another School Day?

An alarm bell rang in my ear. It was another Monday morning. I rolled out of bed and hit the floor with a crash. I managed to crawl to the bathroom and had a shower. I fumbled around putting my school uniform on and made my way downstairs.

'Morning,' I said to my mum through a giant yawn.

'What are you doing up so early?' she questioned. 'And what are you doing in your uniform?'

'Don't ask silly questions, Mum!' I replied as I walked out of the door with a slice of toast.

What had got into her? I thought to myself. She probably thought it was a Saturday or Sunday or something.

I went out of the gate and headed down the road to begin my usual journey to school. It seemed unusually quiet. Maybe I was early. My mum did say that I was up early. I headed for the local corner shop to get my supply of sweets to help me survive the immensely boring day at school.

'Hi there, Barry. What are you doing up so early? I thought you would be having a lie-in,' said the shopkeeper, Mr Howard.

'Why would I have a lie-in? I'm off to school,' I told him.

'Ahhh, right, extra revision, okay, see you later, Barry.'

'Bye.'

Extra revision? What was he talking about? He was probably losing it in his old age.

I went around the corner to enter the school gates. The playground was empty. I looked at my watch. 8.20. I was on time. Then my heart sank, it was Saturday!

Callum Lawrence (14)
Smithdon High School, Hunstanton

24-Hour Le Mans

After completing the Le Mans with a finishing place of second, John Harrows and Peter Gildsing give their account of the race - 24 hours on the harrowing 8.5 mile course.

Words: John Townsend

JT: So gentlemen, I'm astounded - an excellent race - could you both give us an idea of the track and conditions?

JH: Ah, well ... hmm ... it's an 8.5 mile circuit with every twist, turn and hairpin you could possibly imagine - and with over 20 other cars on track it doesn't help.

PG: Conditions were a bit hairy with the track being wet 70% of the time, but with rain tyres on it wasn't too difficult.

JT: Crikey! And what speeds were you travelling at?

JH: Well along the back straights we could get the car up to 230mph or more -

PG: And we averaged at about 145.

JT: Amazing, and you were racing for Maserati - could you give us a bit of info on your wheels?

JH: Well, the 3200 GT is a fast car in road form - 180mph tops - but the souped-up model we were driving is powerful to say the least. It has a massive V8 engine delivering a wacko 712bhp at 7,500 revs. It can do 0-60 in 3.5 seconds and will bomb all the way up to 240mph.

PG: You can feel the G-force kicking in as you leave the pits in a cloud of tyre smoke.

JT: That's quite a nice car. Were you involved in any nasty shunts?

PG: Nothing apart from the occasional graze - but number 17 Ferrari managed to plough through a barrier at 150mph!

JT: Was he hurt?

JH: Paralysed from the neck down, but they say he will pull through.

JT: Ouch. Have you any advice for the beginners out there?

JH: Yeah - always wear your seatbelt.

PG: Your life comes first.

JT: Thanks for your time lads. I hope Maserati win next time.

JH: Cheers.

PG: Thanks.

Fred Marsh-Allen (14)
Smithdon High School, Hunstanton

Guitar Star

About four years ago I would say. That's how long I've been playing guitar for, but I never thought of it as a career until now. I thought of it as a hobby more than anything else.

My first guitar was a cherry-red encore electric. I have still got it today along with my steel string acoustic and black cruiser electric. I got my first one about four years ago for Christmas; I played it and played it, but I didn't get any better, so Mum and Dad said I could have lessons.

My guitar teacher was called Darcy he was American and a little weird but he did teach me how to play guitar. After a year and a half I found myself learning the same stuff over and over again, so I quit. I decided to teach myself to play guitar. I know it sounds weird but it is possible. If you've got the right mentality you can.

Last year I had a great time and a rough time which in its own way gave me loads of inspiration for songs to write; even though I had never tried it before. I thought it might help. It didn't but I made a great song out of it and have the opportunity to record it. I can't sing that well but who cares as long as I can record it and it sounds good.

I think stepping back and taking a look at what you have done right and wrong in your life is the best form of inspiration a person can get. I think everyone knows what they want to do when they get older; but they think it's just a dream and will never happen. Well it's not if you get off your backside and do something that revolves around what you want to do. If you want it so badly, go to the dream because it isn't going to come to you. I'm going to record my song and see if I can reach my dream and you should too.

Jenna Hussey (13)
Smithdon High School, Hunstanton

The Possessed Car

A car doesn't start by itself, or does it? The first thing I noticed was the spluttering noise of a leaky engine coming to life. Plumes of thick smoke poured from under the garage door and made me choke. The doors shook with the engine's vibrations. More smoke glided out of the garage, making it difficult to see. The gleam of the headlights sliced through the fumes like a knife. I heard a crashing as paint tins fell to the ground as the car reversed. Suddenly the engine stopped, leaving deadly silence. Looking round I saw Sam walking towards me.

Two days later my excuse for a brother called down to me from upstairs.

'Go and fetch my footie will you?'

Turning around, I strode over to the garage. Reluctantly I pulled the doors open and that was when I saw it. The car's radiator grille looked like bared teeth and the headlights flashed as if daring me to come closer. I could see the football on the back seat; my trembling hands grasped the handle.

I grabbed the football and heard the locks click down with a metallic thud. The snaky seatbelt snapped into place. The handbrake eased off and I saw the gearstick manoeuvre into first. The car shot forward out of the garage and raced off down a busy road. Full-blast funeral music came on as the car swerved down a country lane.

I smashed the window and jumped out just in time to see the car hurtle into a ditch.

Matthew Kemp (13)
Smithdon High School, Hunstanton

The Death Of Achilles

Soundlessly, Paris crept through the Trojan groves. Sword raised. Leather sandals barely disturbing the tall grass. He could smell the musty aroma of the olives and could hear the quiet mumbling of talking. His heart filled with hatred as he recognised the voice of his sister, Polyxena, and the baritone of his nemesis.

He fumbled for an arrow and placed it to his bow, drawing the hemp cord back towards his ear. The muscles in his back and shoulders strained with the effort it took to keep the yew weapon trembling in readiness.

He hesitated. Every arrow that had ever hit this warrior lying vulnerable before him had been deflected. Every blow dodged. Every cut had left no mark. Achilles was invincible.

Despairing, Paris lowered his bow, he could not hurt this son of a goddess. He sat back and let the wind tug idly at his clothes.

The couple were chatting idly.

'Why don't you have any scars?' Polyxena suddenly asked.

Paris couldn't believe his luck.

'I'm invincible,' Achilles whispered, 'except ...'

Paris leaned forward.

'For my heel ...'

Triumphant, Paris drew his bow. His arrow flew like a dove released from a cage, it arced and soared. Like a swallow it dipped and dived to the ground.

In the heavens, great war god Apollo saw the imminent miss and so, tired of fighting, snatched the arrow and plunged it into Achilles' heel.

Below Achilles felt only surprise as the poison seeped through his body and stole his life.

Alex Hayes (14)
Thomas Mills High School, Woodbridge

A Snail Tale

I'm just a simple snail. I come and go not much to say. Sometimes I eat the green vegetables that grow in the garden, or snooze inside my shell, hoping that I won't be bashed in with a rock. Humans do that, you know. And then they throw you over the garden wall with a *whoooosh!* hoping you may smash some more.

I'd be the first to admit I'm a simple snail. Once, I was nearly eaten by a blackbird, and my whole life flashed before my eyes; snail is born, snail eats, snail potters around the vegetable patch for the rest of life with goals no higher than, 'I'm going to reach that cabbage by Tuesday!'

But this got me thinking. *What if I wasn't a simple snail with small ambition? What if I were a … a human? I could sleep in a warm, cosy bed, visit the sea, play with my friends! Watch television or ride a bike! Imagine that! Going faster than 0.001mph for a change.*

But then I thought, *hey? Who'd want to go to school anyway? Learn maths, history? Who'd want to get a job? Meet deadlines? Have emotions causing you to change what you wear, calculate what you eat, choose who you hang around with? It's all rush, rush, hurry, hurry, do this, do that, never pausing for a moment to think. Hey? Where am I going?*

No, I'd much rather be a simple snail, pottering around my garden … *munch.*

Rebecca Walker (14)
Thomas Mills High School, Woodbridge

A Day In The Life Of A Mother

My little girl was killed today ... shot ... for what? For being in the wrong place at the wrong time. Five years old, barely a child, she wasn't to know ...

I sent her to market with her brother this morning. She was smiling. I stayed home to clean the house.

Three months ago, our country was taken by foreign soldiers - 'liberators' - but things could not get any worse. Looters, riots - we try to fight back but they shoot us down, call us terrorists. It's our country! But my girl, she didn't understand. Locked in the house for weeks, a prisoner of my fear, she needed to escape, just for a while.

So I let her go ...

There was a car bomb, my son tells me. Chaos ... we lost each other ... then the shooting started. She was scared and hurt and helpless - she ran straight into a gunfight.

Her brother carried her to me, her lips pale, her lifeless eyes damp, like my cheeks, with tears, her skin stained with blood and dirt.

I cradled her, fell to my knees ... clung onto her, my baby, my little baby ... just five years old ... barely a child ... is this my fault?

Who will lose a loved one tomorrow? They say they are here to help, but how can I forgive the soldier ... American, British, I'll never know ... who gunned my little girl down?

I'll bury her tomorrow in her home; in the Iraqi soil she was born on ... how can I ever forgive him?

Hannah Gillott (16)
Thomas Mills High School, Woodbridge

The Hinton Diamonds

Detective Inspector Grouse strode through the double doors, pushing them with such force that they slammed against the walls and swung back at him. Too late. They didn't hit him. He was already halfway through the office when it started. The shouting, the screaming, couldn't they do anything on their own?

'Sir, we've got a lead on those fingerprints.'

'Sir, your wife has called, she wants you home by seven tonight.'

'Mr Smith wants to see you.'

It was the people in the office. They were always talking, never working.

He slumped down on his chair in his office. The soft, cold leather felt refreshing on the clammy arms of the detective. It was quiet in his office, a tranquil place; you could just make out the soft hum, like a bee, from the office staff. He looked down onto his desk; the new case had been placed above the stack of others.

The Hinton diamonds had been stolen last Friday night. They were out at a party when it happened, no one saw anything. The only reason they were being put at the top of the pile was because of the amount of money. Detective Inspector Grouse hated people like that.

Inspector Grouse was a short man, though he was rather chubby. He had a thick, brown mass of hair above his lip. It was almost suffocating it. The new work experience students had even given it a name. That's another thing the inspector hated - teenagers. They were always drunk and extremely rude to the older generation. He was also bald on the top of his head. He just said that it was thinning, but it shone so brightly, that's the thing you noticed about him first. That and his facial hair.

The peace was destroyed.

People were knocking on the door, but it was one person in particular. Johnson. He was Grouse's partner. They were completely different. He was loud, cheerful, friendly, everything that the inspector wasn't. He let him in and it started. It didn't look like he was going to be home by seven.

Aimee Plumridge (14)
Walton Community School, Peterborough

Get On With It!

He did not know what to write about for his English homework, which had to be in on Monday and it was half-seven on Sunday evening. His mum was yelling at him to 'get on with it' but his sister was watching television, which was a major distraction.

His mum turned it off and bellowed, 'Get on with it!'

He had run out of excuses not to do his homework, but unluckily he had run out of ideas on what to write about. His mind had gone completely blank. He started to really, really stretch his sentences out about his homework in which he had to write two hundred and fifty words. (At this point he kept counting how much he had left.) His stomach hurt because he was hungry so he got up to get an apple. None of these distractions worked, so he simply gave up, watched television and then went to bed. The lesson being - never give up unless it's half-eight!

Thomas Seager (12)
Walton Community School, Peterborough

The Far Future In The Past

Once, millions of years ago, there was a race of people living on Earth in peace and harmony with all the types of aliens you could dream of. They had all the gadgets like robots and other amazing gizmos that people dream of having in the distant future. They had spaceships and flying cars and an almighty senate.

However, there is always an evil dark lord who wants to rule the world and mould it to their form. This evil lord was called Dr Dinos who, as his name suggests, was a scientist and in charge of Earth's droid armies. But, where there's evil, there's always a good side with better skills and weapons like laser swords that could shoot electricity or charge up to shoot a captive net. These soldiers were called Ninten knights who had mastered special powers from within them called 'the sense'.

Dr Dinos had a perfect plot which, if he did not get his way, could start universal war. His plot; he would create monsters that could survive any weapon except natural disasters, like comets or volcanoes erupting, by mixing certain lizards and other animals together to create what he called 'dinosaurs' which were mighty and powerful creatures. They would be bred for only one reason - to overwhelm the Ninten knights.

Soon, Dr Dinos had found a way to create a number of types of dinosaurs, each one more powerful and terrifying than the others. Soon he had made enough to take over the planet with. Especially with his droid army behind him creating more by the day.

Soon he revealed his plot to the Ninten knights, giving them one chance to join him with ten dinosaurs behind him and thousands of droids as well. The Ninten knights refused the offer and the army attacked. The Ninten knights had no chance They put up a good fight but none prevailed. Many of the knights were on missions somewhere in the galaxy and Dr Dinos would deal with them later.

However, he did not get his real target of the Ninten master, Mardo, who was the most powerful knight in the whole universe and could train more knights. His plan was going perfectly.

Next he went to the senate and revealed his plan but the lights and loud noises had made the dinosaurs go crazy. They wrecked everything then stormed to destroy all of the cities. Mardo heard this and contacted some people he knew that had bombs, he told them to fire at the planet.

A giant rocket came down from the sky and destroyed all the buildings and everything else except for the dinosaurs.

Finally, when the dust settled, it was a paradise of green and blue, perfect for the dinosaurs to reproduce and live peacefully, except when the meat eaters were hungry! It would be a paradise for the next million years until an earthquake, volcano or meteor came to wipe them out.

The surviving knights kept training more knights, hidden somewhere in the world until evil lurked its head again.

Bryan Hoadley (12)
Walton Community School, Peterborough

Jewel's Adventure

A long time ago, there lived a rich king and his daughters, Emerald and Jewel. They often received gifts and had expensive jewellery and paintings, but Jewel's favourite was the mirror her mum had bought her before she'd disappeared. It reminded Jewel of her so it was very precious.

No one knew how her mum had disappeared, but they reckoned it was the work of Oedius, the king's enemy. Everyone was scared of him as there were rumours that he had magical powers. Everyone suspected he was plotting against them as no one had heard of him in a long while. They were right, for something strange was about to happen.

One dark, stormy night, one of the 'guards' sneaked upstairs into Jewel's room. He glanced at Jewel's mirror and had the perfect idea. Then there was an ear-piercing scream ...

When Jewel woke up, Emerald had disappeared completely. She searched everywhere, but there was no sign of her. When Jewel sat down in her room, she looked in her mirror and gasped. For there was her sister's reflection, grinning at her.

'Hi Jewel,' Emerald said.

'But how ...'

'Oedius trapped me in your mirror. He's ruling the kingdom now.' A tone of sadness took over her voice. 'Dad's dead. Oedius killed him.'

'No ... no! Dad's not dead!'

'I'm sorry,' Emerald said.

Tears of anger rolled down Jewel's face.

'But we can find him in here. He's alive in the mirror, but not in the real world. Do you want to come with me?'

'How do I get in the mirror?'

'Just step in slowly and you will get in.'

So she did and they walked off into the distance ...

Heather Garton (12)
Walton Community School, Peterborough

Star Paws
(An extract)

Chapter 1: Cats Of The Galactic Enterprise

On the Death Maw, Darth Tabby and his storm tomcats were plotting a plan. It was against his worst enemy, Doberman Kenobi, from planet Kennel. The plan was to trap the ambassador in the royal embassy.

Then a ship landed on Death Maw. The storm tomcats surrounded it in wonder. With a loud *ching*, Doberman Kenobi and his padworn learner, Luke Skybarker, attacked the storm tomcats but one got away. The one that got away went and told Darth Tabby who said to himself, 'Maybe we can get him without the plan?'

Chapter 2: The Day Of War

This is the day, the day that Luke Skybarker had been dreading for months - four months to be exact. He had seen them as nightmares in his dreams. The war would be the thing that killed his most loved one and to him that was his sister, Lela Skybarker …

Ashley Mulbregt (12)
Walton Community School, Peterborough

Iolanthe

Her hair was dark, so dark it shone almost blue when it caught the sunlight. Her face was pale and elegant, with stunningly high cheekbones. We all expected her stare to be dark too, but the eyes set into that perfect face were the brightest blue we had ever seen. Her stare cut into you like a laser beam and left you reeling. As she walked across the yard, hundreds of pairs of eyes and whispers followed her. Her blouse wasn't white, like the rest of us. Hers was ebony, turned up at the sleeves and tight. On most it would have looked like they were trying too hard, but this girl was like a queen, and instantly we were all her subjects.

She didn't wear a blazer or a tie, but no one noticed. It was her skirt our eyes were all drawn to. Long and black, it combed the floor as she walked. It looked to be made of sea foam, or cobwebs, the way it moved and swept around her like a cloud of bats. She would sit at the back of every classroom, her face blanketed under her hair. It was only in the yard we saw her, always walking from place to place.

Some said she was a witch, others claimed she was a vampire. I simply believed she was lost in herself and walked constantly to find the path to lead her back to reality. Iolanthe.

Hannah Lewis (13)
Walton Community School, Peterborough

Eminem

I am going to take you through the things that people seem to miss when talking about the controversial rapper, Eminem. From 1997 when Eminem became a household name, after coming second place in the rap Olympics, he was said to be a racist, homophobic person who hated everyone. The reason for this was that his lyrics displayed uncontrollable anger and a traumatised life!

His whole life has been a roller coaster with the troubles of having two daughters and not making ends meet, and a wife that was a crack addict. I think the main things that annoy Eminem and his fans are that if he says he's going to kill his wife with a rifle, haters automatically believe him, but if you see some film with Arnie in it shooting everyone, no one thinks that he's actually going to do it, so why is it one rule for Em and another for everyone else?

I think another thing that antagonises him is that even though he has been accepted into the rap culture, the freest part of the rap (battling) is now getting too dangerous. I quote, 'I ain't tryna have none of my people hurt and murdered'. He is talking about the dangers of battling and how there's no point with rap as the lyrics just get escalated.

His rapping career may have affected his daughters nearly as much as it affected him. While he was away rapping with Dre, his daughters were at home with his drugged-up wife or had a nanny looking after them. He has one daughter and one that was his niece, but he adopted her and she is now his daughter. Eminem also had to explain to his daughters that his wife (their mother) had run off and was hiding from the police. As he is not the best talker, he wrote a song about it called 'Mockingbird'.

Eminem has beef with many people but these were not his fault. The most famous beef he has is with Ray Benzino, who is part owner of 'The Source Magazine'. What happened was that Eminem was releasing music and Benzino was writing reviews, then he wrote loads of harsh reviews and made diss songs, so Eminem came back with some of the best diss songs he's made yet - 'Nail In The Coffin'!

The reason I have written about different parts of Eminem's life is because I want people to see that he is not a gay hater (proven by the fact that he's sung with Elton John) and that he is a loving, caring father. I do not see why people can't see the real Marshall for what he is - a great rapper who came from the streets to the big time.

Callum Westbrook (13)
Walton Community School, Peterborough

Dear Diary

Dear Diary,

Today I bombed half of Berlin. It wasn't a pretty sight, but Hitler deserved it - he had taken over Poland and bombed London. The Blitz has got worse. Hitler dropped three butterfly bombs on London today and then one ordinary bomb on us as well. My cousin died saving his country in the First World War, I will do the same for mine.

The people were very worried today. I know they are already scared but this is probably made them doubly scared with 16 air raids in one day, I was pretty frightened myself and I am meant to be saving them.

I took my wife to buy some sewing things down at the shops. Everyone kept hassling me in the shops. They were asking why we had gas masks and when we'd finish the war, but I couldn't tell them.

My uncle died today. Hitler got him and poisoned him. He put my auntie in a playhouse, but my cousins are safe in Australia and I have to write to them tonight to tell them.

I am flying over to America tomorrow to speak to the President about how we are to attack Hitler in a way he won't suspect. When we go to America we will be going to the White House and then going to the beach to compare how bad they are getting hit. But now I have to see my people at a conference.

Goodbye.

Lots of love, Winston.

Saskia Bailey (12)
Walton Community School, Peterborough

That One Thing

'It almost killed me!' Amy said, as she scrambled to her feet.

Amy Smith and her best friend, Claire, had found a tired, derelict, old house by the South Bank River near where they lived. They were both fifteen years old and didn't really fit in at school for various reasons, though they both did extremely well. They'd both known each other from the age of one and a half and neither of them had really got to know their parents. Both of their parents mysteriously disappeared without a trace, after returning from a meal in Liverpool.

'I can't believe that beast almost had you, Amy!' exclaimed Claire, as they sprinted as fast as they could from the rundown house.

'I know, I was petrified. I honestly didn't think that I was going to make it out -' Amy stopped dead at mid-sentence in disbelief. 'Well, you know, out alive.'

Claire and Amy both lived at the same children's home in South London and had many fun times and adventures with the other orphans. Though one thing they both did was to pray for their parents who they believed to be 'up above'.

Claire and Amy still worry to this day that the beast that almost 'had' Amy three years ago was still in that same derelict, rundown, old and tatty house!

It was now the year 2005 and life at St Catherine's Children's Home (orphanage), South London, was normal - that was bar one huge thing that had changed for good.

Things would never be the same between Amy and Claire. This one thing had destroyed both of their lives. It was highly unlikely that they would even look each other in the eye again. This one event that could never be undone, this one treacherous thing that had ruined one of the closest friendships ever to have been formed ...

Victoria Morland (13)
Walton Community School, Peterborough

Loch Ness Monster On The River Thames

Have you ever been to Scotland? Ever thought you've seen something called the Loch Ness Monster? Think again. The real 'Nessie' is to be found, not in Scotland, oh no, it's on the River Thames.

A young boy, Bruce, and his dad were on a fishing trip on a warm, summer's evening upon the River Thames. Bruce's dad had just gone into the tent to fetch some more bait. Meanwhile, outside, Bruce was just about to cast his rod out when something caught his eye. Something *big* had caught his eye! Bruce called to his dad. He came sprinting out, thinking his son had caught a 'monster'. Well he'd done just that. Bruce and his dad stared in amazement as this 'monster' had just yanked Bruce's rod out of his hand, gobbling it up. The creature was horrible, it was green, rough-skinned, yet slithery. This gigantic 'sea snake' swam off, cool and unbothered, slowly sinking down as a submarine would do in an ocean.

Many years had passed and there had been many more sightings of this 'beast'. It was on the TV and papers but no live footage of it existed. Although all this happened, many people still think it's a 'fairy tale' including Bruce's mother.

Alfie Bell (13)
Walton Community School, Peterborough

A Day In The Life Of ...

Dear Diary,

We are in the bomb shelter again, we can hear the planes that drop the dreaded bombs soaring over our heads. Every time one of the bombs crashes into the battered London streets, the dust falls off the ceiling. This little shelter can't last much longer.

Mum screamed at us to get under the table. I think she was more scared than we were. There was an explosion so loud it shook the walls around us. The ceiling shook and dust fell in huge amounts, then it went deadly silent. Edward, my little brother, started crying as another large bang exploded almost directly above our heads.

Edward was very quiet when he asked Mum if we were going to get out of this war alive. I hate him, I wish he would shut up saying these things. His words are always there in my mind, they make me think of all those things I want to say to different people I may never get to do it, I may never get to say sorry for all the bad things I have said and done.

Mum asked what was on my mind, I stared at her face. Her lips were trembling. She acted so strong but I could see that if I did say anything that had just been racing through my head, she would crack and I couldn't look after Edward on my own.

'I'm fine, Mum,' I said with the most sincere smile I could manage.

Mum smiled back and picked up Edward and put him into bed and tucked him in.

Mum cries at night, I hear her when I'm in bed. I hate this war, I wish it would stop. I want my dad to come home, I want us to be a normal family again!

Goodnight Diary, I'll try and sleep. No doubt I won't. I might have something better to write tomorrow.

Jade Wheeler (12)
Walton Community School, Peterborough

Suicide Match

Clyde Connelly dead. The best team still won. The best goalkeeper took racist comments. The best manager helped them win it.

With Lazio taking the first goal could Harchester get back? They could as in the 60th minute Curtis Alexander hit back at Lazio with an amazing goal. However, something ruined this chance for Harchester United. Something came flying in from the crowd. A coin was lobbed at Woods (44) - the game was abandoned with 15 minutes to go as missiles were thrown in from the crowd.

The UEFA took this into consideration and started an investigation, it took 3 days until Woods made an emotional appeal to UEFA to replay the match. The match was replayed yesterday under closed doors. The pubs were full as Lazio went into the lead before Harchester made a comeback with 2 goals, 1 from Andrews and 1 from Alexander. The pubs went mental and Harchester, with only a handful of people watching, went through to the next round.

Matthew Andrews (13)
Walton Community School, Peterborough

A Day In The Life Of Chyna Bonham

My alarm usually wakes me up about 7am, constantly beeping at me until I finally move to press the snooze for another 5 minutes.

I missed my mum at first, but I suppose it was worth it! After all, I got to live like a star, until the football trials came to the horizon. The most exciting change happened. I went to the trials to see if I would become the next Rachel Yankey for England or to follow my dream and play for the mighty Reds, Manchester United ladies' side.

The first thing I have to do in the morning now is go for a 3 mile run which completely drains me of all my energy. Then I lift weights for 45 minutes. After all that I have my breakfast, all before 7am prompt. As you might know, I did make it in the trials and with flying colours as well. Scouts from all over the country were interested but I went with instinct and chose Manchester United. As a result I have been very lucky to be chosen to play for England Ladies.

My favourite part of the day is training - it's wicked. I drive to the training centre at Carrington in my black Bentley GT which my sponsor - Perkins Engines - has generously provided me with as I'm representing Peterborough. Training lasts two and a half hours and after that I have to go to a regular health spar to cool down from all the hard work. This brings me to about 12pm in my day, so I sit down and have my lunch, usually with my sister who is a beautician, that my manager makes that whole squad eat. Then I usually do my daily shop at Tesco. This takes me to when I just mess around by having a kick around and watching TV. Then it comes to bedtime where I settle down and finally fall asleep.

My favourite memory is the first game. It was the best! But there was one letdown; my best friend from primary school was in the line for the opposition! I was amazed, in fact, very. This is what pushed me to the limit to try and score. Luckily enough I did score in extra time with minutes to spare and that's what won us the game. A lucky shot from the 18-yard box and boom! A 1-0 win against our greatest rivals. I was later named player of the match! This was definitely my best game!

Chyna Bonham (12)
Walton Community School, Peterborough

Prison Breakout!

Yesterday evening, a gunman, Nigel Harrods, broke out of the newly built prison in London.

Sighting

The police need to know if there are any sightings of him. He has brown hair with a moustache and doesn't speak very good English. He was wearing grey tracksuit bottoms with a black top with holes in. People need to be aware of this problem. The police are out on the streets of London looking for the mad criminal.

Safety

Police say that citizens in London, mostly in Trafalgar Square, need to avoid going out on the streets, especially with children. The council advise people to lock all the doors and windows when at home. Please do not be scared about this, this is just for citizens' safety.

A woman has phoned up and said that she had seen a possible sighting of the gun criminal. This is what she said: 'I saw a man going mental, wearing the clothes that have been described; when I saw this man I got very worried and rushed home though I could see the rotten man from my bedroom window'.

Punishment

When the mad criminal is found he will be sent back to prison immediately. The police will carry on searching. So until further notice, be very careful!

Georgia Cavender (12)
Walton Community School, Peterborough

Robbery Of Chelsea's Star Frank Lampard

In the early hours of Wednesday morning Chelsea's player and Barclays' Premiership Player of the Year's house was robbed by vicious villains. The football star and his pregnant fiancée were in bed while the robbery took place.

Asleep

A computer, a television and two of his luxury cars were taken, also four of his windows were smashed. These were Frank's words: 'If anyone has any information about my cars and possessions please contact your local police'.

Police Constable Morinio had this to say: 'I can only say the words that Frank has said, but if anyone comes forward and gives us any information, they will get a reward'.

Worried

Frank will be appearing in training soon but obviously not in one of his luxury cars. The Chelsea star is very worried that someone has been in his house and that they could come again.

Chris Ogden (12)
Walton Community School, Peterborough

The Scream

Long, long ago, not knowing precisely how many years, there lived a girl called Meenakshi, but her friends called her Mina. Mina was a very beautiful girl; she had long, brown wavy hair, hazel eyes, fair skin and rosy-red lips. Her life was perfect in every way but she had a deep, dark secret that only she knew about.

It all started one summer's evening when her parents went out to the village ball. They had just gone when somebody knocked on the door. Meenakshi went to answer it and there stood her cousin Vijay. She was pleased to see him but something was wrong. He was looking at her in a cold but weird way.

He casually stepped forward and grabbed her hair with all his might and said, 'You are so proud of your beauty and I am going to take it away from you.' Just then he let go of her hair, whispering something under his breath and walked out.

Mina was still shocked about the pain he caused her by pulling her hair. She started to wonder why Vijay had behaved like this and what exactly had he muttered under his breath before he left. Suddenly Mina heard her own name and there stood her mum all worried. Mina rushed to her and asked her what the matter was. Her mum told her that Vijay had killed himself.

A few years later on Mina's 16th birthday she was walking on the bridge when she thought she saw a bald person behind her. When she looked in the water she saw that it was really her. She was bald and so ugly. Where had her beauty gone?

Just then she heard a deep, loud voice from behind her. It sounded like Vijay's but how could it be? He had passed away a few years back.

Suddenly she realised that it was a curse by her cousin.

All at once with no warning the sky started to bleed, she heard a scream and then it started to echo in her mind. The river started to flood and splashed freezing cold water on to her feet. Mina heard her evil cousin's voice for real this time, she looked up into the bleeding sky and saw his face; he was cackling like mad and shrieked, 'I said I would take away your beauty and now I have, taken it away.'

And that's when Mina screamed!

Sonia Ferdous (12)
Walton Community School, Peterborough

Vamphalla

Vamphalla is said to be where a vampire goes when they need to feast on human blood. Legend has it if you go in there living and breathing, you come out undead, or not at all. If a vampire goes there without a human to feast on, they are reaching the end of their life span, unless however, they have managed to find the key to true immortality, in which case they go there for a special visit or to warn other vampires who are likely to give their secret away.

Even though people know that they might get killed if they go to Vamphalla, they go there because there is a slight chance they will come out again, but undead. This means that they can live for a few hundred years more, or they could live forever.

In Vamphalla vampires rule by order of how long that they have been undead. If anyone challenges this authority they get killed. Once in Vamphalla (so legend has it) a young boy of 8 once found the place by following his heart and wandering wherever he wanted to go.

He now stands as one of the most powerful vampires of all time. He is the vampire that lays the rules out, it's as simple as that from where he stands. He must have discovered true immortality because he's been alive for almost 25 thousand years ...

Hayley Clark (12)
Walton Community School, Peterborough

The Castle

One day me, Mark and Amy went on a school trip. Everyone piled off the coach and walked to the door. Then the guide, who was standing there said, 'My name is Ali, before we go I have to warn you there are ghosts, they were knights who fought over a girl. One night one kissed her, the next day he was never seen again.'

We were walking around the castle and then we looked for Mark but he was not there, so we went to find him.

Meanwhile Mark had found a ghost and he was following it around, then he lost it. We found him looking around for something.

'What are you doing?'

'Looking for a ghost,' said Mark, then he ran away. He bumped into a wall …

'Mark, where are you?' said Amy.

'Down here,' shouted Mark.

We walked down the stairs, it was very dusty and we couldn't see him.

When the dust cleared, Amy cried, 'There is a body!'

Mark was leaning against it and there was a letter. Mark opened the letter and read, 'I will get you'. We ran out of there and ran to find the guide.

Everyone was on the coach.

'Mark, Amy, Lucy, get on the coach,' said the teacher.

'In a minute.'

'Was that true what you said about the ghost?' they asked Ali.

He winked.

'Come on,' said the teacher.

We started to walk and as we looked back the guide had gone …

Laura Cliffe (14)
Walton Community School, Peterborough

Black Magic

I looked up to the sky then back again. The sky was swirling with black and grey clouds, white flashes reached out towards me every minute and every minute the flashes became bigger and brighter. I looked as it, restraining my gaze from the evermore violent sky. It lay there motionless. What was it? Fear and confusion argued angrily inside me. It was too much emotion to handle. I froze. A wild crack followed by cackling witches' laughter interrupted my thoughts.

The only tree for miles, which looked dead anyway, had caught fire. It wasn't just me it had woken up though, the black veil that had surrounded him (which I now know was human and a boy the whole time) lifted, which was soon replaced by a dull white glow but within minutes became a blinding white light snatching him from view. I stood there once again frozen.

I hadn't asked to be here. I wouldn't be here at all if it were up to me. When I was 10 I started having weird dreams about me being in different places with a book in my hand and the wind blowing my black hair in my face but I just stood there looking. The book's cover was made from black velvet with strange silver patterns covering it, it was like flower vines without the flowers, the sky was covered by a tremendous storm, a flash of lightning struck behind me and I woke.

Those dreams went on for years and now that I stand here six years later, with my book of black magic in hand, the mess I have created all around me, I know what those dreams meant. The flash of lightning was the boy who came out of nowhere; I am at the end of my dream, I finally know what will happen next …

Jessica Scully (12)
West Hatch High School, Chigwell

Nasty Neighbours

This lesson was going on forever; each minute seemed like an eternity. Mr Scott was standing at the front of the class, scribbling down words on a whiteboard, long words which I was too tired to make out. My eyes focused on my watch - *tick-tock, tick-tock.* At long last the bell went. I jumped out of my seat and headed towards the pegs to confirm our after school arrangements with my friend Rosie. 'My house at five then,' I smiled.

'See ya,' she replied, in a sweet tone.

As I opened the house door I found a note on the side. It read: 'Had to go to work, food in microwave'. I helped myself to the pasta Mum had left me soon to find another note that read: 'Help me'. Why would my mum need help? Was she in serious danger or was this just a sick joke? Thoughts rushed through my mind ... horrible thoughts.

Just then I received a text from Rosie. 'Sorry can't come round 2nite, neighbour's birthday party, bye!' I kept reading the text. Why were there exclamation marks on bye? Suddenly the word 'neighbours' popped into my mind. That was it. My tiredness was swamped away by a sense of adventure.

I climbed over my neighbour's fence and saw a figure up ahead. It was Mum. She looked shocked. I grabbed her hand and led her back home. Together we phoned the police and told them how our nasty neighbours had threatened my mum to try and get the number to our safe. It was amazing how such an ordinary day turned out to be life-threatening.

Safoora Safaei-Keshtgar (12)
West Hatch High School, Chigwell

Bubbles' Day Out

I woke up in the morning dreaming about the day ahead. I love going to the fair, especially with my best friend Tom. He's known me since I was just a little bear and we've been friends ever since.

We started the day with some tasty chocolate croissants - they were so delicious. I know for some families a trip to the fair is just an ordinary day out, but for us it is the start of a new adventure. As Tom was getting dressed I was left stationary in the front porch next to an old bunch of wellies. Tom's evil little sister then came in and started swinging me by the legs. *Oh no,* I thought, *last time I had eight stitches.* She then dropped me on my head which was extremely painful.

The journey lasted only ten minutes long. When we arrived we all went to our own separate areas. Mother, who was holding the little brat, reminded us to be back by six and to not get lost. Me and Tom rushed straight to the big dipper - it's our favourite ride. After six rides on the big dipper we went to buy candyfloss and a hot dog. As Tom got to the front of the queue I was scooped up by a pooper scooper. I tried to scream but my mouth was stitched up. The man saw me and put me in lost property. When Tom found me he said, 'I'm never going to lose you again.'

Charlie McCann (12)
West Hatch High School, Chigwell

My Netball Match

The crowd eagerly watches on, cheering our team, jeering at the opposition. I stand proud of my wing attack position.

My heart is thumping in my chest, longing to escape imprisonment. Goosebumps engulf my pale skin as the bitter wind's arms reach out, grabbing and pulling me forward causing me to stagger. The grey clouds don't scatter around the sky but conceal the sweltering sun's rays and the clear blue sky. As I glare at the referee, I turn to see the dull, lifeless ground. One girl kicks a minute stone and sends it zooming forward like a rocket across the surface, skipping and grazing the grey slabs. I turn, the referee clenches her whistle and lifts it to her dry lips, it seems like slow motion to me but that's just my nerves. However, I'm determined to win. The referee forces the whistle into her mouth, her chest inflates as she take a large breath.

Whoo! the whistle blows.

I sprint forward like lightning to the aid of Daniella. She passes the ball, it flies towards me. I leap up into the air gracefully and as elegant as a swan and landed gently on my tiptoes. I look at whom to pass to next.

The pitch seems a blur, the opposition marking all the blue bibs (my team). I struggle to see them. I constantly hear, 'Pass to me, pass to me.'

Thoughts rush around in my head in that split second, questions such as, *who's free? Where shall I pass?*

Abigail Lennard (12)
West Hatch High School, Chigwell

The Watchtower Dream

How long ago had it been? I don't know. I have lost all track of time since it happened. I was only 8 years old when that night came. It was a normal day, nothing different. Then came the evening. I went to sleep and then found myself standing at an entrance of a maze.

Where was I? I looked around and before I could figure out what was happening, something huge was racing after me like the speed of light. The only thing I remember was running. I kept running until I was sure it had gone. I realised what I had to do. It was like a game. I had to run through the maze to the stairs at the end which led to the tower.

I looked around. It was like a weird version of a play area. It had loads of different colours. I was quite near the tower and from then on I was running, thinking all the time, *maybe this is my ticket out of this dream.* I was running past tons of different creatures. I was running up the stairs as quick as I could. I froze. In front of me was a very strange old man. He turned to me. Suddenly flames rose around his staff ready to fire at me, then something hit him. It was one of the strange animals which had made him lose his aim and ended up with him surrounded by fire. I had worked it out. He was the one causing my dreams.

Then from out of the flames I heard a 'Help!' There was no way I was going to help someone that put me through torture. The only thing I heard in the background was, 'You will pay.' Then as he burned the whole place was covered in darkness.

I panicked. I tried to wake up. But I couldn't. I was stuck in a watchtower dream.

Jack Farley (12)
West Hatch High School, Chigwell

Myths And Legends Retold

'Up the stairs, the first door to the left.'

'Thank you Mr Keen.'

Arthur and Elsie climbed up the stairs chatting about their day.

They opened the ancient door and noticed the rocking chair in the corner was swinging with a monotonous rhythm. *That's odd,* Arthur thought as he went down to get the luggage.

Elsie sat on the bed and closed her eyes. Suddenly she was overwhelmed by noises, knocks at the door, a telephone ringing, radio blaring and the rocking chair moving. Elsie was frozen, *I must be dreaming.*

At 11.30pm Elsie and Arthur went to bed.

During the night Elsie jolted out of her sleep. At the end of her bed she saw a dark-haired woman wearing a wedding dress. In the blink of an eye the woman had vanished. Elsie woke Arthur and told him what had happened. 'Oh Elsie, you've been dreaming,' he mumbled.

Next morning Mr Keen asked, 'Did you sleep well? Everything alright?'

'Yes, but my wife had a strange dream. She saw a woman standing in her room,' explained Arthur.

'Was she wearing a wedding dress?' Mr Keen asked.

'Yes,' replied Arthur.

'Oh, she appears every year on that day. Her name was Clara, she died on her wedding day in a terrible fire,' explained Mr Keen.

Arthur walked slowly to the car. 'Well Elsie, I knew you were special, but ghosts!' he blurted.

'What? Oh my!' Elsie sat motionless.

Arthur started the car.

Hannah Sibley (12)
West Hatch High School, Chigwell

A Day In The Life Of Me: Betty The Ragdoll

I'm Betty the ragdoll and you wouldn't like to be me …

My day starts around seven o'clock. Chloe jumps out of bed and grabs for me, pulling my knotty golden hair away from my scalp. She dangles me by my feet and runs into Mum's room. Her deafening cries burst my delicate eardrums but she doesn't know that.

Now it's time for breakfast. Chloe has not got any manners whatsoever. She slurps up her porridge with her hands and I feel the slimy mixture over my smooth pale face.

She laughs at me like I have no feelings. She says to her mummy, 'Betty has sticky stuff on her face but I didn't do it,' and then Mum says the dreaded word 'washing machine'!

Mum grabs me by a lock of my hair and throws me in. The loud clicking of the dial makes water rush out of the roof and the machine starts to fill up with bubbles. Then the monster rotates like a roller coaster. My locks of hair are drenched with soapy water and my mouth is full to the brim with froth. I'm doomed but then it stops, it's over. But wait, Mum grabs me out of the machine and takes me outside into the sunny weather. She clips my hand onto the washing line with a peg. My hand is in such pain but nobody knows how I feel.

Peri Ozkeskin (12)
West Hatch High School, Chigwell

A Day In The Life Of A £5 Note!

So there I was all crumpled up in a random purse. It was quite uncomfortable actually. There were pennies all over me, fighting and squabbling over who would get the most space. I felt quite miserable because one of the pennies was calling me fluffy because my queen had fluffy hair but I didn't really get it because they have the same queen too. So there I was just waiting to be spent. I could just about see through the purse and I could see that we were waiting in a queue. I could smell the chlorine and that's when I realised that we were at a swimming pool, (I was a bit worried though because I had forgotten my bikini). The last thing I knew a giant hand reached in to grab me. I tried to dodge it but it was no good, I was trying to struggle free dangling 3ft from the cold, marble floor and then I was handed into a dry, wrinkly hand and I did not like it one little bit.

I was stuffed into a cash register and I didn't know anyone. Another five pound note was moaning and groaning at me because he said I was squashing him. I mean, I'm not that heavy, am I? I was wishing that I was back with them annoying little pennies, there were still other pennies here but they weren't as annoying.

I had a good look around and did you know that you can tell a lot about a note's personality by the way it looks, but oh well, it's what I'm going top have to go through.

Danielle Woodcock (12)
West Hatch High School, Chigwell

The Haunted School

'What was that?' I gasped.
 'It's probably just a spider, put the lights on.'
 'Ouch!'
 'Now what?' Tom moaned.
 'I've bashed my knee,' I said as I turned the lights on. They flickered on and off. Then I recognised the usual boring classroom in the Victorian building alone the school grounds.

Tom ran to the teacher's desk and opened the top draw. He pulled out a silver yo-yo and did an evil laugh.

Suddenly there was a scream coming from the girls' toilet. I looked at Tom, scared and worried. He was looking at me with a cunning smile and one eyebrow up. I quickly said to him, 'Let's go home, Mum's probably worried.'

He said, 'Exploring time.' He ran into the toilets and he whispered, 'Come on, chicken.'

I followed him. He'd gone. All I could see was a napkin. There was a faint figure crying for help and flooding the toilets. I ran back into the classroom. I wiped the sweat off my head and looked up. The Victorian desks were crawling and chattering towards me. I crouched down.

I opened my eyes. Nurses were wandering around. There was Mum.
 'Where's Tom?' I asked.
 'He's missing.'
 Where did he go? Maybe into another world …

Vriddhi Chopra (11)
West Hatch High School, Chigwell

Animal Shelter Burns Down And Clever Dog Saves Hamsters!

Yesterday a dog saved two hamsters from getting burnt in a fire in an animal shelter!

In Harlow Animal Shelter, a very clever bulldog got two hamsters out of the burning shelter. Dog, Trevor, opened the metal cage which the two hamsters were in with his teeth and carried them out on his back.

Residents living nearby smelt smoke and heard the fire alarm in the shelter. Harold Pane, who lives next door to the animal shelter called the fire brigade straight away.

As soon as the fire fighters got to the shelter, nearly all the animals were out of the building. People around were helping the animals, but a lady got too near to the smoke and had an asthma attack. She is in hospital and is now in a safe condition.

When the fire was put out, the shelter was destroyed. No one knew where the animals would be kept, so the local residents took some of the animals home with them.

Now local schools have been raising money to build a new and improved animals shelter. Hopefully by the end of June 2005, the new animal shelter will be up and running. When the new shelter is done, it'll be named after the brave bulldog, Trevor. So thanks to the residents and schools the animals will be back home shortly.

Emily Green (12)
West Hatch High School, Chigwell

Loch Ness Monster, What Loch Ness Monster?

It is Saturday, the greatest day of the week! I jump out of bed and look out of my window. The loch looks fresh and tranquil. Nothing lives in it, except a few fishes, but they're not going to bite your leg off, are they!

I creep into my mum's bedroom and jump on her, knocking her glass of water over and waking her from her deep sleep. I run into my room and scramble into my jeans, jumper and T-shirt, and make my way down the old oak staircase. I slump into my seat at the table and try to stuff as many Coco Pops into my mouth as possible. I stand up, giving myself indigestion, but it doesn't matter, today's my day for exploring the hills.

'A wee bit of fresh air,' Mum says.

I tumble to the door and out I go into the Scottish hills. I stroll down the path and through the mahogany gate and onto the base of Mount Tabadabu.

An opening in the rock comes upon me and I decide to investigate. It comes through onto the loch, as ever fresh and tranquil, but suddenly I can feel a slight rumble in the ground and I spot two eyes that should belong to a hypnotist. Something about them makes me just suddenly stop in my path. Then a murky green hump appears, just peeking out of the deep blue water. Could my mum's stories possibly be true? Is there a Loch Ness monster?

Amy Cross (12)
West Hatch High School, Chigwell

The Undead Basement

It all started one hot summer's day. James was enjoying a cigarette in the back garden. He had been doing this all day for most of the week. The only other thing he'd done, other than sleeping and smoking, was clean his basement, for all the petrol had leaked out from the boiler. He normally did this just before he went to bed.

It was 11 o'clock, he was still smoking in the back garden, but stayed a bit longer. He lit the last cigarette of the pack and called it a night. After getting ready for bed, he remembered to go down to the basement to clean the petrol. With cigarette in hand, he went down the concrete stairs into the darkness ...

He got down to the bottom and switched on the light switch; it flickered three times then came on. He was still smoking his cigarette when he walked over to the boiler, picked up his brush and bucket of water. He started to mop the floor. Then he dropped his cigarette, and the floor behind him was set alight. The fire was blocking the stairs from him. He shouted and shouted, 'Help me ... help me!'

Some people came, but just stood there; the fire was getting closer. The fire got to him and set his shirt alight. Just before he died, all that the people could hear from him was, 'I'm going to make you pay for this when you come down here.'

Ever since, anyone who has gone down there has died ...

Michael Beswick (12)
West Hatch High School, Chigwell

Mushrooms Attack

It all started in a small town called Elderbrook, in the cottage of Mrs Crimsby, a very quiet woman who didn't come out of her house much. She was only ever seen when she went to pick mushrooms from Sweepstake Forest, which laid on the outskirts of the town.

One day, Mrs Crimsby was out in the woods when she came across three mushrooms; strange-looking mushrooms. They had a shine to them. She walked slowly closer, then she knelt down. They began to glow softly, then brighter. The mushrooms started to grow, they were soon as tall as Mrs Crimsby. They grew arms and legs and facial features. The mushrooms swallowed Mrs Crimsby in one. Some people say they heard her shouting from inside.

The mushrooms charged out of the forest into the village. They ran around in what looked like panic. The villagers were also panicking, running and screaming. The mushrooms by then were eating the café. Some of the villagers ran to the town hall.

As they were quarrelling over what to do, one man stepped up and called out his plan to get rid of the mushrooms. He said, 'The only thing mushrooms don't like is being cooked.'

They all agreed. The villagers ran over to the café as quickly as possible. A man started waving his hands and the mushrooms chased him. He ran towards the forest, which had been set alight by the villagers. The man jumped into a bush and the mushrooms were burnt and shrunk. From then on, they never went into Elderbrook Forest ever again.

Oliver Lumb (12)
West Hatch High School, Chigwell

Them

They were coming to get me. All of them. The whole gang. I turned back to take a quick glance, and they were running towards me. I ran as fast as I could, my feet taking big strides. My arms were trembling like a leaf. I didn't know what to do. I could let out a cry for help, but I couldn't speak, I couldn't breathe. I had to stop running. I searched my pockets, frantically trying to find my asthma pump. It wasn't there. Suddenly, everything went black.

When I woke, I wasn't in the place I would have expected. There were wires, tubes, and I could hear beeping noises sounding continuously. It was the hospital. My mum told me everything was going to be all right. I could see tears in her eyes. Dr Mehal was nice. He said I could go home just after they'd done a few scans, but then he took my mum out of the room and had a 'chat' with her. Dr Mehal took the scans and we were able to go home.

On the way home it was completely silent, only until Mum asked about what had happened. I just said I'd forgotten to take my tablet, but she didn't believe me. After that, she asked about the bruises on my arm. I didn't know what to say. I didn't want to tell her about them. They warned me not to tell anyone. But I had no choice, voices were running through my head. I didn't know what to say …

Haniyyah Anwar (11)
West Hatch High School, Chigwell

Chapter One
(In the style of Jacqueline Wilson)

'Isabelle, honey Mummy's going away for a little while. Not far, just for a breather from us,' Dad explained.

'You mean y-you're breaking up?' I stammered.

'No, well sort of, me and your mum, we've been having a lot of arguments lately, agreed?'

I nodded.

'So we think it's best if we spend some time apart.'

'Who's she gonna live with? How's she gonna afford a house? Dad please, please don't send her away again. She'll be better - I'll be better, I promise. Dad?' I fell to my knees and started crying.

Dad put his hand on my head and said, 'It's for the best, sweetie.' Then he walked away.

'*No! No!* I'm going to live with her. She's my mum! I don't believe you, she's your wife!'

'Issy, come on now, get up. You're not thinking straight.'

'Yes I am! Why do you always turn it around against me, so I'm the mad one? You're the one that kicked your wife out!' I stood up, still crying.

'Shut up, Isabelle. I love your mother very much, but adults sometimes grow apart. Honey, I don't always make you seem mad. Stop talking nonsense. You don't want to live with your mum, you know how she treats you. At least I love you.'

'How can you?' I ran upstairs, into my room and vigorously threw my things into my sports bag and zipped it up.

I raced downstairs again. 'I'm going to live with Mum! Goodbye, Dad!'

He grabbed me by the shoulder …

Georgia Harris-Burdis (12)
West Hatch High School, Chigwell

Mysterious Mystery

Ellie went upstairs and went to her room, otherwise she would be late for school. As she walked up the stairs she heard a strange voice coming from underneath her.

The voice whispered, 'Can you hear me? Come here.'

Ellie walked up the stairs, thinking it was her brother playing tricks.

As Ellie reached her bedroom she turned on the light, it flickered four or five times. She walked quickly into her bathroom to brush her teeth. Suddenly Ellie saw a strange reflection in the mirror. She felt something swish by her. A cold chill shivered up her spine, tickling her neck. Ellie looked in the mirror again. She saw her dark brown, curly hair floating up in the air. 'Argh!' screamed Ellie with terror, her heart was beating faster and faster. She ran as fast as lightning downstairs, checking that her brother wasn't there playing ghostly tricks.

Ellie told her mum all the strange things that had happened. She realised it wasn't her mum, dad or brother. After a while Ellie fell asleep on the sofa. Her dad picked her up and took her to bed.

During the night, Ellie woke up and felt a pair of hands touching her feet. She made a sudden movement and curled up under the blanket. She heard another whisper.

'Don't be scared.'

Ellie peeked through the blanket, something strange appeared. It had hair all over.

'Who is it? Go away. What do you want?'

There was no answer, Ellie was petrified!

Ambika Chopra (12)
West Hatch High School, Chigwell

The Angel's Choice

'Can she get better?' I ask my mum, who has tears dropping down her soft cheeks. I can see my baby sister lying there dying, her pale face like a ghost's. The doctor said I could save her, but then a week later, the whole world stopped. I have it too; the disease running through my veins.

Now they are giving me the decision, to let my baby sister die, or to put my own life at risk.

'What shall I do, Mum?' I whisper, wishing I was someone else.

She turns to look at the baby, then at me. My dad is at work; he can't take it.

Tomorrow comes for me and my sister, thankfully. I look into her cot thinking, *how can I choose?* I hold her soft fingers, they slip through mine. I can hear her soft breathing; I want to cry so much.

That night I have a dream, I see her when she gets older, her friends calling her name, 'Ashley'.

The morning comes and today is the day I have to choose. I walk up to the doctor's desk and say what I have chosen.

Now I'm a ghost watching down on her, seeing her every day, laughing. But at night I talk to her. I know that my decision was right, because she is my sister and always will be.

Shannon Maris (12)
West Hatch High School, Chigwell

The Hand

It was a cold, dark night. Gemma had just left her friend Stacey after a night out. Walking home alone, she thought she saw a shadow behind her. She turned, but no one was there. It happened again and Gemma was feeling frightened. Suddenly, a hard, bony hand touched her shoulder and she screamed ...

The hand covered her mouth as Gemma struggled to get free. She was dragged away into the cold night, with only the bony hand for company.

Gemma had no idea where she was. She had fainted with fright, but was now fully awake. She shivered and tried to open her eyes, but a piece of cloth tied round her head was stopping her. Her hands were tied too, and she began to cry.

Then with a creak from the door, Stacey came rushing in to comfort her, but was stopped by the sound of a gunshot. A bullet inserted itself into Gemma's chest. Standing behind them was the man and his hand held the gun, the gun that had killed Gemma. Stacey called 999, but they were too late. The man had gone and although Gemma was dead, her spirit rose. She wanted revenge, but the only way to get it was to follow her cold-blooded murderer.

The killer thought he saw a shadow move behind him. He turned, but no one was there. It happened again and he started feeling frightened. Suddenly, a ghostly hand touched his shoulder and he screamed ...

Joanna Harris (12)
West Hatch High School, Chigwell

Kylie's Cancer Heartbreak

Yesterday, Kylie Minogue was diagnosed with breast cancer. It is tragic news for all her fans as well as her family. The battle may begin with an exploratory operation after a 'small growth' was found in one of her breasts. Because Kylie is at a young age, only 36, she has a good chance of recovery. The survival rate after five years for women under 39 is 77%.

Her father Ron, 65, overcame prostrate cancer four years ago. Because of this, she has been having regular check-ups.

Dannii, her sister, said, 'The news is very upsetting, but we are all optimistic that everything will be OK'.

Elton John said he sent his best wishes on behalf of the UK.

Kylie, who soared from playing Charlene in Neighbours to worldwide pop stardom, drew immediate sympathy from the showbiz world.

Kylie has had many hits like 'I Should Be So Lucky', 'Can't Get You Out of My Head' and many more.

Pete Waterman, who launched Kylie's pop career in 1988, said, 'I am shocked to hear of this news. My heart goes out to her'.

Kylie met up with Olivia Newton John, who has experienced this condition.

Kylie said, 'I am sorry to disappoint my fans. I was looking forward to bringing the finale of the tour to Glastonbury'.

If you think that you have breast cancer, here are some of the symptoms: A blood-stained discharge from the nipple and breast pain that doesn't disappear after your period.

Rebecca Dymond (11)
West Hatch High School, Chigwell

The Irish Fellas

'Us Irish fellas did get up to some mischief, didn't we?' said Patrick in a mischievous way.

Bob and Patrick (or 'Pat' as Bob liked to call him) had moved from Ireland to live in England, because Ireland was a mess.

'Yeah, they were good times,' said Bob, in his usual dopey way.

Suddenly the door burst open. 'I've come to get a debt paid!' The dark figure growled in an aggressive voice.

'Donny, I didn't know you were alive!' said Pat, in a terrified voice as he shrank with fear.

'Well Pat, I *am* alive!'

Donny was the third 'Irish fella'. He had supposedly died in a violent battle with another tribe. When he 'died', Pat had gone off with Donny's little sister, then they had a fight and she had left him. She was condemned as a witch and burnt. (They said it was her magic that turned Bob and Pat to England.)

'It wasn't our fault, really Don!' whimpered Pat.

It was at this point that everything changed. An arrow came soaring through the air and embedded itself in Donny's back.

'Who in Saviour's name was that?' cried Pat.

'I don't know, but I think *He* had something to do with it!' Bob said, pointing to the sky.

They plucked the arrow out of Donny's back. It had an engraving on it which said, *'Keep Safe'*.

A horse neighed, and they heard a cart rattle off ...

Julius Drake (12)
West Hatch High School, Chigwell

Theseus And The Minotaur

His heart pounding, Theseus crept silently around the corner. His lips were dry and cracked; hair matted and eyes wild with fear and adrenaline. The dark, grimy tunnel reeked of blood, and deep into the shadows of the passage ahead, Theseus heard a hysterical scream, and a roar from what sounded like a giant bull. That must be the Minotaur.

The thread was going to run out soon. He prayed that the lair was near. If it wasn't, Theseus thought he might as well give himself up to the Minotaur now. The dagger his father, King of Crete, had given him, was clutched in his hand. It was stained with dirt, and rusted slightly.

There was another low growl. Theseus froze, pure terror flying through his veins, screaming at him to leave. He might just well have done, if he hadn't have seen a shadow pass by. Any sudden movement and he would be dead. He slowly reached for the wall, so he could feel his way back. His fingers connected with something soft and slimy. Theseus recoiled, stuffing his filthy fingers in his mouth to stifle a scream. His fingers tasted of dirt, sea salt and a mixture of other revolting substances. I can tell you now, these were not the type of delicacies that princes such as Theseus were used to.

Suddenly, there was a low rumble behind his ear. He whipped around and screamed …

Lucy Smith (12)
Woodbridge High School, Woodford Green

Goldilocks And The Three Bears

Once upon a time there were three bears, Daddy Bear, Mummy Bear and Baby Bear.

Each morning, the three bears ate porridge for breakfast, but unfortunately, the best before date on the porridge had gone over, so they had nothing to eat. The bears needed to go looking for food, so Daddy Bear called a taxi and they drove into the city.

When the bears got out, they thought they could smell porridge, so following their noses, they came upon a house where luckily, the front door was open. They entered. In the kitchen on the table were three bowls of porridge. The bears sat down and ate it. It was perfect.

After eating, the bears felt tired and went upstairs to take a nap. They squeezed into Goldilocks' small bed and fell fast asleep.

When Goldilocks returned, she noticed that her porridge had been eaten, so suspecting an intruder, she crept upstairs where she discovered the three bears sleeping. Although she was greatly surprised, she had the sense to get her shotgun from the cupboard.

When the bears woke up, they saw Goldilocks and ran down the stairs and out into the street. They did not stop until they reached the bus station. Mummy Bear checked out the timetable, but the next bus was not due for half an hour.

With Goldilocks still chasing them, they tumbled down onto a railway track, where they were hit by a train.

Aidan Scott (12)
Woodbridge High School, Woodford Green

The Digital World

Once upon a time, there lived a boy named Will Smith. He was an undercover police agent, with blue eyes and black hair. He always wore his lost brother's ring. It was pure gold and had a keyhole. Will didn't know where the key was, but he wanted it.

Will had always looked for adventures and had heard about the digital world, where there were riches beyond your dreams.

Will was on a tough assignment, so he couldn't. He had to catch Eddie Murphy, who had stolen a new science project. Scientists didn't tell what it was, but it was something valuable and small.

One day, Will went home and saw an envelope addressed to him. He opened it and saw a message that Eddie was going to be stealing the 25% gold mummy from San Francisco Museum. Will quickly ran to the museum and saw Eddie run off.

Will jumped on his motorbike and chased him. Will shot Eddie's limo and the wheels got punctured, so Eddie got out and they had a fight.

Suddenly, Will's gun fell on the floor and Eddie had Will cornered. Then before Eddie could shoot, a man killed him.

'Thanks ... whoever you are,' said Will.

'The name's John, John Smith,' the man said.

Then suddenly John looked back and hugged Will, because he had found his lost brother.

They went to the digital world as John had the key and the ring was a portal. They lived happily ever after.

Ballal Chaudery (12)
Woodbridge High School, Woodford Green

Hercules' Fifth Labour

Eurystheus grinned as he thought of the fifth labour he had dreamed up to give to Hercules. Eurystheus had told his nephew to clean out the stables of King Augeus, which was hard enough, but Hercules had to do it in one day. It wouldn't normally be hard, except that King Augeus was well known for having one of the largest herds of cows in Greece, and the stables hadn't been mucked out for at least 20 years! He was sure that this time he had thought of a labour that was truly impossible.

A few miles from the stables of King Augeus, Hercules was having a rest. Instead of just taking a shovel to the stables, Hercules had thought his way through how to do it. Doing it the way Eurystheus expected would not be possible. However, Hercules was going to divert local rivers to do the job for him, by washing away the accumulation of filth. Doing it this way was difficult but, for him, it was easier than the usual way.

As he went back to work, Hercules imagined what Eurystheus would say when he returned, having managed the labour. He would be furious, it would be the fifth time he'd gone out with an impossible mission and completed it.

The day he returned and informed his uncle that he had succeeded, Eurystheus decreed that it didn't count as a labour, as he had been paid by King Augeus. He did, however, resentfully praise what Hercules had done.

Jane Holder (12)
Woodbridge High School, Woodford Green

The Lonely Giant

There was once a 500ft monster with light brown hair. Everyone was scared of him, but the thing was he wasn't mean, he was friendly. All he wanted was friends. Unfortunately he was thought of as a scary monster. He was lonely, longing for a friend.

One day everyone rebelled against him and tied him to a tree. The monster started to feel the strain. People were sticking things into him, so he started to shout. Thinking the people would run off, he carried on, but they didn't.

Suddenly from the clouds came a radiant light, with a lady appearing. No one could believe their eyes. It was so bright nobody could really see anything. The lady stood on a cloud and came down. She said to them, 'Say sorry; ask for forgiveness, this beast is harmless. Just get to know him before you judge him. This is your first and last warning. Next time I have to come down, there will be consequences.'

The next day they came back again and were so close to killing the beast, but because the beast was so kind it didn't want to hurt the people. Just like before, the lady came down again. She stuck knives and forks right the way round them and said, 'When this cutlery came at you, what did you feel? Imagine what the giant feels. He just wants to be accepted by you.'

She left them with the guilt of what they had done. Now everyone is the giant's best friend.

Marianne Mahendra (11)
Woodbridge High School, Woodford Green

The Dreaded Nightclub

Rebecca and her girls were sailing the Thames. They were trying to get home; they were lost. Rebecca, the captain of the ship, was tired, the crew nearly drowned in the whirlpool, and then they had to fight the enemy, William and co. That was quite easy, until he called in reinforcements; Sean's gang. They beat them in the end, and only two crew members were injured.

The girls were all resting as they had just finished eating and were tired. Salma, the second in command, went to the captain and said that she had asked a passer-by who had said there was a pier nearby. So Rebecca started to sail. After sailing for ages, they saw a nightclub and thought that they deserved a break, so they went.

In the nightclub there were only a few people, but the music was blaring. The song was 'Crazy In Love'. Rebecca and Salma stood next to each other and started dancing, the rest of the crew copied. After a while they got tired, but found they couldn't stop dancing. Salma screamed as a bolt of pain shot up her back. She still couldn't stop dancing.

Elizabeth, the goddess of food and helpfulness, heard Salma's scream and flew down. She gave the DJ chicken to lure him away. As the DJ was eating, Lizzy turned off the music and the crew stopped dancing.

Elizabeth carried the crew to the ship. The crew were thankful and fell asleep.

Elizabeth Sode (12)
Woodbridge High School, Woodford Green

Thotheka

Thotheka. That was the name of the group consisting of 12 Greek women. They were butch women who were on a mission. They were looking for the dreaded Taou Krakoa. He was a Chinese giant who had invaded their land, eaten their people and crushed their houses into a pile of useless rubble.

The bushes rustled in the wind and the trees creaked and groaned.

'He is near,' cried Melina, the leader.

The ground rumbled and everyone lost their balance. Out of nowhere, there was Taou Krakoa. From Taou's perspective, all the ladies looked like little ants.

Melina stood up with courage in her heart. The sword of her beloved father was in her hand. She was going to kill her father's murderer. 'Leave my country and my people, *now!*' Melina shouted.

Taou chuckled loudly and evilly.

All the rest of Thotheka jumped up and scaled up Taou's body. Melina watched as her women took him down. He lay there helplessly.

'This is for my father!' she shouted. She raised the sword and all the power of her and her father channelled through and she slit his throat and cut out his heart. He was finally dead.

They returned to the village. Everyone stared. Melina raised the heart and everyone cheered and chanted. That night, there was a major celebration and the heart was placed on a stick. Melina's group had defeated everyone's fears. They would always be remembered. Thotheka.

Rebbecca Neofitou (12)
Woodbridge High School, Woodford Green

The Legend Of The El Minatoro Mask

In the heart of Spain, there is a mask, which if you wear it, you would turn into a Minatoro with the strength of thirty strong men. No one dared to go inside the Mastero temple to get the mask because of the two stone guards that protected it. But Lamposkilo, a fiendish young woman who had her face on loads of wanted posters everywhere, wanted pure power so she could rob banks easily, so she decided to pay the temple a visit.

Finally she was at the temple. 'Hmm, no sign of those guards. Oh who cares!' sneered Lamposkilo. 'Ah! There's the mask!' yelled Lamposkilo excitedly as she ran for it.

Creeaakkkkk, it sounded like stone moving. *Crash!*

Lamposkilo screamed when the two guards rose from the ground and Lamposkilo couldn't stop in time. 'Ah, so we finally meet,' said Lamposkilo slyly. 'Take this!' screeched Lamposkilo as she jumped up, shooting her hands into both of her pockets, grabbing the two whips, and she whipped the stone guards until they broke to pieces. 'Boy, that was easy.'

As Lamposkilo grabbed the mask, it blew up and a great net caught her and took her to jail.

'How did you catch me?' Lamposkilo asked the chief.

'Well, I knew you couldn't resist, so I hid the net in the mask and put it there.'

'What about the stone warriors?'

'They're not real stone as you should have realised! Just get in the van now!' yelled the chief.

Ben Marks (12)
Woodbridge High School, Woodford Green